Praise for Anna Schmidt
and her novels

"*A Mother for Amanda* is another jewel by
Anna Schmidt whose characters are realistic
and endearing."
—*Romantic Times BOOKreviews*

"Anna Schmidt's *The Doctor's Miracle* is a
delightful, well-written romance, as usual."
—*Romantic Times BOOKreviews*

"Anna Schmidt seems a natural writer....
Caroline and the Preacher is a story you will
want to pull out and re-read at Thanksgiving,
it's so delightful."
—*Romantic Times BOOKreviews*

ANNA SCHMIDT

A Mother for Amanda

&

The Doctor's Miracle

Steeple
Hill®

Published by Steeple Hill Books™

STEEPLE HILL BOOKS

Steeple
Hill®

ISBN-13: 978-0-373-65204-4
ISBN-10:   0-373-65204-6

A MOTHER FOR AMANDA AND THE DOCTOR'S MIRACLE

www.SteepleHill.com

Printed in U.S.A.

CONTENTS

Books by Anna Schmidt

Love Inspired

Caroline and the Preacher #72
A Mother for Amanda #109
The Doctor's Miracle #146
Love Next Door #294
Matchmaker, Matchmaker #333
Lasso Her Heart #375

ANNA SCHMIDT

has been writing most of her life. Her first critical success was a short poem she wrote for a Bible study class in fourth grade. Several years later she launched her career as a published author with a two-act play and several works of nonfiction.

Anna is a transplanted Virginian, now living in Wisconsin. She has worked in marketing and public relations for two international companies, and she enjoys traveling, gardening, long walks in the city or country and antiquing. She has written six novels for Steeple Hill Books—one of which was a finalist for the coveted RITA® Award, given by Romance Writers of America. Anna would love to "meet" her readers—feel free to contact her online at www.booksbyanna.com.

A MOTHER FOR AMANDA

For your faithful love is before my eyes
And I live my life by your truth.
—*Psalms* 26:3

For all the dedicated souls who serve
as keepers of our glorious national parks.

Chapter One

Chief Ranger Greg Stone woke with a start, instantly on alert, his eyes wide-open as he lay in bed listening. Singing—bad and off-key—splintered the normal silence of the night. He glanced at his bedside clock. Two-twenty. In Yellowstone National Park only the nocturnal animals were usually stirring at this hour. No doubt one of the tourists from a nearby campsite had had a bit too much to drink and wandered into town.

Greg sighed as he sat up and reached for the pants to his uniform. The thing of it was that the singing was coming from a woman. Greg would have expected a male visitor to get drunk and make a scene but not a woman. Her singing was occasionally accompanied by a blast on a police whistle.

As he shoved his feet into well-worn but polished boots the shrill echo of her whistle pierced the night. It was so loud it seemed to come from outside his own window. The woman was going to wake the entire town. Hastily he buttoned his shirt. Greg headed for the stairs, stopping only long enough to check on his ten-year-old daughter. Amanda was a solid sleeper, but this woman's ruckus could wake a hibernating bear.

Bear turned out to be the operative word. As Greg opened the door, he saw a large black bear circling a car parked just outside the unit next to his. Careful to make no sound, he observed the bear's actions from his position just inside his front door. The bear was trying desperately to get inside the car, pulling at the frame, clamoring over the hood, clawing at the windows. Greg frowned and released a grunt of exasperation. No doubt the owner of the car had left food inside, and the bear would use any means he could find to get at that feast.

"Stop that. Stop that right this minute," the woman demanded. "That car is brand-new, you dork. Who's going to pay for the damage you're doing?"

Greg rolled his eyes heavenward and retraced his path through his own house exiting by the back door. Once outside he eased around the corner to his truck and retrieved a stun gun from the cab. Knowing he was downwind of the bear, he worked his way to his half of the narrow front porch. As he stood in the shadows, he caught a closer glimpse of the woman.

She had ventured out onto the adjoining porch, and, in addition to her singing and whistle-blowing, she was madly waving her arms. From the noise she was making, he might have expected someone larger and more robust.

"Shoo," she ordered flinging her hands at the beast as if he were no more than a bothersome mosquito. Then she started to sing again. Her choice was "The Star

Spangled Banner." The bear eyed her and returned to his work. In another minute he would succeed in prying open the passenger side door of the car.

"Just be very quiet and very still," Greg said softly and took particular pleasure in the gasp of surprise his voice elicited from her.

"Oh thank heavens," she gushed when she found her voice. "I have no idea what—"

"*Very* still and *very* quiet," he repeated as he moved into position. He raised the gun and aimed.

"Don't shoot," the woman shrieked just as the bear spotted Greg and paused in his dedication to ripping open the car. Greg fired and the bear dropped instantly and heavily to the ground. "Oh, my stars, you've killed him," the woman whimpered.

Greg put down the gun and headed for the bear. "I've stunned him, miss. He could have turned on you at any moment. Don't you know that you need to stay put if a bear is in the area? Waving your arms and making all that racket, you were taking a foolish and unnecessary risk."

"I thought I was *supposed* to make a lot of noise so he would know I was there," she reasoned.

Greg eased closer to the bear. "You're supposed to make sure there's no food in your car. You were just lucky that he was more intent on getting to the food. He's not going to be so lucky," he added ominously.

"What are you going to do?" Her eyes widened with fresh alarm.

Greg looked directly at her for the first time. It was a stretch to call the person on the porch adjoining his own half of the duplex a full-grown woman. She was barely a hundred pounds and certainly no more than an even five feet tall, but she carried herself with the kind of grace and ease of movement that could only have come from years of working out or participating in some other athletic endeavor. She had blond hair that fell in layers to the top of her shoulders and in the dim light her skin took on an almost translucent quality. Greg's detailed observation of her was the automatic response to years of practice in sizing up humans as well as animals for tips to possible behavior.

"We have to relocate him as far away from here as possible. We have to take him away from what he knows and understands and put him in a place where he'll have to settle in all over again," he lectured as he stood over the bear. "Read the rules, ma'am. If you're going to spend time here, you need to understand that you are the visitor here, not him." He nodded at the bear and scowled up at her.

"I guess I've managed to make quite an impression on my first night," she said softly as she glanced across the street. "So much for my hope to get here and get settled before introducing myself," she added with a smile.

Greg followed her gaze and saw lights on in the apartments where the seasonal help resided. It dawned on him that this dynamo responsible for rousting the entire community out of bed in the middle of the night was the new teacher from Chicago. He'd been hearing about her for weeks. Most of his information came from Amanda who eagerly reported every morsel of gossip she could gather about her new teacher. The book on her, according to Amanda, was that she was very young, very pretty and *very* rich.

Now that he thought of it, he recalled the park supervisor's assistant saying she was assigning the teacher to the vacant duplex. It had never occurred to him that the only vacant duplex was the unit next to his. He frowned and turned his attention back to the situation at hand.

"You should have secured the items in your car before going to bed," he instructed.

"I fell asleep. I meant to unpack, but I was so tired after the long drive," she explained, her eyes on the inert form of the bear. "He'll be all right?"

"He'll be fine—displaced but fine. Hopefully he won't find his way back here. If he does, next time we might not have any choice but to use a real bullet."

"No," she protested as if she actually thought she might have some say in the matter.

Greg glanced up at her. She might be the new teacher, but the fact was she looked too young to be out of school herself and far too fragile to handle life in a wilderness like Yellowstone. Compared to Evelyn Schuller, the woman she was replacing for the year, she had to be a rookie—a rookie who was going to attempt to teach in a place she obviously didn't know the first thing about herself. "Look, Miss…" He searched his brain for the name he'd heard the rest of the staff talking about these past few weeks. All he could remember was that she was the daughter of some big industrialist back in Chicago.

"Beth," she replied, coming down one step of the porch and offering her hand. "Beth Baxter."

Greg accepted the handshake.

"And you are…" she asked.

"Chief Ranger Stone," he replied. Normally he didn't like throwing his title around, but in this case…

"So would I call you *Chief* or *Ranger?*" She smiled a smile that reached her eyes. Greg looked away. The woman was laughing at him. Her full mouth was that close to breaking from a simple smile into full-blown laughter.

"Greg Stone," he said keeping his tone formal and stern. "About the bear, Miss Baxter…"

"Beth," she interrupted and moved in for a closer look at the unconscious bear. "You probably saved my car from total destruction, and I haven't even thanked you."

There was that smile again. It seemed to come over her all of a sudden as if she were incapable of containing it. It lit her entire face, and he had to force himself to look away. Never in his life had he seen a prettier face.

"I probably saved your life. Hopefully I'll be able to do the same for the bear," Greg said sternly. "Now if you'll excuse me, we have a great deal of work to do before he comes to." He headed across the street toward the administration building.

"You're just going to leave him here lying on my doorstep?"

Greg turned slowly and looked at her. "Beth," he began wearily. "That is a three-hundred-pound unconscious black bear. He brings new meaning to the term *deadweight*. I'm going to need some help loading him onto my truck and seeing that he gets to a safe place before he wakes up and realizes that whatever goodies you so thoughtlessly left in your car are still in there. With your permission, I am going across the street to the offices there and call the rangers on duty to give me a hand."

"Can I help?"

Most novices were cowed into submission by now in the face of his stern reprimand. This woman was impossible—she had that big-city arrogance. He'd seen it a thousand times in the tourists who annually traipsed through the park thinking they knew more than the rangers did. "Yes. Once we've removed the bear, you can unload the rest of the belongings from your car and get them inside. That done, hopefully—unless you are inclined to sing some more—you and the rest of the village can get at least a couple of hours of sleep." *There, he had resorted to insulting her outright. That should do it.*

To his amazement, she laughed. "If it makes you feel any better," she called after him, "the bear didn't care all that much for my singing, either."

"I consider myself to be in good company then. Bears are notoriously discriminating in evaluating human traits," Greg replied and then he smiled to himself. He was very glad he had thrown out this last remark while walking away from her. He certainly did not want to leave the impression that he saw the situation as anything other than the dangerous foolhardy thing it had been.

Beth waited for him to return with two young rangers in tow and then sat on the step of the porch she shared with the unit next door and studied the human beast before her. Greg Stone was a take-charge kind of guy, but with an indefinable edge. She had the same sense about him that she had had about the encounter with the bear—she couldn't count on either of them to react according to the dictates of logic.

The chief ranger was tall and well-built. He certainly knew how to fill out that uniform. His close-cropped hair was the color of the bear's fur and his eyes were set deep beneath equally dark eyebrows. The eyes themselves were riveting, defying the object of his attention to look away. She watched in silent fascination as he and his two cohorts made quick work of moving and securing the bear in the back of a truck. There was no wasted action in his spare movements. In another place, another time, he might have been a dancer.

The other two rangers drove off into the night while the Chief Ranger stood watching them go. She sensed reluctance in him to turn around and face her, but he really had no choice. Unless he planned to stand there in the street all night, sooner or later he would have to acknowledge her again. She rested her elbow on one knee and her chin in her hand and waited.

"You can start unloading your car," he said as he walked briskly back toward the duplex. "I'll help."

"I can do it," she replied pushing herself to a standing position and stretching to ease the knots and cramped muscles she was experiencing after the long day of traveling. "You go ahead and try to catch some sleep. I expect you have to be on duty fairly early, especially at this time of the year."

He gave her a questioning look.

"I just mean that this must be the last few weeks of the high season in terms of tourists. I expect you have a lot to keep you busy these days." She could see that he was a little surprised at her observation. "Look, I know I made a big mistake and I'm sorry. I promise you that

I have read the literature carefully. I just didn't expect I'd need to apply it within an hour of arriving here."

He made no reply but stood by the car waiting for her to open the trunk so he could begin unloading her things.

"You know, it feels as if I have just begun a grand new adventure," she said amiably as she opened the hatch, "and frankly in spite of tonight's *mis*adventure, I must admit that I'm quite excited about the year here in Mammoth Hot Springs."

No response.

"I mean, who would have thought that a city girl born and bred who has lived her whole life in high-rise apartment buildings would find herself about to spend a year living and teaching in the wilds of Yellowstone National Park?"

He gathered a load from the car. Beth followed and because she always talked when she was nervous, she continued her monologue as if he had shown great interest in what she was saying.

"My friends and family think I am completely off my rocker," she continued and laughed as she stood for a moment surveying the quiet little town before her. "One thing is for certain—I am definitely out of my element." She laughed.

He didn't crack a smile. There were still a dozen or more boxes to go. Beth gritted her teeth and changed the subject determined to break the ice with this man who would be her neighbor.

"In Chicago, my days were filled with teaching duties at a very exclusive and expensive private school. My students were precocious and, far too often, they were also spoiled rotten." She tried to judge how this news was being received. His face was like untouched granite. "I'm really looking forward to meeting the children here," she added.

He looked at her, seemed about to comment, but then returned to the car for another load of boxes.

"I really love teaching," she told him, "but I was so sure that there was something more I could be doing—something I would never be able to experience in my safe little world there in Chicago. It was as if there was some connection I was missing. My life has been over-scheduled for years between teaching and managing my responsibilities to my family. Did you ever feel that?"

"Not really," he replied stoically.

It was all the encouragement she needed to continue. "The day I saw the notice of the national exchange program, it was as if I'd been zapped by a sign straight from heaven. I mean, what were the chances that I'd be chosen for this assignment? It was like a burning bush or something equally dramatic—I love teaching and felt strongly that there was something more that I was supposed to be doing. Something was already telling me that I would never find the answers by staying in Chicago."

He looked at her with an expression of skepticism, but she ignored it. She was on a roll, talking as much for her own benefit as his as she tried to remind herself exactly why she had just driven straight through from Chicago to get here.

"The opportunity to come to Yellowstone was like a calling, and I feel certain that I am going to discover such new and important things here about the children, about myself and about life in general." She realized how self-serving that must sound to him. "So, I packed up my stuff and here I am," she finished lamely.

"I'm afraid I don't believe in divine intervention, Beth. I believe in what I can see and witness right here on earth, and what happened earlier with the bear could have gotten nasty," he said clearly unconvinced that she grasped the seriousness of what had happened with the bear. "If you were counting on some higher power to intervene, you would have been sorely disappointed—and no doubt you would have ended up with a vehicle beyond repair."

She stared at him, trying to grasp the fact that he had finally responded to her in something other than mono-syllables or cynical looks. One thing was certain, the man had a one-track mind and could clearly care less why she had come or how she was feeling about it.

"Thankfully none of that happened. You inter-vened—possibly at the instigation of that higher power—and I learned my lesson." She pulled a suitcase and a box tied with rope from the car and headed for the house. "I promise not to break any more rules, okay?"

"You have to respect the animals here. This is not Disneyland or Sea World," he warned as he watched her struggle with the heavy luggage. "You are on their turf here, not the other way around." He held up a bag of chocolate candy kisses she'd left on the passenger seat of the car. "If you leave something like this lying around, you're bound to have some unwelcome guests."

Beth set her burden down and sighed. She turned and faced the ranger who was a head taller than she was.

"Yo, Chief Ranger Stone, message received and computed, okay? I screwed up. Judging from the number of lights that went on all around here, the entire staff is well aware of my faux pas. I get to be the newbie everybody can gossip about for the next couple of days. On top of that I get the distinct displeasure of explaining to my father just how I managed to let a bear destroy the paint job on a brand-new car. Punishment accepted. Now, drop it." She turned on her heel, picked up the luggage and attempted a purposeful stride into the house. She failed miserably, weaving from side to side due to her unbalanced load and the fact that she was bone weary.

Inside, she dropped the suitcase and box of books on the floor and turned to go get the next load. Greg Stone was right behind her carrying another large suitcase and two of the boxes. "Where do you want these?" he asked, his face as unreadable as a guard's outside Buckingham Palace.

"Anywhere, thanks." She brushed past him, caught a whiff of his freshly laundered and starched shirt and wondered if he slept in his uniform as she returned to the car for one last load.

"You brought a lot of stuff," he observed as he deposited the last of the boxes on the sofa in the crowded living room.

By now she was hearing every word from his mouth as a reprimand. "School supplies, teaching tools," she said through gritted teeth, wondering if he thought every box was filled with clothes. "Except for that one," she added as she relieved him of the last suitcase. She lowered her voice to a confidential tone, "In here I carry my sky-blue-pink chiffon ballgown and the ruby-and-sapphire jewelry I always wear to church on Sundays. I've asked my designer, Pierre, and my hairdresser, Fifi, to join me here by the end of the week. The butler and upstairs maid I figured I could do without. I mean, what's the sense of roughing it if you don't make a few sacrifices, right?"

He looked so totally confused that she almost took pity on him, but she also saw in his half-believing expression that word of her family's wealth and social position had been part of the information that had been shared prior to her arrival. She hadn't even been here a day and already she had embarrassed herself in front of the whole staff as the novice and city slicker that she was. Suddenly she was exhausted and wondering if she had made the right decision in coming here after all. "Good night, Chief Ranger," she said wearily.

"Good night," he replied and she heard him open the screen door. "You know it was probably a really good idea to leave the butler and maid behind," he observed somberly. "On the other hand, I'm looking forward to church Sunday. I've never actually seen a color like sky-blue-pink before. Good night, Beth and welcome to Yellowstone."

Beth listened as he walked across the porch. She heard the squeak of the door of the unit next to hers. She heard the sleepy voice of a child and the deep rumble of the ranger's reply. She stepped to the open door of her own unit and listened for another voice—a woman's voice, his wife's voice, but then he closed the door and all she heard was the silence of her first night in Yellowstone Park.

Beth stepped out onto the porch and took a deep breath as she let the silence and the scent of the night engulf her. The air was clear and cool for August, and she wrapped her arms around herself for warmth. She sniffed the odor of sulfur and knew the fumes came from the spectacular cascade of terraced springs for which the village was named. She looked forward to the day when she would barely notice the scent—it would mean that she had settled in and become a part of this place.

Maybe it *had* been a mistake coming here. Clearly Chief Ranger Stone would agree with that. She had left behind a career at one of the top private schools in the country. She had also left an active social life built mostly around her position as the only heir to the Baxter fortune, a family fortune that went back three generations. Her father, Thomas Baxter, was one of the most respected and popular businessmen in the Midwest. Her mother, Elizabeth, was a legend in the city for her grace and generosity.

Her parents would never stand in the way of her trying something new, but they had clearly had their doubts about this particular adventure. As he'd helped her pack her car, her father had said only one thing. "It's not too late to change your mind, honey."

"It's Yellowstone, Dad, not the ends of the earth, and besides it's only a nine-month assignment."

Her father had sighed and hugged her hard. "Lately, it just seems as if you're struggling to find your place in this world," he said. "That can be a time when a person might make decisions on the fly and regret them later. I just don't want you to think that you can't change your mind. You spend a month or so there and if it doesn't feel right, come on home, okay?"

She stared out at the quiet little town. She had not expected it to be quite so dark. It wasn't that she had expected streetlights like she knew back home in Chicago, but it was uncommonly dark—inky black to be more specific, like stepping into a great unknown, which was, of course, exactly the case.

It occurred to her that perhaps the reason she had left Chicago was to find a place of her own—a place not first connected to her family's name and history. She was proud of her family and all that they had accomplished, but she had a need to be her own person—to prove to herself that she was strong and capable in her own right.

She listened and heard silence—no cars, no televisions blaring, nothing but the slight murmur of the evergreens rustled by the wind. Across the way, the lights in the other units had been turned out and people had hopefully gone back to sleep. She took another deep breath and closed her eyes, thanking God again for dropping this incredible opportunity in her lap.

She stepped off the porch and into the street. With her head thrown back and her eyes still closed, she spun slowly around. *"I won't let you down,"* she said softly. *"Thank you, God, for bringing me to this wonderful place and thank you in advance for guiding my footsteps in the days to come."* She opened her eyes and focused on one twinkling star that seemed to shine directly on her. It tickled her to consider the possibility that God was looking down and winking at her. Then she heard the cry of something she could only identify as wild and primitive and far too close for comfort. She quickly stepped back inside her unit and closed the door. She was pretty sure the primal cry in the black night was not God talking back to her, and she was even more certain that Chief Ranger Stone would not look kindly on having to rescue her twice in one night.

Chapter Two

In the bright light of morning, Beth surveyed her new home. It was clean, compact, utilitarian and *beige*— there were no other words to describe it. The walls were beige, the carpeting was beige and the well-used upholstered furniture was beige. Even the kitchen appliances were beige. Beth searched through the boxes until she found her grandmother's colorful crazy quilt. She tossed it over the sofa and stood back to admire the effect. That quilt had traveled with her to boarding school, summer camp and college. Its colorful collage of patches had withstood the roller coaster of emotions that were a part of any growing girl's life, and it looked right at home here in this new environment.

"Perfect," she murmured as she returned to the boxes for other items that would make this place *her* place. She longed to bang nails in the walls and hang comforting posters of pristine blue lakes and fields of wildflowers. She had passed a store on her way through town the night before. As she made a list of items she would need, she wished she had packed the crayon-colored dishes that stocked the open shelving in her kitchen back in Chicago. Perhaps she could offset the bland whiteness of the unit's dishes by quilting some colorful place mats. At least the dishes weren't beige. Shelf paper might brighten the cabinets a little, she thought and added that to her list.

She wandered back upstairs to the bedroom and immediately began rearranging the furniture into a less regimented, homier pattern. She spotted an old cane-seated rocker. It was the first thing she'd seen in the place that had a hint of character, and she decided it belonged in the living room. As she wrestled the chair down the stairs, she began to see potential for the place. Rustic, but not impossible.

"Yoo-hoo," a woman's voice called out a few hours later as Beth unpacked books and loaded them into the too small bookcase built into the end of her kitchen counter.

"Come in," Beth replied as she gave up trying to cram one more volume into the tiny space and stood to greet her visitor.

"Hi, Beth, I'm Connie Spinner," a tall angular woman of about forty announced as she crossed the room extending her hand in welcome. "I teach the first graders and my husband, Al, is on the school board? Big galoot, kind of the *aw-shucks, ma'am* type?"

Beth smiled and wiped her hand on her jeans before accepting the welcoming handshake of the other woman. "Of course, I remember him. I try to remember anyone who gives me a job," she said.

Connie laughed. "Honey, you had the job on paper.

Offering to come to Bozeman for an in-person interview just about blew everybody here away. The school board decided it would be downright rude not to meet you face-to-face if you were willing to go to all that trouble." She stepped back and surveyed the room. "Not much to look at, is it?"

"Oh, it has some real possibilities," Beth said with as much enthusiasm as she could muster after a morning spent scrubbing cabinets and trying to arrange the available furnishings into some semblance of a comfortable and welcoming living space.

"You're being way too kind and polite. The good news is that we might be able to supplement these ragtag furnishings a bit if you tell me what to look for." Connie spotted the piles of books. "Bookcases would be my guess for a start. You sure did bring a lot of reading material."

"Those are mostly materials and workbooks for the school. If the bookcase situation there is better than here, then I should be okay." Beth smiled. "How about a cup of coffee?"

"A quick one. I have to get back to the store before the tourists overwhelm Al. He gets to gabbing and before you know it, people have either given up on ever getting checked out or they've walked out without paying. Either way we lose business and here at the end of the season every sale counts." She pulled a pad of paper and pencil closer as she perched on one of the two mismatched bar stools next to the counter. "So, at least one more bookcase. What else?"

"A floor lamp for next to the rocker there?" Beth didn't want to push her luck but…

"Floor lamp. How about for the bedroom? Have you got lighting up there because those ceiling things will blind you for sure if you're planning to read in bed."

Beth smiled. "I wouldn't turn down a nice bedside light," she admitted.

Connie wrote it down. "What else?"

Might as well address the subject up front, Beth decided. "How about a nice bear deterrent?" she said.

Connie looked startled and then gave a hoot of laughter. "Oh honey, don't you worry about that. There isn't a person in this place that couldn't have just as embarrassing a story told on them—including Greg Stone."

"I can't imagine him ever not doing things by the book and being as perfect as his freshly pressed and starched uniform," Beth said.

"Greg Stone? By the book? The man has broken more rules in his day than any of us. He was born and raised in the park system, knows just about every inch of this place and sometimes it goes to his head a bit. He can be something of a rebel, but he knows his stuff."

"Well, he certainly wasn't cutting me any slack last night."

Connie frowned. "He's changed some. Goes back about a year and a half. His wife died—cancer. He'd just been made Chief Ranger when she got the diagnosis. I think Greg grew up real fast that day. I expect we all looked at life a little different after Lu died." She sat for a long moment staring at the notepad in front of her.

Beth's heart went out to the woman who had clearly lost a good friend. She also thought about Greg Stone and remembered the child's voice from the night before.

She handed Connie a mug of steaming coffee. "I'm so sorry for your loss," Beth said softly.

Immediately Connie brightened. "Thanks, but the fact is that it's true what they say about time healing all wounds. Lu certainly wouldn't want people sitting around remembering her with mournful faces. 'Live life or lose it,' she used to say even before she got sick. It's sound advice. "

"Has time healed all wounds for Greg?" The words were out before Beth could stop them. She blushed. "I'm sorry," she hastened to add. "This really is none of my business."

"Honey, in a community as small as this one is, you'll soon learn that everything is everybody's business," Connie assured her. "It's only natural that you'd wonder. After all, Greg's daughter, Amanda will be one of your students." She paused for a minute as if casting about for the right words. "Greg is… Time may not have been as kind to Greg as it has been to the rest of us."

"And his daughter?"

Connie grinned. "Amanda is a treasure. Sometimes I think she took the whole thing better than us grown-ups. Lu did some good work helping Amanda prepare for the end and all." She reached across the counter for the sugar bowl and dumped three teaspoons of sugar into her coffee and stirred it briskly. "Have you been over to the school yet?"

"I thought I'd get things settled here first and then go over and start setting up things for next week's opening day," Beth replied glad to be off the subject of the tragic loss of the ranger's wife.

"Come on. Let's go ahead and get some of these supplies over there now. You may as well get the lay of the land right away. I'll walk you over to the school. I want to check on something in my classroom on my way back to the store. Besides, there's not much more you can do here anyway, right?" Connie picked up one of the boxes plus her coffee and headed for the door leaving Beth no alternative but to do the same.

Just outside the school, Connie spotted Greg. "Hey, Stone, come on over here and give us a hand," she called as she and Beth juggled the boxes of books.

Beth watched the ranger's approach. Was it her imagination that he proceeded toward them with some reluctance? Reading his expression was impossible since his features were hidden in shadow thanks to the wide brim of his hat.

"Connie. Beth," Greg said politely as he took the large box Connie was carrying and then turned to Beth. "You can put that one right on top," he instructed.

"As long as you've got everything under control, Greg, I'll leave Beth in your capable hands and run on ahead. I just want to check to be sure they finished painting in my room and then I've got to get back to the store." Connie turned her attention to Beth. "Now you stop by the store later and say hello to Al, okay? Meanwhile I'll see what I can drum up in the way of furnishings for that place of yours."

"Thanks, Connie. Thanks for stopping by." Beth was actually reluctant to let the woman go since it meant she would be alone with Greg. Clearly he had not revised his opinion of her much from the previous evening's encounter. On top of that, he looked as fresh and starched as usual while she'd been unpacking all morning and felt dirty and in need of a good shower. She brushed back her hair and tucked the tail of her T-shirt into her jeans.

"Could you get the door?" Greg said politely after they had followed Connie inside and gone past her room to a room at the end of the hallway.

"Oh, sure. Sorry." Beth rushed to open the door for him. "Just put them down anywhere. They must weigh a ton. I could barely manage one of them and…oh my,…"

Beth walked slowly around the sixth-grade classroom, trailing her fingers over the worn polished desks, studying the displays on the bulletin boards and taking note of not just one, but three, computers in the corner of the room. "I can see I'm going to have some major shoes to fill," she said softly. "Clearly Evelyn Schuller loves teaching as much as I do."

"Evie Schuller was born to teach," Greg replied as he sat the heavy boxes down with a thud. "She regularly goes after the Washington bigwigs to get the latest equipment for these kids. She's determined that they won't be behind when they leave here and head for the mainstream school up in Gardiner."

"Well, I'll just have to do whatever it takes to live up to her standards," Beth stated.

"Evie was certainly in favor of your selection," Greg said and she could feel him studying her as if he didn't quite understand why *anyone* much less the revered teacher would think Beth could do the job. "Not that there were that many other applicants. Not too many people are anxious to spend a winter in Yellowstone if they know anything at all about how isolated and shut down things can get."

Beth understood that there was an unasked question there somewhere. She waited.

"Do you have any idea what you've let yourself in for, Miss? It can get pretty lonesome here once the tourists leave and things shut down. There's no night-life, no excitement to speak of."

Beth sighed. So, here it was again, the assumption that coming from the city she must be used to life in the fast lane. "Well, of course, I can't know for sure since I've never lived through a winter here, but I think I'll be okay," Beth said and she knew she sounded a little defensive.

"Why would you leave what was surely a comfortable life in Chicago?" Beth guessed that Greg was asking a question that had been the topic of discussion among other park employees. "I mean, the city must be a pretty exciting place to live," he continued considering each word. "I would imagine you might miss that. On the other hand, I've seen people come here because they're running from something." He pinned her with his gaze.

"I'm not running away from anything," Beth assured him and then decided she might as well test the waters. "Do you believe in God, Ranger Stone?"

Greg locked his hands behind his back and walked the length of the classroom as if on patrol. He glanced at the colorful bulletin boards and then settled on staring at the view from the windows. "It's been said that you could bring the biggest atheist in the world here to this place and inside a week, that person would be a full believer."

"That wasn't the question," Beth replied. When he

said nothing, she continued. "As I mentioned last night, I think that God brought me here. I'm not sure why yet, especially now that I've seen Evelyn's classroom. I thought it was to make some difference for the children, but now I have to think it might be something else."

He remained silent as if waiting for her to continue, so she did.

"Back home in Chicago, I felt this…restlessness—for lack of a better word. With my work, myself, my life in general. That's when I saw the announcement of the exchange program. It seemed to be just the right solution."

Greg scowled at her. "I hope you aren't about to tell me that you've come here out of some misguided intent to *find yourself.*"

"No. That's not what I—"

"The children will need your complete attention," he said sternly interrupting her before she could explain.

"Of course. I just meant that—"

"Beth, please believe me when I tell you that I fully appreciate the romanticism that is often attached to Yellowstone. There is a powerful mix of ingredients at work here—incredible scenery, awesome power of nature, the last real frontier in a country that has based its entire history on conquering new frontiers. All of it can add up to expectations that may be unrealistic. For a tourist—here for a few days or a week—there's no harm in the fantasy. For someone who will reside here for a number of months and have responsibilities that affect the lives of our children, such fantasies can be dangerous."

Beth stared openmouthed at the tall ranger. She

thought about what Connie had told her about how much he had changed since the death of his wife. She tried to convince herself that somewhere under all that starched rigidity was a living, breathing, feeling human being who was not immune to the power of a moment. She tried to tell herself that in time she would prove to him that she was every bit as qualified as the woman she was replacing for the year.

"If there's nothing else you need moved, Beth, I'll be going," he said and headed briskly up the center aisle toward the door.

"Ranger Stone," she called after him. He paused but did not turn back to face her. "Just so that we are clear about one thing here—I am an experienced and respected teacher. I am very good at what I do, just as I'm sure you are. In my business, a little imagination goes a long way toward making for a successful day. I'm sorry if your work in these glorious surroundings no longer seems to afford you the same opportunity."

Without another word, he left the building. Beth stood at the window of her classroom and watched him stride across the compound. As he walked away without a backward glance, she felt the tiniest suspicion that there might be an element of truth in what he said. Other than Connie, Greg Stone was the only other person she'd met here. She had deliberately left behind everyone and everything she cherished to spend this year in a place where she knew no one and where the surroundings and life-style were a far cry from anything that even remotely resembled what had passed for normal in her life so far. The whole idea was definitely more daunting in the light of day than it had been the night before.

That afternoon, Beth decided she'd better do something about her car. She drove back to Gardiner, the small community closest to the northwest entrance to the park, hoping to find a dealership or at least a qualified shop to repair the damage the bear had done to her car.

When she had called her parents to tell them of her safe arrival, she had skimmed over the extent of the damage and had definitely left off the part about the scratches being caused by a bear. She drove through town twice before settling on a service shop near the edge of town.

"Hi," she said to the pair of scuffed cowboy boots protruding from under an ancient pickup truck. "Can you help me?"

A woman of about fifty rolled herself out from under the truck and squinted up at Beth as she wiped her hands on a grease-covered rag. "That all depends," she said.

Beth waited. The woman waited.

"On what?" Beth asked politely.

"On what you need help doing," the woman replied.

"My car has some paint damage. Do you handle that sort of thing?"

"Paint damage? Let me take a look." She got to her feet and walked out to where Beth had left the car parked near the garage door. "Left some bear bait inside, did you?" The woman didn't seem to expect an answer as she strolled slowly around the car. "More than one?" she asked.

"Pardon?"

"Bear. More than one bear?"

"No. Just one."

The woman clicked her tongue against her cheek and shook her head sadly. "Gonna need the full works," she muttered more to herself than to Beth. "You like green?"

"Green?" Beth was beginning to feel as if she'd walked into a foreign land where she clearly did not understand the language.

"I've only got green—dark like the evergreens. Nice."

"I see. You know, maybe if it's that big of a job I should go to Billings or Bozeman."

"Suit yourself," the woman replied and walked immediately back into the garage where she lay down on the dolly and slid back underneath the pickup.

"Can I use your phone?" Beth asked. "I'll charge the calls to my calling card."

"Suit yourself," the woman repeated.

Beth turned and walked smack into the chest of Chief Ranger Stone. It was turning out to be a delightful day.

"Problem, Beth?"

"Nothing I can't handle," she replied primly.

"Stone? Is that you?" The dolly rattled out from under the truck and the woman smiled broadly as she leapt nimbly to her feet and pumped Greg's hand.

The man actually smiled. "Hello, Gracie. How have you been?"

"Been missing you, you big long drink of water. It's about time you stopped by." She punched him hard in the arm and cackled with delight. "Did you hear about this one here?" She waved a hand in Beth's general direction. "Got her car tangled up with a bear. Look at the mess he made of that paint job. Looks like a brand-new car, don't it? Pity."

"Can you help her?" Greg asked.

"She don't want green. Green's all I got in stock."

"I see." Greg and the woman called Gracie continued to consider Beth's car as if she had suddenly become invisible. "What's wrong with green?" he asked and Beth realized the question was aimed at her.

"Nothing. It's just that—"

"She's not from around here, Greg. If she thinks she can do better up in Bozeman or Billings, that's no skin off my nose."

"Gracie's the best there is," Greg told her.

"I'm sure she's very good but as you can see the car is red."

"And?" Greg waited.

"And…it's red," she repeated lamely.

"So, it will be green or it'll rust. Seems a pretty simple choice. Trust me, you do not have the time to go all the way to Bozeman two or three times and even if you did, how would you get back and forth while they've got your car?"

Beth had to admit that she had not considered that.

"Let me show you the color, sweetie," Gracie suggested kindly. "I didn't know you was a friend of Greg's. We can order anything you want, but let me show you the green, okay?"

"Sure," Beth replied not wanting to appear rude.

"It's real nice," Gracie continued as she rummaged through an overstuffed desk. "Ah here. These are the color charts and I got this one."

It was a very nice shade of deep green. Beth studied the chart and the manufacturer's claims. "It is nice," she admitted.

"It's recommended for your make and model," Greg noted as he read over her shoulder. "When can you do it, Gracie?"

Gracie shrugged. "Could have it finished for you by Tuesday week."

Greg and Gracie turned their attention to Beth.

"If you like, you can leave it now and ride back with me," Greg offered in that stiff formal way he had of speaking to her.

"How much?" Beth asked, clinging to her last hope for refusing.

Gracie did some figuring with a stubby pencil on a grease-smeared and torn piece of paper and handed it to Beth.

Beth could not believe the figure. "How much for your labor?" she asked.

"I figured that in," Gracie replied and waited.

It was a ridiculously low figure. "Is there a guarantee on the workmanship?" she asked, knowing she was being impolite but they were talking about a car worth about what she would be paid in salary for the year.

Greg cleared his throat. "I will personally guarantee the work," he said. "If for any reason it does not meet your satisfaction, I will pay to have the car repainted somewhere else."

"Bless you, son," Gracie murmured.

Beth saw no way out. "Green it is," she said and turned to take a last look at her beautiful red car.

Gracie grinned. "You won't be the least bit sorry, darling. I'll just need the key."

Beth worked it off the ring and handed it to the mechanic.

"See you soon, Gracie," Greg said as he leaned down and kissed the woman on the cheek. "Ready?" he said in Beth's general direction as he headed back toward his truck.

"See you Tuesday week," Gracie called.

"Don't you need a downpayment?" Beth asked reaching for her purse.

"Heck no, sweetie. I know where you hang out, and I got Greg there to track you down if you try to skip town." Gracie walked Beth to the passenger side of the truck as if they were old friends. She opened the door for her. "You be good to this little lady, Greg Stone."

Greg tipped his hat. "Yes ma'am," he replied and shifted into gear. "Just thought you'd like to know that it's a pretty good hike from here to Mammoth," he said as they headed down the highway. "I'm sure you had it all worked out how you were going to get back in time for school to start next week, but it would have been quite a hike since there's no car rental place in Gardiner."

Beth slumped farther down in the seat. The one thing she had always hated more than anything was appearing stupid. She now amended that to be that the one thing she hated more than anything was appearing stupid in front of Greg Stone.

He drove in blessed silence for several miles giving Beth the time she needed to compose herself and begin to take an interest in the sights around her.

"I see some gold but no reds or coppers in the turning of the leaves. Do they come later?" she asked.

"Autumn color west of the Mississippi tends to be a little less splashy. The gold on those quaking aspen there pretty much has to make up for the lack of other fall colors," Greg replied.

Beth saw that he was more comfortable with conversation about the park and certainly it would make the trip go faster if they talked about something.

"They are beautiful," she agreed. "Those white trunks against the deep green of the evergreens, and just look at the way the leaves shimmer and rustle with just the slightest breeze." She laughed. "Thus, the name *quaking,* I suppose."

They left the aspen behind and entered a forest of very tall, very skinny evergreens.

"Lodgepole pines," Greg explained before she had a chance to ask. "They grow to be about one-hundred feet tall and stay pretty thin in diameter. They cover most of the forested areas of the park."

"They are so tall and elegant in their thin stately beauty," she said. "Some of their trunks are blackened. Have they been burned?"

"Scorched in the fires of '88 but these made it. Other places there are whole stands that were completely destroyed. It's one of the things you're likely to see as you travel the park. A couple of recent isolated fires have left some forests pretty much ghosts of what they were. The trees are still standing—the trunks are, but it's important to remember that they are deceptively sturdy and secure.

Beneath the soil of the burned out trees there is no root system to hold them."

"That's so sad."

"Not really. Fire is a natural thing in a wilderness."

"Fascinating." She settled back and watched a flock of Canada geese fly overhead. They were no doubt on their way to the Yellowstone River. In the meadows were herds of bison grazing and in the distance she saw pronghorn antelope frolicking in the field.

"This must have been what it was like when the settlers headed west," she murmured more to herself than to him. "These are the sights they saw. It's absolutely awesome." Her voice shook with emotion.

Greg glanced over at her. His hat was on the floor between them and the wind ruffled his dark hair. She was aware of his deeply tanned hands on the steering wheel—strong hands that might have belonged to such a pioneer and it struck her that in his own way, Greg Stone was a frontiersman.

Confused by the emotions she felt, she focused her attention back out the window. "Oh, look, that elk herd is twice as large as the one in town. They are magnificent. Look at the way the male stands there keeping watch."

Greg pulled into an overlook and shifted into neutral. "That's his harem. He's making sure some other bull doesn't come along to challenge him for his women."

"Really?" Beth was fascinated at this piece of information.

"It's the rutting season for many of the species. The males stake their claim on the females and defy any other male to come along and challenge that claim. That's what all the bugling you've been hearing in town is about."

Beth felt a growing respect for the ranger. "Tell me about your job. What exactly does a chief ranger do?"

He actually laughed. "Rangers at all levels wear a variety of hats. We are the police, firefighters, animal handlers, naturalists, cowboys and medics. For the human animal we also have to sometimes play the role of parent, guide and psychologist."

"You mean for the visitors to the park."

"There are visitors and there are tourists," he said with a touch of regret. "Unfortunately, we mostly get tourists."

"What's the difference?"

"For tourists the average stay in the park is a day and half. You can't really do much except hit the highlights in that short of a time."

"And visitors?"

He looked straight ahead at the road as he pulled out of the overlook. "Visitors stay longer, but they still leave eventually."

"Like me?"

"Yes, ma'am."

Chapter Three

Several of the children had stopped by the school on the pretense of helping her set up for opening day. Beth understood that the children were driven by curiosity. Based on her one-sided conversation with the chief ranger the night she arrived, she had no such illusions about him.

"Mrs. Schuller always kept the reading books on that shelf," one of the girls instructed as Beth prepared to move them to a bookcase on the other side of the room.

"I don't think that Mrs. Schuller will mind if I change things around a bit," Beth replied. "Where do you think we should set up the science corner?"

The children were alternately shy with her and curious about what kind of year they could expect.

"Mrs. Schuller put it there," the same girl announced.

"I think that's perfect," Beth said and saw the girl smile.

Her students ranged in age from nine to eleven. Connie had warned her that the older children would not hesitate to be quite outspoken about how things were to be done. Beth was amused by the way that they made sure that their conversation was peppered with comments that began, "Mrs. Schuller always…" or "Mrs. Schuller used to…" She tried to encourage them to talk about how school had been before and what they might expect now that she was there. They were clearly coming from very different lives from the children she had taught in Chicago. Their comments gave her insight into their concerns and anxieties about how the year with her might go.

"Okay, I think we've made some real progress here today," she said. "Thank you, children, for stopping by to help. I couldn't have done it without you."

She glanced up and saw Greg Stone standing in the doorway to the classroom. "Everything all right here?" he asked in that serious gruff voice that seemed to be his signature.

"Fine," Beth replied. She wondered if the chief ranger was checking up on her. "Haven't seen a bear all morning," she added and saw the children's eyes widen in surprise.

Greg frowned. "Just checking."

Now that she knew about his wife's death, Beth could not deny that she was curious about the man. She was touched by his efforts to raise his daughter on his own. Her first instinct had been to find some way to be helpful especially since she was living right next door. She had considered and then rejected several ideas. She could invite them over, but that might seem too forward. She could host a party and include them, but other than the Spinners, she really didn't know anyone well enough to invite them for a party yet. It occurred to her that the other children had given her the perfect solution.

"Oh, Chief Ranger Stone," Beth called out as he turned to leave, "please tell Amanda that she's welcome to stop by any time. The other children have been quite a help to me, but they tell me that Amanda has some wonderful ideas as well. Isn't that right, children?"

Four heads nodded in unison as they turned from Beth to Ranger Stone as if they were watching a tennis match.

The ball is in your court, Beth thought and smiled.

"I'll let her know," he replied and hesitated.

"Was there something else?" Beth asked.

He glanced at the children. "No, that'll be all," he said and left the room. It did not escape Beth how he had dismissed her when he was the one leaving.

Over the next several days, Amanda continued to keep her distance although Beth had seen the child watching her comings and goings. Once when Beth smiled and waved, Amanda had pretended not to see her and concentrated all of her attention on straightening the curtains of the living room window on her half of the duplex. Connie had told Beth about Amanda's close relationship with Evelyn Schuller, so Beth had decided to let the little girl come to her rather than trying to seek her out. She wondered if Greg had influenced his daughter's opinion of her new teacher. It was definitely clear that he had his doubts about Beth.

By the time Sunday came, Beth had actually grown used to the sight of elk grazing in her front yard and buffalo—or bison, as the locals preferred—wandering across the road. She had also met several other human residents from the village. Everyone was polite, but it was clear to Beth that at least some of the others shared Greg Stone's reservations about her.

"Good morning, Beth," Connie called out as Beth approached the park's chapel. As usual the gregarious woman drew Beth into the circle of park employees standing outside the doorway. She introduced her to the other three teachers and their families. "We were just talking about this weather."

"Greg says we could see snow before the end of the week," Al noted, "but you sure couldn't predict that judging by today."

"It is glorious," Beth agreed as she spotted Greg Stone coming across the compound with Amanda.

"Good morning, Greg," Connie called drawing his attention to their small gathering.

He smiled, then glanced at Beth, nodded and headed straight for the church. Amanda hurried along beside him, matching his long strides with three of her own. But Beth saw the little girl look back at her and she thought she saw her smile. Beth was determined not to let another day pass without direct contact with the ranger's daughter. By all indications from the other children, Amanda was a leader in the classroom. It would not be wise to wait until school opened to have her first encounter with Amanda.

Once the service began, Beth knew that she was going to find a spiritual home in Yellowstone. The park chaplain, Harry Dixon, led the services. "Look out these windows," his bass voice boomed. "There before you is all the evidence you'll ever need that there is a God—a living God, a loving God, a God who is not immune to being a bit of a show-off when it comes to His handiwork."

The congregation chuckled, for indeed the sky had never seemed as blue or the clouds as pure white or the mountains as magnificent as they did on this morning.

Reverend Dixon was a silver-haired and silver-tongued dynamo who ran the service as if there would never be enough time in the world to accomplish all of God's work. Beth liked him immediately and counted him among the many blessings she'd already encountered in coming to the park. As she listened to his sermon, she felt such a sense of certainty that coming here was indeed the right choice.

She caught a glimpse of Greg Stone's face as Reverend Dixon made the point that each person was a resident of God's world and in God's care. There was an almost imperceptible tightening of the ranger's jaw, a slight frown that creased his forehead. She recalled something he had said that first night.

"I don't believe in divine intervention, Beth."

She hadn't known about his wife's death then. Now she felt the full impact of those words. Had Greg turned away from his faith when his wife died? If so, why on earth was he standing up there singing in the church choir?

According to Connie, he attended church for Amanda's sake. He was polite to the minister and others, but everyone knew that he had severed all emotional ties with religion the day he buried his wife. As the minister invited everyone to stand for the closing hymn, she studied him closely for further clues. When he stood with the rest of the choir, he focused on the hymnal before him and indeed seemed to be going through the motions of singing rather than paying attention to the words.

Previously, she had only thought of him as tall and somewhat rigid. Now she saw that he had a lean athletic body, skin weathered to a permanent and very attractive tan by days in the outdoors and facial features that were at once fascinating and a little intimidating. She also saw a certain weariness—not physical exhaustion—but something that told her he was worn down mentally and emotionally. Her heart went out to him. She was especially intrigued by the undeniable presence of laugh lines at the corners of his deep-set eyes. Those indelible creases told a story—a story of happier and more carefree times for the oh-so-serious chief ranger.

Beth imagined a younger Greg Stone playing football or perhaps basketball. As an athlete, she'd no doubt that he would have been a fierce competitor. Once the game ended, she wondered, had he put aside his "game face" and celebrated with his teammates, laughing at some joke or ogling the cheerleaders? That kind of easy camaraderie was harder to imagine than the image of him driving for a goal.

She felt sad that he had lost not only his wife, but also the faith that would have helped him endure that loss. Then as she watched, an incredible thing happened. For one of the few times since she's met him, Greg Stone smiled, revealing not only the aforementioned laugh lines but also a most engaging dimple at the corner of his mouth.

Beth followed the line of his gaze to the second row where Amanda stood for the closing hymn. She was making exaggerated hand motions urging him to smile as he stood in the back row of the choir and sang the final verse of the hymn with special gusto.

After church everyone gathered for coffee and cake in celebration of another successful and safe park season.

"In the next few weeks, you won't be seeing much of us, Beth," one of the rangers explained.

Beth was aware that the young man was interested in her. She smiled. "Why is that?"

"Time to shut things down for winter," he replied.

"Yes, this is the last Sunday we'll have the company of our seasonal staff," Connie said as she glanced around the room. "They'll all be heading back to college or their winter jobs," she added with a poignant sigh. "I'll miss them."

Al put his arm around his wife's shoulders. "Connie has this habit of adopting every kid who comes through here," he explained. "She goes through this every year."

"You're the same way with the tourists," she replied. "Al gets so caught up in meeting new people every day during the season that it takes him a while to settle into the quieter routine."

"It's hard to imagine there not being so many tourists around," Beth said recalling how they crowded the streets and how their vehicles lined the main roads. "I must admit that I'm looking forward to that."

"Well, before you know it, we'll be down to a skeletal crew," Al said. "You'll be able to roll a bowling ball down the middle of town here and not hit a thing except maybe a bison," he said wistfully.

"Oh, stop it," Connie chided. "You love the quiet as much as the hubbub and you know it."

Al grinned.

The two of them reminded Beth of her own

parents. Their good-natured sparring told the story of a strong marriage, like the one Beth hoped to find for herself some day.

"Well, I for one will be much busier in the week ahead," she said. "School starts tomorrow. I can hardly believe it." Then she grinned sheepishly. "The truth is, I can hardly wait."

"I'm not sure the children share your enthusiasm," Connie replied with a chuckle, nodding toward the place where a group of the older children were watching Beth with barely concealed curiosity and concern.

"Would you folks excuse me?" Beth said with a smile. "I think I have some work to do in putting the children's minds at ease."

Greg Stone worked the room, saying his goodbyes to staff members who would be leaving, touching base with rangers who would manage the schedule of closing facilities during the coming weeks and trying to keep his eye on Amanda.

Ever since Lu had died, he knew he had become overly protective of his daughter. "Dad, I am not a *baby*," Amanda reprimanded him regularly always with a dramatic sigh of exasperation. He would be glad when school started, and he could be sure of her whereabouts for at least the greater part of the day.

He glanced up from his conversation with the park supervisor and saw Amanda standing with three other children, listening to the new teacher. Judging by Beth Baxter's animated hand motions and facial expressions, she was telling quite a tale. The children were fascinated and Greg moved closer to hear what she was saying.

"Well, he was just about the biggest bear I ever saw," Beth said in an awed voice, her hand stretching high over her own petite height. She smiled that smile he had noticed that first night—the one that took over her entire face and seemed to radiate from somewhere deep inside her. "In fact, he was the only bear I'd ever seen outside of a zoo," she added.

"Did he rip open your car?" Dougie Spinner demanded.

Leave it to Dougie to want the graphic details, Greg thought and smiled.

"He tried and he had these long, long fingernails," Beth said curling her own manicured fingers into claws to demonstrate. "He used them to pry and pull and claw at the door." She shuddered at the memory.

"What did you do?" Amanda's best friend, Sara, asked breathlessly.

"My mom said you sang and blew a whistle," Dougie interrupted.

"I did," Beth confirmed.

"She said it must have been just about the worst singing ever heard," Dougie continued. "One of the rangers said if he'd been that bear he would've either run off to the woods or come up on that porch and put you out of your misery."

The children held their collective breaths, suddenly aware that Dougie had repeated gossip he shouldn't have and that the new teacher's feelings were bound to be hurt.

Greg watched and waited.

She laughed. She laughed so hard that the children

started to laugh as well. "Your mom was right," Beth confirmed between gulps of laughter. Then she regained control and became quite serious. "Do you want to know a secret?" she asked in a low confidential tone. The children naturally gathered closer and Greg strained to hear. "One of the reasons I had to leave Chicago was because I sang so loud and so bad that the mayor couldn't stand it any more and told me to leave."

"Chicago's a big place," Sara observed, clearly impressed.

"Not as big as Yellowstone," Dougie declared, equally as determined not to be overly in awe of the new teacher. "You made that part up. So what happened next with the bear?"

"My dad saved her," Amanda announced. It was her first contribution to the animated discussion.

Greg watched as Beth focused her full attention as well as the full radiance of her smile on his daughter. "Yes, he did," she said softly, and added, "Why don't you tell them the rest, Amanda?" In that moment Greg knew that Amanda had been won over, at least for the time being. He stood nearby and listened to his daughter relate the rest of the story even though she had slept through the entire incident. He smiled at her minor embellishment of the facts to make him seem like a real hero.

All the while he was thinking that he liked Beth Baxter a little better for giving his daughter this gift. He looked at her and when her laughing eyes met his, he looked away, confused by feelings stirring deep inside him, feelings that were both faintly familiar and oddly discomforting. Feelings that he had thought were long dead.

* * *

Later that night Greg sat on the side of his ten-year-old daughter's bed listening to her prattle on about this and that in an obvious attempt to delay the inevitable. "Amanda, it's time for you to close those big blue eyes and go to sleep," he said gently as he tucked the covers high around her shoulders.

"But, what do you think she'll be like in class, Dad? The new teacher? I like Mrs. Schuller—she's nice. Maybe the new teacher won't be so nice, you know? Just because she *seems* nice doesn't mean anything," she added in the tone she had evidently picked up from listening to adults evaluate a new person.

"The new teacher has a name, and she is only here for a year, Amanda. Mrs. Schuller will be back next year."

"I guess," Amanda agreed reluctantly, "but I don't understand why Mrs. Schuller had to choose this year to go. Next year I'll be going to school in Gardiner with the other big kids."

Greg studied his daughter as he brushed the bangs away from her forehead. Could it possibly be that her concern about the change in teachers went deeper than simply getting used to someone new? Her mother had been dead for well over a year, and while Amanda seemed to have accepted the massive change in both their lives, Greg also knew that he had been too consumed by his own grief in the early months to be much good to his daughter. More recently, his emotions had settled into a kind of dull apathy as he focused every fiber of his life on his work and his daughter's happiness. Could it be that Amanda's questions about

the teacher were really about not wanting another un-
expected change in her life?

"And why does she have to live right next door?"
Amanda said sleepily. "It's bad enough being the kid of
the chief ranger without living right next door to the
teacher. The other kids will think I'm being given
special favors," she groaned.

"It'll work out," Greg promised, knowing he had
promised the same thing when Lu had been dying of
cancer.

Amanda grunted and pulled her favorite stuffed dog
firmly against her chest. "Sure, Dad," she mumbled and
then she was asleep.

Greg sat there a minute longer watching his daughter,
noticing for the hundredth time the way she curled one
arm protectively across her body the way her mother
had in sleep. And for the hundredth time he wondered
why a God who was supposedly loving and kind would
so cruelly take away a mother at a time when her child
needed her most. He hoped Beth Baxter would have
sense enough to realize that in spite of her lively per-
sonality and high intelligence, Amanda was vulnerable.
She could be easily hurt. Could someone as obviously
inexperienced in the ways of a harder colder world as
Beth Baxter was possibly understand that?

Beth could not believe how excited and nervous she
was on the opening day of school. Ordinarily, she was
not an early morning riser, but she woke before dawn
and cooked herself a full breakfast. As she sat on the
porch wrapped in a blanket against the chill of the

morning and savoring a second cup of coffee, she studied her surroundings.

She had been in Yellowstone less than a week, but already she was beginning to think of it as *home*. She waved to a group of park rangers and naturalists on their way to work and they waved back. There was a real sense of community in living here. One of the other teachers had warned her that like any small town it had its downside. People gossiped and knew more about your comings and goings than was usual in a city, but in spite of that everyone she had met had told her that they would not want to live anywhere else.

Beth heard the now familiar squeak of the screen door on Greg Stone's place as it opened and closed. "Good morning," she said softly not wanting to wake Amanda.

He turned, clearly surprised to see her. "You're up early," he observed.

She grinned. "Couldn't sleep. I never can the first day. Anyway, now I'm kind of glad. It's been wonderful sitting out here in the quiet watching the sunrise."

Greg glanced at the sun and frowned. "Thunderstorms coming this afternoon," he said.

Beth followed his gaze across a cloudless sky. "How on earth can you tell that from a sky so purely blue?"

He held up a sheaf of papers he held in one hand. "Overnight weather reports," he told her. She thought she saw a hint of a smile, but then immediately he frowned. "You do know, Beth, that thunderstorms can be quite sudden and dangerous here in the park? They can come up without warning—even on a day like this. Anyone out in the back country can be caught completely unaware."

"I thought I would let the children get one day in the classroom under their belts before dragging them to the outback," Beth said dryly, wondering if she would ever have a conversation with the ranger that did not involve a lecture.

"It's not like Chicago where you can dash into a building for cover," he continued. "Here, you're exposed to the elements."

"No, it's not like Chicago at all," she replied dreamily as she sipped her coffee. "I can't tell you how wonderful and free I feel here. And how welcome people have made me feel."

"You must miss your friends," he said.

"Of course. But what's happening between me and the people here is unlike anything I've ever experienced." She saw that he was skeptical of her enthusiasm. "No, really, I mean it. All my life I've always had to assess whether someone was being nice to me because they liked me or because they wanted to be closer to my family, or more specifically, my family's money. Here, that's not even a consideration."

"People here are well aware of your family's wealth," he said quietly.

"But that's the point—they know and it's just a fact like that I come from Chicago or that you're their boss. It doesn't mean that's who *you* are as a person." She realized that her normal penchant for openly sharing her thoughts and feelings was making him distinctly uncomfortable.

He cleared his throat as if preparing to make a speech. "The original topic was storms, Beth, and how you will need to conduct yourself should you and the children—".

She sighed. The man had clearly missed his calling. He was a born professor with a natural talent for lecturing. "I have an idea," she replied. "Whenever I take the children out on a field trip, we'll make sure that you or one of the other rangers are along with us. How would that be?"

"Could you, Dad?" Amanda asked excitedly as she came out onto the porch still in her pajamas. "That would be so cool."

"I certainly want to involve the parents as much as possible in the educational activities of the children," Beth continued, taking some pleasure in watching Greg struggle with his determination to refuse her and his unwillingness to disappoint his daughter.

"Come on, Dad. Say you'll do it," Amanda urged.

"We'll see," Greg replied. Then he lifted his daughter high in his arms and grinned. "Is this what you've chosen to wear for the first day of school, young lady? Because, frankly, I would have thought your new chinos would be so-o-o cool."

Amanda giggled with delight as her father carried her back inside the house. "Aw, Dad, sometimes you are so weird."

Beth swallowed the last of her coffee and listened to the excited and muffled chatter of the child getting ready for school. She heard the clang of dishes and pans as Greg prepared breakfast and heard his bass replies to Amanda's constant stream of questions and commentary. She remembered the way his face had softened and lit with love when he had lifted his daughter and teased her into laughter in that brief moment on the porch. It was the second time that Beth had caught a glimpse of another side of the frequently austere, un-smiling ranger. It was a side of him that at the moment only Amanda seemed able to reach, but one that was definitely intriguing.

Chapter Four

Beth hadn't been in the classroom more than an hour when she realized that she had underestimated the challenge of teaching two different grades in one classroom. She had those children in fifth and sixth grade while the rest of the teachers handled those children from kindergarten through fourth grade. She felt a bit like a pioneer schoolmarm, only these children were definitely modern-day students wise beyond their years to the ways of adults. Fortunately, they were mostly well behaved although the older ones were unable to hide the fact that they had serious concerns about Beth's ability to live up to Mrs. Schuller's standards.

Doug Spinner tested her once or twice by causing disruptions when her back was turned. She handled the situation by asking Doug to take charge of the slower reading group in completing exercises in comprehension while she worked at getting the other children settled into projects. To her delight, it worked. Back in Chicago her directions would have been met with a dramatic sigh or worse, further testing of the boundaries. But Doug's innate politeness and respect for adults kicked in immediately. He herded the youngsters to one corner of the room, passed out workbooks and pencils and strolled back and forth checking their work as if he'd been teaching for years.

During recess Amanda and some of the other children were kicking a soccer ball around. As it came rolling toward Beth, she automatically trapped it and sent it on its way back to the group then returned to writing down ideas that she hoped would make her classroom routine function more smoothly.

"Miss Baxter?"

Amanda stood before her, the soccer ball lodged firmly under one arm. "Do you play soccer?" she asked squinting in the bright sunlight.

"I played in college," Beth said.

"Could you teach us?" Doug chimed in as he edged closer.

Beth was surprised. In Chicago, soccer was the sport of the day for most boys and girls. In many neighborhoods it had largely replaced Little League baseball and football in popularity. "I could try," Beth agreed.

"Al-l-l right," Doug murmured pumping one fist.

"We'll have to work out a time schedule for practices," Beth reminded them. "Why don't you hold a team meeting during the afternoon recess and come up with a plan?"

"We don't have a team," Amanda said. "There's just the three of us," nodding toward Doug and Sara.

"I see." Beth pretended to consider the situation. "So,

you're telling me that Jeffrey Thompson and the Quentin twins aren't interested?" She glanced toward the other three older children from the class. Jeffrey was a shy bookworm type, definitely unathletic with his glasses and overweight frame. The Quentin twins were eleven-year-old girls whose interests seemed to run exclusively to hairstyles, clothes and boys—not necessarily in that order. The object of their affection at the moment was clearly Doug Spinner.

Doug's eyes grew large with amazement. "They don't play," he protested.

"So, am I to understand that you've invited them to participate and they've said they'd rather not?" Beth watched the exchange of looks between Doug, Amanda and Sara, saw them struggle with an answer.

"We never asked," Amanda admitted finally.

"I'll do it," Sara volunteered eager to please. She took off across the small schoolyard before either Amanda or Doug could stop her. Doug gave an audible groan.

"You know, I really hope they agree to play," Beth said. "It will be so much more fun if we can have a real game, three-on-three, don't you think? I was thinking that for starters the two of you ought to be appointed captains since you already have some knowledge of the game. Also, keep in mind that some of the children from other classes may want to join in."

"We get to choose players?" Amanda asked.

"For starters," Beth agreed. "Assuming they want to play."

"I take Sara," Amanda announced immediately.

"No fair," Doug challenged.

"Yes, fair. Now you pick," Amanda retorted obviously pleased with herself.

"Then you have to take Jeffrey too," Doug argued.

Amanda beamed. "Okay. I guess that leaves you with the Quentin twins." Then she giggled. "They're going to *love* that, Dougie," she teased as she ran back to the classroom.

Beth suppressed a smile. Amanda Stone was one bright little girl. It was going to be a real joy having her in class.

"How was school?" Greg asked later that day as Amanda set the table and he stirred the spaghetti sauce.

"Okay," she replied with a noncommittal shrug.

"Small class this year," Greg commented knowing that this was one of the years when the school board had elected to combine classes to cope with the lower enrollment. Next year Amanda would attend classes in Gardiner where the class size would be more normal.

"Miss Baxter is going to teach us soccer," Amanda said.

"Really?" His calm reply was in direct competition with the flood of thoughts that raced through his mind. In the first place, he had promised to teach Amanda soccer, but with his work schedule and various crises to handle over the past couple of months, he'd kept putting her off. He wondered how many times he was going to disappoint his daughter as he struggled to be both mother and father plus manage the largest national park in the continental U.S. In the second place, Beth Baxter—in spite of her appearance of fitness—did not seem like the type who would engage in a sport like soccer. She might chip those perfectly polished nails.

"She's pretty cool," Amanda continued as she put the hot garlic bread in a basket and set it on the table. Then she giggled.

"What?" Greg asked, smiling at his daughter's obvious amusement.

"She made me and Dougie captains of the soccer teams—that means we got to choose up sides. I chose Sara, of course."

"Of course," Greg said trying hard to think who else might be available to take part in a team sport. "Who did Doug choose?"

Amanda crowed with laughter. "That's the best part. When I took Sara, he got mad and said I had to take Jeffrey Thompson so he was left with…" She was laughing so hard she simply couldn't get the words out.

"Well, don't keep me in suspense. Who's on Dougie's team?"

"The Quentin twins."

Greg immediately saw the reason for his daughter's delight. The Quentin girls had shadowed Doug Spinner for the better part of the summer. If Doug was around, one or both of them was sure to be nearby. No matter what the poor kid did, he could not shake those two adoring females. Greg laughed with Amanda.

"Miss Baxter really is pretty cool," Amanda repeated once she had gotten control of her mirth and turned her attention back to her spaghetti. "I think she'll do fine."

Greg knew that for his daughter, this was tantamount to declaring that Beth Baxter was the greatest thing since sliced bread. "Well, if you need some help with soccer, things have started to quiet down now. I have some time."

Amanda's eyes lit with delight. "Really? Can I go tell Miss Baxter after supper? I mean like you could coach one team and she could coach the other and it would be the most funnest thing. Of course, you should probably coach Dougie's team. He's going to need a *lot* of help." This last sent her into a fresh wave of laughter, and Greg thought that it had been too long since he and Amanda had shared such a wonderful time together. It crossed his mind that in one sense he had Beth to thank for providing the fodder for this moment.

By the end of her first week of teaching in Yellowstone, Beth was beginning to rethink the idea that she had made a wise choice in coming. The leisurely pleasure of time to enjoy the park, to wave to her neighbors and to fantasize about what her life would become had changed dramatically. She spent long hours at the school and at home adapting lesson plans to the needs of these children. Recently she'd been so busy that she'd barely had time to see her neighbors or any adults at all. What had seemed like a decision blessed by the angels as she sat on her front stoop that first morning had quickly become one that was colored by innumerable doubts.

For one thing, she daily realized how little she really knew about living outside of a city environment. The children seemed to know more about the plants and animals than she did, and she found herself staying up half the night memorizing facts and preparing lessons in order to stay two steps ahead of them. She took her teaching seriously and was concerned that her lack of knowledge would somehow rob the children of a level of teaching she thought they deserved.

On top of that, she was a little lonely. It wasn't that the other residents weren't warm and friendly. It was that they were so busy with their own lives. Their work demanded enormous dedication. Connie sympathized and reminded Beth that in a place like Yellowstone, the permanent staffers were used to seeing people come and go. They were aware that Beth would only be in the park for this one season.

"Just wait until everything finally settles down for the winter," Connie assured her. "That's when things start hopping in town here—lectures, concerts, book discussion groups and amateur theater. Honey, you'll start to wish you could find a few minutes to yourself."

Beth thought about Greg, who certainly didn't seem to mind being alone when he wasn't working. He always came straight home from work regardless of what hour that might be. Once or twice she had been outside her unit or on her way home from catching up on some work at school when he came home. He was always polite, but never seemed inclined to want to stop and visit as others did. She thought again about inviting him and Amanda over for supper, but wondered how such an invitation might be read—by the ranger and by others in the small tightknit community. Also, she didn't want to put Amanda in the awkward position of appearing to be receiving special attention.

At Connie's suggestion, Beth had asked Sandy

Quentin to tutor her on the wildlife and plants of the park. Sandy was a naturalist for the park system and her husband Sam had happily given up the practice of law to run a hardware store in Gardiner. She was also a born matchmaker sprinkling each session liberally with hints that this ranger or that naturalist was certainly eligible and would be a great catch if Beth would be at all interested. Beth began to understand why the Quentin twins might be so interested in boys. Their mother was always trying to pair Beth up with one of her single friends.

To Beth's surprise, whenever Sandy brought up the idea of her dating someone in the park, the face that came to her mind was that of Greg Stone. She actually found herself holding back from asking questions about him, not wanting Sandy to think she was interested. As Connie had warned her, living in Yellowstone was like living in any small town, and Sandy was a charming but eager gossip. Beth knew that all it would take was for her to ask one question about the rugged chief ranger and rumors would spread like wildfire. She told herself that her fascination with Greg was his close proximity in living in the other half of the house and at the same time the clear message he gave off that it was best she keep her distance.

Unlike her father, Amanda was another story entirely. With each passing day, the little girl became more fascinated by Beth. She often came to school early and stayed late to help with the setup of materials and the cleanup afterward. At times like this she would chatter away about whatever might be on her mind. Her conversation was liberally sprinkled with phrases like "Mom used to always say…" or "Before Mom died…" as if it were perfectly normal for a child's mother to die so young.

The first time Amanda had mentioned her mother, Beth had been quick to say how sorry she was and she'd been racking her brain for something appropriate to add about why such things sometimes happen even to wonderful little girls like Amanda. Instead, it was Amanda who comforted her.

"Don't be sad," she had said. "I was sad for a very long time, but now that I'm older I understand that God sometimes needs a special person like Mom. He wouldn't have taken her unless He really really needed her, and He must have figured that Dad and I could manage okay on our own—at least until He and Mom decide on someone new."

"Someone new?"

Amanda had nodded firmly. "Oh, yes. Reverend Dixon told me that he was very sure that one day someone would come along and me, Dad and the new lady would be a whole family again." She had smiled at the thought. "And the best part is that I'll know Mom picked this lady specially for us. That kind of thing takes time, you know."

Beth had resisted asking what Amanda's father thought of all this. She had also marveled at the wisdom of the park chaplain in finding a way to explain the unexplainable in terms that would be comforting and acceptable to a ten-year-old. She wondered if he'd been able to offer anything approaching the same level of comfort to Greg.

One evening as she left the school after her session with Sandy, Beth saw Greg working a soccer ball back and forth with Amanda and Doug across the playground. She put down her books and walked across to the field for a closer look.

"Concentrate, Amanda," Greg called to his daughter whose face was a portrait of focused intensity as she worked the ball with her feet. "Defense, Doug," he coached. "She's coming for your goal."

Beth grimaced as Doug aggressively went after the ball, but Amanda held her own, jostling him, turning her body with natural athletic instinct to protect the ball. Beth resisted the urge to cheer. When Amanda finally lost control of the ball it rolled straight toward Beth.

"Toss it here, Miss Baxter," Doug shouted waving his hands.

"Oh, goody, now we can play teams," Amanda shouted. "Come on, Miss Baxter, girls against guys."

"I don't think…" Greg began.

"You don't think what, Chief?" Beth shouted over her shoulder as she began working the ball toward the goal at Doug's end of the field. Admittedly it was a bit more difficult controlling the ball as she ran in a jumper that reached her ankles than it would have been in jeans. Still, she was determined to give it her best effort.

"Come on, Ranger Stone," Doug cried as he dashed after her. "She's gonna score."

Amanda gave a whoop of delight and came running alongside Beth. Beth grinned down at her and in that split second Greg was right there in front of her stealing the ball and heading for the opposite end of the field. She couldn't be sure but she thought he had actually chuckled at his clever maneuver.

"Not so fast, hotshot," she muttered as she caught up with him from behind and kicked the ball cleanly away and toward Amanda. "Go, Amanda," she shouted and laughed at the expression of total shock on Greg Stone's face.

"Mom, Dad," Doug shouted as he spotted his own parents on his way down the field to catch Amanda. "Come on."

In minutes it was a three-on-three game, women against men. Connie Spinner was a crafty player, and she easily manipulated the ball into position for Amanda to score the first goal. The air was punctuated by the excited shrieks of the three females as they danced and high-fived one another in the middle of the field.

"Aw, Dad, you let her get by you," Doug moaned.

Al Spinner ruffled his son's close-cropped hair. "It's getting dark, son, and I imagine you've got home-work." He glanced over at Beth and raised one questioning eyebrow.

"He certainly does," Beth said. "Book report," she reminded him.

"Oh, man," Doug muttered and trudged off the field with his parents.

"Hey, Dougie, you want to stay for pizza with me and Dad?" Amanda took off after her friend, leaving Greg and Beth alone in the center of the field.

"I've noticed that Amanda is always watching out for the other children," Beth said when the silence seemed to stretch too long for comfort but neither of them had moved.

"Yeah, she's a terrific kid," Greg agreed.

"It's a very adult thing for her to do," Beth added.

"She's had to grow up fast," Greg said and his tone left no doubt that there was no point in pursuing the conversation.

The sun had set and in the gathering shadows she couldn't read his expression. "Well, it's getting late," she said bending over to pick up the ball. When she handed it to him, their fingers brushed and it seemed like so much more than a simple touch. Beth told herself that she was reading too much into an innocent and perfectly natural gesture.

"Did you eat?" he asked.

Suddenly she felt like an awkward teenager, unable to find her voice. She shook her head and waited for the invitation she very much hoped would come.

"Hey, Spinners," Greg shouted across the field. "Come on in. There's plenty of pizza." He started toward the duplex. The Spinner family and Amanda came from the opposite direction. Beth remained standing in the middle of the playing field. "You coming or not?" Greg asked.

"Oh, you mean that invitation included me even though my name is Baxter not Spinner?" she teased.

"Well, if you need an engraved invitation…"

"Nope. I never turn down food especially when somebody else is cooking. You *are* cooking, aren't you?" She fell into step alongside him. "I just hope you're a better cook than you are a soccer player," she added after a moment.

He actually chuckled. "You know I let you win," he said.

"No way."

* * *

Greg watched Beth make herself at home in his kitchen. He listened to her easy banter with Connie and Al, heard the sound of her laughter invading the silence of his house. He smelled the scent of her perfume as she sat next to him eating pizza. When a bit of tomato sauce caught on her lower lip, he thought about wiping it away, touching her and recalled the way their fingers had touched when she handed him the soccer ball. He shook off such fantasies and tried to concentrate on anything else—anybody else. For someone so petite, she certainly knew how to fill up a room.

After everyone had devoured the pizza, Beth and Connie insisted on clearing the dishes and they were soon engrossed in conversation about teaching. Amanda came up to Beth to ask a question about Chicago, and Greg watched as Beth reached out and tucked an errant strand of hair behind his daughter's ear. That simple gesture—so natural, so tender—drew him to her more than anything he'd seen her do or heard her say. Something about her natural instinct to nurture his daughter touched Greg deeply and roused emotions he had suppressed for months. For the rest of the evening he felt shy and uncertain around her, unable to meet her eyes in the normal course of the evening's adult conversation. He was grateful for the buffer of Al and Connie.

He told himself that he was grateful when the evening ended early, and at the same time wondered why he was trying to think of a reason for her to stay. Connie and Al were anxious to get Doug home to finish his book report, and Beth took the opportunity to leave as well. Greg saw Amanda look at him, and knew that she wanted the teacher to stay.

"Amanda and I were glad for the company," he said in answer to everyone's chorus of appreciation for the pizza. He walked with them all to the door and watched as Al and Doug headed across the compound while Connie stopped to finish a conversation with Beth. "Good night," he said.

The two women looked at him and smiled. Greg stepped back inside and closed the door.

"Do you like Miss Baxter?" Amanda asked.

"Sure. She's a nice lady." He thought about her touching Amanda's hair.

"I mean, do you *like* her?"

"Why do you ask?" Greg hedged, banning the memory of the woman's tenderness from his mind. He knew where Amanda's line of questioning was headed, and it was not a topic he was prepared to discuss.

Amanda studied him for a minute, then shrugged. "No reason," she said and started clearing the last of the dessert dishes.

"I'll do that, honey. Finish your homework and get your shower. You need to wash your hair tonight."

"My homework's all done."

"Then go take your shower while I clean up here."

Amanda headed for her room. "I like her more and more and I think Mom would like her, too," she said softly but loud enough so that he couldn't miss it.

Greg frowned as he listened to the sounds of Amanda in the shower and dried the last of the glasses. Beth Baxter was slowly but surely worming her way into his daughter's heart. It wasn't that he thought she had any diabolical intention but the fact remained that Amanda was drawn to her in a way that was different from her attachment to any other adult. The problem as he saw it continued to be the fact that Beth was here for the school year and then she'd be gone. Amanda had already lost her mother. It wouldn't do for her to become attached to Beth and have her leave, too. Letting go of someone you loved hurt too much—he ought to know.

Clearly, Amanda had other ideas about the role that Miss Baxter was to play in their lives. As he combed the tangles out of her freshly washed hair, she chattered on and on about things at school—things that largely had Beth's name coming up every other sentence.

"So, I told her that you'd be glad to help out. You will, won't you, Dad?"

He'd been lost in his own thoughts. "Will what, honey?" He braided the top section of Amanda's thick hair, one more skill he had acquired since Lu's death.

Amanda gave an exasperated sigh and rolled her eyes. "Come to class and talk about plants and animals and stuff."

"The naturalists usually handle that sort of thing."

"Well, Miss Baxter says that she wants to get us in the big classroom before winter comes. Anyway, I told her you would know the very best places to go and that you knew all about every animal in the park. And, that you could name most every tree and flower, too."

"What's the big classroom?"

"The park, Dad. Miss Baxter says it would be a crime to be surrounded by all this nature and spend all day inside a stupid building—well, she didn't say *stupid building*. She was telling us today all about the big fire that happened before any of us were even born. She showed us awesome pictures. I bet you know all about that, don't you, Dad?"

"Come on, Amanda, it's time for bed." He held back the covers for her. He'd been only twenty-two years old when the fire had raged through the park in 1988. Nothing the rangers and volunteers did seemed to work. He remembered the heat and the devastation as if it had all happened yesterday.

"You just *have* to come talk to the class," Amanda pleaded as she climbed into bed and settled a lineup of stuffed animals for the night. "I promised and Mom told me it was really awful to break a promise."

"We'll see, honey. It's late. Get some sleep."

"Miss Baxter said she was pretty sure that you knew everything there was to know about the fire and anything else that had to do with the park, so will you do it?" Amanda looked up at him to see if her words had had any effect. "She said I should ask you and she said it would be wonderful if you agreed. She said it just like that—*wonderful*."

He leaned over and kissed her. "I'll check my schedule."

"I'll tell Miss Baxter to come see you in your office or maybe we should just have her come over for supper again. That was a lot of fun, huh, Dad?"

"I'll talk to Miss Baxter. You go to sleep."

"She's real pretty, don't you think, Dad?"

"Sleep," he repeated and shut out the light.

It didn't take a genius to see what was happening. His daughter was matchmaking, which might have been harmless enough if she wasn't going to be disappointed in the process. Women like Beth Baxter came to Yellowstone for an adventure—not for a life. In June she would pack up and return to Chicago where no doubt she'd be relieved to get back to her normal routine and where he was certain there must be a line of rich young stockbroker types just waiting to make their move.

Greg sat down at his desk to finish a report. Lu's photograph stared back at him. He picked it up and studied it, feeling a twinge of disloyalty that lately he'd been thinking so much about Beth Baxter. The one thing he had promised Lu was that he would take care of Amanda and do everything in his power to protect her from ever being hurt again. Lu had laughed at him and reminded him that God was in charge and there wasn't much Greg could do about that.

Was that when he had first realized that his faith was reduced to little more than going through the motions? Was it the day his dying wife had reminded him that God was in charge? Was that the first time he had swallowed his protest that there was no God in deference to her need to believe that there was?

He replaced the photograph on his desk and stared at it from a distance. He stood up and walked the short distance next door before he could lose his nerve. Greg didn't have much use for a God who took a vibrant woman in the prime of her life for no good reason. He wasn't about to put any faith in a God who would leave Amanda without a mother. And most of all, he wondered what kind of cruel joke God was playing now by sending a woman like Beth into his life to make him feel things he didn't want to feel and then have her leave again.

Chapter Five

"We have to talk," Greg said without preamble when she answered the door. "Is this a good time?" He tried to ignore the way she had pushed her glasses onto the top of her head, how she was barefoot and it made her seem even smaller and more vulnerable. She opened the door a little wider as an invitation for him to come inside.

Greg felt confusion at the emotions she stirred. Because he was a man determined to maintain control of his emotions, that confusion irritated him. Going inside her place seemed far too intimate a gesture. He backed away from the open door. "If you don't mind, could we talk on the porch here? I just put Amanda to bed and in case she needs me…" he finished lamely.

"Sure. I'll get a jacket," Beth replied.

"And shoes," he said. "It's cooled off quite a bit."

She glanced at her feet and grinned. "Good idea," she said.

Greg returned to his side of the porch and waited. She appeared a couple of minutes later wrapped in a heavy hand-knit woolen sweater and wearing, not shoes but slippers that came to her ankles and were shaped like the face of a bear at the toes. He recognized them as one of the items sold at the town store to the tourists.

She lifted one foot so he could get a better look. "Appropriate? Wouldn't you say? Connie gave them to me one day when I was feeling a little homesick."

He frowned. She wasn't going to make this easy for him. Her quirky smile and habit of sharing the minor details of her life with such abandon turned his resolve as well as his knees to jelly.

"Amanda wants me to come talk to the class," he began.

"That would be wonderful," Beth replied as she hoisted herself onto the porch railing to sit.

"I'll come on one condition," he continued.

"Okay, Chief Ranger," she replied in a deep bass voice that mocked his attempt to keep the conversation on a serious plane. "What are your terms?"

This was not going at all the way he had expected. He cleared his throat and paced the confines of the small porch. "I'm sure you're aware that my daughter likes… admires you very much."

Silence.

"I'm sure you also know that her mother died recently, and that given that fact she is still pretty fragile, pretty impressionable, pretty…" He searched for the right word.

"Spit it out, Greg," Beth said but her voice was tense and she wasn't kidding around now.

Greg tried another tack. "As you observed earlier this evening, Amanda is fairly precocious. Since her mother died, she has taken on a great deal of responsibility. One of the things she has focused on is taking care of me." He cleared his throat again. "Tonight, it occurred to me that given her admiration of you and her desire to see me happy, she might…that is, she has gotten it into her head that perhaps you…and I… I mean, it's completely ridiculous, of course, but I have to protect my daughter, you understand."

The woman was not helping one bit. He was fairly certain that she knew exactly what he was trying to say, however badly, yet she remained as still as Yellowstone Canyon on a winter day.

"Now you listen to me, Chief Ranger Stone," she finally said in a low and dangerously soft tone. "I am quite capable of recognizing Amanda's infatuation with me. I am also sensitive enough to understand that for a little girl who has recently lost her mother the hope that someday there might be a chance that you and she might find someone new is perfectly normal. I know that you think the worst of me, but let me assure you that I like your daughter very much and I would never willingly do anything to hurt her. You can count on me to nip any fantasy she may have of you and me as a couple in the bud." She hopped off the railing and headed toward her front door, then turned and stood at mock attention. "Will there be anything else, sir?"

He'd handled the whole thing badly. "I didn't mean to imply…"

"If there's nothing else, I'll say good-night," she replied.

"One more thing," he called after her just before she

shut the door. "I can be in class on Tuesday morning if that works for you?"

"It doesn't," she replied and shut the door firmly.

He showed up anyway and rather than make a scene, Beth made a great fuss over the honor of having the chief ranger as their guide.

"Yellowstone is the largest of the national parks outside of Alaska," Greg said by way of introduction. "It covers 2.2 million acres with 1,200 miles of trails, over 3,000 miles of rivers and streams and 10,000 thermal features."

"What's a *termal* feature?" One of the fifth graders asked.

"Mud pots, geysers. That stuff," replied Doug Spinner.

"Are we gonna see a geyser today, Chief Ranger Stone?" the Quentin twins asked in unison.

Greg looked disconcerted by the manner in which the children had taken charge of the discussion. Clearly he had expected them to sit like little robots and listen politely and attentively to his prepared remarks.

"Let's give the chief ranger a chance to tell us what he wants us to know and then ask questions, children," Beth said.

Ten eager faces turned their attention from their teacher back to him and waited.

"Perhaps it would be interesting for the children to know about the animals in the park," Beth suggested.

Greg cleared his throat and nodded. He clasped his hands behind him and paced up and down in front of the children seated on the grass. "There are approximately 30,000 elk, 2,200 bison, a thousand or so mule deer, 700 moose, 400 antelope, 600 bighorn sheep, 200 grizzlies plus coyote, otter, beaver and, of course, the wolf population we've reintroduced to the park over the last decade."

Beth saw the children's eyes glazing over as he inundated them with numbers. "Well, children, that certainly gives us a lot to look for. As we travel today you may also wish to watch for the wonderful variety of birds that populate the park. Can anyone name one of those?"

"Bald eagle," Doug shouted.

"Trumpeter swan," Amanda added.

"Osprey," said the fifth grader with the lisp, spraying his neighbor in the process.

"Loon," chorused the Quentin twins and then they giggled.

"Very good," Beth said enthusiastically. "Now, let's go see what we can find and, along the way, we'll also take a good look at the flowers and the trees." She herded the children into the van she had borrowed for the day. "Coming?" she asked as Greg stood rooted to the spot where he had begun his lecture.

Without a word he climbed into the passenger seat.

"Seat belts everyone," Beth called out and was rewarded by a chorus of metallic clicks. "Buddy check," she called and each child reported in the name of his or her buddy for the day. "And we're off," she said cheerfully as she shifted the van into gear and lurched forward. "Sorry about that," she told Grég. "It's been a while since I drove a stick."

"Now remember, children, there are rules if we are lucky enough to spot wildlife while we're out on the trail. What are they?"

"No closer than twenty-five yards," the children chanted, "except for a bear is no closer than a hundred yards."

"And how far is that?" Beth asked.

"A lon-n-g way," the children replied solemnly.

"Perhaps you have some fun facts you might share with the children as we spot various species, Chief Ranger," she said as she navigated the twisting road.

"Fun facts?"

"You know, things they can relate to and therefore, will remember. Like there's a herd of bison—tell us a fun fact about them." She pulled into an overlook and pointed out the herd grazing in the field.

"Bison may look slow and clumsy but even though they weigh nearly a ton—two thousand pounds—they can run at thirty miles per hour. That's three times as fast as a person can run." He looked to her for approval.

She smiled. "Very good."

Gradually he got the hang of interacting with the children. Beth saw that he was both surprised and pleased at their questions and curiosity. She saw that when he permitted himself to loosen up he was funny and a natural teacher. He came up with quizzes for the children as they rode from one point to another in the park. At the geyser basin he made them each choose a time when they thought the geyser would erupt and then clocked it on his watch. Before her very eyes he relaxed and enjoyed not only the children but also the opportunity to show off the park. It was undeniable that the park held a very special place in his heart.

Their last stop before heading home was a meadow

where Greg told them the story of the fire of 1988 and then showed them why the fire had turned out to be such a good thing for the park. He showed them the new growth, the rebirth of plant species that had been overshadowed by the more mature growth of the forest.

"You see children," Beth concluded, "here in the park, there is birth and death and rebirth just as there is in life. The fires seemed a horrible thing when they happened. Yet here we can see that they brought something new and necessary, and that something good came out of this terrible thing."

The children nodded solemnly. Beth looked at Greg to see his reaction realizing that he might have thought she was trying to deliver some message about his anger over Lu's death.

He stared at her for a long moment and then handed her the bouquet of wildflowers he had collected to explain the different species to the children. "Thanks for letting me come along today," he said.

Beth's hand shook as she accepted the flowers. "Our pleasure," she replied softly.

Beth was already in her fourth week of teaching and once she had gotten past that early spat of loneliness, she had settled quickly into a routine that was both rewarding and rigorous.

"Hi, Beth." Al Spinner caught up with her as she walked the short distance from the school to her duplex.

"Hi, Al. How are things going for you?"

Al smiled. "Pretty quiet these days with most of the tourists gone. Connie wanted me to ask you if you'd lead the discussion at tonight's book group? She's got a frog in her throat and can barely squawk much less lead a discussion."

"I'm not sure I'm the right person, Al. I'm new to the group and—"

"Have you read it?"

"Several times," Beth admitted.

"Then you're elected. See you at eight. I'll bring the brownies."

"Now you're bribing me," Beth called after him.

Al waved and continued on his way. Beth turned and realized Greg Stone had come up behind her.

"Hi," she said and her voice was unsteady.

"Hello." He continued to stand there.

"Are you coming to the discussion tonight?"

"Are you leading it?" he asked.

She wondered what the right answer might be to get him to say that he would be there. In the end she settled for the truth. "It looks that way. Connie has a sore throat."

"Then I'll be there." He stepped aside to allow her to pass before heading in the opposite direction toward his office.

"It's at eight," she called after him. "In the meeting room at the admin building."

He nodded and waved but did not break stride.

Beth stood watching him all the way across the compound, her books clutched to her chest like a love-struck teen.

The meeting room filled quickly with a dozen members of the book discussion group. Beth took her place on one side of the circle of chairs and glanced around. He wasn't there. He had probably started working on some report and lost track of the time.

Al called the group to order and dispensed with two short items of business. "And with that, my dear Beth, the floor is yours."

Beth shuffled her notes and smiled at the others. It struck her that several of the people surrounding her had already become good friends. It was hard to believe how quickly the time had flown since her first days in the park. Back in Chicago her family and friends eagerly awaited the tales of her latest adventure.

She began the discussion by providing background information about the author and the writing of the novel that many critics thought was his finest work. Then she launched the discussion.

"I thought tonight that it might be interesting to begin our discussion by talking, not about Bill Cobb, the protagonist, but about his wife."

The door at the back of the room opened and closed. Greg nodded to the others as he took a chair on the fringe of the circle and focused his attention on her.

"What would you say is her primary emotion throughout the novel?" Beth asked trying to ignore Greg's gaze riveted on her.

"Hopeless hope," he said quietly.

"Well, she was hopeful—I wouldn't necessarily say hopeless," Connie croaked.

"Hopeless," Greg repeated. "She knew from the opening scene that he was dying and there was nothing she could do to stop that. The best she could do was be there and hold things together."

If he had delivered his comments in a tone of anger, there might have been cause to dismiss them. Instead he stated his thoughts with dispassion and because everyone in the room knew that he was coming from a place they hoped never to have to be, they listened.

Beth swallowed around the lump that had suddenly formed in her throat. Why on earth had they selected this particular book to review? Shouldn't someone have recognized how painful it might be for Greg?

"I think we have to look at this on a larger scale," one of the naturalists said. "I mean, the author is writing about the death of a life-style, of an era."

"That's true," Greg replied, "but the people count, too. This is about a man and his wife and their children coming to grips with the fact that the life they had thought they would have—the life they had planned—will never be."

Beth saw the way his outward calm was betrayed by his clenched hands.

Everyone was silent. Beth had no idea how to direct the discussion.

"What about this business that Bill kept going back to about his own childhood?" Al asked and with some relief the group picked up that thread and followed it.

Greg remained politely attentive but quiet throughout the rest of the discussion. Beth couldn't take her eyes off him. She had read the popular novel more than once and yet she was seeing it entirely differently. She was seeing it through Greg's eyes, through his experience and she began to appreciate in a way she had never been able to before just how traumatic these last two years must have been for him.

When the discussion ended and everyone broke into small groups to enjoy coffee and Al's brownies, Beth approached Greg.

"Thank you," she said and knew it sounded dumb.

He concentrated on stirring his coffee, even though he took it black. "For what?"

"For helping me see something in a new light, for opening a door on a topic I haven't had the courage to really look at before."

"You mean *death?*"

She nodded.

He smiled. "Actually I thought I was a little over the top. I think I made a number of my friends uncomfortable and that wasn't fair."

"Maybe they were just surprised to hear you make the connection. Maybe it gave them something new to think about as it did me."

He focused all of his attention on her. "You're a very kind person, Beth Baxter," he said softly. "A good person."

"Do you really think that your wife was without hope?" She knew there was a risk in asking. The progress they had made toward forging a friendship was fragile.

"I wasn't talking about my wife," he replied.

"I know, but now I am. Was she without hope?"

He shrugged. "She did what she needed to do to get her through to the end. And I did—and do—what I need to do to get through the days."

Beth wished there were some way she could make

him see that going through his grief alone was the hard way to do it—it would take much longer if he closed his heart to what he was feeling, remembering. From everything she knew about his wife, Beth was positive that Lu would not have wanted this for Greg.

Chapter Six

Beth was putting the finishing touches on the crib quilt she was making for her best friend's first baby. A week had passed since the discussion group, and she had decided that she might as well face the truth. She had a major crush on the handsome ranger and his gruff exterior was part of the attraction. She could not deny that she watched for Greg as she moved around the compound. She listened for his voice in the evenings. Her radar went up whenever someone mentioned his name. She even worried about him when he was gone for what seemed an unusually long time handling business in some other region of the vast park.

Beth smiled as she held the quilt up to the light to examine it for any flaws or missed stitches. Her friend Ginny had been married for five years and had been trying to have a child for at least four of those years. Finally it was going to happen. This time in two months, Ginny would be a mother and Beth would be a god-mother. Beth couldn't help wondering what it would be like to have a child of her own.

"Beth?" The calling of her name was followed by a sharp knock on the front door.

Beth realized that it had started to rain again. It had been raining off and on all day. She had been so engrossed in her work that she hadn't noticed. Glancing out the window as she hurried to answer the door, she saw that the rain was coming down in sheets.

Connie was standing on her porch, shielding Amanda from the blowing rain. "Come in," Beth urged. "Let me get you a towel."

"I came to ask a favor," Connie called as Beth disappeared into the bathroom and returned with two towels.

"Name it," Beth replied as she knelt to dry Amanda's face and hair.

"Greg is out on the trail somewhere. Amanda was staying with us, but we just got a call that Al's mom has taken a fall up at the ranch in Bozeman. We need to head up there right away. Amanda insists that she can stay at home by herself and wait for him, but I wanted you to know in case you heard her moving around or something. Greg should be home soon—we tried rousing him on the two-way but couldn't get through."

"Is that all right with you, Amanda?" Beth asked. "Staying home alone?"

Teeth chattering as she adjusted to being out of the rain and cold, Amanda nodded but a flash of lightning made her eyes widen with anxiety. "I'm not afraid," she said with fierce determination that reminded Beth of Greg.

"I tried Sara's folks," Connie added, "but since it's

Saturday they've gone off somewhere. I hate to leave her, but—"

"I've got a better idea. Why doesn't Amanda stay here with me? She can keep me company since I'm not real fond of thunderstorms." Beth saw that the news surprised Amanda and that the child began to relax. "You and Al go ahead and give my best to his mom."

Connie pulled the hood of her rain gear back in place. "Okay, then it's settled and I'm off." Connie bent and kissed Amanda's cheek then hugged Beth. A car horn sounded and Connie opened the door and waved at Al.

"Call when you get there," Beth shouted as Connie made a dash for the truck where Al waited. Connie waved again and they were gone.

"Did you make this?" Amanda asked and Beth turned to find her examining the baby quilt.

"I'm just finishing it. My best friend back in Chicago is going to have a baby in a few weeks. It's my present for the new baby."

"It's beautiful," Amanda said. "Is it hard to do?" She was studying the pattern of small colorful squares intently.

"It takes some patience but the fun is in figuring out what color or pattern to put where. I could show you how," Beth offered.

"You mean I could make one for my bed…for Dad's bed?"

Beth laughed. "Why don't we start with something smaller like a quilt for your doll there and see how it goes?" She motioned to the doll sticking out of the backpack Connie had left by the door.

"Great," Amanda announced as she ran to get the doll.

Beth pulled out her box of leftover quilt squares. "What's your doll's name?"

"Trudy." Amanda immediately began sorting through the fabric. "She doesn't like red but pink is her favorite color."

"How about blue?"

"Blue's good," Amanda agreed. "This is going to be so much fun," she added with a happy grin.

Beth was relieved to see that Amanda was so engrossed in selecting the fabric that she didn't even notice the rumble of thunder coming closer.

Greg Stone was beat. He'd left the house before dawn, and it felt as if he'd been driving for so long that the seat of his truck was permanently welded to his backside. He stretched his shoulders and neck in a futile attempt to relieve some of the tension.

After he'd stopped by the store and found it closed, he headed up the hill to the Spinner house. Al and Connie lived on the outskirts of the town in one of the single-family homes that overlooked the village. Lu had always wanted to live up there in a house all their own and he had promised her that someday they would. He had promised her a lot of *some days*.

He frowned as he pulled into the Spinner's driveway and saw that the house was as dark as the store had been. *Where were they?*

Knowing Connie's habit of leaving him notes if she couldn't raise him on his cell phone or pager, he left the engine running and made a dash through the pouring rain to the front porch. As predicted a sheet of white paper was taped to the front door. He ripped it free and read it quickly. Amanda was at home. Even though he was less than half a mile from home he dialed the number as he drove back down the winding road.

No answer.

His heart began to beat faster. Amanda was afraid of storms. His hands tightened on the steering wheel. As he turned the corner, he saw that only half the duplex was lit. Amanda wasn't home or if she was, she was sitting in the dark, which wasn't likely. Greg reversed his vehicle and headed back up the hill to where Amanda's friend Sara lived. No one was home there, either.

Fighting the low-grade sense of panic that had become a part of his life since the day he had first realized that he was going to lose Lu and there was nothing he could do to protect her or himself from that, Greg headed for the administration building. Only a skeletal crew remained on duty, and they reported that Connie had called to say that Amanda would be at home.

Where was Amanda?

She must be terrified. Normally a brave little kid, she flinched at every rumble and squeezed her eyes shut at the first flash of lightning. If the storm came at night, she would come into his room and huddle in bed next to him. It was night and the storm was raging and she was nowhere to be found. In addition to his panic, he felt a sense of anger at himself for his own inadequacies in trying to be both parent to Amanda and manager of the park.

Greg left the administration building and headed back to his own house. Maybe there was a message from Amanda. Maybe she had gone off with her friend Sara and her family. Maybe…

He pulled the truck to a halt at the back of the duplex and made a dash for the back door. Lights blazed in Beth's place. He could see her standing at her kitchen sink. She was laughing and talking to somebody.

"Whoa! Major steal," she shouted loud enough for him to actually hear her through the slightly open window. Amanda had told him that Beth was a firm believer in fresh air no matter what the temperature.

The thunder followed seconds later and as he fumbled with the keys to his own back door, he heard a second voice yell, "Go-o-al!" in perfect imitation of the announcer at the Olympic soccer games. This was punctuated by a most familiar giggle.

Greg gulped air as he realized that he could breathe again. Amanda was safe. Not only that, but she was actually cheering and enjoying a thunderstorm. He walked closer to the window and looked in.

There was Beth stirring cookie dough and talking to Amanda who was perched on a high stool sewing something, her tongue firmly locked in one corner of her mouth as she concentrated on the work. It was a scene of domestic bliss that might have come straight off of a Norman Rockwell calendar. To Greg's amazement the wetness on his face wasn't all due to the rain. He swiped at tears.

Beth glanced up to see if there was another flash of lightning coming and looked straight into the eyes of Greg Stone. She screamed and dropped the cookie pan.

Fortunately it was empty. "You scared the daylights out of me," she said as she rushed to open her back door and usher him inside.

"Sorry," Greg mumbled as he shrugged out of his rain slicker and let her take it while he pulled off his soaked boots.

"Daddy!" Amanda caught him in a bear hug around his waist. "Come see what Beth taught me. I'm a quilter," she announced proudly.

"Miss Baxter," he corrected automatically as he permitted his daughter to pull him along to the counter where she had left her sewing.

"I told Amanda that in situations like this one, it would be okay to call me Beth. I hope that's not a problem."

"No, I… Wow, that's really something, sweetheart," Greg said studying the uneven stitching and matching of the fabric squares.

"It's a quilt for my doll," Amanda explained not waiting for his obvious question. "See, Beth made this one for her baby godchild that's going to be born in a few weeks." Amanda held up the crib quilt, then dropped it and ran to the sofa. "And, not only that but her very own grandmother made this great big one here. It's called a crazy quilt. Isn't it just the coolest thing you ever saw?"

"Very nice," Greg said. He glanced around the room as if he had suddenly stepped into a foreign world. He had never actually been inside her half of the duplex since that first night when he'd helped her unload her car. It was a totally different place.

"Did you get my note?" Beth asked.

"Your note?"

"We left a note on the front door and by the phone at your place."

"I was coming in the back…saw you and…"

"Oh Greg, I'm sorry," Beth said as soon as she realized what had happened, how panicked he must have been to get Connie's note saying Amanda was home and then drive up to a dark house. "You must have been so worried. I should have thought to at least leave a light burning."

Lightning flashed and Greg turned to catch Amanda, expecting her to propel herself across the room and bury her face in his side.

"Whoa!" she shouted. She had returned to her sewing and as she stitched, she narrated the storm as if she were a color commentator for some sports event. "One of the angels stole the ball. She's headed downfield. Here comes the other team." The thunder rolled. "Go-o-al!" she shouted pumping one fist high in the air and laughing with delight.

Greg looked from his daughter to Beth and back again.

"Beth told me she used to be afraid of thunderstorms, too, but then her daddy told her that it was nothing but God's angels playing some sport. Today Beth and me decided it was soccer."

"I see," Greg replied but the look he gave Beth stated clearly that he didn't get it at all.

"Every time the thunder rolls Amanda decided that the opposing team had stolen the ball and was headed down field. Lightning is, of course, a…" She motioned that Greg should finish the thought.

"Goal?"

"Not like that, Dad. Beth says the professional announcers say, 'Go-o-al!' real loud and drawn out."

Greg picked his daughter up and started to tickle her. "And do the professionals always giggle after they say it?" he teased.

Beth watched the father and daughter laughing with delight and tried to work around the lump that suddenly seemed permanently lodged in her throat. As was her habit, when she didn't know how else to handle a moment, she started to chatter away as she busied herself with multiple tasks.

"Connie came by on their way to Bozeman and she was going to leave Amanda at home but wanted me to know she was there. I was the one who suggested she stay here. Actually I was really glad to have the company as well as the help. After all, I have these cookies to make for the open house at the school and who was going to lick the bowl for me?"

She shoved a sheet of cookies into the oven and turned to start scooping up a fresh batch. "I just love raw cookie dough and as it turns out, Amanda does too."

"Beth said we had to save it for dessert, though. She's making supper for us and then we're going to sit in front of the TV and just pig out, isn't that right, Beth?"

Beth glanced at Greg to see how he was taking all of this. "Well, yeah, that was the deal if a certain young lady finished all her regular food."

"Sounds like a party," Greg said but his voice was quiet and his eyes were on Beth.

"You're invited, Dad, isn't he, Beth?" Amanda

looked at Beth and locked her hands around her father's neck as he held her high in his arms.

"Am I?" he asked Beth.

Do you want to be? "Of course. The more the merrier." Beth busied herself by checking on the cookies, stirring the pot of chili she'd been heating for their supper and gathering the makings for a mixed salad from the refrigerator. "I hope this is okay," she said. "It's just leftovers."

"With a side of raw cookie dough, I'd say it's pretty near perfect," Greg replied as his eyes met hers. He set Amanda back on the stool next to her sewing and cleared his throat. "How can I help?"

"Oh heavens, no. You've already put in a full day, not to mention the fact we probably scared you to death not knowing where to find Amanda. You must be exhausted." She saw that she had come very close to the truth and paused in her frenzied activity to really look at him. He was bone weary and had gotten soaked in the storm as he searched for Amanda. "Why don't you go over there next to the woodstove and just relax?"

Greg took her suggestion. He walked across the small room—the bare bones, impersonal room she had somehow managed to make homey and welcoming. He took note of all the many little details that surprised him—things about her surroundings that made him take stock of his preconceived ideas about her.

He sat in the rocker and noticed the way she had padded the seat and back with colorful cushions. The beige carpet was splashed here and there with small braided rugs. He leaned back and watched her working in the small galley kitchen. This was no performance for his benefit. Beth was clearly used to spending time in a kitchen. She was accomplished at juggling the many tasks of putting a meal together and baking cookies at the same time. Occasionally she would lean across the counter and make some comment to Amanda about the sewing project that claimed all of his daughter's attention.

Greg frowned. Beth Baxter was not at all what he had expected. She was a city girl, used to high-rises and bright lights and—considering her father's money—probably maids, country homes and private schools. Yet, she seemed perfectly at home in these plain surroundings. He glanced away unwilling to let her see how affected he was by her as he watched her work. Closer examination of the small crib quilt Amanda had spread carefully over the small footstool next to the rocker revealed true craftsmanship, a real work of art.

He leaned back in the rocker and noticed a Bible on the table next to the chair, not just any Bible but an old dog-eared, much-used Bible. He picked it up and opened it to the frontispiece. There, in a childlike scrawl similar to Amanda's own ten-year-old handwriting, were the words: "Presented to Elizabeth Joy Baxter on her tenth birthday. With love and blessings, Grandma Jen."

He closed the Bible and replaced it on the side table. From what he had observed of her in church, he knew that she wasn't faking her deep spiritual roots. It was one more thing that he would never have expected about her. She'd arrived at the park like some drifter out of the night. He'd thought of her as an heiress to a fortune, someone out for an adventure. He had never stopped to imagine her as part of a real family—a daughter, a grand-daughter learning to quilt at her grandmother's knee.

Over the past few weeks as his fascination with her had grown in spite of his determination to fight it, the one thing he had used to console himself was that she was just here—on a lark. He'd convinced himself of that and it had kept him from giving in to his curiosity about her. Yet there was something so permanent about the way she had decorated this place, something about her insistence on surrounding herself with mementos and treasures that were well-used and loved, something about the way she obviously valued the ordinary things in life that spoke volumes.

"Impossible," he muttered as a reminder to himself as he once again felt the now familiar draw to her. *She still clings to the idea that there's some master pup-peteer up there pulling everybody's strings. We have nothing in common—nothing,* he reminded himself, firmly making it almost a mantra to help get him through the rest of the evening.

"Soup's on," she called gaily and Amanda scram-bled to help her bring the food to the small table near the woodstove.

"We should say grace," Amanda announced once she had settled herself in a chair across from her doll. "We used to say grace at every meal before Mom died," she told Beth. "I miss it," she continued matter-of-factly and glanced at her father to see how this little speech was being received.

"Amanda," Greg began.

"I think grace is a terrific idea," Beth interrupted

what sounded like it might be the beginning of a reprimand. "Will you do the honors, Amanda?"

Amanda and Beth both folded their hands in prayer and bowed their heads. Amanda waited. "Dad," she said in a stage whisper, "we're waiting. God's waiting."

Greg had no choice. He folded his hands and bowed his head staring at the steaming bowl of chili in front of him.

"God is great. God is good. Thank you, God, for this food," Amanda said softly.

"Amen," Beth chorused with her. Greg added a grudging "Amen."

The food was flavorful and hearty. On top of everything else, the woman could cook. Greg frowned as he helped himself to seconds on the chili.

"Too spicy?" Beth asked. "You're frowning," she added when he gave her a puzzled look.

"No. Just some passing thought," he replied.

"Da-a-d, this is supper time and we don't think about work at mealtime, do we?" Amanda lectured wagging a finger at her father.

He smiled. "It's an old family tradition," he explained to Beth. "No unpleasant thoughts or worries during meals."

"Mom made that rule," Amanda announced and turned her attention back to her chili.

Beth watched Greg for any sign of pain or grief. Instead he smiled at Amanda. "That's right," he said.

"Mom had a lot of rules like that," Amanda continued. "I mean, she wasn't bossy or anything. She'd tell us that the rules were for our own good. What was it she used to say, Dad?"

"That her rules were intended to help us appreciate what we had while we had it," he answered and his expression and voice both softened as he repeated the words.

"Yeah. I think they were pretty good rules," Amanda declared as she gobbled down the last spoonful of her chili. "I've cleaned my plate. Can we eat cookie dough now?"

"One spoon," Beth agreed. "You don't want to make yourself sick."

"One spoon and two real cookies," Amanda negotiated.

"One cookie," Greg instructed, "and stop trying to con your teacher."

Amanda giggled and very carefully filled a teaspoon to the max with raw cookie dough, then took a long moment to select the largest possible cookie. "Is it okay if me and Trudy watch TV?"

"Trudy and I," Beth corrected. "Would you rather watch a video?"

"Cool."

Beth got the tape loaded into the VCR and gave Amanda the remote. When she turned back to the kitchen, Greg was watching her, his expression unreadable.

"You're thinking again," she said lightly as she began clearing away the dishes.

He got up to help her. "I want to thank you for taking care of Amanda today. I'm sure you discovered that she's terrified of storms and yet you seem to have disarmed that fear completely."

Beth laughed. "The truth is, *I'm* terrified of storms

so I did what was necessary to get us both through the afternoon. I was never so glad to see anyone in my life as I was to see you standing outside my kitchen window." The words were out before she could stop them. Afraid that they sounded too forward she quickly added, "Even if you did scare me half to death."

He smiled a charming shy smile that was at odds with his usual stern and serious demeanor. "Sorry about that. I guess I did come off as something of a Peeping Tom." He picked up a dish towel and waited for her to wash the first dish so he could dry. "It's true that I was a little concerned when I read Connie's note about Amanda being home and then saw that our half of the house was dark," he admitted.

Beth was surprised that he would openly admit such a thing. He must have been truly upset. She chastised herself for not making sure she left word in other places about Amanda staying with her. "I should have called somebody. The least I could have done was driven over to Connie's and added to her note. I'm really sorry." She handed him a plate and their fingers brushed.

"It's okay," he said but he was looking at her hand and she became aware of how close they were standing in the small kitchen. She could actually feel the warmth of him next to her, could smell the scent of his uniform, now rumpled from a day in the field, was aware of the steady solid rise and fall of his chest with each breath he took.

She turned back to the sink, her eyes downcast as she wondered if there was any possibility that he felt an attraction for her on any level. She tried to think of a topic of conversation that might lighten the moment. He rescued her by mentioning the quilt.

"I don't know much about these things, but that must have taken a lot of patience," he said after complimenting her on its beauty.

They were on safe ground. She could breathe again. She smiled. "My grandmother is the real artist in our family. She still checks my work to be sure the stitches are even and I haven't taken any shortcuts."

"Sounds like a tough lady. How old is she?"

"Eighty-five. She called last night to remind me that my friend's baby is due any time now. And, she added that since I had done this fool thing of running off to the Wild Wild West, I had better get this quilt on the next stage out of here if it was going to be there in time for the baby's arrival. She's a real character."

Greg smiled. "I'd like to meet her sometime."

It was a perfectly innocent statement so why did Beth's heart leap with pleasure? "Are your parents and grandparents still living?" she asked.

"Yep. All of them. Mom and Dad retired from the park service about two years ago and moved to Arizona. My maternal grandparents live there as well. My dad's parents are up in northern Montana."

"How wonderful for Amanda to have all of those generations in her life."

"It's been pretty important. And, of course, Lu's family has been around as well—fewer of them. Lu's mom also died of cancer when Lu was a teenager. We knew the history and thought we were keeping a watch on things but..." His voice trailed off and he got a faraway look in his eyes as he stared out the window into the black night.

Beth swallowed hard. "I know this really is none of my business, Greg, but Amanda…"

His attention was instantly back on her, his dark eyes probing hers. "What about Amanda?"

"It's just that this afternoon while I was helping her with her quilt, Lu's name kept coming up and there was a moment when…I got a feeling that she's concerned, maybe even feeling a little guilty."

His hands clenched the dish towel, his knuckles turning white with the obvious effort to maintain his calm. "Guilty?"

Beth swallowed and plunged on. "She told me that sometimes she can't remember what her mother looked like and that at times like that she has to look at old photographs. It bothers her that she can't always recall the sound of her mother's voice. I think that may be one reason why she quotes her mother so much.

"She talks about her a lot at school as well," Beth added when they had sat in silence for a moment.

This time there was no doubt about the pain that she saw cross his face. She would have done almost anything to spare him that, but he needed to know.

She placed her hand on his. "Greg, I know this is hard for you."

For the first time since she'd met him, he seemed at a loss. "I know she thinks about Lu a lot. I try to talk to her, answer her questions…" His voice trailed off. "It's just hard because I keep thinking that the real question she must want to ask is *why*."

Beth didn't know what to say. Was he really saying that he was the one still asking why?

"Back in Chicago, there were two occasions when I had to deal with children who lost a parent," Beth said.

He looked at her with surprise and respect. "Really?"

She nodded. "One boy's father was killed in a robbery as he was leaving his office late one night. The other was a boy whose mother died in a car accident right after she and his father had separated."

"That's awful," Greg said.

Beth nodded. "Yeah. In both cases they were there one minute and gone like that." She snapped her fingers.

Greg glanced at Amanda whose attention was riveted on the movie.

"At least with Lu, we had some time—Lu was able to talk to Amanda, help her through it."

Beth nodded. She sensed that she had given him a new insight into his wife's death by telling him about the others. She decided to push her luck.

"I do have a suggestion—something we used with these children in Chicago," she said softly.

Once again she had his full attention, but this time his eyes were filled with pleading.

Help me.

She knew what it would cost a man like Greg to admit that he could manage a huge national park but he could not find the answer to relieving his child's emotional pain.

"We would help the child make a memory book," she continued as if this were a normal conversation in which he was holding up his end of things.

"A memory book," he repeated.

Beth nodded and removed the towel from his hands,

draping it over the side of the sink to dry and then starting to put cookie dough onto a clean cookie sheet for baking.

"It works best if you and Amanda work on it together. You let Amanda tell a story—a memory—about her mother or your life as a family when Lu was still alive."

"I can do that," he said more to himself than to her.

"You help her find pictures of Lu and herself and you to illustrate the story."

"We have albums," he said. "Lu spent a lot of time putting them together before…"

Beth swallowed. It hurt to see how hard it was for him to talk about this.

"You can also let Amanda draw pictures as you write the story down—or help her do that. Then you put the whole thing into a scrapbook."

She handed him a freshly baked cookie, which he ate in two bites as he considered the idea.

"Sounds like a big undertaking."

"It doesn't have to be. In fact it works better if you do it a little at a time—over time."

"I don't know. Stirring up all those memories…"

She wanted to ask him if he was afraid of his own pain or causing pain for Amanda.

"I've seen it work," she said casually not wanting to insist. "Basically, you just keep repeating that simple exercise until the book is full or until Amanda is satisfied with the outcome. It does help," she assured him.

Greg watched her turn to put the last pan of cookies into the oven. He was as close as he had ever been to confiding in someone the horrors of his own jumbled feelings related to his wife's death. His anger. His pain. His loneliness. His own guilt. *Pull yourself together, man. It's the storm and the scent of freshly baked cookies and this woman mothering your child that you're reacting to. Get a grip.*

"It's an interesting idea. Maybe we'll talk about it—Amanda and me."

He did a little drum rhythm on the counter with the flat of his hands and stood. "Well, it's late." He offered Beth a handshake. "Thanks again for everything."

She looked at his outstretched hand and deliberately took hold of it as if they were holding hands instead of shaking hands. She turned a formal thank-you into something else—something friendlier and more intimate.

"Any time," she murmured as she squeezed his hand and released it. She crossed in front of him to gather Amanda's things in her backpack.

Greg watched Beth kneel to pick up the scraps of fabric and the crudely sewn quilt Amanda had started. She carefully pressed the creases from it with her flat palms and he recalled how those gentle, long-fingered hands had felt touching his. He heard Amanda sniffling back tears.

"I'll never understand how you can watch that movie a dozen times and still cry every time," he teased, glad to have something other than Beth to focus on.

"It's a girl thing, Dad," Amanda said as she shrugged into her jacket and then put her arms around Beth and gave her a big hug. "I had a lot of fun today. Thanks for making up the story about the storm. I wasn't quite as scared as usual," she added with a whisper.

Beth hugged her back and kissed her on the forehead. "It was all my pleasure. You work on that quilt now and if you need help or more fabric just stop by, okay?"

Amanda beamed. "Sure."

Beth stood up and handed Amanda's backpack to Greg. "That offer goes for you as well, Chief Ranger," she said lightly.

"I don't do much quilting," he said and smiled.

"Pity," she replied and he realized that they were flirting and that it felt pretty normal and nice.

Back in his own place, Greg put Amanda to bed and then sat down at his desk to do some work.

A memory book, Beth had called it. He opened the bottom drawer of the desk and took out a photograph album.

It was one of the ones Lu had put together, one she had been almost desperate to finish. He remembered how she had wanted him to work on it with her, and how he had refused. After her death, he had put it away.

In those days the pain of looking at her laughing healthy face and remembering all the good times they had shared had been more than he could bear. As time went on he had thought about the album less and less— until tonight. Beth's words rang as true for him as they did for Amanda.

"Amanda is afraid that she's forgetting her mother," Beth had told him.

As he paged through the album he realized that his own mental image of his wife was fading. He also struggled to recall the sound of her voice, the smell of her cologne. The woman who looked back at him from the pages of the album seemed in her glowing health and beauty to be trying to remind him of something important.

"What was that quote you always used to repeat?" He murmured as he stroked the photograph. "You never knew where it came from but it was your favorite."

For an instant the laughing face seemed alive and he heard her voice clearly. "'Life is what happens while we're making other plans,'" he chanted in unison with the words heard only in his mind.

Then the memory changed. The laughter and soft voice that he heard was Beth's. He thought about her talking to Amanda as they made the cookies and worked on the doll quilt. He thought about how she had laughed at the thunderstorm, and gotten Amanda to do the same. He stared at the photograph again.

"I know what you're up to," he said aloud, "but trust me, she's not the right one."

As if Lu were there debating the point, he added, "Maybe it is time to get on with my life, but not with her."

He paused and turned the pages. "No," he continued as if arguing with the woman in the photographs. "I can't take the chance that Amanda will love her and then she'll leave. You of all people should understand that, Lu," he instructed.

Suddenly he recalled the tiny frown lines that used to furrow her brow when Lu didn't agree with him. It was an image as clear as if he had seen her yesterday.

"I know you don't agree, but this time you're just going to have to trust me," he said firmly and closed the album.

Instead of storing it back in the drawer, he left it on the table with all the framed family photographs. Lu looked up at him from a photo of the three of them taken at Yellowstone Lake.

"Okay, I'll admit that the memory book idea isn't half bad. Maybe I'll talk to Amanda about that this week, okay?" He had just done exactly what he'd always done in the face of those challenging little furrows in Lu's brow. He had offered a compromise.

"Dad?"

Amanda stood at the top of the stairs. Her voice was thick with sleep. "Who're you talking to?"

"Myself," he replied. "Go back to bed, kiddo."

He listened for the sound of his daughter's bare feet retracing her steps to her room.

"I've been working way too hard," he muttered as he switched off the light and headed upstairs to tuck her in for the night.

Chapter Seven

The week following the storm passed in a flurry of activity. The children were quite excited about the upcoming open house at the school and kept coming up with new ideas for decorating their classrooms and entertaining their guests. In the face of their enthusiasm the faculty found it hard to say no to anything within reason that they proposed and as a result found themselves spending a lot of extra time at the school helping the children implement their ideas. The other teachers told Beth that they'd never seen the children get so involved in the open house before.

"Are you moving out of the duplex and planning to just live here?" Greg stood at the door of the classroom.

She hadn't heard him come in, but she was inordinately glad to see him.

"It might be easier," she admitted as she leaned back in her chair and stretched her stiff muscles. "There are just so many things the children want to show their parents and friends. It seems a shame not to try to make that happen when they are so very enthusiastic."

"Not like your students in Chicago?" he asked easing into the room and looking around at the various displays.

Beth laughed. "Heavens no. They would be bored silly with the idea of an old-fashioned open house." She paused. "That's not fair. My students in Chicago were good kids. I was the one who was out of sorts," she admitted.

"Really?" Greg studied her. "I find it hard to believe that you could ever be anything but effervescent."

Beth laughed. "Heavens, you haven't seen me at my worst yet. Trust me, I can be a real pain."

"So why were you out of sorts in Chicago?"

She shrugged. "I'm not sure. As I've told you, I had—have a wonderful life there. A fulfilling career in teaching and a full social life. My family is the best."

"But?"

"But I wanted something more," she admitted. "Doesn't that sound extraordinarily selfish?"

"Not really. Depends on what more you wanted? Money? Fame?"

She laughed. "I think those are two of the things I was running away from."

"Aha. So, when you said on that first night that you hadn't come here on the run, you weren't being entirely truthful."

Beth blushed. "I didn't mean it that way. Just that sometimes being wealthy can be…difficult."

He raised one eyebrow.

She laughed. "Yeah, well you know, poor little rich girl and all of that. How on earth did we get off on this?"

"You started it."

"Lucky you to be the one in the line of fire when I do," she joked.

He smiled. "It's nice to see that it makes you as uncomfortable as my talking about myself makes me."

"Touché. Anyway, getting back to the topic at hand— the open house. It's a lot of work, but also a lot of fun and the children are really excited about it."

"But, it's not only the kids who are caught up in this thing," he mused.

"All right. I'll admit that I've kind of gone a teensy bit overboard, but the kids are so appreciative of everything and that part is also different from the students in Chicago. They tend to take things like this for granted."

She watched him as he continued his tour of the room. "I could turn the tables, you know."

He glanced at her. "How so?"

"It appears to me that you've been spending quite a bit of time at your work these past several weeks. I thought things were supposed to ease up once the high tourist season ended."

He smiled. "Guilty," he admitted softly. He leaned against the side of her desk. "How's Amanda doing?"

"What a question! She's your daughter to the core— an overachiever, a born leader and smart as a whip."

He could not hide his pleasure at her praise. "She takes after her mother."

"Some, probably," Beth said, "but I see a lot of you in her, as well. You're a very good parent, Greg."

"Thanks."

There was a moment when neither of them seemed to know what to say.

"Are you about ready to head for home?" he asked finally.

Unable to find her voice, Beth nodded.

"Good. Me, too."

As they crossed the compound together, he told her about his day. "The northeast pass has been closed all week."

"Why?"

"All that rain we got turned to snow in the high elevations."

"It just seems too early for winter."

He laughed. "I thought you Chicago natives were used to cold weather."

"Well, sure—in January," she replied. "You know *winter?* October—that's autumn."

"Winter comes a little earlier around here, and speaking of that, you need to be aware of the particular cautions you'll need to take—"

"Oh, please not another lecture," she begged.

"Just a short one," he assured her and then proceeded to list all the measures she needed to take before heading out into the park for the next several months.

Beth sighed. He just couldn't help himself, she decided. He really should have been a teacher.

In spite of his growing attraction for the woman, Greg was determined to maintain a purely friendship-based relationship with Beth. He didn't want to offend her or upset Amanda, but he was convinced that spending too much time—especially time alone—with Beth would only increase his fascination with her and no good could possibly come of that.

On Saturday, he was finishing up some end of the season reports when he heard the familiar sound of Beth's distinctive laughter outside his office window. He glanced out and saw her talking to a couple of the park's naturalists. She'd certainly made a place for herself among the staff in the short time she'd been there. They accepted her as one of their own, sought her out to join them in various activities and brought up her name in casual conversation with disconcerting regularity.

She was outfitted for a serious hike complete with water bottle, backpack and walking stick and he strained to hear bits and pieces of the conversation.

"...science unit on trees," he heard her say. "I'm off to collect samples." She waved and headed toward one of the main trailheads.

Greg forced his concentration back to his paperwork. Beth couldn't get into trouble collecting a bunch of leaves. There were at least a couple dozen different trees along the trail she had chosen. She should have all the samples she needed within an hour.

But by late afternoon she had not returned. Greg had watched for her. Thinking he might have missed her or that she might have come back into town another way, he walked over to the duplex.

Amanda was working on her quilt.

"Has Miss Baxter come home?" He asked and hoped it sounded like a normal casual question.

"Nope, but don't worry, Dad. Beth will find her way home. She's really good at maps."

The trouble was, Greg hadn't seen a map in her hand. She'd hiked the trail before—or part of it, but it would be easy to get distracted and make a wrong turn.

"I have to go out on the trail for a bit," he said. "I should be back by six, okay?"

"Sure, Dad."

"Okay, see you later," Greg said and headed across the compound and up the trail he had seen Beth take several hours earlier.

It was one of those days that seem scripted by some Hollywood director. The sky was a cloudless blue, the air sharp and crisp with a hint of cold weather to come. The brilliant golden leaves of the aspens rustled in the October breeze. But Greg Stone knew that a day like this could be distracting for the novice hiker. It was a day when tourists would stop in the middle of the path and inhale deeply, then trudge on deeper and deeper into the park, anxious to discover untold beauty just beyond the next bend or rise.

Even if she had brought a map and paid attention to the markings along the trail Beth could have gotten turned around, think she was headed back toward town and actually be moving farther away with every step. Or knowing Beth, she could know exactly where she was but not care that she was moving away from town.

She always seemed to be going in ten different directions as she juggled the routine schooling of the children, plans for the open house at the school and maintained contact with family members and friends back in Chicago. On top of that, it seemed to Greg that her acceptance by the rest of the teachers and park staff had gotten her involved in all sorts of extra activities—church things plus the book discussion group and a bike-hike club.

Greg picked up the pace, oblivious now to the scenery as he focused on one thing—finding her before dark. He could hear the rush of the waterfall as he climbed the path. His breath was coming in bursts of exertion now and he lengthened his stride to conquer the steep slope of the trail. The water crashed over rocks and dropped twenty-five feet straight down to a pool on the other side. It wasn't the highest waterfall in the park but to a novice caught in its drop, it could be maiming or even deadly.

Greg stood at the summit and looked down, afraid of what he might find on the great flat rocks at the base of the falls.

She was there all right, standing on a large rock in the middle of the gurgling water and quite some distance downstream from the falls. She was gesturing with her hands as if conducting an orchestra or having an animated conversation with someone. Greg half slid and half stumbled down the steep trail. When he reached the base, he moved through the trees and underbrush toward the stream.

"Okay, you can go now," Beth shouted.

Greg paused knowing there was no way she could know he was there since he was coming up on her from behind and the noise of the falls drowned out any sounds he might make.

"Shoo," she said and made the same flinging gesture with her hands that she had used equally as ineffectively with the bear that first night. Then she placed both hands on her hips and faced her adversary.

Greg lifted the branch of a low cedar. All the while his brain raced as he tried to figure out what he would do to rescue her from a bear once again. This time he didn't have a stun gun handy. He searched the shoreline for the source of her dismay.

A large bull elk stood at the edge of the stream staring directly at Beth. Greg grinned.

"Now look," Beth shouted at the elk above the noise of the falls. "I've about had it with you. I really don't need this in my life right now. I've got problems of my own, and I'm not the least bit interested in stealing your harem or joining it. So go away."

The elk did not move. He was still exactly between her and where she needed to go to get back on the trail to town. "You know, Chief Ranger Stone is not going to be happy about having to comb the woods for me after dark. You know how he gets when we don't follow the rules," she added.

Greg bristled and waited.

"Come on, Mr. Elk, give me a break. The guy already thinks that I redefine the word *tenderfoot*. If I don't head back now, it's going to get dark."

The elk rolled his head and appeared to look at the sun low in the western sky.

"That happens you know, like clockwork every day. Sun comes up. Sun goes down." She was squatting now, her hands dangling between her knees as she continued to observe the elk. "Tell you what," she said and stood up. "Why don't I just mosey on over to this next rock…" She hopped one rock closer to the shore. The elk eyed her.

"You see, I really didn't mean to disturb you. I just wanted to get a leaf from that tree there. I teach the children, you know."

The elk made a low sound and bent to take a drink of water.

"Well, maybe it's not as glamorous as being the king of the bull elks but I like it," she said defensively. "And frankly, I'm quite good at it no matter what Chief Ranger Stone might think."

She eased herself onto the next rock. The elk was instantly on alert. "He's not a bad sort—the Chief Ranger," she said as she continued to slowly work her way across the rocks toward the shore. "He's actually quite interesting if you like the stubborn type."

Interesting? Greg took some offense at that. He had been called handsome and attractive and even a hunk and all she could come up with was *interesting?*

"He has this adorable daughter—Amanda? Have you met her? No? Well, she's really special." She was almost to shore and the elk was still watching her but hadn't moved. "Well, it's been a real treat chatting with you, Mr. Elk, but I think I may hear your wife…or harem or whatever calling you for supper." The elk took two steps along the shore in her direction.

"No," she shouted.

The elk froze.

"Look, I'm tired and hungry and I want to go home. I've really bent over backward here, and you're beginning to remind me more and more of our obstinate Chief Ranger. It wouldn't kill you to just turn around and leave. You can come back in five minutes and I promise you, I won't be anywhere near here. Deal?"

The elk gave a snort.

Greg smiled in spite of himself. What was it about this woman that made him want to laugh with delight? Why on earth hadn't he let her know he was standing not ten feet from her? Because he wanted to watch her and listen to her ridiculous patter. Quickly and stealthily he moved back up the trail. Halfway up the waterfall, he stopped and cupped his hands to his mouth and called her name. "Beth. Beth Baxter. Are you out there?"

"Greg?" She sounded relieved.

Greg smiled and felt enormously pleased with himself.

"Down here," she shouted and waved her arms wildly.

Greg acknowledged her wave and chuckled at the way he had fooled her as he retraced his steps down the path to the edge of the stream. "What are you doing out there in the middle of the stream?" he asked gruffly as he held out his hand to help her step from the last rock to the shore.

"There was this humongous bull elk," she said breathlessly. "I was right over there collecting leaves and all of a sudden he comes crashing through the trees and he had this awesome rack and he's doing that bugle thing they do when they think there's somebody trying to steal their women and—"

"I don't see an elk," Greg said pretending to look around. "Oh, you mean that guy way over there?"

"Trust me, five minutes ago, he was right here. Maybe your shouting drove him away."

"If that was the case, why didn't you shout at him?" They had started back up the trail.

"I did," she protested.

No, you carried on a normal conversation with the beast, he thought and grinned.

"Are you laughing at me?" she demanded glancing back in time to see him smile.

"No ma'am."

She continued to climb the steep trail. He tried not to notice how she was equally attractive from behind as she was face-to-face. He tried to think about something else and instead found himself wondering what it might be like to kiss her.

As they reached the top of the falls, she stopped to catch her breath. "He was enormous," she protested as she plopped down in the high grass to adjust her hiking boot.

"I believe you," he assured her. "The elk can be a most *interesting* not to mention *stubborn* beast."

She gave him a strange look and he noticed the color in her cheeks, which he was pretty sure, was new and had nothing to do with the exertion of the climb. He liked having her be the one unsure of what was happening for once.

He knelt and helped her with the knots in the wet laces of her boots. His fingers shook slightly, and he cast about for anything resembling a safe topic of conversation.

"By the way," he said, "I want to thank you for the memory book idea."

"You're welcome. Is it working?"

"There's one problem."

"What?" It was unnerving the way she focused every ounce of her concentration on him.

"Well, I'm still not really sure how to go about it. I mean, I gathered up all the pictures and some letters and drawings Lu made, but after that I'm afraid I'm lost and you know how smart Amanda is. If I try to do this and mess it up, she'll see right through me and wonder what's really going on."

"But gathering all of those things is a wonderful way to begin," Beth praised him.

"Maybe," Greg replied but he sounded anything but sure. "Look, I was wondering if you might be willing to work on it with Amanda. I mean, coming from me she might view it as something she needs to do for me. I thought about what you said, and I agree that it's really important for her to focus on her own memories, not try to help me handle mine."

Beth's expression softened. "Of course," she said and he was pretty sure that tears brimmed. "I'm really touched that you would trust me to help Amanda with something so personal."

"Yeah, well…"

What on earth was happening here? He had never wanted to kiss a woman as much in his life. He stood and offered her a hand up from her reclining position.

"Come on," he said. "We need to make time if we're going to get home before dark."

Beth accepted his hand and peppered him with questions about photos and other sources of materials for Amanda's memory book. As they made their way along the trail it seemed perfectly natural to continue holding hands as the brilliant gold leaves of the aspens fluttered like butterflies around them.

Chapter Eight

Greg lay in bed and watched the slow arrival of dawn. He hadn't had a lot of sleep. In fact he'd noticed that ever since Beth Baxter's arrival in the park, sleep had been in short supply for him.

He considered their encounter at the waterfall and the hike back to town. By the simple act of taking her hand and not letting go, he had changed everything. No longer could he pretend to ignore the way his heart tripped every time he saw her walking across the compound or heard her laughter. No longer could he dismiss the fact that he was always watching for her, watching *out* for her. No longer could he postpone dealing with the fact that he was attracted to her in a way that went beyond mere interest or casual friendship.

"Morning, Dad." Amanda plopped herself onto the foot of his bed.

"Morning, kiddo."

"Are we going to church today?"

"Sure."

"Do you think Beth will be there?"

She always was. She always sat in the third row right where he could see her clearly as he sat in the choir.

"Probably so."

Amanda pulled one of his pillows around and lay down. "I like her—Miss Baxter," she said as she studied the ceiling. "I didn't think I was going to and then I did. Funny, huh?"

"That's the way things go sometimes," Greg replied but his mind was on Beth.

"She always looks so pretty, especially when she's in church, don't you think so, Dad?"

Greg grabbed Amanda and began tickling her. "I think that if a certain young lady doesn't get back to her room and start dressing, we're going to be late."

Amanda giggled and broke away from him. "I'm going," she said, still laughing. "Hey, Dad, how about pancakes?" she called.

He got up and made her pancakes, and continued to think about Beth. He couldn't get the woman out of his mind.

Of course, any idea of an actual romance between them was destined to be heartbreak for somebody. Beth was strong-willed. She was also a firm believer, and that was the real problem.

She would only tolerate his nonbelief for so long before trying to change him. That would lead to arguments. Then she would leave. And what of Amanda, getting more and more attached to her? If he did anything that might encourage Amanda's obvious hope that something might develop between them, Amanda was bound to end up brokenhearted.

Weeks earlier when Beth had surprised him with her quiet perception and understanding of his point of view at the book discussion group, he had permitted himself to consider the possibility of getting to know her a little better.

That night in her place when she had baked cookies and cared for his daughter, comforting her when he wasn't there to do it, he had settled on friendship as the best course. He needed to stick with that. Good-buddy-no-strings friendship. That was the ticket.

He poured batter in nearly perfect circles in the hot skillet and smiled.

The woman had certainly gotten herself in a fix yesterday with that elk. By the time they'd hiked back to town it had been dark, but he'd barely noticed the long hike. Talking to her was getting easier every time they were together. He liked showing off the park to her, liked her curiosity and liked having the answers to impress her.

He frowned as he flipped the pancakes. On the other hand, what if he hadn't come along? She'd still be out there—scared and cold or perhaps worse, injured or maimed. He shuddered. For all her adjustment to the ways of park life, she was still a tenderfoot.

The way he saw it, he had two choices. As her friend, he could either let things take their course and worry himself to death whenever she took a notion to go off on her own, or he could make sure she knew the ropes. Number two was clearly the better choice. If he had confidence that she had been properly instructed, he could relax and stop watching for her every second.

He served up pancakes on a plate and set them in the oven to stay warm.

"Amanda? Breakfast," he called up the stairs as he filled two mugs with coffee and rummaged through his desk for the things he needed. "I have to go next door for a few minutes, okay?"

He gathered his maps and his thoughts. There was nothing to be gained by permitting himself to give in to the sort of romantic attraction signaled by that innocent bit of hand-holding. Even if she were willing to accept him for the nonbeliever that he was, he couldn't very well give up his job or his life in the park to follow her to Chicago. It was simply impractical to think anything could come of a romance between the two of them. And the one thing Greg Stone knew for certain about himself was that he was a very practical man.

Beth had never been much of a morning person. Especially on the weekends, she liked the opportunity to ease into the day, savoring such time-honored rituals as lingering over coffee and the paper and lounging about in her pajamas until time to get ready for church. This particular Sunday she planned to indulge herself to the fullest.

Her adventure of the day before had left her exhausted with aches in muscles she hadn't even thought existed. She hated to miss church, but this was one morning when she definitely needed to heed God's command that there be a day of rest.

She stretched out on the sofa and closed her eyes

then immediately opened them. It was useless. She hadn't been able to get back to sleep since she had first wakened at dawn thinking about Greg Stone— about the way his large tanned hand had engulfed hers, about how being with him seemed more and more the right thing for her. She thought about his laughter and the serious expression that crossed his face whenever he was worried about something. She thought about what a wonderful father he was to Amanda. She thought about the times the three of them had shared—times when they had almost seemed like a family.

She sighed and pulled her knees to her chest in an effort to relieve her aching back. Who was she kidding? Wasn't it obvious that Greg Stone was still mourning his wife? To hear Connie and the others talk, the woman had been about as close to a saint as they come. And he had certainly made it crystal clear that he wasn't interested in getting involved—especially with her.

On top of that, she had to admit that his determination to turn his back on the very faith that could have sustained him through all of this was a problem for her. Beth believed firmly in the necessity of a strong spiritual foundation to see a person through life. Certainly strong shared spiritual values were the basis of any successful relationship. Under other circumstances she and Greg might have had a chance. But Beth had witnessed far too many situations where people went into a relationship thinking they would change each other, and she knew that she wouldn't be able to keep herself from trying to change Greg Stone—to bring him back to his faith.

"Argh-h-h!" she cried aloud in her best imitation of a comic strip character's woeful cry.

There was a hesitant knock on the door, followed by the unmistakable bass of Greg's voice. "Beth?"

Beth glanced down at her rumpled flannel pajamas. She knew they probably were more presentable than her uncombed hair. She cleared her throat to get the sleep out of it. "Coming," she said cheerfully. She winced as she rolled off the couch, hastily ran her fingers through her hair and struggled into her robe.

"Hi. You're up and out early," she said as she opened the door and leaned on it for support as pain shot through her lower back.

"Can I come in?" He held up the mugs of coffee and she saw that he was trying hard to balance them plus a bunch of papers he held clutched under one arm.

"Sure." She swung the door wide and stepped aside to let him pass.

He headed straight for her kitchen table, handed her one mug of coffee and set the other one on the counter. "Cream, no sugar, right?" he said as he turned his attention to arranging the various documents he had brought with him.

"Right," she replied as she cradled the mug to warm her hands and peered over his shoulder at the papers. "What's all this?"

"These are topographical maps of every trail in the park. We don't need to go through each and every one of them today, but we should at least cover the trails closest to town here. The rest we can get to on an as-needed basis." He paused to take a breath and a gulp of his coffee. "This, for example, is the map for the trail you hiked yesterday. Judging by your stiff movements this morning, I would guess that you were unprepared for its steep climbs."

"I'm still breaking in my hiking boots," she offered weakly.

He glanced at her bare feet and then immediately back to the map. "You should wear them some each day," he advised. "Now then, as you will see, I've high-lighted the best route on this particular trail—red is for the short circuit, which is what I would advise for the time being. Once you've gotten a bit more seasoned as a hiker you can tackle the blue and perhaps even the green. You're quite athletic and have clearly had some good training in other sports so it wouldn't surprise me if you could skip directly from red to green."

"Thank you, I think," Beth said dryly. She rubbed sleep from her eyes with the back of one hand and took another sip of the coffee. "You don't mind if I sit for the rest of this lecture, do you Professor?" She perched on the edge of one of the high bar stools near the counter. "Ah, look at this. I have a topographical view of the *topographical* map. Lovely."

Greg frowned. "This is serious, Beth. You cannot just go wandering off willy-nilly with no objective in mind."

"I have never gone off willy-nilly in my life," she pro-tested. "I don't even know what *willy-nilly* is."

"You dropped everything you had going for you in Chicago and came here to Yellowstone," he said quietly. "That certainly qualifies."

Beth pulled herself to her full height, which still left

her several inches shorter than he was. "Well, aren't you the perfect one to lecture someone about life choices? You, of course, have your own life firmly in hand, don't you? That's probably why you're so cheerful all the time."

He scowled down at her. "I'm trying to offer a little friendly help here. Do you understand what could have happened if I hadn't come along yesterday? You could have been out there stumbling around in the dark all night."

"Ha! That's fine advice coming from someone who's been stumbling around in the dark—spiritually speaking—for nearly two years now." *Where had that come from? Why was she getting so upset?* Beth glanced down at her bare toes. "I'm sorry," she said. "That was out of line."

He let out his breath as if he'd been holding it for several minutes. He walked the two paces it took for him to reach the sink and tossed the remains of his coffee down the drain. "I think I know what's going on here," he said.

"Good." Beth let out her own sigh of relief that the tension between them had eased. She smiled. "Maybe you could give me a clue?"

He held out his hand to her and she knew he wasn't offering the formal handshake. Hesitantly, she placed hers in his. "This," he said and his voice was unsteady as he closed his fingers around hers. "This is what's going on."

Beth swallowed hard. "Okay. Should we talk about it?"

He studied their intertwined fingers as if seeking answers. "I'm attracted to you," he admitted.

"But?"

"Beth, you have a life—a real life—out there. You

have family and friends and probably an apartment that you've turned into some kind of country home in the midst of the city. You are the daughter of a very prominent man and you have a position in the community—your community." He released her hand reluctantly.

"Come over here and sit down and let me tell you a little something about that perfect life you seem to have assigned to me." She took a step toward the living room and froze.

Greg was immediately at her side. "Beth, what's wrong?"

"I seem to be having a little problem with my back," she replied and grimaced as a fresh pain shot through her. "I'll be fine. I just need a little rest."

Greg led her gently toward the sofa, removing the back cushions to give her more room. "Lie down," he ordered. "Put these under your knees. A back injury is nothing to take chances with. Why didn't you say something?" He stacked the cushions under her knees and she had to admit that she felt immediate relief. He went upstairs and she could hear him rummaging around in the small bathroom. "There are aspirin in the kitchen," she called.

"Kitchen," he muttered as he hurried back downstairs and toward the galley. "They call it a *medicine cabinet* for a reason," he added under his breath.

"Sorry. I just don't seem to get headaches in the bathroom. The kitchen makes more sense to me."

He rolled his eyes, looking a great deal like his daughter in the action. "Take these." He handed her the pills and held a glass of water to her lips.

She swallowed and made a face. "Yuk."

Greg put the glass aside and pulled the rocker next to the couch. "Okay, tell me the story of little Beth Baxter in Chicago," he said as he settled back, clearly prepared to stay for the long haul.

"You know, it's not all seashells and balloons—being the only child of one of Chicago's most famous couples. Yeah, yeah, I know—poor little me, but believe it or not, it does have its downside."

"Such as?"

"You don't always know who to trust—who your friends are. That may be the worst part."

Her voice had taken on a wistful uncertain tone that surprised him. The one thing he had assumed was that Beth Baxter was always very sure of herself and of those around her. "What else?"

She shrugged. "The usual. It's a pain to be known your whole life as *the only daughter of...*or worse, *the sole heir to the Baxter fortune.*" She actually shuttered with disgust.

"You were a teacher there—you certainly didn't need the work, but you were a teacher."

"I love children. I love watching them learn, being there when the lights go on in their eyes, watching them discover an idea."

"So, why did you leave and come out here? You said yourself that your students there were bright and not so terrible."

She adjusted herself slightly and grimaced at the movement. He resisted the urge to help her. Touching her would not be a good idea at the moment. He was far too attracted to her to risk any contact, and it would shoot holes in his plan to be her friend and nothing more. "I mean, why not just keep on teaching there?"

"In the private school where I taught, the students all come from money and have all the advantages life can give. What they tend to know about the baser realities of life, they've picked up from reading or movies."

"That's natural," Greg said.

"In some ways their lives are actually hampered by their advantages. It can actually stunt curiosity and that can mean that they are less open to the adventures of learning. Not in all cases, of course, but—"

"So you left and came here."

"It's not like I ran out on them," she argued as if he had accused her of something. "They have Evelyn Schuller, after all."

"I didn't say you ran out on anybody."

"It's just that I was getting frustrated and that wasn't doing them or me any good," she continued defensively.

"I see."

"I thought if I took part in the exchange program, it might generate some new ideas in me for how best to reach those students in Chicago and the change in teachers for a year would shake them up a bit, as well. From their letters, I can tell that Evelyn is a hit."

Greg nodded. "How's it working out for you here?"

She smiled. She glowed and he basked in the loveliness of that smile.

"It has been so much more than I expected, so different, so exciting," she gushed. "I mean it, Greg. I never expected to feel such…such a sense of community…."

Her eyes widened as if she'd just made a wonderful discovery.

"That's it," she said more to herself than to him.

"What's it?" he asked.

"It's this place, these people—I feel this incredible sense of belonging, of being accepted for myself in a way I've never truly been able to experience before."

"You make it sound as if your life in Chicago was miserable."

"Oh heavens, no. Don't get me wrong," she rushed to add. "I have a fabulous family—my parents are two of the most down-to-earth people you'd ever want to meet. My grandmother is always reminding us that if the family money isn't used for good then what's the point. We have grand times together and I miss them all terribly, but this place…these people…Connie and Al, Amanda, even you…"

He knew she meant it in a teasing way, but his heart beat in triple time and he had to swallow several times to gain control of his voice. Unable to get a handle on his emotions, he reverted to the safe course. "The exchange program is just that, Beth—a temporary exchange of roles. In a few months you'll head back to Chicago…."

"Maybe I will and maybe I won't," she replied. "I know you don't necessarily believe this but I really think I've been brought here for some purpose beyond just teaching for a year. I haven't yet figured it all out but I have faith that God will show me in His own good time."

If he had needed anything to remind him of the differences between them, she had just delivered it.

"I think you're kidding yourself," he replied with characteristic bluntness. "Even God can't change the fact that you're only here for a short time."

Chapter Nine

"Look, just because your own faith has taken a holiday…" Beth began, frowning. She was working overtime to understand that trying to change him simply wouldn't work. Was it asking too much for him to show a little more respect for her point of view?

She saw that she had hit a nerve. His eyes flashed with irritation, but she couldn't help herself, she kept pushing, asking the questions that she'd wondered about for weeks.

"Tell me, Greg, before Lu died, was your faith strong?"

"What's that got to do with this discussion?"

"Just indulge me—you're questioning the presence of my faith. Why can't I question the absence of yours?"

"All right. Yes, I was a believer."

"And in those times did you never question anything that happened? Wonder why God would permit this or that? Was your life really that perfect and unspoiled?"

"Of course, I questioned things—that's natural." He bit off the words and crossed his arms across his body as he figuratively and literally closed himself off from the discussion.

"And in those days when you turned to God for answers, did you get them?"

"I figured things out," he argued. "I may have thought God was leading me but now I know better."

"What changed?"

He stared at her openmouthed. "You *know* what changed."

"Yes, I do," she said quietly. "What changed is that the questions got harder—more personal. What changed was your commitment to digging for the answers even though it was painful."

This time he turned completely away from her. "This is not a discussion I want to have with you or anyone else, Beth."

"Well, that's too bad, because believe me it's a discussion that one day you *will* have with Amanda. Just how long do you expect her to go along maintaining her own faith when the key influence in her life has turned away from his? Don't you think she knows that you're just going through the motions?"

Greg frowned. "The subject was your mission here in Yellowstone. You have the absurd notion that you might want to stay."

"There's nothing absurd about it," she argued.

"I would remind you that Evelyn Schuller will return at the end of the year, Beth. We can't afford another teacher on staff here. If you've got any notion of staying on…"

He saw the irritation furrow her flawless features. "Ah. Now, I'm the one who is hitting a nerve," he added.

"Did it ever occur to you that the lesson you believe you were sent here to learn might just be to appreciate the life that you left back in Chicago?"

She squirmed her way higher onto the pillows in an effort to assert herself. She succeeded in triggering the pain in her lower back.

Greg appeared oblivious to her discomfort as he relentlessly pursued his point. "Have you thought things through, Beth? Life is hard here. It can be boring. The winters are long, and there's not much to keep a person entertained—especially a person who doesn't have a job."

She bristled and grimaced at the jolt of pain that came with the stiffening of her spine. "I'm a grown woman, Greg. I know life here in the park is different from the life I came from, but trust me, I do a fairly good job of amusing myself. Just because I come from money doesn't mean I expect to be pampered and entertained by others."

"I didn't mean it that way." He sat forward, his hands between his knees. "I only meant that sometimes people romanticize life in the park or in any wilderness setting. There's a kernel of the frontier in every American."

"I can tell the difference between reality and romance," she replied stubbornly.

"Maybe, but Lu—" He stopped. *Where had that come from? He had gotten her off talking about Lu and now here he was back at the topic again.*

Beth gave him her full attention. "What about Lu?"

"Nothing." He stood up. "I have to go. Amanda should have left for Sunday school twenty minutes ago."

"Chicken," Beth muttered and stared out the window, refusing to acknowledge him.

"I'm sorry if I upset you, Beth, but the fact is that you…"

She turned back and looked up at him, her eyes flashing with annoyance. "Not another lecture. Could you just try to refrain from offering me advice? Especially when your own personal life is such a mess, okay?"

"My life is fine," he protested.

"Yeah, right. Try finishing this statement. 'But Lu…'"

He stood there staring back at her.

"Can't do it, can you, Mister I've-Got-My-Life-in-Order?" She turned away again.

Greg crossed the room and opened the door. He stopped for a moment with his back still to her. "Lu romanticized life here. She tried hard to be something she wasn't because she knew I loved being here so much. I always told her that someday we'd leave and live like normal people. But I kept postponing that day because I kept earning promotions. I thought that someday I'd be able to give Lu her dream as she'd given me mine. I thought we had time. I was wrong—dead wrong." He left and closed the door without looking back.

Beth made a move to go after him and cried out in pain and frustration as she collapsed back on the couch. "What does that have to do with me?" she said aloud as if he were still in the room. "I'm not your late wife. I'm telling you that I'm beginning to love the park as much as you do. I'm just this close to telling you that I think I love *you,* Chief Ranger Stone." So much for her resolve to not fall in love with any man whose faith was not as strong as her own.

Why him, God? There are a dozen likely souls out

there—good, faith-abiding men. Why this one? She closed her eyes against the hot tears that stung and threatened to break free.

Giving in to her tears was definitely not a good idea. Sobbing took a lot of back action and she really wasn't up to that at the moment. Instead, she picked up one of the pillows he'd moved to the floor and threw it at the door. "I don't need you or any other man to make me happy, Greg Stone." On the other hand, he was doing a bang-up job of making her miserable.

Connie stopped by with hot soup for lunch. "Greg told us you were down," she said as she bustled around the kitchen. "Everyone at church this morning was ready to smother you with a steady flow of company but I persuaded them to let me take the first crack at it. So, what's your pleasure? Nonstop visitors bringing you an array of baked goods and home remedies—not to mention advice? Or something less dramatic?"

"Definitely the latter," Beth replied with a grimace as she eased herself into a more comfortable position. "Was Greg at church then?"

"He walked Amanda over for Sunday school, then said he couldn't stay—something about paperwork at the office." Connie handed Beth a mug of steaming chicken noodle soup. "You two have a fight or something?"

"Of course not," Beth protested. "Yes," she admitted when she saw Connie's skepticism. "Is it that obvious?"

Connie laughed. "Honey, our first clue was Greg. The man is as transparent as that windowpane when it comes to you."

"He is also the most exasperating, mule-headed, opinionated…"

"Uh-huh. Eat your soup." Connie perched on the arm of the couch and nibbled a cracker. "The way I see it, the two of you are on a collision course, and yet you keep missing each other. It's the most incredible thing. You like him. He likes you. Amanda adores you both. The Lord indeed works in mysterious ways His wonders to perform but I have to admit that this time, the big fella has me completely stumped."

"It won't work," Beth said miserably. "We're too different."

"No, you're too much alike—both of you trying to be noble and think three steps ahead of what's really happening here. You're missing the moment, honey. Snap out of it. Pay attention."

She polished off the cracker and brushed the crumbs off her lap. "Got to run. Somebody will be by later this afternoon with supper. Try to resist the urge to rearrange the furniture until then, okay?"

"Aye, aye," Beth replied with a mock salute. She watched Connie head for the door. "You really think he likes me?"

"Gee, I don't know. Why don't I pass him a note during study hall and see what he says?" Connie teased. She laughed as she left, ducking the pillow Beth flung in her direction.

Beth was running out of pillows.

"Beth?"

Beth's eyes fluttered open and immediately shut

again. It was dark in the room. She must have slept the afternoon away.

"Miss Baxter? Dad and I brought supper." Amanda was kneeling next to the couch. "Dad made turkey sandwiches. I helped."

"That's nice of you, honey. Turn on that light, okay?" Beth blinked at the sudden flare of light in the room. She focused on a tray on the kitchen counter that hadn't been there earlier. "Where's your dad?"

"We forgot the mustard—Dad has this special cranberry mustard he likes on his turkey sandwich. He went to get it." Amanda rushed to straighten the covers as Beth struggled to sit up. "He told me to come on over and wake you up."

"How was Sunday school?" Beth moved gingerly and recorded the fact that she was in decidedly less pain than she had been earlier.

"Pretty good. We did the Good Samaritan lesson today." Amanda grinned. "We're supposed to perform a Good Samaritan act before next Sunday. Do you think this counts?"

"Absolutely," Beth assured her. "Could you get my hairbrush off my dresser?"

"Sure." Amanda took off up the stairs at a run.

"And a pair of socks," Beth called. "In the bureau."

"Okay," Amanda shouted.

The front door opened letting in a gust of the chill night air. Beth looked up at Greg and wondered if there would ever come a time when her heart would react normally to his comings and goings in her life. She didn't think there was much chance of that. "Hi."

"Feeling better?" he asked but instead of coming closer or even making direct eye contact, he headed straight for the counter and began unwrapping the sandwiches and spreading them with mustard.

"Some." *This is going well,* she thought with a sardonic sigh. "Look, I'm sorry about earlier but—"

"Not a biggie," he replied with a dismissive wave of his hand which only served to infuriate her more.

"Beth? Do you want your mirror, too?" Amanda called from the bedroom.

"Sure, honey."

Amanda brought the requested items. "Oh hi, Dad." She made an attempt at fluffing a pillow behind Beth's back. No doubt she had seen the nurses who cared for her mother do the same thing.

Beth pushed herself a little higher on the pillows and risked a glance in the mirror. It was worse than she had imagined. Her hair stood up in funny little spikes where she had slept on it and her left cheek mirrored the pattern of the chenille throw pillow. She quickly brushed her hair and handed the mirror and brush back to Amanda. "Thanks."

"You look pretty even when you don't feel good, doesn't she, Dad?"

Greg glanced up and then back at the sandwiches. "Come pour the milk, Amanda," was all he said.

He brought Beth a plate filled with the sandwich, chips and fresh fruit. Suddenly she was ravenous. "Looks good enough to eat," she quipped and Amanda exploded into laughter.

The sound of childish giggles filling the small close

room broke the tension. Greg smiled at his daughter and then at Beth. "Then, let's eat," he said relieving Amanda of one of the glasses of milk she carried in each hand.

After Amanda had led them in thanks, Beth bit into her sandwich. "Amanda tells me they worked on the lesson of the Good Samaritan in Sunday school today," she said.

"Yeah, Dad, what have you done today to be a Good Samaritan?"

"He took care of me twice in one day," Beth replied before Greg could answer. She watched him to see what his reaction would be.

"It's my pleasure," he said softly.

"That's very good, Dad," Amanda announced. "Mrs. Clark said the best Good Samaritan is the one who doesn't do it for any reason other than because it's the right thing to do. Then it gives them pleasure even as it helps the poor and downtrodden." Amanda's imitation of the oh-so-proper Mrs. Clark was perfect.

Beth giggled at the same time she tried to take a gulp of her milk and ended up snorting the milk out her nose.

Greg grinned. "Very classy," he observed handing her a napkin.

"You know how classy we high-society Chicago girls are," she teased back and was thrilled to see how his eyes softened as he watched her.

"We have cake," Amanda announced.

"Chocolate?" Beth asked.

"Chocolate-chocolate chip," Amanda confided. "Sara's mom made it for you."

"Only if you eat *all* of your sandwich, young lady," Greg instructed.

"Ah, Dad."

In a thinly veiled attempt to disguise the fact that she was only pretending to nibble at her sandwich, Amanda kept up a lively conversation relaying to them the latest gossip about each of the students in the school. Beth smiled because what Amanda failed to notice was that by occasionally taking a bite of the sandwich, she was in fact finishing it. She saw that Greg had caught on as well and between the two of them, they peppered Amanda with questions to keep her talking and eating.

"Look at the time," Greg said finally. "Guess we'd better head back home, kiddo. School tomorrow."

Amanda looked stricken. "Dad, the cake, remember?" she said in a stage whisper.

"Oh, yeah." He snapped his fingers and then grinned down at her. "Cake."

Amanda giggled. "I'll take care of everything. You stay here and sit with Beth, okay?"

"Works for me," Greg said, his voice taking on a more serious tone.

For what seemed like the hundredth time since he'd first come through the door early that morning, Beth wished she'd had the good sense to struggle into something slightly more becoming than her flannel pajamas.

"How's the back?" he asked as he sat back down in the rocking chair.

"Much better."

He frowned.

"Truly," she assured him. "I think by morning I should be absolutely fine."

"You could take a day off. Connie can sub for you.

She told me to tell you she can pull your kids in with hers—she's done it before."

"I'll keep that in mind. Connie is going to call me first thing tomorrow just to be sure I can hobble over."

He smiled and nodded.

They had run out of things to say, and Amanda seemed to be taking her own sweet time dishing up the cake.

"About earlier…" they said in unison.

"You first," he said.

"I just wanted to say that I didn't mean to snap at you. I know you were just trying to avoid a painful topic, and it wasn't fair of me to keep pressing you." He started to interrupt but she held up her finger indicating she wasn't finished. "What bothered me a lot was the fact that you seem to assume that your wife and I—being women—are somehow dependent on you or some other man for our welfare and happiness. That you must blame yourself for whatever it is you think Lu wanted out of life. My guess is that she had exactly what she wanted—you and Amanda. We each make our own choices in life. Lu did. I do. From everything I've heard about your wife, she was content and happy. She clearly loved you and adored Amanda, and she was a woman of enormous faith. Forgive me for saying it, but I think she would be more disappointed now in the way you've turned away from God than she ever was about living in some house on the hill."

Greg frowned. "Surely you can understand that it's a real stretch for anybody to believe in God when somebody as loveable and young as that little girl ends up without a mother." He spoke through gritted teeth and in a low tone so Amanda wouldn't overhear him.

Beth paused, willing herself to compose her thoughts and choose her words carefully. "Greg, what I understand is that by turning away from God at the very moment when you need His help the most, you put yourself and Amanda in an incomprehensible position—you deprive yourself and your daughter of the very foundation of all hope and comfort." Her voice was low but her tone was intense. "He is there to help you endure these difficult times, not to bring them on you."

To her astonishment, Greg answered her with a wry smile. "I thought you disapproved of people who lectured," he said. He was smiling but his eyes flashed.

"Cake," Amanda announced and both adults put on their best forced smiles for the benefit of the child.

The two of them focused all of the attention on Amanda and as soon as he had consumed the last bite of his cake, Greg stood. "Now, we really do have to go," he said, still not looking directly at Beth. "Miss Baxter needs her rest and tomorrow is a school day, honey."

Amanda kissed Beth's cheek while Greg carried the dishes to the kitchen and rinsed them. "I'm really sorry you hurt your back," she whispered, "but I think Dad likes looking after you."

Beth hugged Amanda. "Thanks for coming," she replied. "I'll see you tomorrow at school."

"Good night," Greg said stiffly from his position near the door. "Call if you need anything during the night."

"Thanks for everything," Beth called. "I'll be fine." She hated this. They needed to finish their conversation. "Greg, I…"

"Good night, Beth." The door closed behind him.

Chapter Ten

A week passed. Then two. The snows were a regular thing now. The northeast entrance to the park was closed for the season. The days turned from golden to gray as the dry leaves crunched underfoot like the wads of paper the children discarded at school.

The seasonal changes weren't the only chilling aspects of life in the park. Ever since that night when Greg and Amanda had brought her supper, Greg had had to work overtime to keep things purely casual with Beth.

"The woman is dangerous," he reminded himself as he stood at his living room window and watched her hurry across the compound on her way to school.

She made him question the things that he thought had gotten him through the terrible months following Lu's death. And most of all, she made him feel hope again.

She acted as if everything was perfectly normal between them whenever they passed on the street or on their way in or out of the neighboring houses.

"Are you completely oblivious to the effect you have

on me, Beth Baxter?" he murmured watching her caress the head of one of her students as together they walked into school.

Greg forced himself to move away from the window and to put any thought of Beth Baxter out of his mind. She was the most infuriating, exasperating woman he'd ever known.

On the night of the school's open house, Amanda was nervous and excited. She had been elected by her classmates to act as the narrator for the program.

The room was getting pretty crowded. Just about everybody in town had come. She spotted Beth across the room looking just as pretty as she always did as she greeted each and every person. Amanda liked the way Beth had of taking a person's hand between both of hers. She'd been practicing that in her room, and some day when she was grown-up she planned to do exactly that same thing. People really seemed to like it a lot.

She checked her script one more time and then looked around for her dad. He wasn't there yet. Amanda sighed. She knew his work often kept him from getting to places on time, especially for fun things like this.

"It's almost time to begin," Beth said softly as she and the other teachers herded all the children to the curtained area they had dubbed as backstage. "Is everyone ready?" she asked.

Every head nodded but no one spoke.

"All right, then. Circle of friendship," Beth prompted.

Amanda and all the other children clasped each other's hands as they formed a circle. They all closed their eyes for a moment until they heard the third-grade teacher's voice say, "Blessings on us all."

"Deep breath," Beth prompted as she demonstrated taking in air and slowly releasing it. "And it's show time," she added with that wonderful smile of hers that made them all feel as if nothing could possibly go wrong.

Amanda stepped out from behind the curtain and into the spotlight. Of course, the spotlight was really just a lamp with a bright bulb in it, but she might as well have been on the biggest stage in the world. Then she saw her father slip into a single empty seat in the front row. He made the motion he often made to him when he sang in the church choir—the one that reminded him to smile. She felt her mouth curve and at the same time she relaxed. Her dad could be such a geek sometimes.

The entire performance seemed to fly by and before she knew it, every class had performed their part and all of the school's thirty-two students and their teachers were standing onstage and bowing to the audience. Meanwhile everyone in the audience was standing and applauding and a few of the rangers were whistling and cheering. It was really something.

"You were just wonderful, Amanda," Dad said as he came onto the stage and hugged her. "Mom would have been so proud of you."

Mom was proud, Amanda thought with pleasure. It was hard to explain to her dad that she often felt that her mom was with her—watching over her, laughing with her, fuming over this or that. Dad didn't much like to talk about things like that—not since Mom died. Amanda really wished she could find some way to make him see that Mom was okay and that just like Reverend Dixon had told them, she was in a better place because in heaven she wasn't sick or in pain anymore.

"I'll get you some punch," Dad told her and moved away just as Beth approached.

Amanda did not miss the fact that he had hurried away just at the time Beth came closer. He did that a lot, but Amanda was sure that he really liked her teacher. It was something grown-ups could be so stupid about. They liked each other but they acted like there was something wrong about that. All of which led her to the conclusion that Beth was special. She smiled at that idea. If Dad thought of Beth as special, then just maybe…

Once she had even hinted to Sara that her dad and Beth might get married. Sara had acted like it was the most amazing idea she'd ever heard.

Amanda went in search of her father. Maybe there was some way she could make sure that he and Beth got a little closer. "Miss Baxter could use a glass of punch," Amanda said as he handed her a cup filled with the rosy-colored liquid. "She's hardly had time to breathe," Amanda added in her best imitation of the way Connie Spinner talked sometimes.

She watched her father watch Beth and saw how his eyes got all soft and mushy when he looked at her. It was the way men looked at ladies on television when you were supposed to understand that they really really liked each other and would probably end up kissing before the next commercial.

"I'll pour her a glass for you to take her," her dad replied.

Amanda had seen that on television too where somebody brings the beautiful lady a drink and then tells her it's from some man sitting clear across the room. She waited until her dad had the full glass in his hand and then she said, "Could you do it, Dad? I just saw Sara and there's something I really need to tell her."

Sara was on the other side of the room but Amanda sprinted toward her, grabbed her and said, "Just pretend that I'm telling you something really serious," she ordered.

Sara's face twisted into a frown of serious concern. Sara was a born actress. Everybody said so. "What's up?" she asked.

"I want Dad to take that punch to Miss Baxter."

The two girls watched as Amanda's father stood holding the punch and looking at Beth. Beth was totally unaware that he was watching her because she was so busy taking care of one of the little kids. But then she looked up, and the first person she looked at was Amanda's dad. The two girls held their breath.

"This is *so* romantic," Sara whispered.

"I know," Amanda agreed. *Take her the punch, Dad.*

Beth smiled and Amanda's dad lifted the punch glass in a kind of a toast like he did on Thanksgiving and New Year's, but he didn't cross the room. He stayed where he was and drank the punch himself.

"I have a surprise for you," Amanda said later that week as she helped Beth clean up after school.

"Really?" Beth was glad that in spite of the fact that Greg had obviously resolved to keep his distance, he hadn't kept Amanda from spending time with her. "I love surprises."

Amanda sighed. "Me, too."

"Well?"

"Tomorrow. I get to go with Dad for his rounds in the park, and he said it would be okay if you came, too."

Beth studied the child. She appeared to be holding her breath. "You asked him if it was all right to bring me?"

Amanda nodded vigorously. "Will you come?"

"I don't know, Amanda…."

"Oh, please say you will. You've been talking about wanting to see the park in winter and now this is only the most perfect chance and Dad said you could come and it could be months before he's not too busy to let us come with him and—"

Beth laughed. "All right, you've talked me into it. I'll call your father tonight to get the time and everything."

"Six o'clock," Amanda assured her. "Dad likes to get going early and then we have the fabulous breakfast on the trail and then we go everywhere—you've just got to see the geysers in winter and then we'll stop for lunch at the winter patrol cabin. Dad will make a fire, and we'll have marshmallows. It's going to be the best day of your whole life, I bet."

"Six?" Beth said. "In the morning? Isn't it still dark then?"

"Yeah. It's so cold you can see your breath and Dad says your words could freeze except for mine. He says I talk way too fast and too much for my words to ever freeze. He brings a big thermos full of hot cocoa, and we sip it along the way. It's just heaven." She sighed as if she had just laid out a trip to a tropical island. "You're just going to love it."

Beth smiled what she hoped was an encouraging smile. She really wanted to see the park in winter. She also wanted to spend time with Greg and get them past this silly impasse. And she very much wanted to make Amanda's day. But, the thought of getting out from under her pile of quilts and dressing in the dark to actually venture outside for most of the day was intimidating, to say the least.

Amanda must have seen her hesitation. "You know, Dad thinks you're a real tenderfoot," she said as she focused all of her attention on cleaning off the chalkboard. "I bet he thinks you'll say no."

Beth knew what Amanda was up to in throwing out this challenge and at the same time her mind conjured up the skeptical face of Greg Stone. The child was right. Greg thought she would make some excuse and refuse to come. That's why he had agreed that Amanda could invite her. He was betting that she would make an excuse and he would win in two ways—he wouldn't have to face her and he wouldn't *lose* face with his daughter.

"Okay, six it is," she said with an enthusiasm she didn't quite feel.

Greg packed supplies into the saddlebags and saddled his horse, then turned his attention to the smaller second horse. Amanda had assured him that her guest could ride although she had remained close-mouthed about which of her friends was coming along. In answer to his question as he tucked her in for the night she had just giggled and said, "You're going to be really surprised."

He chuckled to himself as he checked the cap on the thermos of hot chocolate. Whoever she was bringing, it had been too long since he had spent a day with his daughter and he was looking forward to their trip. Earlier, as he lay in bed waiting for the clock to go off, he'd had the thought that every day that passed took them a little further from the pain of Lu's death. Every day brought them a little closer to feeling normal again, whole again.

He thought about Lu as he saddled the second horse and realized that the usual physical ache he had assumed would be a permanent part of remembering her was absent. He paused and conjured her face and her laughter and her voice urging him to take care. He felt the same sense of pleasure and well-being that he felt whenever he thought of sharing a moment with his best friend who had died when they were both thirteen.

His heart lightened with the realization that he had passed into this new stage of his mourning. The guilt and regret were absent, and so was the familiar rage.

"Hi." A muffled voice croaked the single word from just behind him. "Can I help?"

He turned and faced a very good imitation of a creature from outer space. Only the eyes were familiar. "Beth?"

"Don't you dare laugh at me," she warned. "It is cold, and one thing people who grow up in Chicago know is cold and how to dress for it."

He nodded and strolled around her.

"What are you looking at?" she demanded.

"I'm just wondering if you fall down whether we'll be able to set you upright again? Or with all that padding, will we just have to leave you there until we can let some of the air out of all those layers?"

"You *are* laughing at me," she accused.

He couldn't help it. She looked absolutely ridiculous all done up in a bright-purple down jacket that was a couple of sizes too large for her. Most likely she had borrowed it from Connie. She had obviously used the extra room to put on extra sweaters and probably long underwear. He laughed out loud. "What are you doing out here at this hour dressed like that?"

Her large expressive eyes registered surprise and confusion. "I'm going with you. Oh, I get it. You thought I'd chicken out. Well, I'm tougher than you think, Mr. Chief Ranger." She struck a pose with legs planted apart and hands on her hips. "Besides, Amanda said there would be hot cocoa."

He froze in his tracks.

"Well?" she demanded.

Greg had forgotten the question.

"Is there cocoa or not? Because if not then I'm outta here." She turned and took two steps back toward her unit.

"Dad, stop kidding around," Amanda ordered. "There's cocoa," she assured Beth.

"No wonder the kid was being so cagey about who she'd invited," Greg mumbled.

"You didn't know? But I thought she said it was your idea."

Greg shrugged. "She asked if she could bring a friend. I figured she'd ask—"

"Dougie or Sara," Beth said. "Oh Greg, I'm sorry. I really don't have to…I mean if you'd rather I didn't…"

"Dad, you promised," Amanda stepped between them and gazed up at her father.

Greg looked at Beth. "Do you want to come?"

"Do you want me to come?"

More than anything. "I promised Amanda she could bring a friend. You certainly qualify."

It was not exactly the ringing endorsement Beth had hoped for but she would take what she could get. "In that case, which horse is mine?"

Greg gathered his senses enough to reply. "Well, now ordinarily, I would think Reba here would be for you—smaller more delicate. But with all the weight you've added with those clothes, maybe Skydancer here is the better choice." He patted the neck of his horse. "You don't mind carrying a couple of extra pounds, do you, boy?" he said and then couldn't help laughing again.

He saw that she had caught his joke and was definitely not amused. "That's right, I forgot. You're not exactly a morning person, are you?" he teased as he indicated the smaller horse and prepared to help her mount up.

"My sense of humor appears in direct proportion to the hilarity of the joke," she replied as she tried without much success to get her foot high enough to step into the stirrup and swing onto the horse. The problem was all those layers made what was a fairly routine motion impossible. "I could use a hand," she admitted.

"Give me your foot," he said doing absolutely nothing to disguise his laughter at her predicament as he cupped his hands and boosted her onto the horse. "You do ride, don't you?"

"I ride," she replied through gritted teeth as the horse, Reba, pranced and stamped in the snow and Beth held on trying to get her balance.

"Okay, then. Amanda, come on. You ride behind me, okay?" He mounted his own steed and then held out his hand to Amanda to pull her aboard.

Beth fumbled with the reins that had gotten twisted. "Here, let me help," Greg said and urged his horse forward until he was next to hers. Greg took off his gloves and leaned very near as he straightened the reins and checked them. Beth was aware that he did not move back right away and looked up and into his eyes.

"Thanks," she murmured.

He studied each of her features as if seeing her for the first time.

"Greg?"

"Yeah," he said huskily as if they shared one thought, "we'd better get started." He turned to Amanda. "Ready?"

"Ready," she replied with a salute.

"It can get a little bumpy out there," he said as he studied Beth. "You're sure you can do this?"

"I do ride, Greg," she assured him. "Let's go."

He gently kneed his horse. "You heard the lady, Skydancer. Lead on."

Beth gave a little yelp of surprise and hung on as Reba fell into step and kept pace with Skydancer.

As soon as they were out of town, Greg took one of the old service roads that led them through pine forests in a shortcut to the main road that would lead them into the interior of the park. They passed a small canyon and Greg reined in and pointed. Behind her Beth could look down and see the lights of Mammoth twinkling in the distance as the sleepy little town awoke for a new day.

Greg picked up the pace as they headed on past a group of boulders known as the Hoodoos and onto the open plains surrounding Swan Lake. There he stopped again.

"Listen," he whispered.

Silence and a vast landscape surrounded them.

"Look over there," Greg instructed, his voice still low and reverent as he wrapped his arms around Amanda.

Beth turned and saw the sun rising, streaking the sky with color over Sheepeater Cliffs. An eagle soared across the sky.

"Beautiful, isn't it?" Greg said.

Beth nodded. "I was just thinking about something Reverend Dixon said that first Sunday I was here. It was the most glorious autumn morning, and he said it would be impossible for anyone to look at a morning like that and not believe in God."

Greg didn't make any response and Beth realized that he might have taken her statement the wrong way. "I wasn't…I didn't mean to imply…"

"It's okay. I know what you meant."

"But you don't agree." *Was she determined to ruin the morning?* Beth thought as she willed herself to stay quiet.

Amanda glanced up at her father waiting with Beth for what he would say next.

"Nobody appreciates the majesty of this place more than I do, Beth. That will never change. Coming out here and just standing here looking out at a landscape untouched by humans has brought me enormous peace."

"That's a start," Beth said softly.

"Well, I love this place," Amanda announced.

"Me, too," Beth replied in an awed tone as she took one more look at the sunrise.

When she looked back, Greg was watching her and there was something indefinable in his gaze. Whatever it was, it gave Beth a rush of pure pleasure.

"Got to get going," Greg said reluctantly.

Once again, Beth followed Greg's lead as the horses cantered across the snow-covered terrain. What was happening to her? She'd been here such a short time, and yet it seemed as if the life she had known before was in the far distant past. This was her reality now, her life now—this place, this man.

By the time they made their next stop, Beth was ravenous, but Greg was focused on his work. He frowned as he caught sight of some indentations in the snow.

"Bear?" she asked nervously.

"Poachers," he said more to himself than to her. He helped Amanda to dismount and then slid off his horse. Beth followed suit. Greg bent and examined the foot impressions and hoofprints. "Recent." He took out his binoculars and scanned the horizon for signs of men on horseback.

Poachers brought to mind tales of the Old West when men had routinely crossed property lines and stolen livestock from their neighbors. "Surely, in this day and age…"

Greg's attention turned to her. "It's a wilderness,

Beth. It attracts all kinds—those who respect its population and those who don't."

"But there are laws—hunting permits, boundaries."

Greg gave her a wry smile and she saw that his eyes
expressed a deep sadness. "Some people don't think the
law applies."

The impression of at least two different pairs of boots
was unmistakable. "What will you do?"

Greg scanned the horizon. "They've got several
hours on us." He pulled his two-way radio from the
pack behind him. "Brent?"

Static punctuated the crystal clear air.

"Yeah, boss."

Greg reported the poachers to Brent Moser and
turned his attention back to Beth and Amanda. "Can't
a guy get anything to eat around this place?" he
demanded in mock anger.

Amanda giggled. "Breakfast," she announced as she
reached up and retrieved a canvas pack and the thermos
of hot cocoa from the saddlebags.

Out of the bag came the most delicious cinnamon
rolls that Beth had ever tasted along with bananas, trail
mix and the blessed hot chocolate.

"Heaven," she praised as she bit into a roll. "These
are incredible."

Amanda grinned. "They're Dad's specialty. He used
to make them all the time before—" She paused and
glanced at Greg, suddenly unsure of herself.

"Before," Greg continued gently. "When Mom was
still living. She really loved them."

Amanda's face brightened. "Yeah. She used to say

they were absolutely *sinful,* and she'd get the icing all over her chin just like you have now, Beth." Amanda giggled as Beth hastily reached for a paper napkin.

"Got it," Greg said huskily as he gently stroked her chin and caught the dollop of frosting with his bare finger.

Beth felt herself blush but she could not take her eyes off him even when she was aware that Amanda was staring at them both.

"Mom also said that she would never trust a woman who wouldn't eat one of these rolls," Greg said.

"Yeah," Amanda recalled, "she said that anybody who was more interested in their weight or how they looked than eating such a delectable treat was abso-. lutely not to be trusted." Amanda's voice took on an adult quality that was no doubt a perfect imitation of her mother's inflection.

"What did she say about a woman who asked for seconds?" Beth asked, her eyes still locked on Greg's.

He grinned. "The question never came up. Nobody can eat more than one…so far." He was throwing out a challenge.

"Yeah, nobody can eat two," Amanda chorused catching onto the game.

"Oh, really," Beth replied as she fingered another of the giant rolls. She lifted it and took a small bite. "It's very good," she commented as she took a second bite. "Sinfully delicious," she added as she took a third.

With each bite she took, Greg's eyes widened. "You'll make yourself sick," he warned.

"But I'm not breaking any park rules or anything, am I?" she asked as she took another tiny bite.

"Come on, Beth," Amanda cheered, jumping up and down and clapping her hands.

Beth was having a lot of trouble making a real dent in the roll, which seemed to get bigger rather than smaller with each bite she took.

"Your bites are getting smaller," Greg noted with satisfaction. "We'll be here all day if you eat at that pace. Give it up, Beth, and let's get back on the trail."

Beth forced herself to take a larger bite. She was beginning to understand the perils of gluttony, but she was determined to win the challenge. "Let's make this contest a little more interesting," she said. "If I finish it, what do I get?"

Greg roared with laughter and Beth thought her heart would leap right out of her chest with the thrill of hearing him laugh with such abandon. "An enormous stomachache for starters."

Beth shrugged as she carefully wrapped the remainder of the roll and put it in the pocket of her jacket.

"Ah, don't give up," Amanda protested.

"I'm not," Beth replied. "It occurs to me that there were no rules about time so I assume that as long as I finish eating the roll by, say the time we get back to town, I'll have met the challenge?"

"You can't…that's not the way…" Greg sputtered.

Beth grinned and put her arm around Amanda. "You had your chance to lay out the rules. Too bad, so sad. Now, weren't you anxious for us to get going here?"

Greg muttered something under his breath that Beth was certain was best not heard by herself or Amanda.

She winked at Amanda and the two of them toasted each other with cups of hot cocoa.

Once they were back on their horses, Beth realized that Greg was traveling at a much slower rate. She knew that he was still on the lookout for signs of the poachers even though he kept up a lively commentary, indicating points of interest as they traveled through the park. An hour later, he reined Skydancer in hard, knowing Reba would follow his lead and stop as well.

"Stay here," he said tersely as he lifted Amanda onto Beth's horse and guided Skydancer toward a clump of trees.

"Some people just don't understand," Amanda explained as she watched Skydancer break a path through the powdery knee-deep snow. "They aren't bad people, really. They just don't understand."

Beth put her arm around the little girl as they both watched Greg reach the trees. He knelt, then stood and pulled out his two-way radio again. They couldn't hear the conversation but everything about his body language said that he had found something he didn't like.

As Skydancer followed his own footsteps back to them Greg scanned the sky. The wind had picked up, and the gray day had gotten noticeably darker. "There's a storm on the way," he said. "We'd better head for shelter."

"What's over there, Dad?" Amanda motioned toward the clump of trees.

"The poachers killed a moose for the antlers," he replied.

"Did you call Brent?" Amanda asked as if this were nothing new.

Greg nodded.

Tears glistened on Amanda's cheeks. "I hate those bad men, Dad," she whispered. "I know that's wrong, but I can't help it. They are bad."

Greg glanced up at Beth. He seemed at a loss to know what to say.

Beth hugged Amanda. "It's really hard to understand these things sometimes, Amanda, even for grown-ups." She looked up at Greg and saw that he was as deeply saddened as his daughter was by the senseless killing of the moose.

"We'll get them, honey," Greg promised.

Amanda's lips tightened. "I just don't understand it. We're all God's creatures, isn't that right, Beth?"

"Yes, even the bad guys."

Amanda blinked in disbelief and she opened her mouth to protest that remark.

"Remember what we talked about in school," Beth reminded her quietly.

Greg watched them both with interest. "What?" he asked.

"It's important not to get angry at others when they do something we don't understand," Amanda said.

"I see," Greg replied but clearly he didn't see at all.

"These men made a very bad decision today, Amanda," Beth said. "They may have thought they had a good reason even though we know they didn't."

Amanda nodded. "We'll just have to educate them," she said with a very grown-up sigh of exasperation. "Right, Dad?"

Greg looked from his daughter to Beth and back

again. "Right," he agreed even though he was obviously still unconvinced. He studied the darkening sky. "Come on. Let's get the two of you to the patrol cabin."

The horses seemed to fly across the snow as Greg set his sights on the sheltered cabin the rangers used as an outpost for some of their winter duties. They both reined the horses to a halt near the front door.

"You two unload the stuff while I get the place opened up." He unlocked and opened the thick shutters, then headed around the side of the small cabin and returned a few minutes later with his arms loaded with firewood.

The one-room cabin had been recently used as evidenced by the fact that the snow had been shoveled away from the door. Inside everything was in pristine condition, and Beth took notice of how well stocked the cabin was with cans of food, blankets, reading materials and a two-way radio. A ladder in one corner of the room led to a loft space.

"Sometimes a patrol can get snowed in for several days," Greg explained when she commented on the variety of canned goods lining the shelves. "We'll probably be here for the night—or at least the two of you will."

She took notice of the four kitchen matches laid out in order on the edge of the stove.

"The last occupant is responsible for making sure there is kindling and that matches are laid out ready to start a fire," Greg explained. "In the cold and dark, it's imperative that a ranger be able to feel for the match and get the fire going as quickly as possible."

His brow furrowed and she had the urge to brush it smooth with her fingertips. He looked tired and worried. "We'll be fine," she assured him.

"I have work to do, and as long as Amanda can stay with you I won't have to ruin her day. Do you mind? I may not get back tonight," he said.

"It's all right," she assured him and turned to Amanda. "Top bunk or lower one?" she asked.

"Top," Amanda declared with a grin. "Can we make s'mores?"

"Possibly, if a certain young lady eats every bite of her dinner."

"Canned beef stew?" Amanda looked skeptical.

"Not your favorite?" Beth asked.

Amanda made a face and both Greg and Beth laughed.

"To tell you the truth," Beth confided, "it's not exactly at the top of my list, either, but then we pioneer women can't be picky. We must be brave and keep the home fires burning, right?"

"And make s'mores?" Amanda added hopefully.

"And make s'mores," Beth agreed.

Greg smiled. "Let me show you how to keep the fire going."

Beth rolled her eyes. "Another lecture," she muttered and grinned at him.

After Greg had shown Beth the basics, he pulled on his parka and gloves. "You'll be fine," he said as if he needed to assure himself.

But will you? she thought but didn't want to ask questions with Amanda there.

"He'll be okay," Amanda promised her and Beth

wondered at the little girl's instincts for reading grown-up minds.

Beth stood at the door of the cabin with her arm around Amanda. The little girl waved to her father as he mounted Skydancer and took off after the poachers.

Beth truly felt like a pioneer homesteader watching her man ride off into the sunset. "Keep him safe," she murmured as he crossed a rise and disappeared from sight.

Chapter Eleven

It took Greg three hours to track the poachers to where they had crossed the park boundary back into Montana. They would be back no doubt, but there was little he or the other rangers could do but patrol the boundary on as regular a basis as possible until the poachers returned.

That was a good plan but the problem was, the park was understaffed. Funding for extra rangers in the winter months had never been a priority even though Greg had gone to Washington himself to present their case to a senate subcommittee. He took one last look around to see if the poachers had left any evidence that might be helpful in identifying them, then mounted Skydancer and headed back toward the patrol cabin.

As he rode along, he considered the thought that had come to him early that morning. He was no longer mourning for Lu. He would always miss her, but the long period of mourning was over. He examined his thoughts and felt only complete comfort. Lu had been gone now for nearly two years. He had coped by focusing everything on his work. Lately that hadn't seemed like enough, and he had compensated by taking on even more work.

Then Beth had arrived. From the first she had made him feel things that made him uncomfortable in her presence. He sensed something about her that spelled danger or risk. He had been determined to keep his distance and had failed miserably.

In spite of his best efforts, in spite of the impossibility of the entire idea, he was struggling mightily against falling in love with her. And yet loving her was not an option—for either of them. There were so many problems, any one of which might have been surmountable, but taken together they spelled trouble.

Even so, he couldn't wait to see her, to get back to the cabin where she would be waiting for him. The very image of that made him smile and push Skydancer even harder. He imagined her with Amanda, the two of them playing some card game or reading a story or perhaps baking something. His visions of domestic bliss made the trip go faster. He chose not to ruin his fantasies by considering what the future might hold. For now, he wanted to savor the moment—the day he had awakened to find the familiar ache in his heart healed and had known that he could love again.

An hour's distance from the cabin it started to snow—a light steady fall that he knew meant they were in for several inches before dawn. He pressed on.

It'll be good to be home, he thought and it stunned and pleased him to realize that by *home* he meant wherever Beth and Amanda were. His feelings were deepening by the hour, much like the snow around him.

It was dark when he crossed the last ridge. He was relieved to see smoke coming from the chimney, meaning Beth had managed to keep the fire going. He was mystified to see the addition of several small bonfires around the perimeter of the cabin. "Come on, Skydancer, let's get down there and see what this incredible, if sometimes slightly crazy, woman is up to now."

As soon as he reined in Skydancer and dismounted, Beth and Amanda opened the door to the cabin and Amanda rushed out to meet him. Beth's eyes were wide with relief. Amanda's were equally alive with excitement.

"There was a bear, Dad," she announced as she flung herself at him and hugged him hard. "And the wolves were howling and howling and howling. Beth built fires like the pioneers used to when they traveled west on the wagon trains."

Beth had not moved. She was smiling, but it was the sort of tight, brave smile that did not reach her eyes.

Greg pulled Amanda next to him and walked toward the house. "You okay?" he asked Beth.

She nodded but seemed paralyzed with fear.

"Honey, why don't you fix me some tea?" he said to Amanda who rushed to do his bidding. He turned his attention back to Beth. "Come here," he said softly as he pried her fingers away from the door frame and hugged her hard.

She gave a shuddering sob and buried her face against his shoulder. "I thought…I was so afraid that…"

"Sh-h-h. I'm here now. It's okay." He stroked her hair and waited for the shivers that racked her body to subside.

"He was a monster," Amanda said as she brought the tea—a cup for him and one for Beth, as well. "We were pretty scared, but Beth told me stories about women who went west in the old days and how sometimes they had to be the ones who kept the home fires burning, right?"

"That's right," Beth replied with a weak smile as she wrapped her shaking hands around the mug of tea and let the steam bathe her face.

"Where did you see the bear?" Greg asked. Sometimes bears would try to break into the cabin for the rations. He mentally berated himself for not preparing Beth for that possibility.

"We heard the wolves first and then they just kept it up and we couldn't decide if they were coming closer," Amanda explained. "Then we decided to build the campfires while it was still light. Beth did a great job, didn't she, Dad?"

"I thought I'd get back sooner," he said. "I'm sorry." He sat beside her, rubbing her back, trying to ease the tension that bunched the muscles of her shoulders and neck.

Beth looked up at him, her eyes calm and lovely. "It's okay," she replied and managed another smile that was a little closer to her usual sunny grin. "We frontier women are tough, aren't we, Amanda?"

"How did you come up with the campfire idea?" Greg asked, his own mood lightening in direct proportion to hers.

"I saw it in a movie," she admitted. "It was probably dumb."

"Not at all. It showed real initiative."

"Dad is real big on initiative," Amanda confided as if Greg had suddenly gotten up and left the room. "He'll even forgive a mistake if you at least show some imagination."

"I'll have to remember that." Beth looked at Greg who was grinning at her. "The bear was up on the rise just sort of standing there, watching us." She shivered.

"It gave us the williams, right Beth?"

"Willies," Beth corrected gently. "It gave us the willies."

"Did he come closer?" Greg asked, his expression filled with concern and worry.

"No. Maybe the fires helped?"

Greg shrugged and then he grinned. "Obviously it beats singing and blowing a whistle."

"Dad! That's just mean," Amanda chastised him.

Beth laughed and once she started she seemed unable to stop. "Maybe a whistle should be standard equipment here in the cabin," she said between bursts of laughter.

Then Amanda started to giggle and Greg started to laugh and before long the three of them were collapsed onto the bunk that served as bed and sofa for the tiny cabin. Finally, they got control of themselves and the atmosphere in the room returned to normal.

"You must be starving," Beth said as she pushed herself off the bunk and headed toward the small cook-stove. "I made the stew," she said proudly.

"And biscuits," Amanda added proudly pointing to a pan of biscuits that were flat and unevenly cooked.

"Smells terrific and I am famished. Let me just take care of Skydancer and wash up."

While they ate, he filled them in on the hunt for the

poachers. He tried to downplay the danger for Amanda's sake, but he saw that Beth understood that he had been at perhaps even greater risk than she had that long afternoon. It touched him to see the concern in her eyes and at the same time he wanted to reassure her that he knew how to handle himself in these situations.

"I have a good crew," he said.

"I know." She focused on clearing the dishes.

"We know what we're doing," he added.

She nodded and her hand shook slightly as she scraped a plate. "It's just really the first time I've thought about there being danger from humans," she said softly. "Somehow that's different from the animals."

"Yeah, I know. It's easier to forgive the animals. They're just doing what they have to do to survive."

"Maybe these men are, as well," Beth suggested.

"I doubt that."

"We really don't know. They could be out of work and looking for a way to feed their families or pay their rent," she said.

Greg studied her. "You have this knack for always seeing the good, don't you?"

It wasn't a reprimand, but she understood that her ability to look for the reasons behind acts of destruction or misfortune bewildered him.

Amanda yawned noisily.

"Bedtime, scamp," he said.

"Aw, Dad," she protested but stumbled over to the bunk beds and sat on the lower one to take off her shoes.

Greg helped her get ready for bed and lifted her onto the top bunk. He pulled the rough blanket over her, topped it with a down sleeping bag and kissed her good-night. "Love you," he murmured.

"Me too, love you," she mumbled and was asleep.

Beth watched the scene play out and felt tears sting her eyes. It was so wonderful to see them both safe, to know that Greg was there in case the bear or wolves returned.

"Hey, what's this?" he said softly as he turned away from his sleeping daughter and saw her tears.

"I really don't know," she replied with a shaky laugh. "Just a long day, I guess."

"I really appreciate the way you watched after Amanda today, Beth."

"She did as much for me."

"I know you must have been so frightened, and I'm sorry. I should have prepared you for some of the possibilities."

"You had your work to think about. In the end we were fine."

"But you were scared."

She nodded and the tears came in earnest. "And I was worried about you," she admitted. She knew it was the release of all the tension and anxiety she had endured through the long afternoon and evening, but her inability to stop blubbering was embarrassing nevertheless. "This is stupid," she said and brushed impatiently at the tears.

"Come here," he said and for the second time that night she walked straight into his embrace.

They stood in the middle of the small rustic cabin, their arms around each other as he rocked her slowly from side to side. Undone by this gentler side of him focused entirely on her, she continued to cry. Her tears soaked the front of his flannel shirt.

"Hey," he coaxed and gently lifted her chin with his forefinger so that she was looking up at him. "It's all right," he assured her and she saw that he wanted to kiss her.

"Greg," she whispered and stroked his cheek.

He bent to meet her lips and they shared their first kiss—a kiss of such gentle tenderness that they were each struck by its fragility and preciousness. Beth could feel his heart pounding beneath her palm and knew that her own heart beat in unison with his. She was a woman who had led a charmed life. Yet, never before had she felt so cherished.

When the kiss ended, he continued to hold her, his lips resting against her temple, his breath a gentle breeze on her hair.

There is something so right about all of this, Greg Stone. I don't know where we will end up, but we are connected. God has brought us together at a time when we each needed a friend. Whatever happens next, I'm putting my trust in Him and so should you, she thought, but knew if she said the words aloud, it would startle Greg and spoil this moment—a moment she knew she would treasure for the rest of her life.

"You must be exhausted," he said finally and stepped back but continued to rest his hands loosely on her shoulders.

"I am a little wiped out," she admitted. She glanced at Amanda sleeping peacefully in the upper bunk and then at the lower bunk. She could not control the blush that stained her cheeks as she realized that there were two of them and only one remaining bed.

"There's a sleeping bag," he said as if reading her mind. Then he cleared his throat as she had learned was his habit whenever he was uncomfortable with the way things were going. "I should bring in some wood for the fire."

"I'll help. After all, I was the one who used up the supply setting those ridiculous fires." She reached for her parka.

"Stay here. Maybe heat up the last of the cocoa. I'll get the wood." His voice had taken on that tense tone he sometimes used with her.

"I'll—"

He opened the door and she was silenced by the sudden influx of bitter cold and snow. The wind howled—or was that the wolves?

"Be careful," she said as the door blew shut behind him.

In seconds she heard the steady beat of the ax splitting logs. She stood at the cabin's front window and watched him work. He attacked the logs with a fierceness that was both thrilling and a little intimidating. She wondered what he was thinking, and thought she probably knew. Kissing her had been a mistake—a betrayal of his beloved wife.

Beth turned away from the window and checked on the sleeping child. Then she poured the remainder of the cocoa into a small pan and heated it on the stove. She couldn't imagine how they were going to get through this night. They had made real progress toward forging a friendship, but the kiss had changed everything. Where would they go from here?

She heard the steady rhythmic beat of Greg splitting the logs and then silence, followed by the sound of him stamping snow off his boots at the door to the cabin. She hurried to open the door for him.

"I made the cocoa," she said for lack of anything else to say.

He nodded and stacked the firewood near the stove. Then he pulled a length of rope from his parka pocket and tied one end to the post of the bunk beds just below where Amanda slept.

"What's that?" Beth asked as she divided the cocoa between two mugs and handed one to him.

"Privacy." He fixed the other end of the rope to the other bedpost. Then he draped a blanket across it curtain-style. "You're not the only one who learns from going to the movies," he explained.

Beth smiled. "Clark Gable and Claudette Colbert."

"Normally I would sleep up there in the loft, but given what you've been through, I'll camp out on the sleeping bag over there on the floor, and you—"

He grimaced as he tightened the rope.

"What's wrong?"

To her surprise, he smiled—it was a sheepish grin, but a smile nonetheless and it seemed as if the tension that had crowded into the small space with them since they kissed had eased.

"It's been a while since I chopped wood," he admitted. "I've rubbed a doozy of a blister."

Beth held his hand and examined his palm. "My heavens, Greg. What were you thinking?"

He covered her hand with his, forcing her to look up

at him. "I was thinking about you…us. What were you thinking while I was out there playing macho man?"

Beth ducked her head shyly. "Same thing," she admitted. "I'm sorry…" She began.

"We need to talk," he said at the same time.

"You first."

He looked at her. "What have you got to be sorry about?"

"I…falling apart…being so silly…"

"That's not why I kissed you."

"It started out that way."

"Yes," he agreed, "but it changed."

"How?"

Her eyes searched his expression for clues to his mood.

"I wanted to," he said softly and caressed her face with his injured hand.

She closed her eyes and savored his touch.

"I want to again," he added softly.

She nodded. "But we shouldn't," she said finishing what she was certain he was thinking. "Not until we figure a few things out."

"Such as?"

"You're the one who has set limits," she reminded him.

He sighed heavily. "We can't ignore the fact that you are only here for a few months, Beth."

"You see, that's one of the differences between us," she replied. "You focus on my leaving and I think about the time I am here—now, tomorrow, next month."

He nodded. "But if we let our feelings…if we give in to…we have to consider Amanda."

"I am considering Amanda. She's happy. She likes

me. She likes doing things with me and with you. What's wrong with that?"

"Nothing at all, as long as that's as far as it goes."

"And what if it went further?"

"We both understand that there's another piece of this that has nothing to do with Amanda," he said.

Beth nodded. "Faith," she said. "Belief." She felt him tense.

Their fingers intertwined and neither of them seemed to know what to say.

"Where do you keep the first-aid kit?" she asked huskily.

"On the shelf next to the door," he replied but did not release his hold on her.

"What if we tried it again—kissing?"

Beth looked up at him in surprise. She smiled. She knew he was only trying to lighten the mood. He was a man, after all, and there had been that spark of something between them. He was flirting with her.

She lifted his wounded hand to her lips. She could feel his eyes on her as she tenderly kissed his palm. "You mean like this?"

"That's a start."

"And that's as far as we're going to go," she said lightly. "I'll get the first-aid kit." The one thing she knew she couldn't handle was any kind of casual affair between them.

This time he let her go.

As expected the kit was well-stocked and in no time she had cleaned the wound and applied a soothing ointment. She wrapped his hand loosely in gauze. As she worked he sipped his cocoa and said nothing.

"There. That should help." She replaced all the materials in the first-aid kit and returned it to the shelf. *Now what?* She thought nervously.

"I'm going out to check the horses," he said shrugging into his parka. "Why don't you go ahead and get ready for bed?"

She understood that he was actually leaving to give her some privacy for performing her bedtime routine. The cabin had a portable toilet, and Amanda had shown her how to melt snow and heat it for washing herself. There was a kettle filled with steaming water on the back of the stove.

By the time Greg returned she was just getting under the covers of the lower bunk.

"All set?" he asked as he sat on the edge of the bed and tucked her in.

She nodded.

"Good night then," he said huskily and bent to kiss her forehead. "Thank you again for taking care of Amanda, Beth. I honestly don't know what I would have done without you."

"We make a good team," was all she could think to say. "I mean, Amanda and me."

He smiled and brushed a strand of hair away from her cheek. "I know what you mean, Beth. I think we make a good team, as well—the three of us. Amanda and I are both lucky to have you as our friend. Good night."

Beth knew that she should be thrilled at his compliment. He was telling her that they were friends. Friendships could last across the miles. Friends visited each other from time to time. For the first time since she had met him, he wasn't reminding her that she was leaving in a few months. Still, the confession that they were friends led to the obvious understanding that that was all they were—or ever could be.

He stood and pulled the blanket curtain into place. She heard him stoke the fire and spread the sleeping bag. She heard him take off his heavy boots and settle in for the night.

Remembering the kiss, she put her fingers to her lips and wondered how they were going to manage the next several months.

Chapter Twelve

Beth woke to the sound of voices and horses snorting and stamping outside the cabin. She also recognized the smell of bacon frying and biscuits baking. Light seemed to flood the cabin through the small window. In the bunk above her, Amanda grumbled and pulled the covers over her head.

Beth peeked out from the cocoon created by the blanket curtain and blinked rapidly as she tried to adjust to the sudden glare of the light.

"Rise and shine," Greg called out. "We've got company."

Beth noticed that he was fully dressed, the sleeping bag had been cleared away and he was stirring something on the stove. He had removed the gauze that covered his blistered palm.

"Dad, it's not a school day. I get to sleep in," Amanda protested in a muffled voice from under the covers.

Greg slid the pot to one side and headed for the door. "Two women in my life who aren't morning persons may be more than I can handle," he commented and laughed when both Beth and Amanda protested the sudden influx of cold air that accompanied his opening the door. "Come on in, guys. Coffee's on," he called cheerfully.

Beth suddenly realized that there were people outside who would soon be inside and she was still in bed. She scrambled to her feet and tried to straighten the tangled knot of the clothes she'd slept in. It was hopeless. Her sweatpants were twisted around her legs and the socks were half on with the toes flopping crazily with each step she took.

"Morning, Beth."

Brent ducked his head to clear the doorway as he entered the cabin. He was followed closely by Todd Roberts, another ranger. "Sorry to disturb you."

Beth realized how this must look to the two rangers. She wondered how she could possibly explain that it had all been platonic. She looked to Greg for help and realized he would be no help at all. The man knew exactly what she was thinking, and he was enjoying her discomfort.

"Let me get you some coffee," she said as the two rangers took off their parkas and gloves.

She handed them each a mug of coffee and poured one for herself.

"The poachers came back last night," Brent told Greg and in that one sentence he erased all trace of Greg's good mood.

"I was afraid of that when I heard you coming. Did they make a hit?"

Todd nodded. "Yes, sir. A bull elk."

Not my bull elk, Beth wanted to protest. Her hand shook as she served up the eggs, biscuits and bacon.

"The trail is still really fresh. They must have come in early this morning," Brent continued. "The snow will slow them down quite a bit."

"You think we can get them?" Greg studied the younger rangers. "There's no time to get backup in place before we go."

"Yes, sir, I do. We'll have to act fast but I'm sure we can," Brent replied.

"Let's get going then," Greg said as he tossed back the last of his coffee and reached for his parka. "Amanda?"

A tousled head popped out from beneath the covers. Clearly, Amanda had been listening. "Yes, Dad."

"Time to go."

Instantly, Amanda was off the bunk, dressing and packing her gear. Beth helped her finish dressing and insisted she eat some breakfast. "Five minutes," she told Greg.

He turned back to confer with the two rangers. They spoke in low urgent tones and Beth realized that with the poachers still out there, even five minutes was asking a lot.

"You two go on. I'll take Beth and Amanda back to town and come in from the other direction," Greg instructed. He held up his two-way radio. "Stay in touch," he added as the rangers bundled up and left the cabin.

"Hurry, Amanda. We need to get started," Beth said softly as she checked to be sure that the matches were in place for the cabin's next visitors.

Amanda shoved the rest of a biscuit in her mouth and

grabbed her parka. Beth had just washed the last of the morning dishes and replaced them on the shelf when Greg returned from closing and locking the shutters.

He glanced around the cabin checking for the matches and kindling and saw that everything was in order. "Good work," he said and pulled Amanda's hood into place and fastened it under her chin. "Are you ready to ride, partner?" he asked with a grin.

"Yep," Amanda replied and headed for the door.

Beth saw that in spite of the smile he had given his daughter, Greg's expression was grim. He was frustrated that the poachers had struck again. "I wish there was something I could do," she offered.

He wrapped his arm around her shoulder as they headed outside together. "There is. Once we reach town, could you take care of Amanda until I get back? It could be a couple of days."

"Of course." She would have walked over hot coals for the man. Asking her to care for Amanda was like giving her a gift instead of asking a favor.

Greg checked one last time to be sure that the cabin was secure. He had saddled the horses, and they stood ready and waiting as if they, too, understood the urgency. Beth mounted her horse and waited while Greg lifted Amanda onto his and got on behind her.

"All set?"

Beth gave him the thumbs-up sign and he nodded and headed out. Reba trotted to keep up with Skydancer's pace.

Beth understood that this would be no leisurely trip to catch a glimpse of the park's winter garb. Instead, everything flew by as if the world had suddenly been thrown into fast-forward as they moved from trot to full gallop. Amanda closed her eyes and hung on.

They had been riding for some time when Beth realized Greg was slowing down. She looked up and saw a rider coming toward them.

"It's Brent," Greg shouted.

"We've spotted them," Brent reported as soon as the two horses were parallel. Both men dismounted and walked a little away. Beth followed suit telling Amanda to stay with the horses.

"Todd's keeping watch but they're pretty close to the border—playing it cagey," Brent reported.

"Did they spot you?"

Brent shook his head. "I think we stand a good chance of surrounding them and getting them with the evidence before they can get out of the park." Once caught, the rangers would take the poachers back to Mammoth where they would be kept in jail until they could appear before the U.S. magistrate who served the park.

Greg nodded and turned his attention to Beth. "Do you think you can take Amanda on Reba there and make it back to town?"

Beth glanced nervously at the vast white wilderness surrounding them and nodded.

As usual he had read her mind and he took a step closer. "We'll get you to a marked trail. I'll radio ahead and have one of the rangers start out from town and meet you. As long as you follow the markers, you'll be fine."

Beth nodded again.

"You do know I wish there were some other way," he said.

"I know. We'll be fine. Don't worry about Amanda. I'll take good care of her."

"For once I should be seeing that someone takes care of you," he said and touched her cheek.

"It's okay," she managed to say around the lump of emotion that had formed in her throat. He helped Amanda onto Reba, and Beth pasted on her bravest smile. It would not do to panic now. Greg had promised a marked trail, and she believed him. It didn't matter that everywhere she turned everything looked the same. She would follow the markers and before she knew it they would be home.

"Ready for a new adventure?" she asked Amanda with a heartiness she really did not feel.

"Cool," Amanda shouted once Greg had explained the plan.

"Don't rush," Greg advised as they stood next to the horses. "You've got plenty of daylight." He pulled out his radio and called headquarters. She heard the instructions to send someone on the trail. Then he pulled Beth a little away from Brent and Amanda. "I'm going to make this up to you. I know that I've got to stop counting on you to be there for Amanda and me."

"Because I'll be leaving," she finished his thought.

"Because it's not fair," he corrected. "If there was any other choice…"

"We'll be fine. Really." She wanted to reassure him. She wanted to touch his haggard face. She wished there were more she could do to make it easier for him to do the job he needed to do.

"I'll make it up to you," he promised again.

She laughed. "I'll hold you to that. For somebody who thought I was a rank tenderfoot a few weeks ago, you sure are putting me to the test," she teased.

Her reward was his smile. "I may have jumped to some incorrect assumptions," he admitted sheepishly. "On the other hand, you were singing to a bear and later on I caught you arguing with an elk. You have to admit that's pretty questionable behavior." He reached to embrace her then, aware of the others, changed his mind and withdrew his hand. "I have to go."

"I know. Don't worry. Amanda will be fine. I won't let anything happen to her." She didn't want him thinking about them when he needed to focus all his attention on what was potentially a dangerous situation. "Just take care of you," she added.

This time he did stroke her cheek with his gloved finger.

Beth reached up and covered his hand with her own. "You'd better get going. Brent keeps glancing at the horizon as if he's expecting the enemy to come over that rise at any moment."

Greg laughed as they walked back toward the others. Brent was already on his horse and had helped Amanda transfer from Skydancer to Reba. Greg helped Beth onto Reba more because he needed to touch her than because she needed the help. Then he mounted Skydancer and signaled for her to follow them.

"Here goes nothing," she muttered to herself as she urged Reba onto the trail Skydancer was breaking. Amanda was smiling as if she were on some grand adventure.

Too soon they reached the trailhead. Without breaking Skydancer's pace, Greg motioned toward the marker, and Beth signaled that she saw it and understood. Greg waved and took off, but Beth noticed that he watched over his shoulder to be sure that they were safely started on the trail.

As she navigated the trail, she replayed the sight of him riding off like some warrior into battle. Once again, she was afraid for him. What if the poachers had guns? What if they had spotted Todd and taken him hostage? What if something happened to Greg?

Watch over him and bring him home safe, she prayed silently. She glanced at Amanda and felt a renewed determination. Her job was to make sure she got the spunky little girl home. There, they would wait together for Greg's return.

Greg was glad that conversation was not an option as he and Brent rode hard toward the point where he expected the poachers to be. He needed to focus on what lay ahead, but thoughts of Beth kept crowding in around his concentration on the job to be done. Beth standing in the doorway of the cabin. Beth facing her fears so that Amanda would not be harmed. Beth overcome by tears of stress and tension. Beth in his arms. Beth's lips meeting his. Beth tenderly dressing his blister. Beth sleeping. Beth waking. Beth. Beth.

What if there was some possibility they could have a future? What if she stayed after the year was up? Why would she do that? What could he offer her?

Brent Moser signaled him as he turned off the main

trail. Greg almost missed the cut. He shook his head, willing himself to pay attention to his duty. The poachers would be armed. They would not surrender willingly. They had too much to lose.

Minutes later, Brent slowed his horse to a walk. Absolute quiet surrounded them. It was impressive and at the same time, eerie. In a place where peace and quiet were commonplace, this quiet seemed too perfect, almost artificial. Brent spoke in low tones on the two-way radio.

"Todd has our position, sir," he reported. "The poachers are working along the north boundary as we suspected."

"How many are there?"

"Only two."

Greg nodded. "Radio for extra backup to help with the arrest and transport and let's go in."

Brent did as he was told. "Todd reports that he called for the extra rangers, and they should be in position."

Greg held out his hand for the radio. "Good work, Todd."

"Thank you, sir." The ranger's voice crackled through the static. "We're ready at this end."

"Then let's go. Give us twenty minutes to get into position on this side and then make your move." He handed the radio back to Brent and motioned for the younger ranger to follow him.

The fact was, Greg loved his work. He couldn't imagine living and working anywhere other than the parks—maybe not Yellowstone forever, but the wilderness was his calling. If anything were to develop between them, how would Beth adjust to that?

* * *

A sense of alarm that escalated with every minute gnawed at Beth as she strained to see through the lightly falling snow. She tried to recall the topographical map Greg had brought her. This trail had been the one he showed her. She tried to recall the landmarks he had noted. Had she passed the place where the trail split off to the falls? Had she come to the small cluster of mud pots yet?

The last trail marker had been slightly askew, and she had made a choice and turned to the right. Maybe she should have gone straight. Maybe not. Surely there should be a marker soon. She squinted, trying to see any sign of color in the relentless white-gray-and-brown landscape.

She glanced at the sky, which had grown steadily darker in the last half hour. She slowed Reba to a walk and considered her options.

"Are we lost?" Amanda asked.

Beth looked at the child. She was perfectly calm. The question had been delivered in a matter-of-fact tone that signaled her certainty of the answer.

"Maybe," Beth hedged.

"So, what's the plan?" Amanda looked at Beth with such complete confidence that Beth swallowed her fear and smiled.

"Well, there are a number of possibilities."

"We could go back to the marker," Amanda suggested.

"That's an idea," Beth agreed but the blowing snow was already covering their tracks. Trying to find their way back might only result in their becoming more lost.

"We could stay here and wait for the ranger to find us."

"That's probably not the best choice," Beth said. She glanced at the sky.

"Yeah, probably not. It's getting late and that means the temperature will drop and with the snow and all we should probably keep moving," Amanda reasoned.

Out of the mouths of babes, Beth thought. In the face of Amanda's absolute certainty that Beth would find a way to get them home came the courage Beth needed to take action. Greg was counting on her.

"Maybe if we make our way to that ridge ahead we can see over a greater distance and figure out where we are. What do you think?"

"Works for me," Amanda agreed. "Maybe we'll see Dad and we can set a flare or send smoke signals. He'll be so-o-o surprised." She giggled with delight.

Beth would have liked to share in her pleasure, but the fact was she was becoming more certain by the moment that such antics might actually be essential to their survival.

Please, God, she prayed, genuinely scared now.

She hoped that the ridge wasn't as far in the distance as it appeared. "Hang on, honey," she called to Amanda as she urged Reba off the trail.

As she rode, her mind raced. At least on the ridge, there were trees. That meant wood for a fire. She could start a fire to keep them warm and perhaps it would also serve as a signal for those who would be looking for them. Trees also meant shelter. Hopefully there would be some good tall evergreens. She could settle Amanda in the shelter of the trees and...

Reba stumbled.

"Is Reba okay?" Amanda asked and this time she didn't sound quite so confident.

Beth nodded. "Maybe we should let her wait here though. The slope might be slippery. Let's gather the extra blankets and some of these supplies, okay?" She fought the sense of rising panic and tried not to think about Greg and how she had failed him in the only task that mattered. Amanda was in danger—from the cold and the elements and it was all Beth's fault.

Amanda looked out toward the ridge and back again. "The snow is getting deeper."

"I know, honey, that's why we need to get going. Here, wrap this around you." Beth handed Amanda a blanket and began stuffing supplies from the saddlebags into a backpack. "Okay, let's go. Just keep walking toward those trees there. I'll be right beside you."

Amanda struck out, but slogging through the freshly fallen snow was exhausting and it took a long time to make any progress at all.

"Beth?" Amanda's voice sounded small and scared in the silence of the wilderness.

"What is it, honey?"

Amanda turned to face Beth and made no attempt to hide the huge tears that trickled down each cheek. "I'm scared," she whispered.

Beth wrapped her arm around Amanda's shoulder. "I know you are, but we're going to be all right. Here, follow in my footsteps. That'll be easier."

"How do you know that we'll be okay?"

"I just know it. God will—"

"I know God is supposed to take care of us, but sometimes I wonder."

"What do you wonder?"

Amanda took a deep breath. "Sometimes I wonder why God lets scary stuff like this happen in the first place—I mean if He's in charge of the whole world and all, then how come—"

Beth stopped and turned Amanda so that they were face-to-face. "Now, listen to me. I believe that there is a reason for everything that happens to us—good things and bad. Sometimes it's very hard to understand that reason but in time we begin to see why it was a part of God's plan for us."

Amanda frowned. "You mean like Mom dying?"

Her words were not delivered with malice or anger and yet they felt like a blow to Beth's psyche. "That, too," she replied through clenched teeth. "Right now though, we need to figure out the best way to get through what's happening to us at this moment, today, and one day we'll be telling our friends and our children and grandchildren about this day and we'll realize that there was a reason for it. But first we have to live it, understand?"

Amanda's teeth had started to chatter. "I guess," she replied but she sounded anything but convinced.

"Okay then, on to the ridge," Beth shouted with a bravado she was far from feeling herself. She stepped off in an exaggerated marching step. "Coming?" she called.

"Coming," Amanda replied and Beth's heart twisted as she looked behind her and saw the little girl bravely following in her footsteps.

Chapter Thirteen

"Call for you, Chief," Brent Moser handed him a two-way radio. "It's Taggert back at dispatch."

Doris Taggert was a park veteran. She had worked with Greg's father and Greg knew if she was asking for him, instead of simply relaying a message through Brent, something important had happened.

"I'm here, Dorie. What's up?"

"Just had a message from Becker. He's traveled almost to the trailhead, and there's no sign of Beth and Amanda."

Greg's heart paused and then started to pound in triple time. "Where's Becker now?"

"Waiting for orders. He thought he might have missed them somehow and radioed to see if they had made it back to town." There was a pause. "They haven't."

"Tell Becker to retrace the trail. I'll come in from the other direction."

"Got it."

Greg and the other rangers carried off the arrest of the poachers without incident and recovered enough hides and antlers to put them in jail for a very long time. Now he sent the others to complete the routine of the arrest while he went in search of Beth and Amanda. As he pushed Skydancer hard, taking shortcuts wherever possible to cut the time and distance, Greg considered the possibilities.

It's probably something simple, he thought, but knew that this was unlikely. He visualized the trail, thinking through every turn of it, counting off the markers in his mind. *Where did you turn off the trail, Beth?* He reached the place where he had left her. The fresh snow had covered the tracks. Greg swore and fought against the renewal of the old familiar bile that God would permit such things to happen to people like Amanda and Beth while He was off letting poachers kill innocent beasts on a whim.

"*Why?*" he shouted. "*Why them? Why do this again?*" He knew that what he really meant was *Why do this to me again?*

He felt shame that his thoughts focused on his own pain when Beth and Amanda were out there somewhere.

"*Help me,*" he whispered. "*Come on. We'll work the rest out later. Just help me now. I'm begging You, for their sake.*"

He closed his eyes and sat back on Skydancer. He waited. For what, he didn't know. Perhaps for his racing heart to beat more normally, for his shattered brain to function reasonably again.

And suddenly, he knew exactly where she had made the wrong turn. He saw it in his mind's eye as clearly as if it were spotlighted before him. He had seen the marker at that point earlier in the fall and had made a mental note to have it turned so that it clearly pointed the right way for the cross-country skiers who would rely on it to move them safely through the park in winter. But the snows had come sooner than expected, and he had been distracted by other concerns. The sign had remained untouched… and pointing in the wrong direction.

"Thank you," he whispered raggedly and swiped at the tears that etched the exhausted plains of his face. *"I owe you one."*

He reached the crossroads of the trail, saw the twisted sign and turned Skydancer sharply in the direction he was sure she had followed. As he rode, he found himself continuing his silent entreaties to God to get him to Beth and Amanda before anything happened to them. Unlike when Lu was dying, this time his anger was directed at himself rather than God. This time, if anything happened to them, it would be his fault. His prayers came from deep within his soul.

God, I know I've been away, but Beth's faith in you has always been constant. Don't make her pay for my mistakes, for my lack of faith, for my anger. Please, help me find them before it's too late.

Thunder rumbled in the distance. Greg fought against the urge to curse the heavens. Was this God's response? The sky grew darker in the direction he was headed. He thought of Beth and Amanda and their fear of thunderstorms. It was one thing to face a storm from safe inside a warm solid house. It was quite something else to be lost, cold and probably terrified and have to deal with thunder and lightning as well.

Please, Greg chanted again and again as the wet sleet

and snow pelted him, making visibility nearly impossible and travel treacherous. He resisted the urge to bargain with a power greater than himself. In the face of his own inability to find Beth and Amanda, he had resorted to his faith. God had answered that first prayer to help him find the right path. Perhaps He would answer this one as well.

In that moment Greg understood that he had never truly stopped believing. He had only turned his back. If he turned around now, would God still be there for him?

In the unending whiteness of the snow, in the distance, he thought he saw a flash of movement. He reined Skydancer in and impatiently wiped sleet and ice from his face. Was it his imagination?

No. It was a horse. It was Reba. His heart leapt with joy then plummeted again. There was no other sign of life as the first bolt of lightning split the sky.

"I'm so scared, Beth," Amanda shouted shakily above the sound of the wind and thunder.

"I know you are, Amanda. Please be brave for just a little bit longer—just until we reach those trees up there, okay?"

Amanda nodded and her grim little face broke Beth's heart. *Please, let there be another patrol shelter or the town or something we can get to and be safe and warm,* she prayed silently as she willed herself to put one foot in front of the other, breaking a trail for Amanda to follow.

Slowly she made her way up the steep hill working her way in a serpentine pattern to find the easiest route and stretching her hand out to bring Amanda along as she climbed. She heard the rumble of thunder and the howl of the wind in the leafless trees.

As the wind gathered force, the trees began to sway, knocking against each other. They sounded like hollowed bamboo poles tapping out an ominous rhythm.

"Amanda, come here," Beth shouted above the thunder and wind as the first lanky tree lost its fragile grip and fell with a clatter on the hill behind them.

Amanda screamed and raced forward. Beth grabbed her hand and stumbled on a horizontal path hoping to get out of the stand of trees. It was useless. They were completely surrounded. Beth wrapped her arms around the terrified child and dropped them both to the ground as trees fell like dominoes all around them. Even though the weight of the trees was lessened due to their thin diameter and hollowed core, Beth knew that with so many trees falling, she and Amanda were in real danger. Lightning streaked the sky and thunder roared nearby.

Please God, not Amanda, Beth prayed fervently. *What would Greg do if he lost Amanda, too?*

She pulled the child more firmly against her, shielding her with her own body as the storm raged. A tree fell just above their heads followed by another that caught Beth squarely across the shoulders. She bit her lip to keep from crying out as pain rifled down her left arm.

As suddenly as the storm came, it passed, leaving behind a path of felled trees, one terrified little girl and a woman who suddenly found she could not move her left shoulder.

"Are you okay, Amanda?"

"I think so," came the quavering reply. "I'm really cold though and hungry, too."

Beth considered her next move—that was assuming she could move. With her good right hand she checked herself for any other injuries and discovered a small lump in the pocket of her parka. She smiled.

"You know what I just remembered?" Beth asked as she rolled slowly away from Amanda and tried not to let her see how much pain that caused her. "Check my pocket," she encouraged. "Go on."

Amanda got to her knees and reached inside the pocket of Beth's parka. "Dad's cinnamon roll," she cried with delight as she held up the smashed, partially eaten roll as if it were pure gold.

Beth grinned. "Go on. Eat it."

"We'll share."

"No, you go ahead. I'm not that hungry." The truth was, she was beginning to feel a little nauseous from the pain and hoped she wouldn't pass out before she could signal for help.

"Now, honey, check that pack we dropped up there when the trees started to fall. I took an emergency flare and some matches from the saddlebag."

Amanda scrambled up the hill and Beth used the time to drag herself to a more comfortable position. Her left arm was useless, hanging limply at her side. With her right hand she spread the blankets they had used to wrap themselves in, doubling them over and over to form as much of a buffer as possible between her body and the snow.

"Beth, guess what?" Amanda shrieked from the top of the rise.

"What?"

"I can see the town. It's way over there, but I can see it."

Thank you, God. Beth closed her eyes in silent prayer then opened them immediately. There was no time to waste.

"That's wonderful, honey. Bring me the flare and matches so I can show you what to do."

Amanda approached slowly. "You're hurt, aren't you?" she asked and tears brimmed on her lashes.

"A little, but we're going to be fine. Now watch closely. I want you to take the flare to the top of the hill and light it like this. Wait for the wind to be calm before you strike the match. Be very careful and don't burn yourself. Then come back here, okay?"

Amanda swallowed hard and nodded. "I can do that," she said but her voice was a whisper. "Are you going to be okay?"

Beth understood the child's reluctance to leave her. It was partially rooted in concern and partially rooted in fear. "Tell you what. You go up there and set the flare and I'll sing. That way, you'll know I'm okay."

Amanda giggled. "That's silly."

"I know," Beth grinned. "That's what makes it fun."

"Okay, I'm going. Start singing." She headed up the hill and Beth started to sing.

"Louder," Amanda called.

Beth belted out a show tune and as she concentrated on singing loud enough for Amanda to hear and keeping the little girl in her sights, she realized that she wasn't thinking about her pain. She also realized that she was absolutely certain that someone would find them—they would be rescued and everything would be all right.

Thank you, she whispered.

"Beth? Keep singing," Amanda shouted as she reached the crest of the hill.

Greg was still examining the tracks around Reba when the storm hit and he spotted two people struggling up the hill through the snow. They were quite a distance away, and he knew they would never hear his shouts above the wind and thunder.

He forced Skydancer to travel as far as possible across the new and blowing snow then left the horse and struck out on foot. The snow was well over his ankles and in places had drifted to knee-height. He ran whenever he could, slipping occasionally but scrambling forward on all fours if necessary, all the while calling out to them.

As he slogged through the snow, he saw Beth shelter Amanda with her own body as the two of them hurried around the side of the ridge and disappeared from Greg's view.

"Beth," he shouted. "Stay down."

It was useless. They had not spotted him yet. He concentrated all of his energy on covering the distance between them. *Just give me a chance, God. That's all I'm asking. Let me get there in time. Help me.*

Greg glanced up. He still had half a football field to cover before he reached the base of the hill. He paused to catch his breath and heard the first tree crash to the ground, followed by another…and another…

"Beth! Amanda!" He ran toward the hill, watching in horror as two trees crashed directly on the spot where he had last seen them.

"No-o-o!" he roared and this time his tears flowed unchecked.

The storm passed as suddenly as it had come. The stillness that followed held no comfort for Greg. He plunged on, climbing the ridge, stumbling over the fallen trees as he rushed toward the spot where he had last seen them.

As he rounded the hill, he heard the most beautiful sound this side of a choir of angels. He heard singing. Bad and off-key. And over that he heard the sound of his daughter's laughter.

"Thank you, God," he murmured, then paused and fell to his knees. *"Thank you for saving them and for not giving up on me."*

His radio crackled and he clicked it on. "Dorie?"

"Just spotted a flare, boss," the dispatcher reported then gave the location.

"That's it. I'm here but send the extra help just in case."

"Roger."

Greg clicked off the two-way radio and turned his attention back to the place where he had heard Beth singing. It was quiet now.

He got to his feet and started to run, falling and stumbling in the snow and bumpy terrain. He ran the gauntlet of fallen trees as deftly as he had mastered the obstacle course of old tires that his college football coach had insisted he run every day.

"Amanda!" he cried as he ran and waved to his daughter on top of the hill. "I'm coming. I'm right here."

Amanda waved back. "Daddy! Beth, look. It's Daddy. I told you he would come. I told you." She started running and sliding down the hill.

Greg's heart soared as he spotted Amanda and realized that she was safe and unharmed. Once again Beth had cared for her, put her own life in danger to protect her.

"Beth," he shouted as he searched the hillside for her. When he saw Beth's lifeless body, the fear that gripped him was paralyzing.

Please, he prayed. *Please let her be all right.* He put one foot in front of the other, forcing himself to move away from his own fears and toward Beth.

"Daddy," Amanda called. "I set off a flare."

"Wonderful, honey. I'll be right there, okay? Just stay right there and watch for someone to come. Dorie is sending help."

"Okay. I hope they come soon. I'm pretty cold."

"It's on the way. They saw your flare, and they're coming," he shouted to her, but his attention was riveted on Beth.

She moved slightly, and he was so relieved that he sprinted the last several yards. She moaned as he moved the tree that had obviously hit her and gently rolled her to her back. "Beth? I'm here. It's going to be all right. Can you hear me? It's going to be all right."

Beth heard and saw everything through the haze of her pain and slipping in and out of consciousness. She found it impossible to believe that Greg had somehow miraculously found them. She figured she must be hallucinating. The one thing she knew was that she had to make sure Amanda was all right. Keep her warm. Get her to safety.

"Amanda," she called and knew that it came out as only a whisper.

"Amanda is safe," Greg's voice told her. An angel no doubt making use of Greg's voice to bring her comfort.

"Blankets." She pushed at the blankets beneath her wanting to get them free so that Amanda could wrap herself in them.

"I know that you're cold, Beth. Just give me one more minute to check the extent of your injuries. So far we seem to be dealing with a broken collarbone and some nasty bruises. There's a lump on your head. Stay with me, love. Help is on the way."

"They're coming, Dad!"

Beth distinctly heard Amanda's excited voice shouting from someplace above her.

"Good," she murmured.

"Beth says that's great, honey." Greg shouted.

"Did you catch the bad guys?" she managed around the thickness of her tongue and dry mouth. Might as well talk to this apparition.

"Got 'em, ma'am," he replied.

"Good," she murmured and felt herself sinking once again into unconsciousness.

"Stay with me, Beth. Come on. Open those beautiful eyes and look at me."

She concentrated on doing what he asked of her.

"That's it," he said and continued working on her arm and shoulder. "I just need to get this secured until we can get you to proper medical help, okay?"

She tried to nod but her head felt too heavy for any such gymnastics.

Greg. Was it possible?

With her good hand she reached up to touch the face that hovered above hers. The face lined with concern. The face with a day's growth of stubble. The face she had wanted more than anything to see. He wasn't a hallucination. Greg was here. He was in charge. Amanda was safe, and Beth could finally permit herself to slip into the bliss of sleep.

Chapter Fourteen

Beth woke to find herself at home in her own bed. She could hear talking downstairs. She smelled something wonderful cooking on the stove. She was hungry and sore. She glanced down and saw that her left arm had been immobilized. She ached all over and had no idea how long she had slept.

She had vague memories of the arrival of the other rangers. Excited voices shouting orders as she was lifted onto some sort of litter and transported back to the village. She had images of Greg looking worried and voices talking quietly in the background of her semiconsciousness.

There had been a moment when she had opened her eyes and willed them to focus. She had seen Greg sitting by her bed with Reverend Dixon. The minister was talking softly to Greg, and Greg was nodding and listening intently. Then an amazing thing happened.

Greg bowed his head as if in prayer. Reverend Dixon placed his hand on Greg's shoulder and bowed his head as well. His lips moved. Greg's lips moved. That's when Beth had been certain that she was either dreaming or dead. Whatever else might have happened, Greg did not sit with Reverend Dixon and Greg certainly did not pray.

But she was alive, perhaps more alive than she had ever been in her life and she had things to do. She rolled to the side of the bed and attempted to sit up.

"Whoa. That wouldn't be your best move just yet," Connie said as she came through the door with a tray of food.

Beth fell back on the pillows. "I just need to take it a little slower," she said. "Hand me my robe, okay?"

"Not on your life. You're going to stay put for at least a couple of days. Then we'll see about getting up and around."

Beth frowned. "I need to check on Amanda and let Greg know that—"

"Amanda is fine, and Greg knows everything he needs to know. Heaven knows he's spent enough time over here. Now eat a little of this soup I made or my feelings will be hurt."

Beth gave in and ate the soup plus two pieces of homemade bread.

"Well, it's good to see you haven't lost your appetite," Connie teased her.

"Greg must be furious with me," Beth stated aloud the one thought that was uppermost in her mind.

"Greg? Why on earth would he be angry with you? Honey, he blames himself for the wrong turn. He saw that marker weeks ago and meant to straighten it and never got around to it. When they carried you in here last night, all I could get out of him was that all of this was somehow *his* fault."

"Was Amanda hurt?"

"Not a bit. She was cold and tired and hungry, but she was so tickled that she had climbed that hill and set that flare you would have thought that she'd conquered Mount Everest. Greg is letting her think that she's the sole cause of the rescuers finding you."

"She's so brave." Beth's eyes filled with tears. "I really adore that kid. If anything had happened to her, I don't know how I could ever have forgiven myself."

"Here now, none of that. Everything turned out just fine." Connie bustled around the room taking the tray away, straightening the covers and fluffing pillows. "If you're up for some company later, I happen to know a certain chief ranger and his daughter who have been stopping by every half hour to check on you."

Beth caught a glimpse of herself in the dresser mirror. "I can't see them looking like this," she moaned.

"Then let's get you bathed and into something more fetching than those flannels, okay?"

Greg paced the small living room of Beth's duplex. What could be keeping Connie? She had promised that as soon as Beth had had a chance to eat and freshen up a bit, she would call for him. One more minute and he was going upstairs to see for himself that she was really okay. He glanced at the clock on a shelf above the woodstove and willed the seconds to tick by.

"You can go up now, but just keep in mind that she's pretty wiped out yet and needs her rest. Don't go lecturing her because she scared the daylights out of you," Connie instructed as she carried the empty tray to the kitchen.

Greg nodded as he glanced up the stairs and waited for Connie to complete her instructions.

"Well, go on," she urged.

Greg took the stairs two at a time then stopped. He needed to compose himself. After all, just because he had come to a decision about the two of them didn't mean that Beth would understand or even agree. He knocked on the door frame.

"Come in," she said.

She was sitting up in bed, and she looked like an angel. Her blond hair glowed against the dark denim of the sheets. Her beautiful face was scratched but radiant as always. She was wearing a pale-blue night-shirt and he had to resist the urge to gather her into his arms and kiss her.

"How are you feeling?" he asked and thought that there was no way he could possibly have come up with a more geeky opening.

"Much better," she replied. "How's Amanda?"

The atmosphere in the room was laced with polite small talk with an undercurrent of tension he could have cut with a knife.

"Fine."

"I'm so relieved."

Silence as they stared at each other.

"She can't wait to see you," he said finally. "In the meantime, I'm afraid she's embellished the story quite a bit with her friends. Apparently according to what she told Doug Spinner, she was quite the hero." He smiled and edged a little farther into the small room.

"Oh, but she was a genuine hero," Beth protested. "There was no way I could have set that flare and if she hadn't…"

Tears welled in her eyes making them even larger and more luminous than usual. In two steps he was by her side, sitting next to her on the bed as he held her uninjured hand in both of his.

"Greg, I am so sorry, I—"

"Beth, if there were any way I could take back these last—"

They spoke in unison and then stopped.

"I need to see Amanda," she said. "I need to see for myself that she is indeed safe and uninjured."

"I'll bring her by later, but Beth, you did everything you could. I watched you put your own safety at risk to protect her. How can I ever thank you for that?"

"Oh, Greg, don't you understand that I love Amanda. I know it's impossible to love her as much as you do, but she is so very, very special to me. You should have seen her out there. She was so wise and brave and you would have been so proud."

He pushed her hair away from her cheek and then ran his hand down her face as if assuring himself that she was indeed all right. "We've been so very blessed," he said softly.

Beth's heart beat in double time. He had said *blessed,* not *lucky* or *fortunate. Blessed.*

"Yes, yes we have," she replied. "It could have been much worse."

He seemed about to say something but held back. "You should get some rest." He stood. "I'll come back later and bring Amanda."

Beth nodded and lay back against the pillows. "Promise?"

He smiled and bent to kiss her temple. "Promise."

She watched him go. There was something different about him, something that went beyond relief that their misadventure had ended well. She couldn't put her finger on it, but there was a marked change in his manner. He seemed... She searched for the right word and found it. *Peaceful.* He seemed at peace with himself for the first time since she'd met him.

Beth smiled. It was a step in the right direction, she thought as she gave in to the effects of the medicine.

"Hi, Beth," Amanda said tentatively as she entered the room the following afternoon. She looked a little anxious as she approached the bed.

"Hi, yourself, kiddo. How are you?"

"Fine." She was carrying a box that was filled to the brim. She waited at the foot of the bed. "Are you going to be okay?"

"Absolutely. I'll be back in the classroom by next week."

Amanda studied her closely. "You look okay," she said.

"Amanda, I'm not sick." *This isn't like your mom,* she wanted to assure the little girl. "I hurt my shoulder, and I'll be just fine. Remember when I hurt my back?"

Amanda nodded.

"It's like that."

"Oh." Amanda continued to wait at the foot of the bed.

"What's all this?" Beth indicated the box Amanda carried and patted the side of the bed inviting Amanda to join her. "Come on up here and show me what you've brought."

Amanda set the box on the bed and climbed up, settling herself cross-legged at one end. "These are things about my Mom. Dad wants me to put together a memory book. He thinks you can help me." She grinned. "What I really think is that he's trying to find a way for me to keep you company while you get well."

"It's a good idea—making a memory book—and I can definitely use the company," Beth said. "Show me what you've got."

They spent the next hour spreading out the photographs and mementos that Amanda had collected. As she displayed them for Beth, she told the story behind each item.

"What a fabulous collection, Amanda." Beth fingered the photographs nearest her. It was the first time Lu had been so real to her. "Your mom was very beautiful," she said softly.

"Here's the book Dad got me to put it all together in."

"Very nice," Beth said. "How do you plan to begin?"

Amanda began laying out the items in order, making stacks of photos and other treasures that would correspond to her own life from birth to her mother's death.

Beth looked at each photograph, listened to every story. How could she ever have thought that she might someday fill the void this incredible woman had left behind? No wonder Greg's grief had run so deep. From everything Amanda was telling her, Lu had been a devoted mother—one able to put aside her own illness in her zeal to make certain that her child would one day understand and accept her death.

Beth considered her own role in Amanda's life. What was she to this girl other than someone she enjoyed spending time with? What could have ever given her the idea that Amanda might one day accept her as a part of her life? What had Beth been thinking to imagine that in just a few short months she had the ability to make that deep of an impact on Greg or his daughter?

"Oh, this is a good one," Amanda squealed as she uncovered a photograph of her parents rolling around on the ground under a sprinkler held by Amanda.

Greg found them deeply engrossed in the memory book project when he stopped by after work. He had heard Amanda's excited voice as soon as he entered the house. She was laughing and he picked up enough words to know which story of her mother she was sharing with Beth.

The memory book had been exactly the right thing. Beth had known when he hadn't that Amanda sometimes struggled with her own memories of Lu. He climbed the stairs, smiling as he heard Amanda relate the story of the day Lu had dragged him into the sprinkler to cool off after he'd come home grousing about some dumb move from Congress.

He stood at the door and observed Beth's blond head almost touching Amanda's dark hair as they pondered some piece of the project. *Mother and child,* he thought.

"And how are the two bravest women in Yellowstone doing today?" he said as he entered the room.

Amanda giggled. "Dad says that I make us sound like some kind of superheroes," she told Beth.

"Well, one of us definitely was," Beth replied. "I don't think I could have made it all the way up that steep hill in the snow and lit that flare."

Amanda grinned. "I had to strike three matches before I got it lit."

"The important thing is that you succeeded, honey," Greg said. "Help came and that's what we needed."

"It was really just like in the movies when the good guys come to rescue the beautiful lady. When those rangers came charging over that ridge on their horses and there you were in Dad's arms…" She sighed dramatically. "It was so cool."

In Dad's arms. Beth blushed. She remembered that moment, remembered thinking that this was exactly where she belonged.

"Amanda and I have been working on her memory book," she told Greg in an attempt to change the subject.

"So I see. Remember what I said, sport. Save a few pages at the end, okay?"

"Sure, Dad. I'm going downstairs. Mrs. Spinner was making cookies. I'll save a couple for you," she called and then giggled at her own humor.

As soon as she was gone, Greg began putting the photos and other items back in the box. "Connie tells me you'll be getting up tomorrow."

"Finally," Beth said. She felt suddenly shy with him. She tried to remember just how much of a fool she might have made of herself in the past few days.

"Maybe we could go for a drive in a couple of days.

If it wouldn't tire you out too much, I thought maybe we could head up to Gardiner for dinner on Saturday." He was focusing on the task at hand.

"I'd like that." *Was this an actual date?*

"Just the two of us, okay?"

"Okay." *No, not a date. He had told her he would make it up to her for getting Amanda safely home. This was his way of living up to that promise.* "You don't have to do this," she said lightly.

"Nope, I don't. Neither do you, but will you come?"

Once again she was aware of a change in his general mood. "Sure," she replied.

He smiled. "Then it's a date. I'll pick you up at six, okay?"

Had she missed something? He was acting so strange—happy. Maybe it was just relief that this time everything had turned out all right.

"Six is fine," she said. She wondered how she was going to make it through a whole evening with him without Amanda as a buffer to her true feelings.

He picked up the box and bent down to kiss her forehead. "See you then. Don't overdo it on your first day."

"I won't."

He got as far as the door, then turned around and looked back at her. "Good night, Beth."

"Good night."

She heard him go downstairs, heard him whistling as he went. She heard him stop in the kitchen and talk to Connie and Amanda. She heard the three of them laughing. He was genuinely happy and she was down-right miserable.

* * *

Beth spent the next couple of days helping Amanda work on her memory book after school. At the same time they talked about their ordeal. Beth wanted to be very sure that there would be no residual effects of that experience.

"Dad says that it was God who kept us all safe until he could get there," Amanda reported. "He told me that I must remember that he never would have remembered the sign being wrong or found us so fast if God hadn't taken him by the hand."

"Your father really said that?" Beth's heart beat a little faster.

"Yeah. When we got back here and he was sure the doctor was taking care of you and he thought I was asleep, I heard him call Reverend Dixon. Next day Reverend Dixon came by the house and they talked for a really long time and Dad cried. I never saw him cry except when Mom died."

Beth made no comment but her mind raced. Was it possible that during their ordeal Greg had found his way back to God? If so, then it would all have been worth it. Even her own disappointment that she had made more of the relationship than was possible could be eased by the realization that Greg had found his faith again.

"And *then*," Amanda continued, "yesterday morning he gets up and he's singing and he said something about God being in His heaven and all's right with the world. Weird."

Definitely—but a good sort of weird. Beth found new

reason to look forward to the dinner out with Greg. If Greg had found God, Beth wanted to hear all about it.

On Saturday, she was dressed by five and waiting for Greg to call for her. She had been up since before dawn and busied herself catching up on her schoolwork and writing thank-you notes to everyone who had brought food or stopped by to check on her during her recupera-tion. The minutes crawled by. Even a two-hour nap in the early afternoon didn't seem to help.

Finally she heard the door to Greg's unit open and close, then his footsteps on her porch and finally a knock at the door. She forced herself to walk calmly, normally across the room.

"Hi," he said. He was wearing regular clothes and a Cheshire grin. He looked wonderful.

"Hi. I'll get my coat."

He held it for her, placing it gently over her shoul-ders to cover the sling on her arm. As they left the house, he took hold of her elbow. He touched her as if she were fragile, taking care not to jostle her arm and shoulder.

As they drove he made normal conversation about his day, about the substitute teacher and tales he was hearing from Amanda about how Doug Spinner was putting her to the test. He asked in-depth questions about the doctor's prognosis and plan for Beth's recovery, frowning and nodding as she laid out the regimen of physical therapy the doctor had advised.

At the restaurant, he made suggestions about the menu but let her order on her own. As their food was delivered, he told her funny stories about some of the regulars dining at the restaurant and especially about Gracie, the auto repair shop owner.

Over dessert and coffee, Beth decided to seize the moment. She had rehearsed her part carefully. She would gently introduce the topic of his return to faith and let him take the lead.

"Amanda tells me that you met with Reverend Dixon, that she saw the two of you praying together." *So much for easing into things.*

He looked surprised and then smiled.

"Guilty," he replied as he shoved down another bite of cheesecake.

"So?"

He shrugged.

"You're not going to tell me what happened?"

"I realized that I had been a class-A dope."

"End of story?"

"That pretty much sums it up," he replied. "Are you going to eat the rest of that cheesecake?"

She pushed her half-eaten piece across the table toward him. "Come on, Greg. What really happened? I mean I'm so glad for you—for Amanda. It's wonderful news."

He seemed incapable of suppressing his grin. "It is, isn't it? I mean, when I think of the time I wasted being angry and all bent out of shape because of my own selfish idea that somehow this was about *me.*"

"It was about you," Beth said. "That's the point."

His expression grew serious and he pushed the empty dessert plate to one side as he reached across the table and took her hand. "No. It never was. It was about Lu.

She was the one in pain. She was the one having to say goodbye to everything and everyone she loved and held dear. She was the one who died."

"And you were the one left behind."

"Yeah, me and Amanda and a gazillion other friends and family members who would have the memory of her to carry with them, the example of her extreme courage to hold up as a model, but who would go on with their own lives."

Beth didn't know how to respond to that. All she could think was that her instincts had been correct. Lu was a saint—a woman whose own strong faith had not only seen her through her darkest hour but everyone she knew and cared for as well.

"When I was out there on that trail, trying to find you and Amanda, I realized that I couldn't do it alone and that made me understand that what I had been trying to do ever since Lu died was do everything alone."

"That's true, but…"

"I was sitting out there trying so hard to find you, to think through how to find you. All around me was nothing but snow—a blank canvas in a way. I was so scared and so frustrated and so angry at myself."

"What happened?"

"I prayed—not anything official, you understand. It was pretty unorthodox when I think of it, but it was there in my subconscious—the need for help, the cry for help."

"Oh, Greg…"

"That's when I remembered the marker and suddenly I knew exactly what had happened. I knew exactly how to find you."

"That's incredible," Beth whispered and her voice cracked with happiness for him.

"It didn't stop there," he continued. "I was racing Skydancer across the terrain and once again it seemed as if everything were monochromatic—white and more white. Then out of nowhere, there was Reba with her red horse blanket, stamping and snorting like she was trying to signal me. It was like a mirage—just there."

"But you know you would have found it eventually once you were on the right path."

"Oh, God wasn't done testing me yet." Greg laughed. "I looked up and there you were struggling through those lodgepole pines and I saw the storm coming, saw you take Amanda under your wing as you went around the side of the hill."

"I never saw you. If only I had seen you coming."

He squeezed her hand. "It wouldn't have helped. I saw the trees start to fall, and then I couldn't see either you or Amanda anymore. I thought God had devised the worst kind of punishment for my arrogance in turning away from him."

"But God doesn't work that way, Greg," Beth protested.

"No. I discovered that He has quite a sense of humor."

"How so?" She was intrigued by his story, thrilled by his obvious joy in the telling of it.

"Just when things seemed to be the most bleak, I heard you singing." He laughed. "It was every bit as awful as that first night although you had chosen something easier than the national anthem this time."

"I beg your pardon. I thought I was at least passable."

"As my grandmother is fond of saying, my dear, you

cannot carry a tune in a bucket, and yet it was the most beautiful sound I think I ever heard. Choirs of angels could not have been more magnificent than the sound of your croaking voice."

"You make me sound like a frog," she snapped but she smiled.

"A beautiful frog," he added looking deep into her eyes. "The most beautiful frog this prince has ever met. When I heard that sound, I fell to my knees, thanking God that you were all right. Then I saw Amanda on top of the hill—it was as if my prayers had been answered. I knew then that God had brought you into our lives. I understood for maybe the first time that He had a purpose in doing that. I finally accepted the fact that if I continued to try to fight Him on that, He was just going to keep proving to me over and over again how important you are to us—to me."

Beth fought to control the tears of happiness that filled her eyes. "I am so happy for you, Greg."

"Do you remember telling me that first night you came here that you thought God had had some purpose in mind in sending you?"

Beth nodded. "You didn't believe me," she recalled.

Greg laughed. "Frankly, I thought you were out of your mind. You were exactly what I did not want in my life right then."

And now? Beth held her breath, daring to hope that perhaps things had changed.

Greg's expression sobered. "I'm trying to tell you that I was wrong about so many things, Beth. I have been fighting so hard to stay in control—in what I thought was control." He chuckled. "The truth is, my life has been completely out of control ever since I first learned that Lu wouldn't make it."

So, there it was at last. The admission that losing Lu had devastated him. "She's still with you, you know," Beth said softly. "Just as she is with Amanda. I can see it in the photographs, hear it in the stories Amanda tells about your life in the days before Lu died."

"Lu is gone," Greg said with no anger or distress. "Amanda and I will always carry her in a part of our hearts, but our lives need to move forward. Lu would want that. God wants that."

"It's taken you a long time to get to this place, Greg."

"I couldn't have done it without you."

So, friendship it would be. Someday it would be enough, but tonight it made Beth a little sad—as if something precious had been lost.

"I'll be right back," Greg said releasing her hand and standing. "More coffee?"

Beth nodded and Greg signaled the waiter.

"Wait here," he said as he headed for the door.

Beth was surprised to see Greg leave the restaurant, but he returned a moment later with a large thick book under his arm. When he placed it on the table and removed the protective covering, Beth recognized it as Amanda's memory book.

"Amanda and I wanted you to see this," he said pushing the album toward her.

"She finished it already?"

He nodded and watched as she slowly turned the

pages. "She still wants to add a couple of stories, but this is the way she wanted it and you said that it was best for her to decide when it was complete."

Beth nodded as she slowly turned the pages. She recognized the flow of the book, recalled each story. She saw the creativity Amanda had shown in putting it together—the way she had angled and cropped certain photos to tell a story without words.

"Isn't it wonderful?" she said as she studied each page.

She had almost reached the end of the album when she turned a page and saw a picture of herself. And then another. And another.

"Where did these come from?" she asked pleased to see them but mystified at their inclusion in the memory album.

"Amanda took some of them. Connie took those that one day when the kids were playing soccer. These over here are from the open house at the school."

"But why? They belong in a different album, not this one."

"Look closer."

She did and saw that Greg or Amanda or both of them were in most of the pictures with her and if they weren't, Amanda had created a wonderful collage to make sure the three of them were together.

"I don't understand," she said as she turned another page and found only several blank pages completing the album.

"There's a note," he said as he prompted her to look at the inside back cover where he had taped an envelope.

She noticed that his hand shook as he pulled the envelope free and handed it to her.

She slid open the sealed flap and pulled out the single sheet of paper:

Dear Beth,

As you can see, there is still room in this album for more pictures—more memories. I have reason to believe that meeting you was a special blessing brought to me by the grace of God and Lu's loving hand. Amanda and I wondered if there might be any chance that you would be interested in helping us fill up this album—and several more—with the memories of a lifetime together.

Love, Greg

Beth read the note twice to be certain she had read it correctly. Her hesitation unnerved Greg completely.

"Okay, I know it's a corny way to handle this and after all we've only known each other a few months— although frankly it seems as if I've known you forever or at least wanted to know you forever and Amanda adores you, of course. I mean, the thing of it is—"

"Just ask me," Beth whispered praying that the question he would utter was the one she wanted so very much to hear.

He reached across the table and took her uninjured hand in both of his. "I love you, Beth—more than I thought I could ever love anyone again. You have brought me such peace, such joy, such understanding.

You have taken my daughter into your home and your heart and given her the love and nurturing she needed most. Please say that you'll stay. Will you stay and be my wife and Amanda's mother?"

"Yes," she replied immediately and saw that he was surprised. "Yes. Yes. To both questions."

Chapter Fifteen

Amanda had attended several weddings in her short lifetime. The park was a popular site for such events and as the daughter of the chief ranger she got to watch a lot of them. On the other hand, she had never actually been a part of the wedding party. She wondered what she would wear and dreamed of a white lace gown that reached all the way to the floor and made her look like a princess.

"What do you think they'll be like?" Sara asked, interrupting Amanda's daydream.

Amanda frowned. "Not sure," she replied and sighed heavily.

"My dad says that rich people are different from the rest of us—that's the way he said it—*the rest of us.*"

"Beth isn't different," Amanda said defensively.

"I know, but Dad said—"

"Your dad can be wrong you know."

"Hey, don't get mad at me. I'm just saying—"

"Sorry."

There was a silence as the two of them sat on the floor of Amanda's bedroom stitching on the quilts they were both making for their dolls.

"When are they coming?" Sara asked.

"Tonight."

Sara nodded sympathetically. "They'll be like your grandparents, right?"

"Plus a great-grandma. Beth says I'm going to love her grandmother. She says I'm to call her *Nana.* That's what she calls her."

"That's so cool," Sara sighed. "Just think. You're gonna have all those grandparents plus a bunch of great grandparents and this new great-grandma. That's really so cool."

Amanda's mood brightened slightly. She hadn't thought of it that way, and her real grandparents were coming to town for the wedding as well. If things didn't work out with Beth's parents, it wouldn't be so bad. After the wedding they'd head on back to Chicago and she'd probably only see them about once a year. In the meantime she had her real grandparents and she *knew* they loved her.

"Yeah, it is pretty cool at that," she admitted.

Beth stood at the gate watching the plane taxi into place. She glanced up at Greg who stood stoically at her side. She knew exactly how he felt. A week earlier she had been in his shoes, meeting his family for the first time. She had been unprepared for the sheer numbers of them—parents, grandparents, siblings—some with families of their own, aunts, uncles, cousins. There were even a few members of Lu's family who had maintained close ties and who showed up to meet Beth.

In those first moments of meeting she had seen in their smiling-but-wary expressions that they were as concerned as her own family about what seemed to them to be this sudden decision to marry. But within an hour, she felt as if she had found a wonderful extended family. Greg's mother was a fabulous gourmet cook and promised to share her recipes and secrets with Beth. His father was as gregarious and happy-go-lucky as Greg was quiet and studious.

Greg's sisters were shy at first, but soon fell into an easy pattern of sharing stories of their own wedding adventures and offering Beth advice on how best to handle their brother as well as help with the wedding itself. The most delightful part of all was seeing Amanda with her cousins and realizing what a wonderfully rich reservoir of family she already had to sustain her and with whom she would always be able to share her joys and concerns.

The gatekeeper announced the arrival of the plane from Chicago. Beth took hold of Greg's arm. "Smile," she urged. "They won't bite."

He nodded but there was no change in his expression and he continued to nervously turn his ranger hat in circles as he held it.

"Here they are," Beth said under her breath. "Mom! Nana! Dad!" She ran to meet them suddenly aware of how long it seemed since she had seen them, of how much her life had changed in only a few short months.

"Where's young Amanda?" Nana wanted to know.

"We left her at home. We thought it might get late and it's a long drive and—"

Greg stepped forward and extended his hand to her father. "Dad, this is Greg Stone."

Her father shook Greg's hand and she could see that the two men were sizing each other up. Then Greg nodded politely to her mother. "Pleased to meet you, ma'am," he said.

"My stars, Beth wasn't kidding around. You are gorgeous," Nana announced.

Greg looked startled and then he grinned and then he laughed and all at once the tense mood was broken and they were all laughing.

"You'll have to excuse my mother, Greg," Elizabeth Baxter told him. "She absolutely never beats around the bush."

"There is no earthly reason to live this many years if you can't say exactly what's on your mind," Nana declared. "I'll bet there's been a time or two when you wished you could sound off to some of those pesky tourists who traipse through that park of yours, don't you, son?"

"Yes, ma'am." Greg replied.

"Let's get the luggage," Beth suggested. "We've got a long drive."

Without her orchestrating a thing Greg fell into step beside her father, politely inquiring about the trip and easily joining in the discussion of the safe topic of sports.

Beth walked arm in arm with her mother and grandmother. "Well?" she asked quietly.

"He's…" her mother began and searched for the right words. "He's not at all what I was expecting."

"He's much better," Nana interrupted. "My heavens, child, you found a keeper with this one."

Beth laughed. "You've been with him for five minutes, Nana."

"I can tell," she insisted. "This one is blue chip all the way."

"I agree," Elizabeth added quietly. "I'm not sure why but I have the most wonderful feeling about this marriage now that I see the two of you together."

Amanda had watched them arrive from her position at the window of her upstairs bedroom. It was hard to really see them well, but it was clear that Beth's dad was almost as tall as her own father and that her mother was the exact same size as Beth except she had this really beautiful snow-white hair that she wore in a really short cut that made her look like a cross between a fairy god-mother and Tinker Bell.

But most of all her attention was drawn to Beth's grandmother. There was something about her quick sure movements that attracted Amanda immediately. Then she looked right up at Amanda's window as if she'd known she would be there. She waved and headed straight for the front door carrying a large white box.

"Amanda?" she called in a strong deep voice. "Come see what I've brought you."

Amanda was fascinated. The woman was older than her own grandparents and yet she seemed so full of energy. She bustled around the small living room, taking off her coat and a beautiful scarf she had tied around her neck. Then she kicked off her shoes and settled herself on the couch, legs folded under her as she tapped the large white box. "Open it," she urged.

Amanda approached the box and untied a wide satin ribbon. Inside there was so much tissue paper that she thought she would never get to whatever was beneath it. Then she saw it—a beautiful lace dress, the color of the palest pink rose. Carefully she lifted it out of the box, letting it unfold.

"Do you like it?"

All she could do was nod. *Like it? It was the most beautiful dress she'd ever seen—even on television. It was absolutely amazing.*

"It's really cool," she said softly.

"There's another in case you prefer another color or different style."

Amanda turned her attention back to the box and discovered the second dress. This one was white with a rainbow of narrow pastel ribbons threaded through it at the neckline and hem. It was equally as beautiful as the first.

"Or you could keep them both—wear one for the rehearsal dinner and the other for the ceremony."

"I'll have to check with my dad," Amanda said as she looked back and forth between the two dresses.

"Easily done," the woman replied. "Why don't you run upstairs and put one on, then come back and model it? We'll have a bit of a fashion show."

Amanda smiled. "Thank you," she said shyly. "They are the two most beautiful dresses in the world."

The woman smiled and leaned forward. She held out her arms and Amanda walked straight into them and returned her hug. "They need a beautiful young lady to show them off properly, and I think you're just the right person. Now scoot, before the others come inside. I want you to dazzle them."

With a giggle Amanda took both dresses and ran up the stairs. She was going to like Beth's Nana very much—not because she brought her dresses so much as that she was a really cool lady just like Beth.

"I'll go see what's keeping Nana and Amanda," Beth said even though no one was really listening. Both her parents were spellbound as Greg regaled them with stories of the vastness of the park, showing them maps and explaining the different ecological regions.

Her father was a shrewd judge of character and she knew that he had immediately seen that Greg was an honorable and upstanding man—a man he would trust implicitly. Her mother was clearly taken by his rugged good looks and his gentle demeanor.

Beth smiled as she thought of how he had changed since the day he had proposed. Gone was the stern manner, the rigid posture and the scowling expression. In rediscovering his faith, Greg had also rediscovered his sense of humor, his ability to view the world as a good place, a place of beauty, and his ability to look upon his fellow human beings with patience and understanding.

"Nana?"

"Oh, Beth, come see," Nana called.

Beth stepped inside Greg's unit and her breath caught. "Oh Amanda, you look like a princess," she whispered.

Nana was standing next to Amanda, a hairbrush in one hand. It was evident that she had just put the finishing touches on Amanda's sleek shining hair by adding a pale pink ribbon that exactly matched the shade of the pink lace dress she was wearing.

"Isn't it the prettiest dress you ever saw?" Amanda asked, reverently fingering the fabric.

"It is that," Beth agreed.

"As Martha Stewart would say, 'It's a good thing,'" Nana agreed standing back to take a long look at Amanda. "What do you think, Amanda dear? This one or shall we try the white one again?"

"I like this one. Is it all right, Beth?"

"It's perfect. I think you may just outshine the bride at this wedding."

"Not likely," Nana said. "Get me that garment bag, dear." She motioned toward a bag Greg had hung on the closet door. "Open it."

"Oh, Nana, it's your wedding gown." Beth choked with tears as she lifted the beautiful gown from its protective covering. "I love this dress."

"Then do me the honor of wearing it. That is unless you've found something you'd rather wear and have for your own."

Beth could not contain her tears of happiness. "I always dreamed of being married in this dress," she said softly. "Ever since I was a little girl."

"Splendid. Just call me Nana, Inc.—Maker of Dreams Come True."

The three of them had a good laugh and then decided that they would surprise the others at the actual ceremony rather than model the gowns for them beforehand.

Later that night after Greg had gone to his temporary quarters in one of the empty apartments across the compound and her parents and Amanda had gone to bed, Beth stopped by her grandmother's room. Beth was staying in Greg's unit with Amanda so that her parents and grandmother could take over her unit.

"Nana?"

"Come in, child," Nana was in bed. She laid her book aside and patted the covers beside her. "Are you very, very certain about this man?"

"Very, very," Beth assured her.

Nana grinned. "Good."

"I wanted to ask a favor," Beth said.

"Of course."

"Well, since Deanna is due any minute and won't be able to be my matron of honor, I was wondering—I mean I know it's unorthodox—but would you do me that honor?"

It was the first time in her entire life that she ever recalled seeing her grandmother at a loss for words. Tears filled her pale-blue eyes, and she placed her delicate hand over Beth's. "Your mother will think this is most unusual," she warned.

Beth laughed. "Mother has been dealing with my unseemly actions since I was four. She'll come around. Will you do it?"

"Absolutely. As Amanda likes to say, 'It will be so-o-o cool.'"

They had chosen the Saturday after Thanksgiving for their wedding day, and the long holiday weekend was filled with activity. It seemed as if everyone in the park was involved.

On Wednesday, the children and some of the mothers surprised Beth with a bridal shower.

On Thursday, both families gathered at the ranch where Greg's grandparents lived to celebrate Thanksgiving.

Friday flew by in a flurry of prewedding activity. The park supervisor had given permission for the wedding and reception to be held in the magnificent old lodge at Old Faithful. Connie had taken charge of plans for the dinner following the ceremony and had recruited a team of park residents to assist her. That night members of the wedding party gathered at the lodge for the rehearsal. The informal dinner following the rehearsal was a joyful event in itself as the families shared the childhood and teenaged misadventures of the wedding couple.

Beth found herself pulling back a little, wanting to savor each moment, to observe it and preserve it.

"You're unusually quiet," Greg said as he joined her on the edge of the family circle.

"But not in a bad way," she assured him. "They're all so precious, aren't they? These moments of our lives."

He nodded and put his arm around her, pulling her closer to his side. "Look over there." He pointed to where Amanda and the other children were gathered around Beth's grandmother. Their faces were rapt with wonder as she told them some tale.

"Nana should have been an actress," Beth said with a laugh. "She's certainly a born storyteller."

"Amanda loves her already." He turned her so that they stood face-to-face. "Tomorrow is the day. Any second thoughts?"

"None. You?"

He pretended to consider. "Nope, can't think of a single one."

"Then let's get married."

Greg stood next to the impressive stone fireplace that soared forty feet into the seven stories of lodge-pole rafters that formed the lobby of the lodge. His father stood beside him as his best man. He watched as his mother and Beth's mother were both escorted to their seats that were next to each other in the front row. Beth had insisted there be none of the usual fool-ishness of one side being seating for family and guests of the bride and the other for the groom. "We are fam-i-ly," she had sung dancing around the lobby with Amanda.

The music changed and Beth's beloved Nana started down the aisle. She was dressed in a gown of deep-rose-colored silk and she looked decades younger than her eighty-five years. She winked at Greg as she took her place across from his father.

Next came Amanda. Greg's breath caught. His beloved daughter was dressed in a beautiful gown of pale-pink lace. Gone were her usual jeans and chinos. Her thick-soled shoes had been traded for a delicate pair of slippers. Her hair, usually caught into a hap-hazard ponytail, fell sleek and shining to her shoulders. She carried a basket of rose petals that she scattered along the aisle as she slowly advanced toward him.

He smiled at Amanda as she took her place next to Nana, then followed everyone's gaze to where Beth walked slowly down the aisle on the arm of her father.

A thousand images raced through his mind. Beth singing at the bear. Beth in the fuzzy bear slippers. Beth stealing the soccer ball from under his nose. Beth laughing with Amanda. Beth making dinner in his kitchen. Beth in his arms. Beth. Beth. Beth.

He saw in her eyes that she, too, was remembering the events that had brought them to this moment. That morning he had been up before sunrise and looked out his window to see her sitting on one of the benches that surrounded Old Faithful. She was wrapped in blankets, wearing the funny slippers and warming her hands and face over a steaming cup of coffee. He had stood at the window for a long moment cherishing the idea that he was gazing out at his future. He had never been more certain of anything in his life than he was of his love for this woman and the wonderful life they were about to begin together.

As the geyser erupted with its usual punctuality, Beth lifted her mug of coffee saluting the spray of steaming water. Greg considered the appropriateness of the symbolism—the geyser came and went without fail whether or not anyone was paying attention. Life was like that. These last several months he had permitted it to go on around him, without him. He would not make that mistake again. Beth had shown him the importance of appreciating every moment.

Beth and her father reached the altar. Greg stared at her, unable to believe his good fortune in finding this woman, knowing luck had had nothing to do with it. A far greater power than simple good fortune had brought them together. He smiled at her and received the reward of her glorious smile in return as Reverend Dixon cleared his throat and began the service.

"Well, now, I think it's safe to say that there are at least a dozen people in this room—myself included—who saw from the beginning that this was indeed a match made in heaven."

Everyone chuckled appreciatively.

"Who gives this woman to be married to this man?"

"Her mother and I do," Beth's father replied in a strong firm voice. Then he kissed Beth's cheek and took his place next to Beth's mother.

"And, in a bit of a twist on the traditional," Reverend Dixon continued, "I am compelled to ask, who gives this man to be married to this woman?"

Amanda set her basket of flower petals down and stepped between Greg and Beth. "I do," she announced as she clasped both their hands and then joined them together.

"Then it shall be done," Reverend Dixon said softly as Amanda stepped back to her place near Nana. Beth and Greg continued to hold hands as they turned to Reverend Dixon and as they began the age-old ritual of exchanging promises and vows, there wasn't a dry eye in the house.

* * * * *

Dear Reader,

Several years ago I made my first trip to Yellowstone
National Park. It was late fall and a quiet and wonderful
time to be there. Slowly, the park was readying itself
for the long winter ahead. The Great Fire had just
happened a couple of years earlier—the scene at the
end of this book where they run among the falling
lodgepole pines actually happened to me!

Our parks are such a national treasure—a gift from
the Great Spirit that reminds us more than anything
else of how fortunate we are to inhabit this incredible
land. One night when I returned to the Yellowstone
Hotel after a day spent hiking the beautiful Yellowstone
Canyon, I was raving about the magnificence of this
particular landmark in a park filled with such wonders.
A woman looked up at me and quietly commented,
"You've never been to the Grand Canyon, have you?"
And she was right—I hadn't. When I did go a few years
later, I saw what she meant. It was an equally incredible
yet very different reminder of the awesome gifts we
have around us that have nothing to do with material
wealth and everything to do with being richly blessed.

I hope you enjoy *A Mother for Amanda* and that if
you have never taken the time to visit one of our great
national parks, you will do so—there's bound to be one
near you somewhere. In the meantime, please don't
hesitate to write to me. I would love to hear from you
as I work on my next tale of Love Inspired.

Blessings!

Anna Schmidt

THE DOCTOR'S MIRACLE

Come, let us cry out with joy to Yahweh,
Acclaim the rock of our salvation.
Let us come into His presence with thanksgiving,
Acclaim Him with music.

—Psalms 95:1–2

To the healers and the survivors

Chapter One

Rachel Duke blinked at the lights and smiled at the audience. She took a deep breath. Just one more song and she might win the talent search. Unbelievably, she stood in the midst of a dream coming true. She settled herself onto the high stool a stagehand had placed in front of the microphone and waited for the audience to recover from the rocking fervor of the last performer.

Her last number—the one that had won her the spot as a finalist in the talent search for new faces at the Grand Ole Opry—had been a rousing gospel classic. She had gotten the audience involved, and when she left the stage they had given her a raucous ovation that included cheers and whistles. She could see that they were anticipating something similar, and she hoped her change of pace would not disappoint them.

As she strummed the strings of the guitar to check the pitch and to capture their full attention, she saw Doc McCoy hurrying to the seat she had reserved for him. She nodded in his direction even as she caught sight of the tall, dark, bearded man following him. That would be Doc's son, Paul McCoy.

She had tried to assure Doc that she was fine on her own and there was no need for him to be there, but he had insisted.

"I'm not about to miss your big night, Rachel," he had announced. Doc had served as surrogate father for Rachel and her siblings ever since their parents had died when Rachel was twelve.

"Doc, Paul will be exhausted. It must take hours to fly from Kosovo, not to mention the connections and delays. He's going to be anxious to get home."

"He's young," Doc had replied cheerily. "You young folks bounce back. Just look at you—battling this bug these last few weeks and still determined to get up there and knock 'em dead."

Rachel understood that her recent bout with the stomach flu had gone on too long in Doc's opinion. "I'm feeling good. You need to concentrate on Paul."

But he had come anyway. Rachel glanced again at the father and son. If outward appearances were any indication, Paul had changed quite a bit since high school. Refusing to break her concentration, Rachel deliberately turned her attention to the opposite side of the hall where the judges waited.

"I want to thank y'all for the chance to sing for you again. This is a song I wrote last spring and haven't yet had a chance to perform…until tonight. I sure hope y'all like it," she said as she launched into the musical introduction. "I call it 'This Little Child,'" she added, as she began to hum along to the echoing timbre of the twelve-string guitar.

She sang the first verse with her eyes downcast, concentrating on the movement of her fingers. As she reached the first chorus she glanced at the audience and saw that she had made the right choice. She relaxed and allowed her gaze to return to Doc and Paul McCoy.

Doc was leaning forward, listening intently and smiling at her. When he saw her look his way, he gave her a subtle sign of encouragement. Doc was her biggest fan, and she was suddenly very glad he had insisted on coming.

Paul McCoy, on the other hand, was understandably less than thrilled to be there. After all, he'd just gotten off a flight from Kosovo where he'd spent the last several months treating refugees in the camps there. Like Doc, he was also a doctor, but he definitely marched to a different drummer than his father did. Paul had headed for Chicago as soon as he finished medical school. There would be no third generation of McCoy doctors in Smokey Forge as far as he was concerned. His focus had been research. The Kosovo thing had happened a few months earlier, and Rachel never had gotten it straight why he'd suddenly left a prestigious position at a top teaching hospital in Chicago to go halfway around the world.

All she knew was that he was coming back home for an indefinite amount of time to help Doc out. The rumor mill in Smokey Forge had it that Doc secretly hoped he could get Paul to stay for good. Doc was getting along in years, and ever since the death of his beloved wife, Mary, he'd been at loose ends. Publicly he claimed that Paul was just going to be around long enough to lend a hand until Doc could find a partner who would take over the practice and let him take life a little easier.

Doc continued to smile at her and nod in time to the music. Paul was slouched in his seat with his eyes closed. Rachel frowned. She didn't care how exhausted he was, nobody was going to sleep through her performance. With a renewed energy she hadn't felt in all the long, hard weeks of preparing for the talent search, she concentrated on raising the level of her performance a notch.

> And God was there
> And God could see
> This little child
> Was really me.

When she saw him open his eyes and sit up straight in his chair, she smiled and began the second verse. But her voice faltered slightly when she felt the full power of his dark eyes watching her. Paul McCoy had always been handsome in a dark, slightly intimidating sort of way. In high school, he'd had the respect of every male student and the heart of every female, but he had kept to himself—a serious student and top athlete who stayed away from school dances and social events.

The man watching her from the second row bore little physical resemblance to that boy she remembered from high school. The eyes that had stolen hearts with their burning intensity stared at her now. They did not glow with passion as they had in high school. They were dull with what she assumed was exhaustion and something more. In them she saw pain that bordered on

despair and she wondered what he had seen in Kosovo
that had brought him such sadness.

Certainly, her heart broke every time she saw a report
on television or read a story about those poor uprooted
and displaced souls. She couldn't imagine what it must
be like to actually be there trying to help. It was the faces
of the children that really touched her most. Those faces
had been the inspiration for the song she had chosen to
perform for the finals.

> And God was there
> And God could see
> This little child
> Was really me.

Paul McCoy had watched Rachel Duke cross the
stage and noted the resemblance to her older sister
Sara—the one he'd had the crush on in high school.
He'd seen her glance at his father as they hurried to their
seats and knew that Doc had done the right thing in
coming. As she started the usual patter with the audience
while she tuned her guitar, Paul had slumped farther into
his seat on the aisle.

"She's made the finals," Doc told him, having obviously picked up this bit of news from the person on the
other side of him.

"Great," Paul replied and fervently hoped that this
meant they had arrived for the grand finale of the show
and would soon be back on the road for home. At the
moment, he wanted a hot shower and a soft bed with
clean linens a lot more than he wanted to hear the Duke

kid sing. As she fingered the intricate melody of the song, he slouched farther into his chair and closed his eyes. At least she had chosen a ballad, he thought.

He had shut his eyes, prepared to make it through the next hour with as little effort as possible. He was exhausted and emotionally drained from having to leave behind unfinished work in Kosovo. Not that he could ever have really finished his work there. Every time he thought they were finally on the verge of a breakthrough in the numbers of people in need of medical care, a new flood of outcasts arrived. In spite of an end to the fighting, the new arrivals seemed more desperate than any of the masses of refugees who had come before.

Gradually, as he surrendered to the fatigue and frustration of the last several days, the music broke through the armor he had constructed for sheer emotional self-preservation. Her voice was deep and low and so rich that it seemed impossible to come from the skinny young redhead onstage. She demanded attention in a manner that was at the same time subtle and insistent. He opened his eyes and focused on the ceiling as if in doing so he might actually see the sounds floating over the hushed auditorium. He found himself straightening, sitting upright, leaning forward as his eyes locked on the waif with the huge guitar who sat alone in the center of the vast stage.

He tried dismissing the words as so much religious drivel and found he could not. He listened as if hearing a master storyteller weave a tale that was at once familiar and haunting. She sang of children lost, wandering and in need. He thought of the children in the inner-city of

Chicago where he had worked before going abroad. He thought of the children that his father drove deep into the hollers (as the locals called them) and valleys of the Tennessee mountains to treat for free because they had no money to pay. For the first time since stepping onto the plane leaving Kosovo, he permitted himself to think of the children in the refugee camps. He thought of ten-year-old Samir and felt a tear escape the outer corner of one eye. He let it find its way down his cheek unchecked as he stared at the woman onstage.

There had to be a way to get the kid out of there, to get as many of them out of there as possible. The countryside was still riddled with land mines. Forget the land mines. Just drinking the water could be hazardous. He'd seen too many of the children—fatherless, motherless, alone in a place that had little time to be concerned about whether or not a kid lived or died. He'd been torn—having to choose between them and the aging widowed father who needed him, the father who had never before asked for his help. In the end, he'd come home. Sami had stood at the chain link fence watching him go. It was the only time Paul had seen the kid cry.

"You'll be okay," Paul had assured him.

"I want to come with you," Sami had pleaded, sounding for the first time like the ten-year-old kid that he was.

"Your mom needs you here." *And my dad needs me there.* It was a cheap trick, reminding a ten-year-old of responsibilities he shouldn't have. Paul felt that he, too, was abandoning the boy.

As the last note of Rachel Duke's song sailed high into the upper balcony and faded, there was utter silence for a split second before the audience roared its approval. People stood and applauded and cheered. Rachel Duke stepped forward and released the strap of her guitar. She smiled uncertainly in Doc's direction and then she collapsed onto the stage, her guitar landing next to her with a discordant thud.

In seconds the stage was alive with people crowding around her.

"Call 911," someone yelled as Paul leaped onto the stage.

"I'm a doctor," he said in a tone that parted the crowd without question. When he reached Rachel she was unconscious and so still that his heart skipped a beat. "Dad?"

"Right here, son," he heard Doc reply.

"Let's get her off this stage," Paul said. "Are you in charge here?" he asked the guy in the tuxedo.

"I can help," replied another man, who seemed far more capable. "I'm the stage manager for the theater. You can bring her backstage."

"Rachel? It's Paul McCoy. Can you open your eyes?"

Well, of course, I can. The fact is I don't want to. How embarrassing to have my big moment and pass out cold! I poured everything I had into that performance, and now this!

"Rachel?"

He had a nice voice. I'd forgotten that. It was surprisingly gentle when I might have expected a more brisk professional tone. Maybe little Paulie McCoy had inherited his father's quiet, soothing bedside manner.

"Let's get her backstage."

Rachel felt his arms go around her, lifting her. This was too much. "I can walk," she croaked, opening her eyes and finding her face too close to his for comfort.

"No doubt," he replied. "But humor me anyway." There was no hint of humor to be found in the grim, determined set of his bearded jaw. His deep-set eyes were shadowed with fatigue and seemed to dare her to test his patience.

"I'll go get my bag," she heard Doc say.

Paul carried her offstage and into a dressing room, and she could hear the emcee announcing that it was just a case of nerves and nothing to be concerned about. As Paul deposited her on a sofa and closed the door, she heard the emcee introducing the last finalist.

Paul returned to sit next to her and immediately began probing the glands under her chin and along her throat. His hands were large and warm. She felt the color rise to her cheeks.

"Bet you didn't think you'd be called into action the minute you stepped off the plane," she said in a failed attempt to lighten the moment.

"Shh," he said and frowned as he counted her pulse. "How much do you weigh?"

"Probably somewhere around one twenty," she replied.

"Probably somewhere around a hundred and five would be closer to the truth," he replied with just a hint of a reprimand. He lifted her hands and studied her unpainted nails. He frowned slightly, then patted her hands and released them. "You know, in spite of what you young women think, there *is* such a thing as being too thin."

"I…" She started to protest.

"Believe it or not, there are still people in the world who don't have enough to eat," he lectured.

Her eyes flashed in irritation. "Yes, I do know that. Perhaps you might remember that some of them live right here in the good ol' U. S. of A."

"Are you saying you don't get enough to eat?" Cynicism dripped from every word.

So much for bedside manner, Rachel thought and then spoke to him as if she were dealing with one of her third-grade students.

"I'm saying that you don't have a monopoly on understanding that some of us have more options than others. I'm saying that I would be as ticked off as you obviously are if I thought someone had deliberately starved herself for no good reason." She paused for a breath and delivered the clincher. "I'm *saying* that I am *not* anorexic or bulimic or anything like that, okay?"

Paul's mouth opened and shut, then opened again as he prepared his retort and then seemed to reconsider it.

"What's the verdict?" Doc asked as he entered the room and opened his medical bag.

"Not sure yet," Paul replied, stepping aside to permit his father to take over.

"What are you thinking?" Doc asked as he pulled out his stethoscope. "She's been fighting this stomach virus for the last few weeks, and we've just not been able to help her shake it."

Rachel closed her eyes again as she heard Doc relating the gory details of her illness as well as the measures they'd taken to address the symptoms. She could hear applause.

"Look, I'm fine, really. I want to know what's happening," Rachel said and tried to stand. She stumbled, and Paul caught her. She swallowed a nervous giggle as it suddenly dawned on her how many of her girlfriends in high school would have been thrilled to find themselves in the arms of Paul McCoy not once but twice in a single evening.

"Why don't I go see what they decide and you get back on that sofa, young lady?" Doc said, handing Paul the stethoscope. "You're in good hands here."

Before Rachel could stop him, Doc was gone. She faced Paul again. They traded wary glances. "How about a truce? We'll chalk your bad mood up to a long plane ride and mine up to nerves and embarrassment at falling flat on my face in front of a panel of judges I really wanted to impress."

"It was the music they were to judge, not you," he replied with maddening logic as he donned the stethoscope and prepared to use it. "Take a deep breath." He listened and moved the stethoscope. "Again."

She did as she was told. "In the first place, they may have come to judge the music, but since the music comes from me—this mouth, these fingers…" She saw that he was frowning again. "You know, you're making far too big a deal of this," she protested.

He ignored her protest and continued to listen. "Okay, regular breaths now."

"I've had a little bug, and you're right to a point. I mean, I'll admit that I probably could have eaten more nutritious meals, but…"

"Again, deep breaths and this time, try not to talk,"

he said quietly as he moved the cold metal just inside her blouse.

She studied the man before her and tried to relate this person to the boy she'd known. He'd been in her sister Sara's class, four years ahead of Rachel. He had always been very serious, a kid determined to come to his own conclusions rather than simply accept the rules of others. His attitude quickly earned him the label of rebel in the small, conservative community. The adults tolerated him because of their respect for his parents. The kids idolized him.

Paul never seemed to notice one way or another. The opinions of others clearly did not interest him. She tried to recall a single time Paul had permitted his carefully cultivated facade of coolness to slip. Then she did remember a time, and it made her smile. It was the day he had asked Sara to the prom. Rachel had been with Sara, and Paul had stammered and blushed so badly that he'd barely been able to get the words out. She decided to hold on to that image of him as a weapon in combating his efforts to intimidate her now.

"That was quite a performance out there," Paul said as he sat back and hung the stethoscope around his neck while he reached for a small penlight from his father's bag. "Follow the light without moving your head," he instructed as he moved the light back and forth, up and down.

"Thank you, I think. I mean that's the kind of thing a person could take either way. Sort of like what my mom used to call a left-handed compliment."

"Possibly." He put the light away and considered her

for a long moment. "I have friends in Chicago who are performers. It takes a tremendous amount of energy to stay in top form. They all work hard at keeping themselves in excellent shape—diet, exercise…"

She sighed heavily. "Look, you keep hinting that I have an eating disorder. I don't," she assured him. "I eat like a horse, and bluntly put, I keep it all down. I've had this little virus lately. Other than that…" She could see that he was definitely not used to being talked to in this way.

He repeated the gentle probing of the underside of her jaw near her ears with his fingertips. "Any soreness or tenderness there?" he asked.

Warmed by the sensation of his gentle touch, Rachel shook her head in response. She knew he was not listening to her protests.

"Good." He found pen and paper on the dressing table and made a couple of notes. "Tell me about this virus."

"Nothin' but a good ol' fashioned stomach flu," she replied. "You know, throwing up, stomach cramps—all the usual attractive symptoms."

"How long did it last?"

"Doc told you—" she began, but he interrupted.

"Yes, he did. Now I'm asking you."

"It comes and goes."

He glanced up, and there was the slightest flicker of surprise in his expression. "For how long?"

"I guess it first came on about four weeks ago."

"And the most recent episode—before tonight, that is."

She laughed. "Tonight had nothing to do with the flu, Paul."

"Let me be the judge of that. Have you had previous incidents of dizziness or fainting associated with this?"

"Of course not. Maybe a little light-headedness from time to time—a couple of times, but this is the first time I've ever fainted in my life. It's not something I plan on repeating any time soon, I assure you."

He attached a blood-pressure cuff to her arm and began pumping it. "That's a little high," he said, more to himself, it seemed, than to her.

"I get a little nervous seeing doctors," she said. "Look…"

He motioned for her to be quiet as he counted her pulse again.

"So, you're *that* Duke," he said as he let go of her wrist and replaced the blood-pressure cuff in Doc's bag. "Now I remember. Dad always had some problems with you. I think I remember that there were a couple of times when you made it pretty clear that you didn't care a whole lot for doctors. That was you, wasn't it?" He remembered the freckle-faced kid she had been, with a temper to match her red hair. "As I recall, you actually bit him once for giving you a shot."

She stared at him. "Let me guess. You were absent the day they taught bedside manner, right?"

"The man had to wear a bandage for a week."

She blushed. "I apologized for that. Mama made me write a note and hand it to Doc personally."

"Well, I promise not to give you any shots. On the other hand, I would like to get you home as soon as possible and run some tests. Maybe draw a little blood. I mean, if you're telling me you aren't anorexic, I'd like to find out a little more about this virus." He began packing up his father's equipment as if her agreement were a foregone conclusion.

"I might need to stay here," she replied. "If I win," she added shyly.

"I wouldn't advise that."

"If I win the competition, I have a contract to perform," she explained as if talking to a not-so-bright child.

"Unless you get some rest and proper food, you're going to end up in the hospital," he replied as he snapped the bag shut.

Rachel decided she would take the matter up with Doc. After all, Paul was not her doctor. She relaxed on the couch and waited for Doc's return.

"Do you also sing country rock?" Paul asked. He had sat down in a chair across from her and stretched out his long legs. She understood that he, too, was deliberately closing the subject of her health, at least for the moment. "It seems to be all the rage these days."

"Strictly gospel," she replied automatically as she continued to consider her options should she win the contest.

He raised one eyebrow in surprise. "Really? Nothing but gospel?"

"Why does that surprise you?"

"I guess I just assumed that someone young like you with all that ambition would perform in the venue most likely to give you national exposure. Gospel is not exactly what wins the top Grammy awards."

She flinched defensively. "Well, it's what I do and there's always a first time."

"Sorry. I don't mean to offend you. Even though I'm

hardly the model churchgoing type, I happen to enjoy gospel singing very much."

"For the music rather than the message, I assume?" she asked.

He shrugged. "It's not easy for a Smokey Forge boy to admit that he's strayed from the faith." He could not imagine why he would confide such a thing to her.

"That's too bad—I mean that you've strayed," she said, studying him long enough for him to feel slightly uncomfortable. "Admitting it is the first step toward getting back."

"Perhaps for some," he muttered as he stood and paced the small room. Instinctively, she knew that the simple words covered some deeper unspoken message.

She nodded. "It's definitely not terminal. People drop out all the time, but sooner or later, they find their way back. You will, too. God will see to that."

Paul pinned her with his dark eyes. "I know it's impossible for others to understand, but perhaps if you could have seen some of the pain and suffering I've witnessed…" He shook his head and turned away.

"So, then why did you come back home? Why leave Kosovo?" she asked when the silence between them had gone on too long.

"Dad needs some help until he can find someone to take over the clinic after he retires, and… Who knows why any of us make the choices we do?" A slight lifting of his shoulders was the end of his response as Doc opened the door and looked from her to his son and back again.

"What's the verdict?"

"I don't want to jump to conclusions, but there are a number of things that are coming together here." Paul moved closer to his father and spoke in low tones as if she were sleeping or had left the room. "Loss of weight, fatigue, an elevated heart rate and higher than normal blood pressure. This virus that she's been fighting. Is there something going around town?"

Doc shook his head. "A few cases of food poisoning about a month ago."

"I want to run some lab work, but at the very least when an otherwise healthy young woman has dizzy spells, we're dealing with something that shouldn't be ignored."

"Rachel, you never mentioned these dizzy spells," Doc said sternly.

"You're both overreacting." Rachel stood and this time she didn't need anyone to steady her. "It's nerves and burning the candle at both ends and forgetting to eat. All easily fixed. What happened out there, Doc?"

Paul read his father's face and knew she hadn't won.

"Close second, honey," he said softly and handed her the envelope with the cash prize he had collected for her.

"I see," she said softly as she fingered the envelope.

Paul watched her take a moment to digest the news. Then she turned and looked at them both with a dazzling smile. "Well, can a girl hitch a ride home with you two doctors? I should get back so I can teach tomorrow, and Paulie here wants to siphon off some blood for his tests."

Paul couldn't have been more surprised at her reaction to the news. He might have expected tears and gnashing of teeth, not having to hurriedly gather his jacket to follow her and his father down the hall.

On her way out, Rachel took time to congratulate the winner and thank each judge. She hugged the stage manager, who held her close and said something that made her laugh. There wasn't a trace of self-pity in her, Paul thought as he observed all of this. Rachel Duke was pretty poised for a kid straight out of the hills of Tennessee who had just performed on the biggest country music stage in the world. She was not at all what he might have expected.

Chapter Two

❧

"**Y**o, Dr. Paulie, how 'bout leaving some in the tank?" Rachel protested with a grin as Paul prepared to fill a second vial with blood.

It had been a busy week since they'd all returned from that night in Nashville, and she had finally come to the office to permit him to draw blood for the battery of tests he had ordered.

"Just one more," he replied. Rachel had always been the cute one in the Duke family. Her sister Sara was more serious, and Maggie, the eldest, cast into the role of mother for her siblings when their parents died, had taken to her part as earth mother with relish. When she was a child, Rachel's antics had been in keeping with her life as a much-loved child. As an adult, he would have expected the harder knocks of life to dampen some of her enthusiasm. Apparently, they hadn't, or else she had lived a sheltered and charmed life.

"You're not going to find anything, you know," she

assured him. "I'm feeling better already. It was just nerves and the remnants of that flu."

She might be cute, but she was also opinionated. It always came out in an upbeat way, as if she had some secret source for inside information. "The flu does not commonly last four weeks or more," he replied, stating a fact. "Nor does it generally appear, go away and then appear again. At the very least you are borderline mal-nourished and dangerously exhausted." He didn't add that she had also just had what he assumed was a major disappointment in losing first place in the talent search, and such things took their own toll.

She put on a mock frown. "Gee, Dr. McCoy, the patient feels fine, and she's having no symptoms. Here's a radical thought—maybe she's not sick anymore? Maybe she just needs a week or so and a couple of hot fudge sundaes to get back on her feet?"

"Don't you ever have a bad day?" he asked, studying her closely for any sign that she was putting on some kind of act to cover more serious symptoms.

Rachel shrugged and grinned. "Life's pretty amazing."

He made no reply to that as he released the elastic tourniquet on her arm and pulled out the syringe.

"I'm a quick healer, Paul. Always have been," she assured him, refusing a bandage. "Looks like you could have used one earlier yourself."

She pointed to the place on his chin where he had nicked himself shaving that morning. Her finger came just short of touching him, and he wondered why that disappointed him. "I'm a little out of practice."

"How come you took off the beard?"

He shrugged. "I just let it grow out in Kosovo. Not a lot of time for shaving over there." He tried to make light of it. Instead he found it hard to disguise the painful memories that came with any thought of his experience there, much less the guilt he couldn't shake at having left his work unfinished. He had shaved because every time he looked in the mirror, he found himself back there. He could hardly expect Rachel Duke to understand that.

"So, was it as bad as all the reports say?" For the first time all morning, her expression was serious and filled with concern. Her voice was low and soft as if she wanted to know but didn't want to intrude.

Paul stifled an urge to give a sarcastic laugh. "What reports? Kosovo is pretty much forgotten ever since the fighting stopped. The media have lost interest."

"I'm sorry. It's understandable that you might not be ready to talk about it. It must have been pretty awful." She paused and then put her hand on his. "You know, sometimes it really is good to talk these things out. I mean, stuffing all those memories and feelings inside…" She saw something in his expression that stopped her from finishing her thought. "On the other hand," she said, deliberately changing her tone as well as the topic, "I know that Doc is really glad you decided to come home for a while before heading back to Chicago."

"I'm not sure I'm going back to Chicago," Paul said and wished he hadn't. He wasn't ready to share his plans and he didn't want to raise false hopes for his father. What was it about her that had him blurting out these things? "That is, it could take some time to get somebody in here to help Dad. Besides I could use some time to take stock." There, he'd done it again.

Rachel laughed. "Some things never change, Paul McCoy. You always were one to go off somewhere alone to lick your wounds or plan your next move. It was a huge part of your charm when you were sixteen. We'll have to see how it plays now that you're twice that."

She stood and headed for the door. As she passed him, she playfully ruffled his hair. "Welcome home, Dr. McCoy."

A couple of days later he found himself warmed by the memory as he squinted at the slide under his microscope and then sat back and thought about the kid he had known. Rachel had been all arms and legs as a youngster and shown none of the promise of beauty that she had grown into as an adult. She'd always been tagging along with her older sisters, even on that awful day when he'd finally worked up the nerve to invite Sara Duke to the prom.

He realized now that it was Rachel's face rather than Sara's he recalled most clearly from that day. He recalled her look of fascination at his stumbling, bumbling attempt to impress Sara Duke with his coolness. In that moment he had dropped his carefully constructed facade of the serious, studious loner and revealed to the world his desperate hope that Sara would say yes. Rachel had seen his vulnerability that day, and she couldn't have been more than fourteen. Earlier this week, he had once again exposed his vulnerability to her, and she'd picked up on it just as quickly as before.

The idea that Rachel Duke could see right through him was a little unsettling.

He glanced out the window and back to the slide he'd been holding. It was a glorious autumn day, and for reasons he couldn't quite grasp, he suddenly felt like enjoying it. No doubt, Rachel would assure him that this was a positive result of all those dreary months in Kosovo. Still, taking a break for a walk over to the café for a sandwich seemed perfectly in order.

"Ruby," he said to the receptionist who had worked with his father for over twenty years, "tell Dad I took an early lunch."

Rachel sat alone on a park bench in the middle of the town square. She glanced through the flaming orange leaves of the maple and grinned. "Well, God, I guess I'm here at the burning bush. You know, I thought it would be easier to accept not winning the other night, but the truth is I really wanted that contract. I'm trying hard to understand why You think I ought to be happy just staying here in Smokey Forge, teaching the kids and playing the local revival circuit, but…"

She shook off her objections. "Sorry," she said meekly. "It's just I'm trying to understand what it is I'm supposed to do. I mean, You gave me this talent, and surely…"

She took a deep breath. She knew better than to debate with God. "The thing is, I could use a little guidance here if You're not too busy with other things right now." She closed her eyes for a minute, then opened them and saw Paul McCoy walking across the square toward her.

"This is Your answer?" she whispered, glancing heavenward for assurance. "This is Your sign? Paul McCoy?" She watched Paul coming closer and took a deep breath. "Well, okay, but I don't get it. I don't get it at all."

"Rachel?" Paul covered the distance between them and looked around. "Who are you talking to?"

"God," she replied without hesitation, and taking in his look of abject disbelief, she added, "We chat from time to time. I think He sent you to Nashville the other night just in the nick of time to rescue me, and now, at this particular moment, so I guess we need to talk—at least until I can figure out your part in all of this." She patted the bench beside her to indicate that he should sit down.

"I see."

She understood that he didn't see at all and that he was amused by the situation. She was used to that, although it made her sad that so many people did not have the kind of open loving relationship with God that she had known throughout her life.

"So what does God want from me?" he asked.

"A great deal, judging by the fact that He entrusted His children in Kosovo to your care, not to mention all those poor people in Chicago and now everyone here in Smokey Forge."

"You're not making a lot of sense," he said. She noticed that he had begun to frown the moment she mentioned Kosovo.

"Well, it's just that you were supposed to be in Kosovo or Chicago. I was hoping to be in Nashville, and here we are. Doc tells me I have the flu, but you right away see that it might be something else. Makes me reconsider some of my symptoms."

"You're still not feeling well," he finished quietly, and studied her.

"I'm feeling fine, but the way you reacted the other night and now drawing these blood samples and all, I'm guessing you think this is more than just the garden-variety stomach flu. I'm also guessing you might have seen something similar in Kosovo?"

She was pretty perceptive for someone untrained in medical science. "I'd just like to know more about what led up to your passing out the other night."

Rachel nodded. "I can't really say. I mean, I've always been so healthy," she said softly. "I was just so sure that it was just getting over this bug and the excitement of the performance and all, but it's beginning to make sense that it might be something more. I mean, for me to have so little energy is unheard of—ask anyone in town."

"I'm afraid prior good health plays no favorites in people becoming ill, Rachel, although that is certainly in your favor when it comes to getting well. Tell me what's happening."

She had his complete attention now, and it was disconcerting. "It's weird. Most of the time, I'm feeling great and then out of the blue…I just feel…I don't know…punky."

He blinked. "Punky?"

"Yeah, not really sick but less than my best. I still don't seem to have much energy. I mean I eat like a horse—honestly." She glanced at her flat stomach.

"Punky." He repeated the word to himself.

"It's a family thing," Rachel explained. "That's how Mom helped us describe our symptoms when we were kids."

"I'm going to need a little more to go on than that," he said, but his voice was more gentle than normal.

"What about the blood you took the other day?"

"Inconclusive," he replied, and frowned again. She could see that Paul McCoy still liked to have clear-cut answers to problems.

"But what do you think?" she asked after a moment.

"If you're not anorexic—which, believe me, I am not convinced you're not—is there any chance you could have come in contact with some contaminated water?"

To his surprise, she laughed. "Me? Heavens, no. Ask anybody in town, and they'll tell you I am religious about drinking the bottled stuff exclusively. Abigail down at the market orders a case of it every week just for me. It's my one vice."

"It's not unheard of for bottled water to become contaminated. Can I get a sample to check?"

"Well, sure, but how could that possibly relate to what you saw in Kosovo?"

"While I was there, we saw a number of cases of this certain type of parasite. You have a lot of the same symptoms. I contacted a friend of mine in Chicago who has been researching this parasite. He's quite interested in the idea that it might have shown up here as well as overseas."

"Doc treated a few other people around the same time that I got sick, but they had symptoms that were more like food poisoning."

Paul nodded. "The symptoms are pretty similar in milder cases. I take it those people recovered quickly?"

She nodded. "Why would that be? I mean why would theirs go away while mine came and went for weeks, and why didn't anybody else get it—if it's in the water, then…"

"It's probably not the water you drink. It may not even be water that's local to here, but there has to be some common element." He was talking more to himself than to her.

"Okay, so what do we need to do?" she prodded.

"Let's start by testing the water. In the meantime I'd like to prescribe some antibiotics for you, just as a precaution."

Rachel reached into the canvas bag that served as her purse. She handed him a half-filled bottle of water. "Is this enough to test?"

Paul nodded and took the water. "I'll call in a prescription to the pharmacy as soon as I get back to the office."

"If you don't mind, Paul, I'd like to keep this between us, at least until you know more. Maggie's already in serious mother mode ever since I first got sick." She blushed and gave a nervous little laugh.

"Having somebody to watch over you doesn't sound like such a bad idea."

"I know it's silly but I've worked pretty hard to break the apron strings, so to speak. My sisters have finally started to view me as a grown-up. If Maggie gets the idea that this is anything serious…" Rachel rolled her eyes.

"I really don't think you need to be overly concerned, Rachel, and by the way, believe it or not, I understand about your need to break away," Paul said, and made a sound that bordered on a chuckle. "How do you think it was for me, being the only son and grandson of the doctors who have treated everybody in town for decades?"

"Why, Dr. McCoy, are you suggesting that we're two of a kind? Imagine that," she replied and stood to gather her things. "Well, I've got classes in an hour. I'll stop by the pharmacy after school."

"Do you have to get back right away?" he asked. "Have you had lunch?"

"Paul, I do eat. You don't have to feed me," she assured him, the mega-watt smile firmly in place.

"I'm not asking in my professional capacity," he protested. "Honestly. I haven't eaten and if you haven't, then why not eat together? You can catch me up on all the gossip."

She looked at him with suspicion. "Since when do you have any interest in gossip?"

"Try me. Maybe I've changed."

Rachel laughed. "Oh, I get it. I bet you just want to get the scoop on Sara—she's not married, you know."

"Really?"

They walked across the square together.

"She's still gorgeous."

"No doubt."

"You might have a shot," she added. "If you play your cards right."

"Hmm."

She punched him hard in the arm. "If we're going to do lunch, Paul McCoy, you're going to have to stop talking in doctorspeak."

"But I am a doctor. That's the way we talk."

"You're also a red-blooded American male who once

had a serious case of the hots for my sister. I don't believe for one minute that you aren't curious about what's happened to Sara since you ran off to medical school."

"And, as I recall, you were always this sassy kid who drove your sisters crazy."

"A sassy kid who was usually right," she retorted with a grin as they entered the café together.

After lunch Rachel taught her afternoon music classes at the school and stayed late to give some private lessons. She thought about the possibility that Paul and Sara might actually strike up a romance and liked the idea very much. Sara was far too serious and enmeshed in her work. She could use a little love in her life—a little happiness.

Rachel was humming as she climbed the hill to the house where she had grown up and now lived with her two older sisters and younger twin brothers when they weren't off at college. Nothing would make her happier than for each of her two sisters to find true love. Then maybe they would stop worrying about her and she could get on with her life—and her dream of spreading God's joy through her music. She wondered what Paul McCoy's dream was. She wondered if he even thought in terms of fulfilling a dream. As close as she and her sisters had been to Paul's parents, she realized that he had usually been absent when the two families got together. He'd always had some excuse—basketball practice or a paper that was due. Once he'd left Smokey Forge for college and medical school, he hadn't come home very often, and then his visits had been short.

Paul McCoy was an unknown entity in the unique dynamics of their two families. She doubted that anything would change now that he was back in town.

Maggie was sitting on the porch swing grading papers. Rachel squared her shoulders, put on her brightest smile and willed herself to walk with a lightness she didn't feel. The long afternoon of teaching and the short walk from the school had sapped her energy. One thing she had to agree with—she needed to rebuild her strength.

"Hi," she called out to Maggie as she climbed the porch stairs. "What's new?"

"Not much. Sometimes I feel as if I've graded these same papers a hundred times before," Maggie replied with a laugh. "You look a little done in."

"I'm just a little tired."

"Honey, you've been *a little tired* for over six weeks now. What did Paul say about those blood tests?"

Rachel considered her options. She had never been able to outright lie to Maggie, so her best bet was to stick as close to the truth as possible. "He's going to give me some medicine—antibiotics—just as a precaution."

Maggie studied her, looking for any sign of deception. "Maybe Doc should have another look at you."

"Doc isn't going to find anything different. Honestly, Maggie, Paul does have an actual degree and everything."

"Well, I just think that Doc knows your history. You've lived your entire life at ninety miles an hour and you seem intent on doing that until the day you drop. At the rate you're going that'll be sooner rather than later."

Rachel grinned. "Maggie, it's going to be okay.

You'll see," she assured her big sister. "I'm going to rehearse awhile," she called as she entered the house, allowing the screen door to bang shut behind her. "I've got to get ready for the revival over at Codger's Cave this weekend."

"You could skip that," Maggie said. "You could actually take a few days to just sit on the porch here and strum your guitar or read a book."

"Can't let folks down if you're able to be there," Rachel replied. "You're the one who taught us all that."

"Me and my big mouth," Maggie grumbled to herself. She could hear Rachel gathering her music and guitar and heading out the back. "Be home for supper," she called as the phone rang. She waited for the second ring to see if Rachel might come back to answer, but she was already halfway across the yard, headed for the path to the mill. With a resigned sigh, Maggie pushed herself off the swing and went inside to answer the phone.

"Maggie? Hi, it's Paul McCoy."

"Well, Paulie, how nice to have you back home. I hear you saw my baby sister earlier today. Want to tell me why she's so thin and tired?"

"Now, Maggie, you know as well as I do I can't discuss that with you," he said, his tone strictly business.

Maggie laughed. "I thought it was worth a shot."

"Is she there?"

"No, not right now. You just missed her. Can I give her a message?"

"No, nothing important. I'll catch up with her later."

"You come on by any time—how about supper tonight? Sara will be here. The twins are off at college, but Mattie came in for a few days. He's got himself a girlfriend, and it's beginning to look pretty serious. Seems impossible, but there you have it. She's coming to meet us all tonight so you might as well be there, too. Matt will be as nervous as a cat in a room full of rocking chairs. Maybe having another male here will help. So, you'd be more than welcome."

"I'll see how things are going at the clinic," Paul told her, not wanting to commit to the evening.

"Don't stand on ceremony," Maggie replied. "Just show up. There's always plenty of food. We sit down around six."

He promised again to think about it and hung up. He tried to figure out why on earth he had not turned down the invitation to supper. It had certainly never been difficult before. In fact, it had almost been automatic. It surprised him to realize that not only was he considering the invitation, he was looking forward to it.

"Ridiculous," he muttered as he gathered the notes he'd made on Rachel's bottled water. Clearly, he had considered the idea because that would be an obvious way to see Rachel and tell her the water was clean. He certainly didn't need to go to supper to accomplish that.

"Ruby, tell Dad I've gone for the day," he said as he hung up his lab coat and headed for the door. "I'm going to check on a patient."

He left the clinic that occupied a storefront office on Main Street and drove through town. He had no idea where he was headed, but he hadn't wanted to raise further questions by asking Maggie how to find Rachel. Her comment about trying to break out from under the shadow of her sisters' achievements had struck a chord with him. How well he remembered the pressure he'd put on himself to live up to the spotless reputations of his father and grandfather. Rachel deserved a chance to make her own decisions and follow her own dreams.

As he drove through town, he saw a number of people he'd grown up with. They waved or called out to him, and he waved back. He realized that it was certainly not as difficult as he might have thought to come here. Actually, it was even pleasant to feel part of a community that went beyond hospital walls, to be in a place that was so completely normal and safe after what he had witnessed in Kosovo.

On the outskirts of the small village was the charter elementary school that the parents of the Dukes had started before they died. Maggie and Sara had taken over after they finished college. Knowing that Rachel taught music at the school, he wondered if she might possibly be there even though classes were out for the day. A car was in the lot so he pulled in and headed for the entrance.

"Paul McCoy, look at you."

Sara Duke was every bit as beautiful as Paul remembered, but he felt nothing of the spark he had always wrestled with upon seeing her in high school. "Did you dump me for some other guy yet?" he said as he walked up the path to the school.

"Maybe. I could hardly be expected to stand around waiting for you to decide to come home where you belong," she replied. Then she hugged him. "You look great. How's Doc?"

"Firmly in charge of things, but glad to have me home, especially now that Mom's gone. I think it got pretty lonesome for him rattling around in that big ol' house."

Sara nodded. "He was so excited when you agreed to come back until he could find someone to join the practice. That was a really hard thing for him to do, you know. Ask for your help. He knew how important your work was to you and he felt guilty about taking you away from people who needed you more than he thought he did. He talks about you constantly—a very proud papa."

"That's embarrassing," Paul said with a grin and glanced around, hoping to catch a glimpse of Rachel.

"Well, now, obviously you didn't just stop by to chat. How can I help?"

"I thought maybe Rachel might be here."

"Rachel? No, I haven't seen her. Maggie called and said you'd given her a prescription for some antibiotics. She's going to be okay then?"

Paul nodded. "I just forgot to tell her one thing— nothing major. I was driving by and saw your car. I thought she might be here."

Sara smiled with relief. "That's really sweet of you, Paul. I have no idea where she is. Did you check up at the house?"

"Maggie said she left a little while ago."

"Then check the old mill. She goes there sometimes to play her guitar and write her music. She's probably rehearsing for the revival she's playing this weekend over at Codger's Cove."

Paul turned to go. "Thanks, I'll do that."

"Hey, we're all getting together for supper at the house tonight. Why don't you come?"

"Maggie already asked me," Paul replied and waved as he hurried to his car.

When Paul reached the mill, he saw Rachel sitting by the stream. She was playing her guitar, and he thought he had never seen anyone who looked more at peace with the world than she did. He envied her that. It was one of the things he had come back to Smokey Forge to find.

"Did you write that?" he asked when the last chord had died away.

She jumped at the sound of his voice but immediately composed herself. "It's just something I'm working on."

He sat on the bank of the creek a little away from her. "I got the preliminary results from the water test. They were negative."

"That was fast."

He shrugged. "They're not as conclusive as the results I'll get back from the state lab, but I've set up a little lab in the clinic, and the initial results are in."

She glanced at him then studied the tumbling creek. "So, if it is the parasite, it's not from the water."

"At least not from that water."

"It's the only water I drink," she reminded him.

"Yeah. I was wondering about that. It raises some interesting questions."

"Such as?"

"Well, if you only drink bottled water and this is a waterborne parasite, and it wasn't in the water you drink…"

"Of course, it could have been in a bottle I drank several weeks ago, couldn't it?"

He admired the way her mind worked. "Or you might have come in contact with the parasite in some other manner. I understand that you're performing at a revival this weekend?"

"Codger's Cove, but I don't see what…"

"Do you eat or drink at these things?"

"Sometimes."

"Just to be on the safe side, take your own food and water with you this time, okay?"

There didn't seem to be anything left to say, and yet he made no move to leave.

"I really liked that melody you were playing when I came. Could I hear it again?"

She nodded and nervously strummed the guitar. She was used to performing in front of large crowds of people as well as friends and family members, but the thought of playing in front of Paul suddenly made her shy. She fingered the tune for several bars.

"It goes on like that," she said.

"I was surprised when Dad told me that not winning first place meant that, at least for now, you were going to give up trying to make it as an entertainer," he said.

"I never aspired to be an entertainer in the way I think you mean it," she replied.

"You tried out for a performing contract at the Grand Ole Opry," he reminded her.

"I remember that," she said with a grin. "I was there."

It took him a few seconds to realize that she was gently teasing him.

"Well, yeah, but isn't that why you did it? I mean, don't you want to be a big-time star some day?"

"Not really. I thought that if I won the talent search it would be a sign that God wanted me to take that route in spreading His message through my music." She shrugged. "He obviously has some other plan in mind, and now I just need to wait and see what that might be."

He considered this for a minute. "You won second place," he reminded her.

"And maybe one day that will lead to something, but for now, I am a teacher of music and I write songs. It's a very good life." She punctuated her summation with a strum on the guitar. "Why did you decide to be a doctor?"

"We're not talking about me," he reminded her.

"Maybe we should," she replied and met his gaze.

Chapter Three

He hesitated. Her directness was surprising and unsettling.

"Come on," she coached, "I'll help get you started. Back in Chicago you…" She made a pulling motion with her hands as if towing a boat to shore. "Come on. There must have been some reason you dropped everything and took off for Kosovo for three months."

"Back in Chicago I was spinning my wheels," he said matter-of-factly, and was prepared to leave it at that. But she remained silent, watching him, waiting for more. "The hospital was mired in bureaucracy, and making any kind of real difference was next to impossible." He stopped and bowed his head to avoid her gaze.

"So you left," she said quietly.

He glanced away. "Do you play a lot of these regional revivals?" he asked, signaling an end to any further personal conversation.

"But why Kosovo?" she persisted, ignoring his attempt to change subjects.

He frowned. "I couldn't tell you. The opportunity came up. It was a spur-of-the-moment decision, and once I was there…" He was obviously prepared to leave it at that as he strolled closer to the rushing stream.

"I think God sent you there, just like He's brought you home now."

Paul turned and faced her. "I don't believe that, Rachel," he said sternly. For the first time her determination to draw him out seemed shaken. "Look," he continued, "I know that stuff helps a lot of people—clearly, it's meaningful to you, but…"

"It's not about whether it helps or not," she argued stubbornly. "It's just the way it is. It's the way the world works."

He stared at her for a long moment, and in his eyes she saw such sadness that it was like watching a person in great pain.

"No, Rachel. Believe me, I know how easy it is to buy into that when you've lived your whole life in these mountains, but it's not the way the world works. The world can be horrific and cruel. It's filled with people whose only concern is for themselves and the power they can wield. It's filled with nations who have hated each other for so long that they can't even remember where it all started."

"If everyone believed that, nothing would ever get accomplished. People would just throw up their hands," she said with absolute certainty and no rancor. "And by the way, it's very unattractive, you know—that big-city snobbery that says you can't know the world until you've walked the mean streets."

"I am not a snob," he protested, but she could see that she had succeeded in breaking his somber mood.

"Yes, you are, and in some ways you always were, Paul McCoy. Fortunately you were gorgeous enough to get away with it."

"So, you think I'm gorgeous?" he asked, his face a mask of seriousness. Still, she did not miss the hint of mischief in his deep-set eyes.

"I used the past tense," she reminded him. "You *were* gorgeous for a high school senior and in comparison to the rest of the local talent in those days."

He actually laughed, and she realized it was the first time she'd really heard him laugh out loud. She liked the sound of it.

"Why, Dr. McCoy, beneath that gloomy exterior, could there actually be a sense of humor?"

"Let's get back to your condition," he said. "Just because there was no contamination in the bottled water doesn't mean we stop looking for the cause. With your permission I'd like to track your case. It would be a major step forward for my friend's research if this turned out to be the same parasite he's been tracking in Kosovo."

"You want me to be a lab rat for your friend's research?"

"Yeah. Something like that. Contributing to Dan's research project could give me a chance to help the people I left in Kosovo. Will you do it?" His eyes reflected some of the fire she remembered from the old days.

She stared at him, looking for any sign that he was joking. What she saw was a man who was totally serious. "This is going to be like looking for a needle in a haystack. Why not just accept that I had it and move on? Why does it matter how I got sick if we know what it is and can treat it if it comes back again?"

"If there were others in town showing the same symptoms, even if their cases were milder than yours, I'd like to include them in our effort to gather data. Anything that we can learn about your case as well as the others would be helpful."

"Including those children you saw with the same symptoms in Kosovo?"

He nodded. "Well, sure. Frankly, it would be nice to feel like I'm still helping even though I'm over here now."

"Do you regret so much that you left them?"

"A little torn would be closer to the truth. I'm not saying I didn't make the right decision coming home to help Dad, but…"

"But your work there wasn't finished," she added.

"No. On the other hand, if we can discover the source of the parasite here, Rachel, then I can have the best of both worlds—doing what I need to do to help Dad and helping my colleagues continue to fight at least one condition in Kosovo."

She was flattered that he obviously had no reservations about trusting her. Paul had always been extremely cautious about involving others in his projects.

"Well, listen to this, God," she said to the blue skies above in a perfectly normal conversational tone. "I can help Paul help those kids over there and not even leave town. Of course, that's why You brought him back here in the first place, right? That and the fact that there are people here who need him, too." She nodded knowingly as if she could both see and hear the unseen third party, then she turned to Paul.

"Works for me," she said with a smile. "Number-one lab rat at your service, Doc. How do we begin?"

"Maybe supper would be a good idea. You seem to be having some serious hallucinations. Maggie and Sara have both invited me, and if we leave now we can just make that six o'clock sit-down time Maggie gave me."

"Ah, you've seen Sara."

"Yeah, I stopped by the school."

"She practically lives at the school," Rachel said in a tone that made it clear that she thought her sister could find better uses for her time.

"Well, she always was dedicated to whatever project she took on."

"Is that why you liked her in high school?"

"Hey, what is this—the third degree? I thought we were going to eat." He loaded her guitar into the back seat of his car, then held open the passenger door for her.

There were already several cars in the driveway when they arrived, so they had to park on the road and walk the rest of the way.

"They're all on the porch," Rachel said, and Paul heard a hint of nervousness in her tone. "I mean they'll wonder how we came to be together."

"Yep. Folks in town have already been speculating about the two of us. I'm pretty sure our having lunch earlier today was major news. Ruby knew it by the time I got back to the office. Now supper at your sister's?" He gave a shocked intake of breath that made Rachel laugh. "What *is* going on here?"

"You know, actually…" An idea was beginning to take shape. Maybe if Sara thought Paul was attracted to her little sister, she would pay more attention. "What do you say we give them something to really talk about?" she suggested with a mischievous grin. She took his hand as she led the way to the porch. "Come on, Paul, live a little," she chided when she saw him hesitate. "Just follow my lead. It'll be fun."

"I'm not good at *fun*," he muttered.

Rachel chose to ignore that last statement. "Hey, everybody, look who I found down by the old mill-stream," she called gaily as they climbed the warped steps of the front porch.

Paul sensed that everyone had already been discussing the two of them as he and Rachel had come up the hill from the car. He knew that Rachel was trying to play on that curiosity. What on earth was he doing here, and how had this pint-size dynamo coaxed him into being part of her scheme? He let go of Rachel's hand and turned to Maggie. "Am I still invited for supper?"

"That depends," Maggie said with a stern frown.

"On what?"

"On whether or not you've been keeping something from me, young man."

"You mean this?" Rachel asked, grabbing his hand again and holding it aloft as if he'd just been proclaimed the winner of a prizefight.

"It's all over town that the two of you had lunch together—now you show up a few hours later holding hands?" Maggie shook her head in mock disapproval.

Paul shrugged. "We got to talking and, well, you know your little sister here—she's pretty hard to ignore. Actually, we found out we have a lot in common."

"Well, I'll be," Sara murmured, but she looked pleased. Rachel sighed. This was not going at all the way she had planned. Sara was supposed to be cool to the idea of a possible relationship between Rachel and Paul. Instead, she was clearly delighted.

"Now you listen to me, Paul McCoy," Maggie continued sternly. "If you think you can come on back here to Smokey Forge and bring your city slicker ways with you and take advantage of my baby sister, you'd best think again."

"Oh, Maggie, lighten up before you scare the poor guy off," Matt said as he crossed the porch and offered his hand to Paul. "Welcome home, Dr. McCoy. This is my girlfriend, Lisa, and we'd both like to thank you for taking the family spotlight off of us."

Paul nodded at the pretty young woman seated on the porch railing then turned his attention to Matt. "I think your big sister there is a little upset with me," he said in a stage whisper.

"Nah. She's just trying to embarrass you."

Paul looked at Maggie for confirmation and was not surprised to see her burst into laughter as she hugged her brother. "I never could fool this one," she said. "He always saw right through me. Well, come on in. Soup's on. Let's eat."

At the supper table Maggie made a big deal of arranging the seating so that Paul and Rachel were next to each other. Meanwhile Rachel worked hard to keep

Paul's attention focused on Sara, asking her questions about the school, telling Paul how Sara had single-handedly gotten grants to keep the school running when funding had run low. She saw that he was impressed and she liked the fact that he and Sara seemed to talk easily. Maybe her plan would work, after all.

"I've made a special celebration pie," Maggie announced, presenting her lemon pie with its lightly browned meringue piled high on top. "This was to be a pie to celebrate Rachel winning second place at the talent show, but perhaps…" She eyed Rachel and Paul.

Rachel blushed. "That's real nice, Maggie. Thanks."

After the table had been cleared and everyone had pitched in to make sure the dishes were done and put away, they all sat on the porch talking and drinking coffee until nearly ten.

"I'd better go," Paul said. "Thank you, Maggie, for inviting me."

"It's good to have you home," Maggie assured him.

He turned to Rachel. "Walk me to my car?"

No, Rachel wanted to protest. *Ask Sara.* But Sara had already busied herself collecting the last of the coffee mugs and taking them inside. Rachel saw Sara give Maggie a nudge and indicate that she should also come inside.

"Sure." They walked across the yard, aware that Rachel's family was watching them. "Sorry about that," Rachel said.

"What?"

"I was just trying to have a little fun with Maggie and take some of the pressure off of Matt. I'm afraid that things got a little out of hand back there, and now Maggie and Sara think we're…you know…a couple."

"Yeah. Bummer."

"I'm serious, Paul. You don't know my sisters. By morning, they'll have us in a full-blown romance. They're probably peeking out the windows and wondering why you don't kiss me good-night."

He grinned and stroked her cheek. "Why, Ms. Duke, I thought you'd never ask," he said and leaned in to kiss her gently on the forehead. It was hard to say which of them was more surprised at his action.

"I…didn't mean…you…" Rachel sputtered as she felt the soft warmth of his lips on her forehead. "Just go," she whispered, taking a deliberate step away from him. She couldn't tell him she wanted to match him with Sara. That would make things just too awkward between Sara and him.

Paul got into his car. "I had a good time tonight, Rachel. I'll see you tomorrow. Get some sleep," he ordered. "I want to get started on collecting our data. The first thing I need to get is a thorough history of where you've been that you might have picked up the bug. I'll be by at seven to take you to breakfast."

"You don't need to feed me."

"I can see that. I don't know when I've seen a woman pack it away the way you do at mealtime," he teased. "If I didn't suspect you had been infected by a parasite, I'd wonder where you were putting all of that food."

"I have a very high metabolism," she said, huffing, "and I don't eat *that* much."

"No, I'd say most young women your age take thirds on Maggie's lemon pie."

"It was a sliver. Don't you have any other patients to harass?"

"Not yet. I'm new in town, remember? Be ready at seven and start thinking about where else you might have picked up this bug of yours."

"I have to be at school by eight-thirty," she called as he drove away.

He acknowledged that bit of information with a wave and kept driving. Rachel stood watching the taillights of his car until he turned the corner.

"You know, other people have important stuff to do, too," she muttered to herself as she walked back up the hill to the house. She glanced at the star-filled sky. "I could use a little help here, You know. I can handle the medical part, but getting him together with Sara is in Your hands, okay?"

Over the next few weeks they fell into an uneasy pattern of working together. Her eternal optimism was disconcerting, to say the least. Paul felt the necessity to instruct her in the science of data collection, showing her that following a rational path did not always end in the answers a person hoped would be there at the end. Undaunted, she kept challenging him. Every time he asked why, she was more interested in *what if*.

Not that Rachel felt she could offer much help, but she found the whole process interesting and she couldn't keep herself from wanting to know what he might have discovered while she was busy teaching third-graders to play the recorder.

Some days she would come out of school at the end of the day and find him waiting for her. Together they would head to the library at the small private college in town. There she would take notes while he searched through the documents and articles he could find on the library's link to the Internet, while he waited for his own computer and files to be shipped from Chicago. As they drove from place to place, he would continue to ask questions and dictate notes that he would later send Dan in Chicago.

While he waited for her to finish teaching, he would lean against his car reading some article in an old medical journal he had found in his father's office.

"You should come inside sometime. Sara's office is right there," Rachel told him once, after her classes were over. She pointed to a window near the entrance. "She always has the coffeepot on."

"This is fine. Gives me a chance to catch up on my reading. Besides, I just got here a couple of minutes ago."

One particularly blustery afternoon, she noticed that his jacket was open, as usual, while she was hastily buttoning her sweater.

"I don't know why you have to be so stubborn about coming inside. Sara has other things to occupy her, and you could read in her office. She won't bite, you know."

"Rachel, I'm not afraid of your sister—anymore, that is. This isn't high school."

"Suit yourself. Go ahead and freeze," she said, grousing as the wind picked up dry leaves and swirled them around her ankles.

"I'm used to it, remember. I used to work and live in the Windy City. Are you going to be warm enough?"

"For the library? I don't know if you've noticed, but that place is usually hotter than Florida in mid-August."

"I've been thinking that maybe we'd take a different approach. I seem to recall that there are a lot of creeks and streams back in the country."

"*This* is the country," she reminded him.

"Naw, this is *town*. I mean back thar in them hil-ahs," he said in an exaggerated drawl.

"Hil-ahs?"

"Hills. Hollers. The sticks?"

He made her laugh. Serious, intense Paul McCoy was making a joke.

"What do you hope to prove?" she asked.

He held up empty glass vials. "Once we collect samples, Dan can test the water and figure out where this bug lives."

"That makes sense. Let's go."

"What? No questions? No buts? I'm shocked, Ms. Duke."

"*Now,* he finds that offbeat sense of humor," she muttered and got into the car.

They spent several afternoons climbing through the hills to remote creeks and streams and collecting samples. All the while she would remind him that she hadn't been in contact with any of the water he was testing.

More often than not, it seemed only natural to stop by the clinic, pick up Doc and head to the farm for one of Maggie's bountiful suppers. Before Paul knew what was happening, he was spending more time at the Duke house then he was at his dad's. Not only that, he looked forward to the evenings he spent there.

After supper, Rachel usually made a point of going off with friends or up to her room to rehearse, leaving Paul with Sara and the others. Sara was very good at asking questions about the research—better than Rachel was. Sara understood the science of what his friend was trying to discover and prove, and Rachel could not help noticing how Paul's eyes lit up whenever Sara asked about the project.

In addition to playing chauffeur and secretary for his research, Rachel still stopped by the clinic for regular checkups and to permit him to draw more blood.

"You've tested negative for the parasite ever since you started the antibiotics," he told her one afternoon.

"You sound a little disappointed," she teased him.

"Heavens, no," he protested, then realized she was joking. "Cute. You've gained five pounds."

"Where?" she said twisting around to check out her backside. "Well, no more of Maggie's chocolate cake for me."

"The fact that you're gaining back some weight is a good thing," he reminded her.

"Who are you all of a sudden? Martha Stewart?"

"You're singing better than ever," he commented, knowing the way to her heart was to praise her talent.

"You really think so?"

He smiled.

"Oh, you. You'd say anything to make me think you were some kind of miracle healer. You always had this enormous ego."

"And you, as I recall, were always able to charm your way out of anything you didn't want to do."

"I was a very good kid," she protested.

"Uh-huh," he replied with a skeptical lift of his eyebrows.

And that's the way things went. Before Rachel knew what had happened she was working with Paul McCoy to find answers to the mysterious parasite. She didn't fool herself into thinking there might be anything more to it on his part than work. He was a scientist. She had a condition that interested him and was a departure from the routine ailments he and Doc treated at the clinic. He was a man who searched for answers to questions that raised his professional curiosity. On top of that, it was clear that he liked her and her family and enjoyed their company. On the other hand, he was Paul McCoy, dedicated to his work, fated to do great things and destined to do them anywhere besides Smokey Forge, Tennessee. From that standpoint, they were a good match, because Rachel also dreamed of doing great things in bigger places.

For Paul, spending most of his free time with Rachel and her family started the night she decided to have some fun with her family and drew him into her mischief. As a kid Paul had played by the rules, but he was always in control. Rachel's spontaneity and constant good humor kept him off balance, and yet he looked forward to spending time with her. He enjoyed talking about his research with Sara, but he especially liked getting Rachel's unique perspective on his work. She raised illogical questions that would never occur to him.

He thought about her as he had always thought about

her when they'd all been in high school. She was Sara's younger sister—the cute one, the one with the overactive imagination, and these days, the one who made him smile. She made no demands on him or his time. In fact, he sometimes worried that he was imposing too much on her time. They each had a dream to do something bigger with their talent, and he reminded himself that it was important that he not keep her from focusing on her dream while he pursued his own.

He was aware that she was trying to play the matchmaker between Sara and him. He suspected Sara was aware of it, as well, and amused by the antics of her younger sister. The truth was he liked Sara, but any romantic feelings he might have felt in the past simply weren't there. Still, he kind of enjoyed watching Rachel try her hand at matchmaking.

"So, let's talk about this thing you and Sara used to have for each other," she said casually one afternoon after she had dropped off some articles she had copied for him on the school's copy machine.

"If you're referring to that disastrous crush I had on your sister when we were juniors in high school, I would say that it was pretty one-sided."

She shrugged. "Things change," she commented as she stood up and headed for the door. "See you at supper."

Paul had seen her smile to herself and knew that she thought she had planted an important seed.

That night, Maggie had invited more than the usual gang for supper, so the table was full. Several conversations flowed at once, and Paul was aware of Rachel's interest in the one he was having with Sara.

"You've done enough for one day," Paul told Maggie and Sara when they started to clear the table. "Go, sit. Rachel and I have got this."

As they worked together, he waited for her next foray into matchmaking. He didn't have to wait for long.

"You and Sara are a good match," Rachel observed as the two of them finished wiping the dishes. "You look good together."

"Well, that's certainly reason enough to fall madly in love," he replied soberly as if he might actually consider such a thing.

"You know what I mean."

"Not really. Hopefully it takes more than looking good together to make a match."

Rachel sighed heavily. "You should give this thing a chance, you know. You and Sara both. I don't know which of you is the more stubborn."

"Rachel, whatever might have been between your sister and me is long gone—for each of us. We're different people."

"You have a lot in common."

"Why are you so intent on this? I would think the last thing you'd want for either of your sisters is to get mixed up with a nonbeliever like me."

"Maybe Sara would be better equipped to bring you back to your faith. After all, you're both practical types who look at the world through clear rather than rose-colored glasses."

"I wasn't aware that I had asked for help finding anything—especially not my faith."

Rachel shrugged. "You should give it some serious

thought, is all I'm saying. Sara could help. You two could be really good for each other."

She was frustrated by the lack of any real progress in her attempts to throw the two of them together. She couldn't decide if it was because of Paul's indifference to her sister or to his spiritual soul. The truth was she had come to like Paul and she really wanted the best for him. He was a decent man who deserved happiness and contentment in his life. Down to her bones, Rachel felt that he could never be truly happy until he resolved his own self-imposed estrangement from anything spiritual and found somebody who could be there for him while he followed his dreams.

She didn't fare much better when she decided to bring the subject up with Sara later that night. In fact, her sister laughed at her.

"Rachel, stop matchmaking. You've got plenty to occupy you. Paul McCoy and I are friends, and that's pretty much all we'll ever be. He's not my type. More to the point—I'm not his type, either."

"But you're exactly alike," Rachel blurted. "I mean… you know. You both like things neat and organized. You're both serious and studious. You're…"

"Rach, did it ever occur to you that maybe what I want in a relationship is what I'm missing in myself? The fun, the spontaneity. Someone who would sweep me off my feet and be completely and impossibly romantic." She closed her eyes and sighed. Then she immediately opened them and went back to grading papers. "That does not describe Paul McCoy."

"What if he likes you? I mean, are you going to break his heart twice?"

"Paul?" She laughed. "Rach, honey, this isn't high school. We've moved on. We're very different people."

"Well, yeah, he said the same thing, but…"

"Besides, Paul isn't staying in Smokey Forge. One day he'll head back to Chicago or to some other big hospital where he can pursue his career." She reached over and patted Rachel's hand. "You really have to stop trying to rescue everybody you meet, Rach. Believe it or not, some of us are quite happy with the way our life is going, and I'm pretty sure Paul is one of those people."

Maybe so, Rachel thought, *but he sure does frown a lot for somebody who's supposedly happy and content.*

"You've known these people your whole life," Doc reminded Paul in a conversation one afternoon.

"What's up, Doc?" Rachel asked with a grin when she popped into the clinic. She had stopped by to see if Paul had made any progress on his research.

"My son has turned shy on me," Doc reported with a hint of exasperation.

"I'm just not as comfortable as…"

Doc heaved a sigh and ran his hands through what was left of his snow-white hair. "You have no trouble bothering people with your questions about this parasite. Now I want you to do some actual doctoring and…" He paused, composing himself. "Look, son, we're talking about C. R. Snodgrass, for heaven's sake. You played on the basketball team with the man. The two of you were best buddies."

"And I haven't seen him in over twenty years," Paul replied reasonably.

Rachel looked from father to son and back again. "Paul's a little skittish about actually calling on folks up in the hollers, huh?"

Doc nodded. "You'd think a man who can walk down the mean streets of Chicago could…"

"I could go with him," Rachel volunteered. "Is it Emma? Her time?"

Doc shook his head. "Soon. I just thought it would be good experience for Paul to get out there before there's something big like Emma delivering on the kitchen table because nobody's there to bring her into town. I mean, half my practice is out there, not here." He turned his attention to Paul. "Look, son, I know you want to help your friend with his research, but these folks right here need you, too."

Paul cleared his throat, drawing their attention. "The idea of making a house call is a little intimidating."

"And?" Rachel asked.

"And what?"

"And what are you going to do about it?" she asked, then proceeded to answer her own question. "The way I see it, you have two choices. One, you can sit here all safe and warm inside this clinic and wait for them to come down the mountain, which they won't. That, by the way, has never been your style. Or, two, instead of scooping up little test tubes of water looking for a bug that nobody's seen hide nor hair of for weeks, you can use your God-given talent for healing people who are really in need."

As usual, her assumption that his gift was divinely given rankled. "I didn't see God when I was pulling those all-nighters in med school or working double shifts as an intern and resident," he commented with a frown.

"Clearly, you weren't paying attention," she retorted. "Who do you think helped keep you awake and alert?"

He had quickly learned that the only way to get her off the subject was to change it. "These people are different. They know Dad. They think they know me."

"Probably better than he knows himself," Rachel muttered to Doc.

"Yeah. He's spent too much time away from home," Doc agreed.

"Didn't Emma have some symptoms awhile back that might have been the parasite?" Rachel asked Doc, knowing full well that this would definitely get Paul's attention.

"That's right. Well, that in itself is reason enough for him to go up there."

"Did someone leave the room?" Paul asked, looking around, "because I'm pretty sure that I'm still here."

Doc laughed. "If you have half a brain, son, you'll accept this young woman's offer to go along with you. She can smooth the way for you. She can do the talking and you can do the doctoring."

"She can talk, all right," Paul said as he pricked Rachel's finger to draw the blood sample he needed.

"Ouch," she protested. "You enjoyed that."

He permitted himself a hint of a smile and then gave her his wide-eyed attention. "Oh, did I hurt you?"

"We're going to see Emma, so get that through that

stubborn head of yours," she informed him as she pulled her hand away and sucked on the wounded finger.

"Tough lady," Doc commented, and as he left the room he was chuckling.

Rachel stood up. "So, are you going or not?"

Paul stared at her. "You mean *now?*" He glanced at his watch. "It's pretty late."

She laughed. "It's just past four." She turned to get her coat and made muffled clucking sounds under her breath.

"I am *not* chicken," he assured her.

"Then come on," she urged and held the door for him. "I'll drive."

Chapter Four

C.R. had not changed at all. He was still the same easygoing guy Paul remembered. Five minutes after they started to talk, Paul felt immediately at ease.

"Wanna take some shots?" C.R. asked, nodding toward the makeshift basketball goal he'd attached to the side of his ramshackle barn.

"You sure that thing will hold up?"

C.R. grinned. "You talkin' about the basket or the barn?"

As they took turns shooting the ball, they caught up on what had been happening since they last saw each other. C.R. had served in Operation Desert Storm, and that opened the door for Paul to talk to him about Kosovo. For the first time since leaving there, he felt as if someone truly understood what he'd experienced.

Emma insisted on making supper for them. Paul watched how easily she and Rachel moved around the kitchen, talking, laughing, tending to the four young children who crowded in and out of the small room.

Rachel was good with the children, and he suddenly wished he'd taken her up on her offer to come inside the school. Not to visit Sara, but to observe Rachel teaching.

Emma was well into her eighth month, but she barely looked old enough to be a mother once much less five times. The kids brought back memories of Kosovo…the camps…Sami.

"You the doctor?"

Paul looked into the upturned face of a very serious ten-year-old.

"Now, Henry, you leave Dr. Paul alone," Emma said.

"It's okay," Paul said and turned his attention to the child. "Yeah, that would be me." He knelt on one knee to be more at the boy's level. "Can I do something for you?"

"Yep. I need some hep."

"Hep?"

"That would be *help,*" Rachel prompted him quietly as she passed behind him on her way to put the salad on the table.

"What kind of help?"

"I'm working on me a science project, and Teacher says if I can do it the way I'm plannin' I might get to take it to the state competition."

"I'll do what I can."

"After we eat," Emma instructed. "Now, go wash up. You, too, Paul."

Paul was surprised to see that the boy walked with a pronounced limp as he headed down the hall to the bathroom.

"What happened?" he asked C.R. when he was sure Henry was out of earshot.

"Tractor accident last summer. He was visiting my brother. He fell off the tractor on some uneven ground, and it rolled over his foot."

"Crushed some of his bones real bad," Emma added as she carried steaming bowls of food to the table.

"Surely, the doctors…"

"Paul," Rachel interrupted, indicating that he was getting into a topic that was best left alone.

"No insurance," C.R. said quietly.

"And nobody like Doc who'd have been willing to ignore that, knowing somehow, some day, we'd pay him off," Emma added as she dished up pieces of fried chicken onto a platter C.R. was holding for her.

"Done," Henry announced as he came back down the hall, holding up his clean hands for his mother's inspection. "Your turn," he told Paul.

At supper, Paul questioned Emma about her symptoms. "When you thought you had the flu," he reminded her.

"You mean that it might have been some bug she picked up in the creek water?" C.R. asked after Paul had explained his preliminary theory.

Paul explained to them the research his friend was doing and how he had seen the same parasite in Kosovo.

"I'll take a sample of the creek water back to check, but I don't want you to worry. It's the same creek that flows past the mill, and we've been checking that regularly. In the meantime, boil your water before using it for anything. Just to be safe, okay?"

"Can I show Dr. McCoy my project now?" Henry asked. .

"I'd like to see it," Paul added as he and Henry waited for Emma's permission to leave the table.

When Paul saw the plans for the project, he was amazed at the sophistication of the boy's thought process. The two of them spent quite a lot of time examining the model he'd started to build and figuring out other solutions for what the boy was trying to demonstrate. By the time they were ready to leave, Paul had made arrangements for C.R. to stop by the clinic to get some supplies that Henry would need to finish the project.

"I got you this jar of creek water," C.R. said.

"Thanks."

"You don't think the baby's in any danger, do you, Paul?" Emma asked as she cradled her distended stomach.

Paul realized that his talk of parasites had upset her. "Emma, given the fact that your symptoms were very mild and there's been nothing since, I really think both you and the baby are fine. But, tell you what, I'll run the test on this water sample as soon as I get back to town tonight. Then, tomorrow I'll come back and we'll do a full examination of you and the baby. Would that be okay?"

Emma nodded.

C.R. clapped Paul on the back. "Thanks, Doc. We sure would be grateful for your kindness."

It was the first time anybody in town—other than Rachel—had called him *Doc*. Paul found that he liked the sound of it. More than that, he liked the feeling he got when Emma and C.R. looked at him. It was the same look he'd seen people give his father for decades. It was also the look of hope mingled with trust that he'd seen on the faces of the refugees.

* * *

Later, in the car on the way home, he felt Rachel watching him, glancing his way from time to time as she negotiated the winding narrow road she must have driven a thousand times.

"You and Emma are good friends," he said, working at conversation, uncomfortable with her for the first time.

"Best of friends," she agreed. "Emma knows me so well. She inspires me."

"*She* inspires *you?*" He chuckled and shook his head. "I would think that with all your talent and then teaching on top of that, well…"

Rachel shrugged. "I write songs about life. Emma lives life—day in and out."

"She's got her hands full with those kids and another on the way." He shook his head.

"You disapprove?"

"It's not my place to approve or disapprove. I'm just saying that…"

"You seemed to enjoy the children in a distant sort of way, especially Henry."

"He reminded me of someone I knew in Kosovo."

"Samir?"

"Sami. Yeah."

She waited for more, but by now she knew he wasn't the type to volunteer much about his own life, especially the part that had taken place in Kosovo.

"Tell me about him."

He shrugged. "There's not much to tell. He got there just a few days before I left. We didn't have long."

"But he touched you—more than any of the others."

She waited.

"He's about the same age as Henry, but looks younger—small for his age. Skin and bones."

She drove and waited for him to go on.

"He'd been through so much by the time I met him and yet he was always so upbeat. And smart...really smart." He fell silent. "A little like Henry," he added as they approached the lights of town.

"You're good with kids," she commented. "You'd make a good teacher." She pulled up next to his car in back of the clinic, deliberately changing the subject to something lighter because they both had things to do and she knew they didn't have the luxury of lingering over conversation.

"I think you Dukes have the teaching profession pretty well sewn up in this town," he replied.

She didn't smile. She looked at him for a long moment. "Paul McCoy," she said finally as she reached across and brushed the hair from his forehead, "you are one unhappy man. I wish you could see the good that you do—the importance of your work. The way you were with C.R. and Emma tonight—so gentle and understanding. I know you feel guilty about leaving Sami and the others behind, but I believe that God had more important work for you here."

He tried to laugh off the comment, but she was too close to recognizing his feelings of guilt. "It's been a long day," he said as he opened the car door and stepped out.

Rachel decided to drop it, but the fact was Paul McCoy was a good doctor and he was good with the people of Smokey Forge. More and more it occurred to her that maybe God had brought him home to stay. He just needed a reason to do that.

"Do you write to Sami or any of the others?"

"Once in a while."

"Would you mind if I added a note the next time you write to Sami?"

"That would be nice. He'd really like that, but I warn you, the kid is ten going on twenty-five. Don't you dare send him a picture or he'll tell everybody you're his girlfriend."

Rachel laughed. "I'll write a letter tonight and get it to you tomorrow, okay?"

Paul nodded. "You want me to follow you home?"

"Paul, this is Smokey Forge, not Chicago. I'm perfectly safe." She waved and drove off toward home.

She realized that in a way she wished that it *was* Chicago and she did need him to keep her safe.

It was a Saturday morning in late October when Rachel received the call from Todd Mayfield. It was also the day she realized that without her noticing it, Paul McCoy had become her best friend. Todd Mayfield was a talent agent and manager—one of the best in the country music business and he wanted to represent her. The first person she thought about sharing that news with—even before Maggie or Sara—was Paul. That surprised her.

It also surprised Paul when she showed up at the clinic in the middle of the morning with no appointment.

"You okay?" He looked up from adding notes to a patient's file with a worried frown.

"I'm fine. I just got some news and, well, I thought maybe you'd celebrate with me."

"Celebrate?" He blinked and pushed his glasses onto the top of his head where they were instantly lost in his thick, unruly hair.

She might have been speaking a foreign language.

"Yeah, you know, like a birthday party?" She smiled and thought maybe this hadn't been such a good idea. Just because she thought of him as her best friend didn't mean that feeling was anywhere near to being reciprocated.

"It's your birthday?"

"No. That was an example."

He rubbed his eyes, and she saw that he was exhausted.

"Hey, I'm interrupting you," she said as she quickly backed toward the door. "Are you free for supper tonight? Maggie's making chili."

"Yeah, sure, but you didn't come all the way over here to invite me for supper. Now sit down and tell me what's going on." He led her to the straight-backed metal chair, and she sat.

"I got a call from an agent—you know, from Nashville?" She felt suddenly shy about the news. After all, what was the big deal? He was a doctor who did important research and went off to Kosovo to save lives in his spare time. She was talking about a guy who might get her a gig at the state fair.

"And?"

She shrugged. "He's a pretty good agent—good connections. It might lead to something."

He started to grin. "Yeah? What happened to the deal you made with God that it was first place or back to teaching?"

"As I have explained, God doesn't make deals," she reminded him. "But He does send messages, and if we're paying attention, we don't miss them."

"The agent is a message?" Paul was starting to relax and enjoy himself as he always did when he was around Rachel.

"More likely a messenger."

"This is complicated." He was teasing her now.

"Do you want to hear this or not?"

He held up his hands to forestall the force of her irritation, but he did not stop grinning. "So, your big break has come in the person of…?"

"Todd Mayfield. He represents some of the top names in the business." She felt her excitement building. "Paul, he wants to represent *me*."

"Well, of course, he does. Have you heard yourself sing? You're dynamite, lady."

She grinned. "Aw, shucks, Doc, I bet you say that to all your gospel-singing patients."

"So, what should we do to celebrate? How about a picnic?"

"Really? I love picnics," she said shyly.

"Then a picnic it is. Ready?" He took off his lab coat and reached for his leather jacket.

"Today? Now?"

Paul McCoy was almost never given to spontaneity unless it was related to some new theory about his research. On top of that, he would logically assume that the season for picnics had long since passed. "In October?" she asked.

"I think that's the best plan. It's a beautiful day—

October or not. It may be one of the last such days before spring, so we should take advantage, don't you think? Live in the moment. Isn't that what Maggie always says? We have something to celebrate, and there's no time like the present."

They stopped for sandwiches and cans of soda. Paul insisted on adding two gooey chocolate caramel brownies to the feast.

"I think the mill is the perfect spot for this particular picnic," he said. "After all, isn't that where you got your start?"

"You're being really terrific, Paul. Thank you for sharing this with me."

"My pleasure."

As they ate she regaled him with Todd Mayfield's impressive history of taking unknowns to the top of their field.

"Sounds like quite a guy."

She nodded. "And he wants to represent me." She stood up and twirled around and around, her arms flung wide, her head back as she sang the words to the heavens. "It's my dream coming true, Paul. All I ever wanted was the chance to try, and now God has decided to give me that."

Paul joined her in the dance, taking her in his arms and waltzing her around the open meadow next to the rushing stream. As they danced she began to sing— a song of thanks, a song of praise, a song of unadulterated joy.

"Oh, Mr. Todd Mayfield knows a good thing when he hears it," Paul said as the dance ended on a soaring note and they collapsed onto the grass breathless with exertion and happiness. "I'm really proud of you, Rachel," he added as he covered her hand with his.

"I couldn't have done it without you." She laughed. "I mean, imagine what might have happened if I hadn't passed out in front of you that first night." She sat cross-legged in front of him and took both his hands in hers. "Life is filled with such wonderful things like that—me passing out, you being there with Doc. I really think God sent you at that exact moment because He knew I needed your friendship in my life."

"You give me far too much credit."

"No, think about it. What if I'd won in Nashville and not passed out. I would have signed a contract and then halfway through the tour, I might have gotten sick again and then there's your friend and his research and you catching on that whatever I had might be the same as what you saw in Kosovo and…"

"Okay. Okay. Glad I could be of help."

They were quiet for a long moment, sitting together in the comfortable silence that only good friends can experience as they ate the gooey brownies and watched the stream rush past.

"I have to get back to the clinic," he said finally.

She rinsed her hands in the rushing stream, scrubbing at the sticky caramel from the brownies that had oozed over them. She used her wet fingers to scrub her mouth and then turned to him. "Thanks for sharing this moment with me. You made it extra special."

He was staring at her with a very strange look on his face.

"You have that deer-in-the-headlights look," she said.

"You just washed your hands in the stream."

She glanced at the stream. "They were sticky."

"And then you wiped your mouth."

"It was sticky, too." She couldn't imagine where he was going with this. "You're making me a little nervous," she said, and tried to laugh, hoping he would laugh, as well.

"Did you ever do that before? I mean, use the water from the stream to wash up?"

"Well, I don't make a habit of it."

"Rachel, that may be how you picked up the parasite."

It seemed impossible. "It was just a few drops, and besides, this water has tested okay for weeks."

"It may not have been this water. Think. Where else might you have wet your hands or face in untreated water?"

She was prepared to dismiss his theory as far-fetched, and then she remembered something. "Oh, my heavens," she whispered.

"What is it? Tell me."

"Last summer, I played a revival down in Hogan's Gap. They were doing baptisms in the river there—full immersions. There was this little girl, and she was afraid but she wanted so badly to be baptized."

"And?"

"I went in with her. I went *under* with her." She stared at Paul. "That could be it, right?"

"Could be—probably is. I'll call down there tomorrow and make sure they test that water."

"Make sure everybody's okay, too, will you?"

"I promise, and just to be doubly sure, I'm taking a new sample of this creek water with me to test right now. We can't have you getting sick again now that you're on the verge of stardom."

She laughed with pure joy, her good spirits completely restored.

As they drove back to town, Rachel talked and wrote notes and lists on scraps of paper that she pulled from her bag and her pockets. She told him that she needed to think about taking care of her teaching responsibilities, handing them off to a substitute in case Todd wanted her to go on tour. Then she was on to thinking about her song list. Did she have enough? Should she add some songs by other artists?

Paul laughed. "Slow down. You don't even know what this guy's going to do for you. There will be plenty of time to plan when you get that first offer."

"Maybe," she said, but clearly did not believe it for a minute. "On the other hand…"

"You're going to prepare for any contingency?"

She nodded and grinned. "It's the way I operate."

"Is that how you manage to keep all the balls of your life in the air?"

She shrugged.

He laughed. "Go. I'll see you later."

He was still smiling as he put his lab coat on and returned to his work. It was a slow day at the clinic, which meant he had time to make the calls he needed to make to the clinic near Hogan's Gap and to check the water from the mill, as well. He put a slide under the microscope, and what he saw there gave him more pleasure than any lab test he had ever run. The water was clean. Rachel was in no danger.

Rachel could hardly wait for Paul to come for supper. She'd arrived home to find a message to call Todd Mayfield, and now she had even better news to share with Paul.

"Could you just settle down?" Maggie scolded as she tried to work around Rachel. "You're worse than a pesky fly. Here, go set the table." She thrust the flatware and napkins into Rachel's hands and shooed her toward the dining room.

As she set the table, Rachel hummed a new tune that had popped into her head as she walked home from the clinic that afternoon. Nothing could dampen her spirits tonight.

"So, what did this guy have to say when you called him back?" Maggie asked as she brought in a stack of plates and salad bowls and set them on the end of the large dining room table.

"He thinks he might have an opportunity for me to be the opening act for the Wilson Brothers."

Maggie paused and looked at Rachel. She was clearly impressed. "Really?"

Rachel nodded. "I can hardly believe it myself. Can you imagine? I mean, they're like the biggest name on the charts in gospel right now."

"You'd have an audition?"

"Next week in Nashville."

Maggie came around the table and hugged her hard.

"Honey, I am prouder of you than I've ever been of anybody in my whole life."

"I don't have it yet," Rachel reminded her.

"Details," Maggie replied, and Rachel noticed that her sister brushed away a tear with the hem of her apron as she hurried to the kitchen. "Who would have thought?" Maggie said softly to herself. "Little Rachel Duke from Smokey Forge, Tennessee."

Rachel couldn't remember when she had felt so completely happy. She glanced out the window for the tenth time, hoping to see Paul's car. Of course, he probably never even heard of the Wilson Brothers.

She hurried to the CD player and after rummaging through her collection, inserted a disc and turned up the volume. The duo's rendition of "Amazing Grace" filled the house and spilled out onto the porch where Rachel went to wait for Paul.

Paul checked the slide three more times before setting it aside. He pulled out three earlier slides and studied them, as well. They had all tested negative for the parasite. He leaned back and thought about the scene at the stream earlier. His heart had been in his throat the minute he'd realized what she'd done. In that moment he had seen yet again how an instant could change everything. If the parasite had been there, she might have been infected again. Not only that, but it would have meant that C.R. and Emma and the kids were also in danger.

At first when she had washed her hands in the stream, he had laughed, teasing her about being such a messy eater. Even as he watched her wipe her mouth with her wet hands, scrubbing off remnants of the caramel that had stuck to her chin, it never occurred to him to stop her. When he realized what she had done, he felt as if he'd been kicked in the stomach.

He consulted an issue of a medical journal Dan had sent him. It contained the first published studies of this type of parasite.

"In some patients…evidence of a susceptibility to sometimes virulent onset of symptoms…especially if exposure to parasite reoccurs…"

He closed the journal and took one more look at the slide. There was no parasite. Rachel would be all right.

"You coming to Maggie's?"

His father stood at the door, and Paul became aware that the clinic was quiet. Ruby had left for the day, and the last patient had been seen and discharged.

"Yeah. Coming," he said, but he put a few more drops of the water sample on a fresh slide and slid it under the microscope. He had to be one hundred percent sure. His father remained standing at the door, watching him.

"Did you find something new?" Doc finally asked, edging a little closer.

Paul glanced up, then stood to offer his father his place. "Here, take a look."

Doc settled his large frame onto the stool and adjusted the microscope. After a long moment he sat back, removed his glasses and pinched the bridge of his nose. "Where's this from?"

"The mill." He told his father about Rachel's exposure to the water.

"It looks clean." Doc was clearly mystified at Paul's intense study of the sample.

"I know, but what if it hadn't been?" He quickly told his father what had happened earlier that afternoon.

Doc nodded. "Why don't I run up to C.R.'s right away? Just because the water is okay down here doesn't necessarily mean we shouldn't test it up there. I'll take them some bottled water, just until we're sure," Doc said. "You should go on to Maggie's."

Paul glanced at the clock. "I know."

"Son, this is good news—Rachel is fine." Doc was mystified by his son's intense expression.

"I know, but what I need to do now is make sure she's in the best possible shape to take advantage of this opportunity. Remember what happened last time?"

"She was just coming off the virus," Doc reminded him.

"I know, but she doesn't take care of herself at all, Dad. This is her big opportunity. This Mayfield guy could offer her the chance to perform all over the state, and she'd say that was fine and still manage to teach her kids and write half a dozen new songs at the same time."

Doc grinned. "That's our Rachel."

"Well, I'm going to make sure she gets her rest, eats right and starts on a regular program of exercise to build her stamina. She neglects herself something terrible."

Doc gave him a strange look. "Are you sure you can work all that into your own schedule? I mean, you've been spending every free minute helping your friend Dan and staying in touch with your colleagues back there in Kosovo. I won't even bring up the fact that we also have patients here who need you. Maybe I should take on Rachel's care."

"I can do it. I have to do it, Dad." He dumped the rest of the creek water in the sink and missed his father's grin. "She's as stubborn as they come, and I can't really see you jogging down the road with her every evening to make sure she sticks to her exercise."

"Well, if you think that's best," Doc said as if he doubted the wisdom of Paul's choice.

"Dad, I have to do this, okay?" Paul replied, his voice filled with urgency. "I promise you that I won't neglect the others, but Rachel—she's important."

"I understand," Doc said and patted his son's shoulder. "You go ahead. I'll be along later after I go up to C.R.'s place."

Paul nodded and headed out the door. Doc stood there watching him go. "You have to do this, all right," he said to himself as he watched Paul rev his car and spin gravel in his haste to get to Rachel. "But it has very little to do with that little girl being your patient, son. I sure hope you wake up to that before it's too late."

Chapter Five

"Absolutely not. I don't have time for all of that," Rachel declared, and her expression left little room for discussion. "You said yourself that you didn't find any sign of the parasite, and now you're just plain overreacting."

"But, darling," Maggie chided, "if Doc and Paul *both* think that—"

"I have a thousand things to do just to get ready for the audition and that doesn't even begin to address what I'll need to do if the Wilsons decide to let me open for them." She glanced around the room and saw their collective expression of skepticism. "I am in perfect health," she continued and stood up. "Look at me. I've gained back almost all the weight I lost. My nails are healthy. My color is good."

"You're the one who's overreacting," Sara told her. "All Paul is suggesting is that you start doing a little exercise and make a few changes in the way you eat to be sure you are at your best. It's perfectly reasonable."

"Perhaps you can postpone the audition," Maggie suggested. "They would understand that you've been sick."

"I haven't been sick in weeks, and Todd Mayfield does not *postpone*," Rachel said. "He finds somebody else."

Paul frowned. "This isn't a game, Rachel."

"I know that," she replied, and her tone was serious and calm. "This is my life—my dream. I know perhaps better than any of you what it will take to get ready for this. God will take care of the rest."

"Even God likes to have a little help, honey," Maggie said.

Rachel sighed. They were right. She was overreacting, but when she thought about everything she needed to do, the idea of adding to the list was daunting. "All right, I give up. Tell me what you've got in mind, Dr. McCoy. It's clearly the only way I'm going to have any peace at all."

"It's not going to be a walk in the park," he warned her. "You're going to have to follow the regimen I set for you religiously."

"To coin a phrase," she teased.

"You know what I'm saying. We're talking about regular nutritious meals—not your usual candy bar and diet soda for lunch. We're talking about proper rest." He paused as if trying to collect his thoughts. "Oh, and exercise, of course. Also, it wouldn't be a bad idea if you gave up caffeine."

"You're making this up as you go along, aren't you?"

He ignored that. "You're going to have to make choices. You can't keep burning the candle at both ends—teaching, tutoring, writing your music, rehearsing and running off here and everywhere just because this Mayfield guy says so, understood?" Paul asked as if the others had left them alone in the room.

"As long as I get to that audition in one piece," Rachel replied with equal conviction.

"When is it?"

"A week from tomorrow."

There was a long beat during which everyone else watched the couple intently.

Paul was the first to blink. "That doesn't give us much time," he finally conceded.

"My point exactly. Do we have a deal?" Rachel growled like some grizzled politician in a smoky back room. Then she grinned and stuck out her hand for him to shake and seal the bargain.

"I'm going to hound you," he warned.

"So what else is new?" Her hand remained outstretched.

"You're not going to like it," he said as he grudgingly accepted her handshake.

"I expect I'll survive," she replied. "On the other hand, I'm not at all sure that *you* will," she added softly as she turned away to serve the dessert. "You've really got to learn to lighten up, Paulie. The fact is some of this is way out of your control." She turned to the others. "Cake, anyone?"

After supper they sat together on the steps of the porch, sipping their coffee and not talking for several minutes, each lost in thought.

"You saw this parasite recur in Kosovo, didn't you?

That's why you got so worked up when you thought I might have ingested it today?" Rachel asked.

"Yeah."

"Did Sami have this parasite?"

Paul shook his head. "His mother had it, and his sisters. He probably had had a mild case, as well, but he had other problems." Paul frowned. "The fact is, Rachel, we just never know. Things can be going along just fine, and all of a sudden everything changes."

"Are you talking about Sami? Something else happened to him, didn't it? That's part of what frightened you today."

"Maybe."

"Tell me more about him, Paul. How did he get to the camp? Why did he of all of them touch you so deeply?" She shifted a little closer to him and placed her hand in his. "I really think you need to tell somebody about what happened that day he came to camp—the whole story."

Paul took her hand and held it and put his other arm around her shoulders. "It was so cold that day. This fine sleety rain had been falling most of the night and into the morning. Bone-chilling rain—you know, the kind where you swear you'll never be able to get warm again? The sky was gray. The landscape was mud. Even the people seemed pale and colorless. It was like some really overstated Hollywood version of the ravages of war."

"And then Sami arrived," she prompted.

Paul chuckled. "The kid was wearing a red flowered dress when he rode into camp on the back of a wagon with his mother, aunt and three sisters. Talk about a bright spot in an otherwise dismal landscape. He jumped off that wagon as soon as he saw me. Kept hold of the side of it as if the driver might take off with his mom and the others. 'You in charge here?' he demanded in perfect English." Paul laughed at the memory.

"He was wearing a dress? The poor kid."

"The crafty kid. The Serbs were taking all the men and older boys from their houses, rounding them up and killing them. Sami saw them take his father, grandfather, uncles and brothers. He figured out that the way to stay alive was to pretend to be a girl."

"What a clever boy, but how horrible—he's just a child."

"As soon as I introduced myself as the doctor in charge, he motioned his mother and the others over to me. 'They need help,' he said and then he collapsed."

"He must have been exhausted."

Paul was very quiet for a long moment. "He'd been injured by a land mine," he said softly.

Rachel gasped and turned to face him. "No," she whispered.

"One of his little sisters had wandered off into this field, chasing some butterfly or something. Sami had gone after her, knowing there were probably land mines. He made it all the way to her and brought her out, then he tripped on the skirt of that red dress and fell over, triggering a mine. It had happened just minutes before they reached camp. I couldn't figure out why the aunt and the driver of the wagon were so agitated, but only Sami spoke English."

"But he made it. He's alive."

Paul nodded. "He's alive, although by all rights he shouldn't be. When we cut that dress off him…" He shuddered at the memory, then took a deep breath and went on. "The wagon driver had done a pretty good job of bandaging him up, which had stopped the bleeding. We got him on the operating table and did what we could."

"I'm sure you did everything possible," she assured him.

"We had to take off one leg at the knee. The other leg is still all there, but pretty scarred up. The kid won't play soccer again, that's for sure." He delivered this startling news in a monotone that told Rachel more than anything else how much he blamed himself for not being able to do more.

"What about his family?"

"They made it to the camp because of him. You could just see the way things were. Sami had clearly taken charge. His mother was very ill, plus she'd lost everything. Understandably, she'd pretty much withdrawn and given up. The aunt and sisters had no choice but to look to Sami. Part of it was his ability to speak English, but most of it was just pure courage in the face of unspeakable horrors. The kid just refused to allow them to give up." Paul shook his head. "He's one terrific little boy."

"I'm glad you were there for him," Rachel said. "That God brought him to your camp."

Paul grimaced. "Yeah, well, for all the good it did. I saw a lot of children come through that camp, and what I was able to do for any of them was minimal. You find yourself fighting everything—time, the government, the lack of proper medicines and facilities, and of course the general apathy."

"What will happen to him now?"

"His mom didn't make it. She was too far gone physically by the time they reached camp, and she was so depressed. In his latest letter, he told me he and his sisters have been separated from the aunt."

"He's alone, then?"

"Pretty much. Of course, he still has his sisters."

"How old are they?"

"Six and eight."

"He's ten," Rachel said, as if that should matter.

"Almost eleven."

"That's too young for so much responsibility."

"Not in his world, unfortunately," he replied in a voice that seemed to come from far away. "There are a lot of kids like him—kids who have had to grow up too fast. Kids who have seen things that most adults couldn't survive."

"You could bring him here," she said.

Paul stared at her. "It's no use, Rachel. If I could have gotten him out of there, the time to do it was back then. Now…"

"Now he needs rehabilitation. I'm sure he can't get that there. And what about a prosthesis?"

"He's one kid. There are dozens of them just in that one camp."

"You start with one. In time, you can bring others."

"It's hard to get people interested in the world that Sami and his peers inhabit. It's too awful to imagine, and people don't like to think about things they can't fix."

"Well, we have to do something about changing his world, then." Rachel sat up and turned to face him. "I mean it, Paul. We have to get him out of there. We have to get them all out of there."

"It's not that simple, Rachel."

"I know that, but what if you and Doc could expand the services of the clinic—specialize—set up a program to treat injuries? I mean, just think about it. One of the reasons Henry made you think of Sami was his accident. You're drawn to them because they're innocent and they're injured. If you built a place just for the children, we could get grants, we could…"

His head was spinning as the idea rolled off her tongue as effortlessly as water over brook stones. He raised his hands in mock self-defense and laughed. "Oh, no, you don't, young lady. Right now the best thing you can do is take care of yourself and follow Doctor's orders, okay?"

"But…"

He placed two fingers against her lips to silence her. "No buts, lady. You have more than enough on your plate, and if you want to be at your best for that audition, you'd better live up to your part of our bargain. You take care of that, and I promise you that I'll think about your idea—ideas—okay?"

She nodded, and he took his fingers away from her mouth.

"We're going to start simplifying your life," he continued, "not complicating it with more worries, okay?" He tucked a strand of hair behind her ear.

"He's a little boy, Paul," she said softly. "We have to find a way to help him—to help all of them."

"I know that. You're going to just have to trust me and let me handle finding help for Sami, okay?"

"Okay."

They sat in comfortable silence, enjoying the last remnants of the unseasonably mild October evening. She leaned back and rested her head on his shoulder.

"Paul, I'll bet if you could bring Sami here to live with you, Sara could help. She's really good with kids. Together, the two of you…"

"Rachel?"

"Hmm?"

"One of the things you need to take off your plate permanently?"

"Yeah?"

"Matchmaking. You're really lousy at it, so please give it up."

"But…"

"Now I want you to go to bed." He stood up and offered her his hand to help her up, as well.

She laughed. "It's ten o'clock. I never get to bed before…" She saw his expression and paused. "Time for bed," she said contritely. "Can I at least read?"

"You can read as long as it has nothing to do with school or your music."

"How about the Old Testament?"

"Whatever works," he replied, refusing to rise to her obvious bait. He had no doubt that she was serious in her choice of reading matter, but he also understood that she was testing and teasing him a bit by mentioning it.

"You could read aloud to me," she invited as she dusted off her jeans.

That made him smile. "Now there's something that would definitely put you to sleep." He followed her into the house and said his good-nights to Maggie and Sara.

"See that this one gets to bed soon," he directed as he patted Rachel on the shoulder.

"I already have my orders, Doctor," Rachel reminded him.

"I'll expect you to stop by the clinic first thing tomorrow," Paul added. He was all business now. "I want to get some baseline data before finalizing the program I have in mind for you."

"Yes, sir," she replied. "I don't have to be at school until later."

"You aren't coming to school at all," Maggie instructed. "Sara and I have discussed it. You've got just one week to get ready for this audition, and that deserves your complete concentration." She saw that Rachel was about to give her an argument. "I mean it. Between the two of us, we can handle the music. We may not be Nashville stars but we can plunk a guitar and carry a tune when we have to, right, Sara?"

There was no use arguing.

That night, as Rachel lay awake, she started to think about Sami and the other children in the camps. She couldn't get them out of her mind. She envisioned the camps, the terrible conditions she had seen on the news. She thought of the pictures she'd seen of the children who had been stranded there, orphaned or abandoned or ripped from their homes with no future and no place to call home. The expressions on their faces had always tugged at her heart—those brave little terrified faces.

"God, I'm not sure what I can do, but I know You wouldn't have made me aware of Sami unless I'm supposed to do something. Please, help him. He's so very young, and his life has been so terribly hard."

She thought about Paul and imagined him there in the camp walking among the refugees. She thought about the way that he had of striding along, hands thrust into his pockets, shoulders hunched in a manner that seemed to signal a kind of instinct for self-protection. To a stranger, he would appear to be deliberately attempting to keep others at bay. Rachel had seen another side of Paul McCoy. She was pretty sure that Sami had also recognized that deep inside Paul was someone he could count on, someone who cared deeply.

"Henry saw it, too, didn't he?" she whispered

She thought about the night they had spent with Emma and C.R. Paul's trademark reserve had vanished, and the sometimes abrasive exterior that the locals chalked up to too much time spent living in the big city had been missing, as well. The minute he saw Henry limp down that hallway, he'd been totally focused on the boy. She'd seen in his eyes that he wanted—needed—to do something to help. Now she understood that he'd been thinking about Sami that night.

He had treated Henry as an equal—someone to be respected for his unique interests. He had acknowledged the injury but made no big deal of it. It was then that Rachel had fully understood and appreciated that his gift for healing went well beyond simple textbook medicine. He had a talent for listening, an instinct for moving beyond the words to the emotions underneath. Henry, who was painfully shy, had blossomed under Paul's attention. Rachel knew what it had taken for the little boy to muster the courage to talk to Paul at all. She understood that the science project had to be very important for him to have risked such a thing. Most of all, she was captivated by Paul's patience and complete concentration on the child and his needs.

"A person could trust a man like that," she said softly. "And in a world where innocent children get their legs blown off or have tractors roll over them, maybe You sent Paul McCoy to set things right again."

The following morning, when she went downstairs to fix her breakfast, she was comforted by the good feelings she had about Paul and his power to heal.

"Mornin'," she said to Maggie. "Isn't it a fabulous day?"

"Fabulous. Now come sit down and eat. You have to get dressed and get down to the clinic."

"What's this?" Rachel studied the strange-looking food in the bowl Maggie set in front of her.

"Paul stopped by. He wants you to add this to your diet. Roughage. It'll build your strength."

Rachel studied the assortment of grains in the cereal bowl. "It looks like stuff he raked up from some farmer's field." She poked it with a spoon. "What am I supposed to do with this?"

"You can put milk on it and eat it."

"Maybe milk and half a bowl of sugar," Rachel muttered.

"You could have a banana cut up on it. That'll sweeten it and give you potassium, which you probably need." Maggie quickly cut the banana. "I have to get to the school. The heat is stuck on eighty degrees. I expect you to eat every bite of this."

"Yes, ma'am." Rachel took a tiny spoonful of the cereal mixture. "Yuck," she grumbled as she forced it down. "Might as well ask me to eat shredded cardboard."

"It's good for you." Maggie hurried around gathering her books and notes. Just before going out the door, she poured a pale green liquid into a mug and set it on the table. "Green tea," she said. "It's decaffeinated."

"Oh, goody," Rachel said without conviction. She looked at the counter where the coffeemaker usually steamed with freshly made brew. It was still in the same place. It was also empty and recently washed.

"Eat," Maggie commanded as she stopped just shy of leaving the kitchen. "Dr. Paul is waiting."

"I'm eating. I'm eating." As far as Rachel was concerned, Dr. Paul was taking this thing *way* too seriously.

Chapter Six

The clinic's waiting room was filled.

"Flu," Ruby explained when she saw Rachel's look of surprise. "It's running through town faster than melted butter on a hot ear of corn."

"Rachel, go home," Doc ordered gruffly as he ushered the next coughing and moaning patient into the examining room.

"I had a flu shot," Rachel replied, but Doc was already halfway down the hall, and his attention was on the patient.

"Unfortunately, honey, so did a lot of these folks," Ruby reported. "It's a different strain."

Rachel glanced around the small crowded room and saw a number of waiting patients nod miserably.

"Ruby, I need you to call Mrs. Gaussmore's son and have him come take her home. She's too sick to drive herself. Then I'll—" Paul saw Rachel. "Are you nuts?" he asked in a low tone as he crossed the room in two strides and stood toe to toe with her.

"Actually, I'm here for my appointment—the one *you* made me promise to show up for?"

He ran a hand through his hair and took a deep breath. "Sorry. It's been like this since we opened the doors, and I forgot to call you."

"Well, I'm here and Maggie won't let me help at school so what can I do here?" She started to remove her jean jacket.

He took her by the arm before she could get her jacket off and ushered her out to the street. "You can help by quarantining yourself in your house for a couple of days until the worst of this flu runs its course. You don't want to risk catching anything." He glanced toward the busy clinic. "I have to get back in there. I'll stop by to check on you later, okay?"

"Sure," she said, and could not keep the hint of irritation out of her tone. She started to walk away.

"Wait." He caught up to her. "You understand why I'm concerned about letting you be exposed to the flu, right?"

"I understand."

"Then what's with the attitude?"

She released a heavy sigh. "You are *treating* me like somebody who is sick and fragile. I really hate that."

He blinked, and she knew that her reasoning escaped him.

"I will follow the regimen. I will eat the breakfast cardboard…."

"It's high fiber. You need—"

She placed a restraining hand on his arm. "What I *need*, Dr. Paul, is for you to trust that I'm as invested in being at my best for this audition as you are, but this is not the same thing as Sami or even Henry. You are not going to fail me in some way, okay? We're going to do this together—you, me and God, okay?"

"But—"

"You'd better get back inside there before Doc gets overwhelmed. I'm going home and I'll see you later, okay?"

He nodded.

She couldn't help herself. She laughed. "Why, Paulie McCoy, I do believe I have managed to leave you speechless."

Paul could hear her laughter following him as he turned and went inside the clinic. How was it, he wondered, that this woman—so young, so inexperienced in the ways of the world, so innocent—how could this woman walk around dishing out such wisdom?

Back inside the clinic, he smiled. "Who's next?" he asked with more enthusiasm then he'd felt all morning.

If Rachel thought Paul had become a fixture in the Duke household before, she was mistaken. He seemed to show up at every turn. It started later that same afternoon after Rachel had finished telling Sara about her confrontation with Paul at the clinic. He knocked at the back door dressed for a run.

"Do you jog?" he asked when Rachel opened the door.

"Not if I can walk," she replied.

"It's important to build up your stamina," Sara said with her usual serious expression. "A workout once a day could make a difference in the level of your energy, and that can have a big effect on your performance at the audition, Rach. You really need to listen to what Paul is telling you."

Rachel glanced at Paul. "You may have a point. After all, look at what it's done for Paul here." She slowly circled him, ogling his physique in an exaggerated way, and was delighted to see the color rise to his cheeks.

"Are you going to change?" he asked.

"Not likely," she replied with a grin. "Oh, you mean am I going to change clothes so we can proceed with this jogging thing? Well, sure, I'll give it a shot. Do you want something to drink while you wait?"

"That reminds me. Did you drink the green tea I left you?"

Rachel rolled her eyes. "Maggie implied that the tea was her idea." She glanced at Sara, who shrugged her shoulders and gave her a wide-eyed look of innocence. Rachel turned her attention to Paul. "Clearly, my sisters are in cahoots with you."

He did not reply but was obviously still waiting for the answer to his question.

"I drank the tea," she said with a sigh.

"Good girl," Sara said. "You go change while Paul and I whip up a fresh batch."

Rachel groaned and headed upstairs. If there had been any doubt in her mind that Paul and her sister Sara were made for each other, it had disappeared. The man was every bit as overbearing as her sister. Like Sara, he was sure that he always knew best, and he wasn't good at debating the point. Both of them were organized and serious. Once either one of them got focused on some project, they were worse than a hound dog with a fresh bone, never mind that God and other people had different ideas.

She shuddered as she pulled on a pair of stretch pants and an oversize sweatshirt that read Jesus Is Coming—Try To Look Busy. She could hear them downstairs making the tea. She could imagine that Paul would approach the task like Sara did most things in the kitchen—as if it were a science experiment. The two of them deserved each other, whether they were willing to admit it or not.

She pulled her hair high into a ponytail and used it to anchor an old baseball cap that had once belonged to her father.

"Rachel? Are you about ready? We're losing daylight."

"We're not making a movie here," she said under her breath as she squatted and searched under her bed for the mate to her running shoe. "Coming." *No shoe.*

Then she remembered and ran downstairs, one shoe on.

"Were you planning to hop or run?" Sara asked.

"Cute. Last time I wore these I stepped in a big ol' puddle and had to wash the one shoe." She fished it out of the laundry basket and held it up triumphantly.

Paul stared at the found shoe. "You didn't wash both shoes?"

"Only this one was dirty," she answered, and as she laced it up she missed his look of total bewilderment.

"Ready?" she asked as she jogged in place.

"Yes, but you need to warm up." He led the way to the back yard, where he demonstrated a series of stretches and warm-up exercises that he clearly expected her to follow.

"I thought we were losing daylight," she reminded him after he began the fourth exercise.

"A sports injury is preventable if you're properly warmed up," he lectured.

She sat on the ground and wrapped one leg over the other yoga style. Then she proceeded to stretch her legs full out into a split and touch her head to either knee. "Can you do that, hotshot?"

"You youngsters are so cocky," he conceded as he held out a hand to help her up.

She grinned and headed off down the path at a run. "Well, come on, Gramps, at least try to keep up."

He caught up to her easily and let her set the pace. She had a nice easy stride, and after several minutes of running showed no sign of tiring.

"What sports did you play in high school?" he asked.

"I tried out for basketball, but was a total klutz. Then somebody mentioned the track team. I decided to give it a shot and absolutely fell in love with running. The idea of competing against a clock was somehow very inspiring."

"You've kept it up?"

"Not really. Life got in the way—teaching, my music, traveling around to the tent and revival meetings in summer."

"You do that—the traveling around to revivals and such part—for the experience of being in front of an audience, I imagine," he said.

She glanced at him, expecting him to be kidding. When she saw that he wasn't, she spoke in slow, measured tones. "I do that, Paul, because God calls me to do that. He gave me a wonderful gift—a talent that can bring comfort to some and inspiration to others. To *not* go would be selfish. It would be like ignoring all the blessings He's given me and mine."

"Rachel, just for the sake of discussion here, what about the fact that He took your parents when you needed them most? What about the fact that He permitted you to be infected by that parasite last summer? What about all the terrible stuff that *He* lets happen all over the world—to innocents?"

"Now, you listen to me, Paul McCoy, I will not have you blaming God for every terrible thing that happens to people. He gave us free will to make decisions. He also gave everybody else on the planet the same free will. Don't you think that sometimes somebody else's bad decision—like the guy who decided to have one more beer and then get behind the wheel of his pickup and slam it into my parents' car—is going to spill over on a lot of innocent people?"

Now she was breathing hard. Paul couldn't decide if it was the exertion of the run or the breath it took to deliver that sentence. "I thought that was the point. I thought the Big Guy's job was supposed to be watching over people."

"The *Big Guy* does watch over people—even you. I imagine for His own amusement, He occasionally lets you run off at the mouth like you've just been doing, instead of zapping you with a bolt of lightning like you probably deserve."

"Aha, so you do believe He punishes," Paul said with a smug smile.

"He reprimands and reminds. Occasionally, He has

to slug a person in the face to get that person's attention. Personally, I'm waiting for that to happen to you."

"You are a strange bird."

"Could come any day now, the way I see it. You'd better be watching over your shoulder," she warned and sprinted ahead of him, her ponytail swaying from side to side in rhythm to her effortless pace.

One afternoon later that week, during what had become their daily run, there was little conversation. Rachel was absorbed in thinking about the audition, and who knew what Paul was puzzling over. All she could tell was that he seemed more agitated than usual.

"How are things at the clinic?" she asked.

"Okay."

"Are you still swamped with flu patients?"

"Not really."

Rachel glanced at him. He seemed oblivious to her presence, much less her attempts at conversation.

"And how was your day, Rachel?" she asked herself. "Well, let's see, right after I force-fed myself my usual shredded cardboard for breakfast and washed it down with about a gallon of that tasteless-might-as-well-drink-water tea, I got a phone call," she replied taking the other side of the conversation.

She waited a beat to let him jump into the conversation. He didn't. "And who called?" she asked herself. "Todd. You know, Todd Mayfield, my agent?"

Paul grunted, but he was still completely focused on his own thoughts.

"And what did Todd want?" she continued. "Oh, he

just said that if the audition is a success then I'll be leaving on tour in November. The Wilson Brothers are doing a holiday tour throughout the Southwest, and I would be the opening act. But the best part is that he wants to marry me—the sooner the better."

"That's nice," Paul said.

She stopped running and waited for him to notice. Half a block down the street he seemed to realize that she wasn't there. He turned and jogged back. "What's the matter? Are you having pain? Weakness?"

"I'm *talking to you*," she said, hands on her hips.

"I know. I heard you. Todd, the audition, a possible tour. Todd's getting married. It's nice." He waited, looking at her, clearly confused about what all this had to do with her interrupting their run.

"I said Todd wanted to marry me."

He blinked as he took that in. "Seriously? You don't even know each other, do you? I mean, I really wouldn't advise—"

"I threw that in there to see if you were paying attention," she said. "Todd is already married with four kids and a grandchild on the way. He's not exactly my type."

"Why would you say that then? I mean, about him wanting to marry you?"

"I was testing you to see if you were listening."

"I heard you."

"Well, I don't know how they do it up in Chicago, but down here the normal conversation between two people actually involves both people. There's a comment and then a response and most of the time that does not come from the same person, get it?"

"I'm a little distracted."

She started to jog slowly again, waiting for him to come alongside. "That's a start. Why are you distracted—that is, more than you usually are?"

"It's nothing for you to worry about."

"That wasn't the question."

"Really, it's nothing," he insisted.

She stopped running again, and this time she sat down in the middle of the road. "I'm not moving until you tell me, and this is a really dark road once night comes, and there's that curve up there. A car or truck comes barreling around the bend, I haven't got a prayer, and it'll be your fault."

He laughed in spite of his lousy mood. "You do have this way of getting my attention," he admitted.

"What are friends for? Come on, talk," she ordered, crossing her arms and legs as if she were prepared to follow through on her threat.

He pulled out the water bottle he carried and offered it to her. She took a long drink, and he followed suit. "It's just that…well, there's Dad, for one thing."

Satisfied that he was indeed going to confide in her, she got up, and they resumed their run. "Doc? What about him?"

"I hadn't realized that with age he's gotten pretty set in his ways. I made a couple of changes in the way Ruby does things at the clinic—not major things, mind you, just stuff that will make the office run more efficiently, and then I was trying to add some preventive health education stuff to the program."

"That sounds like a good idea."

"Yeah, well, then I started thinking about what you said the other day. Maybe we could expand the clinic—maybe even think about setting up that special program for kids who have been injured in some way. I know that it all requires big bucks and obviously we don't have that. But when I try to talk to Dad about it and about grants, he says he doesn't have time for such things."

"He's got a point. I mean he's always been a one-man show, and now that the town has grown he must be working overtime just to keep up. How's he going to specialize when he's already taking care of everybody in town?"

Paul nodded. "But then, what happens to a kid from a family who can't really afford specialized care? You know, like Henry. Dad's a talented physician, but he could hardly have handled the kind of care Henry would have needed following that accident, no matter what C.R. and Emma think."

"Henry's accident wasn't something they could have prevented, Paul. They weren't even there."

"I'm not blaming them, but if they had had the proper services available here, maybe Henry's foot could have been repaired. I just wish…"

"What?" She felt as if she needed to hold her breath—as if she were at the brink of some wonderful discovery for Paul.

"Nothing. I came here to help Dad find somebody to bring into the clinic, but if we could help a kid like Henry—and there are dozens of farm accidents, not to mention hunting accidents every year just in this area alone. I'd like to do something about that, Rachel. You made me realize that this is not all that different than what I saw overseas. They are children and they need help no matter where they are."

"Did you tell Doc that?"

"Not really, but how can I? It just adds to everything he's already doing. He wants to cut back, Rachel, not add more."

"Maybe he's just afraid that you'll get caught up in trying to help him build a program here and lose sight of your own dreams of getting back to Chicago and your own career. Parents worry about that sort of thing sometimes."

It was his turn to stop running and look at her in surprise. It had never occurred to him that while he'd been mulling over the idea that maybe staying in Smokey Forge wouldn't be so bad, his dad had assumed that his plan was still to leave as soon as possible. "You constantly amaze me, Rachel. I mean that's an incredibly insightful thing to say and especially coming from someone who has gone through most of your life without benefit of parents."

"Ah, but I had Doc and your mom while she was alive. And of course, I had Maggie and Sara—talk about surrogate mothers!"

They began to run again.

"You know, Paul, this is the first time since you've been back that I've heard you talk about your dreams. You've talked about Dan and his research, and of course you've been there for me through everything, but nothing for yourself. If anything were possible, what would you do—to help kids like Henry?"

His face lit with excitement. "I was thinking about a mobile clinic—you know, take the medicine and therapy to them? Maybe one day, we *could* expand the clinic to include a state-of-the-art rehabilitation center— attract the best therapists, build it into a program respected throughout the region, maybe even the nation."

"Now, *that* sounds expensive."

"It would be, but if we could find the funding, we could do amazing things."

"Like what? If you had the funding, what would you do?"

He sighed heavily. "What *wouldn't* I do? These kids—regardless of where they live—are innocent victims of the dangers of the world. The kids in Chicago had to be afraid all the time of drive-by shootings. The kids in Kosovo had the land mines to contend with— that's assuming they made it out of the villages in one piece. The kids here are safer, but they are still around dangerous stuff, like farm equipment and hunting rifles. It's a wonder any of them make it to adulthood."

"Your program would give them a better chance," she reminded him gently.

"We can't prevent the accidents, necessarily. But we could help them rehabilitate themselves. We could give them a better chance at recovering."

"So, this mobile clinic would be some kind of van with equipment that would travel up and down the hills sort of like a library bookmobile?"

He grinned. "Something like that. Sounds like a pipe dream, huh?"

"Not at all. I think it sounds terrific. I mean, wouldn't

it be cool if you could bring Sami over here, get him out of the horrible place, give him his chance? Wouldn't that be incredible?"

He laughed. "You just never see the glass half-empty, do you?"

"That's the gift of faith, Paul. All things are possible—you just have to find the right path." She turned onto a narrow cow path that ran down the hill toward the millstream. "Like this one," she called happily. "Come on. Last one to the stream has to come to church with me next Sunday."

Once again, she had succeeded in breaking his mood and getting him to laugh. "No fair," he shouted as he took off, running hard, pushing to pass her. "And if I win," he called over his shoulder, "then the last one there owes the winner dinner and a movie."

"Going to church will get you a lot closer to realizing your dream than dinner and a movie," she yelled and ran after him.

"Yeah? Well, what if my dream at the moment is a date with you?" He kept running.

She stopped and stared after him in dumbfounded surprise and then heard his laughter. There was no way she could catch him now, and he knew it.

"You'll do anything to win," she called after him. The idea that Paul McCoy might be interested in a date with her *was* ridiculous, wasn't it?

Chapter Seven

"**Y**ou have got to help me," Rachel whispered into the phone two days later.

"Rachel? I can barely hear you," Paul said. "Are you feeling ill?" His voice reflected his usual concern.

"I'm fine. It's just that Maggie and Sara have both decided they need to come with me for the audition."

"That's nice," Paul replied.

"It's a nightmare," Rachel screeched hoarsely. "You know how they are. Maggie will be in full-blown nurturing mode, and Sara—well, Sara will be her usual I-know-better-than-you-do self. I can't *do* this."

"And I can help you by?"

"Say you'll go with me for the audition. *Please.* You don't actually have to go, but just let them think you'll be there to watch over me and…"

"Slow down." He covered a chuckle with a cough.

"Stop laughing. This is serious. Surely you of all people know how they can be. You grew up with them."

"I was blinded by Sara's beauty, remember?"

"Well, get unblinded for a minute and help me out here or, for the rest of your born days, carry around the guilt of my failed audition with the hottest act in gospel." She gripped the phone. "At least have the common courtesy to stop laughing," she ordered, "and help me get out of this mess. The audition is the day after tomorrow."

"I'll go."

"The least you could…"

"I said I'll do it."

"Oh." She paused. "You know, you don't really have to."

"Okay. I'll stay here and work."

"No," she protested and then spoke more softly as she caught Maggie's curious glance from the kitchen. "I mean, I just…"

"Why are you whispering?" he asked in an exaggerated whisper.

"Because unlike you big-city types, we only have one phone in this house, and it sits here in the middle of the downstairs hallway where anyone might wander by."

She could hear the hint of barely suppressed laughter in his voice as he spoke normally. "Okay, what time do we need to leave? What time's the audition?"

"Four in the afternoon."

"Okay, we'll leave early. Take our time so you can relax."

"You mean it?"

"Sure. It'll be fun."

"You don't *do* fun, Paul," she said suspiciously.

There was a pause. "Okay. I was going to be in Nashville Saturday anyway to see a friend at the university. He's done some work with accident victims—adults, mostly. We've been planning to get together to share notes."

"You rat. You could have offered to give me a ride all along."

"I beg your pardon," he replied. "Just a minute ago I was saving you from the fate of spending one of the most important days of your life under the thumbs of your well-intentioned but overbearing sisters."

"Well, when you put it that way, I guess I could hitch a ride with you…as long as you're going anyway."

This time he made no attempt to disguise his mirth. He laughed out loud, and she realized how much she had come to enjoy the sound of it. "You're welcome. Get a good night's sleep, songbird."

"We'll be back before midnight," Rachel promised her sisters as Paul drove slowly away from the house two days later.

"But you'll call the minute you know," Maggie shouted as Paul pulled the car out of the driveway.

"Yes, okay. I'll call," Rachel promised and waved.

"Could you get all the way in the car and fasten that seat belt, please?" Paul instructed. "You'd think you were going on a six-month safari, not a simple day trip to Nashville."

"There is nothing *simple* about this," Rachel replied testily as she flung herself into the seat and tried without success to fasten the seat belt. "I don't think I'm ready. I should have prepared another selection—something more upbeat. They're going to think I'm a rank amateur."

"Here," Paul said as he steered with one hand and deftly clicked the seat belt into place. "Take a deep breath. Go on. Deep." He demonstrated. "Now, let it out slowly."

"It makes me light-headed."

"Good. It's working. Again." He drew in a long breath and blew it slowly out through his open lips.

"You are seriously weird," she said, but she did as he instructed and found she was indeed feeling better.

"Okay, now what?"

"Warm up," he instructed.

"Excuse me?"

"Whatever it is that you do—scales, la-las. You know, warm up the pipes."

She giggled.

"Shall I demonstrate?"

"You're serious? You sing?"

"I happen to have been in the choir at school for at least a week, young lady, before I realized they actually expected me to rehearse." He started to hum and then sing an off-key version of "Coming 'Round the Mountain." "Feel free to join in."

"That's really terrible."

He stopped singing and gave her a pained look. "I'm crushed."

They rode along in comfortable silence. She dozed. He turned the radio on low and enjoyed the passing scenery. Halfway there he pulled into the parking lot of a roadside coffee shop.

"Are we there yet?" she asked sleepily as she sat up and looked around.

"No. I just thought we'd take a short break. How

about some green tea?" He grinned and held up a plastic sandwich bag containing tea bags. "Maggie sent them along. She also instructed me to make sure you had yours with honey."

"She's impossible," Rachel replied, but she said it with a smile, and he knew that she was touched by the caring gesture.

Once they were in the coffee shop, she grew uncustomarily quiet.

"Are you still nervous?" he asked.

She shrugged. "A little. It's probably normal, don't you think?"

He pretended to consider that. "Well, now, let's analyze that. Were you nervous that night at the talent show?"

"Well, of course."

"Are you nervous when you sing at church or at a revival?"

"No."

He stroked his chin as if he had suddenly grown a beard. "Then here's what I'm thinking. If you pretend that you're back home singing at church, you'll be fine."

"Thank you, Dr. McCoy."

"No problem. Now, drink your tea and let's talk about that date you owe me."

"You used that to cheat, and you know it," she protested.

"I did not. It was a bona fide offer, a bet that you lost and one that I fully expect to collect on. How about Saturday?"

"This is Saturday," she reminded him.

"As in next week."

"We'll see."

"Ah, the lady is playing coy with me." He twirled an imaginary mustache. "Well, I always collect on my bets, Miss Duke, so don't try to get out of this one."

"You're playing mind games," she replied and drank the rest of her tea.

He leaned back and studied her. "Maybe. Maybe not. I did make you forget about being nervous for five minutes, didn't I?"

She smiled. "Yeah. You did. Thanks."

When they reached the outskirts of the city, she began to fidget.

"You're going to do fine," he assured her.

"I'm more nervous than I would have imagined," she confessed.

"Maybe because it means so much to you?"

"Yeah, maybe."

He parked in front of the theater, and they both stepped out of the car. He offered to come in with her, but she refused. "I have to do this on my own. Can you understand that?"

"More than you know."

"You go see your friend and talk shop. I've got the number, and I'll call you the minute it's over."

"Sounds like a plan."

She started to walk away, her guitar case in one hand, a garment bag with her dress for the audition in the other.

"Hey," he called.

She stopped and looked back.

He walked the few yards to her and kissed her gently on the forehead. "You're very, very talented, Rachel. If you don't get it, it won't have anything to do with who you are or your talent, okay?"

"Thank you."

"You're welcome. Now, go knock 'em dead, songbird." He gave her a light tap on her backside.

Paul had stopped listening to his friend's explanation of the research he was conducting and started checking his watch. It was nearly six, and there had been no call. Was that a good sign?

Ten minutes later, the phone finally rang as if he had somehow willed it to happen. His friend answered and handed him the receiver.

"Hi."

He could tell nothing from her voice.

"Should I come get you?" he asked.

"Yeah. I'm pretty hungry. Did you guys eat yet?"

They were talking about the mundane. She hadn't gotten it. "Rachel, I'm…"

"'Cause the Wilsons would like us to join them for some of the best barbecue in Nashville."

"Really?"

"Yeah. You don't mind, do you? They want to talk about the tour, and I told them I had to get back tonight. They're cool with that, but they—"

"You got it."

She started to laugh, and it was music to his ears. "Well, yeah, if I can manage to put together an opening act between now and when we leave on tour in November."

"You got it. Oh, Rach, that's really terrific." He didn't stop to analyze why he didn't feel all that happy at hearing the news. After all, it was what she wanted—what he wanted for her. "Congratulations. I'll leave right now."

It was a wonderful evening for Rachel. Paul could see that traveling with the Wilsons would be a family affair. Ezra Wilson's wife was part of the crew, as were several other relatives. They were professionals who knew how to have some fun. But he had some doubts about Todd Mayfield.

He didn't like the way Mayfield looked at Rachel, as if she were a commodity to be marketed like breakfast cereal or the latest hot toy for kids. He didn't like the way he kept talking about changing her clothes and her hair to give her what he called more pizzazz. If there was one thing Rachel had, it was genuine pizzazz. The woman lit up a room. Mayfield talked in terms of promotions and referred to her as a potentially hot property. It was all Paul could do not to punch the guy in the nose.

Rachel seemed enthralled by it all. She listened carefully to everything her new manager told her. She hung on every story the Wilsons told of life on the road. Her eyes sparkled with anticipation. She blushed when one of the Wilson brothers complimented her on her talent for songwriting.

"Honey, it's one thing to sing 'em," Ezra Wilson told her. "Writin' 'em is a whole different ball game, and you write real good stuff, little lady."

"We were thinking maybe you might put your mind to writing something we could all do together," Jonah Wilson added.

"A finale," Todd said with glee. "A grand finale."

Rachel was incredulous. "You want me to write a song for you?" She looked at each of the brothers in turn.

"Yep, and sing it right along with us. How about a holiday song since it's a holiday tour?" Jonah suggested.

Rachel was in shock. "This can't be really happening," she said with a shy shake of her head. "I mean, me sitting here at supper with the Wilson Brothers just like…"

"Ordinary folks, honey," Ezra's wife, Pearl, told her. "That's all we are. We happen to make our living singing songs—spreading the good news. It's not that different from a traveling preacher."

"Except when's the last time you heard of a traveling preacher being paid six figures to do a tour?" Todd gloated.

"It's God's work and God's will, Todd, and don't you be forgettin' that," Pearl said sternly, and Paul saw that she didn't like Todd Mayfield all that much, either.

In the car on the way back to Smokey Forge, he listened to Rachel describe every detail of the audition— what everyone said, how they looked, what they asked and how she answered. He realized that in spite of her joy, he couldn't shake a concern that she wasn't really ready for the bright lights of big-time show business.

"You know, it's not going to be all seashells and balloons out there," he said and regretted it the moment the words were out of his mouth. This was her night. He shouldn't spoil it.

"Well, of course. There are rough spots in any job. I know it can get lonesome out there on the road, but I'm going to be lucky to have Pearl and the others—she's a lot like Maggie, don't you think?"

Paul smiled. "Yeah, she is."

"And Ezra reminds me a little of Doc—same sense of humor, and he just can't help playing the big protector to everybody else. Jonah's a foot taller than he is, but Ezra still treats him like his baby brother."

"I thought you didn't like that sort of thing."

She glanced at him. "What are you doing?" she asked, and her voice had lost all of its enthusiasm.

"Nothing. What do you mean?" But he knew what she meant. He was throwing a huge wet blanket on her high spirits, and he couldn't for the life of him figure out why. "I'm sorry," he said honestly.

"Aren't you happy for me? I thought you, of all people…"

"I'm really happy for you. I'm thrilled for you."

"But?"

He covered her hand with his and squeezed it. "Don't mind me. I am truly happy for you."

They drove for a while in silence through the dark night.

"I'm an insensitive idiot," she said quietly after several minutes. "Here I've been going on and on about my day and I never even asked about your meeting with your friend at the university. What did you find out?"

"There's not much to tell. We compared notes. I checked out some research he's doing."

"On injuries from accidents?"

"Yeah. He's started to do some preliminary research for an international organization on injuries from land mines."

"Not in this country?"

"No. Overseas. The Middle East, mostly. He's on

the verge of getting some major grant dollars. He might be interested in working with me on building a rehab program."

He turned off the interstate and headed for Smokey Forge. "Hey, why are we discussing all this serious and depressing stuff? You have made a major step forward in your career today. I am so proud of you, songbird."

She sighed and stretched. "It is pretty awesome, isn't it?"

"Yeah, who would have thought—me driving around with a real live country music star."

She giggled and punched his arm, but he could tell that he had succeeded in returning her thoughts to the wonder of the day just past.

The time raced by, and Rachel had never been busier or happier. She worked with Todd Mayfield and his staff to develop and perfect her opening act. She rehearsed for hours and accepted every opportunity to try out her songs in front of an audience. Maggie and Sara recruited a college senior doing his student teaching to double as the music teacher for the rest of the term.

Rachel spent as much time as possible with Paul, relying on him for advice on her selection of songs, her choice of wardrobe and how to conduct herself in the interview. Even though Paul was as busy as she was, he and Doc still came for supper at the farm several times a week, and he called a couple of times a day.

"It's like a dream coming true in fast forward," she said one day when he called after she'd had a particularly exhilarating rehearsal.

"You're the one who's working to make it all happen," he reminded her. "Don't forget that."

"Gee, wonder what else or *who* else might be responsible."

He was silent.

"Prayer works, my friend," she said happily. "You should give it a try. What if I told you it could help you find a way to get the money you need for the mobile unit? Think about it. Now, hang up the phone so I can get my beauty rest."

Beauty rest was the last thing she needed, he thought.

"Tomorrow's the big day." The closer the time came for her to leave, the less he wanted her to go. He told himself that he was just worried about her. She was inexperienced, and he would hate to see the tour end up being less than she had expected.

"Yeah. It's pretty amazing."

"The time will go really fast," he said, even as he thought how interminable it was going to seem not seeing her for the next two weeks.

"I wish…" She paused.

"More wishes? I thought they had all come true," he teased.

"Yeah, well, I'll miss you."

For a minute, he thought that she might be saying more. *Don't be an idiot,* he thought. *In all the weeks you've known her, there's never been the slightest hint that she views you as anything other than a friend.* "You'll be fine, and there's always the phone."

"It works both ways. I mean, if you need a friend…or something."

"I'll keep that in mind. After all, you still owe me that date, lady."

She laughed, but made no reply.

McCoy, you're an idiot. "I'd better let you go and get that rest," he said aloud. "That tour bus will be pulling into town bright and early tomorrow."

She didn't want to hang up.

Neither did he.

"Good night, songbird," he said softly.

She hung up and saw Sara standing in the doorway of the kitchen.

"I'm gonna say this just one more time—you're nuts for not seriously going after that guy," Rachel said as she passed her sister and headed upstairs.

"Maybe you're the one who should go after him," Sara replied.

Rachel laughed. "Yeah, right. That's really gonna happen." But she couldn't help blushing with pleasure at the thought. Perhaps if she took him up on that date thing, it might lead to something. "On the other hand," she said aloud, "why complicate a perfectly incredible friendship, right, God?"

There were three large buses parked outside the town hall. The bus belonging to Ezra and Pearl was at the front. The bus was awesome. It was outfitted with a full kitchen, which was Maggie's favorite part. She and Sara had both insisted on inspecting the vehicle for themselves. Sara was outside with the driver looking over the tires and the engine.

"Look at this," Maggie whispered excitedly as she

ran her hand over the stove and refrigerator. "It's incredible and so compact."

"The boys like their home cooking, especially when we're on tour," Pearl said. "Jonah's bus is the same size, but he spends a lot of time riding up here with us. His wife is expecting pretty soon and won't be going with us on this tour. Now, Rachel, honey, this is your space here." She pulled aside an accordion-pleated door and revealed a small sleeping area.

"That's really nice. Thanks." She glanced out the window.

"He'll be here, honey," Maggie assured her.

"It's okay. We said our goodbyes last night." She smiled and turned to Pearl. "It's my friend Paul—you know, the doctor?"

"Oh, he's a cutie, that one," Pearl said, gushing. "Don't let him off the hook, sweetie."

"But he's not…that is, we're just really great friends."

"Uh-huh," Pearl said, and nudged Maggie. "I'll just go be sure the boys are ready to head out." She held the door for Sara, who was just coming to see the interior. "You folks take your time here."

As soon as Pearl left, Maggie held out her arms to Rachel. "My baby sister," she said, her voice choking a little as she hugged Rachel hard.

"It's only for two weeks," Rachel assured her.

"You'll call every night?" Sara added, joining the circle and hugging them both.

Rachel nodded, her eyes misty as she realized that this was really about to happen.

Someone cleared his throat, and she looked over

Maggie's shoulder to see Paul standing in the door of the bus.

"I think there are some people out here who'd like to say goodbye," he said.

Rachel went to the door and looked out to see what looked like the whole town gathered in the town square. A sign that read Rachel Duke, Our Very Own Singing Star was stretched across the front of the bank. Her students launched into a song as Doc presented her with a bouquet of flowers. "Break a leg, honey," he said, then looked confused. "Does that work for you concert singers as well as people in the theater?"

Rachel hugged him hard and assured him she accepted all forms of good wishes. She turned her attention to the other townspeople gathered to see her off.

"This is really too much," Rachel cried as she waded into the crowd and happily accepted the hugs and good wishes of the people she had known all her life.

"All aboard," Todd Mayfield shouted, looking at his watch.

Rachel turned and found herself face to face with Paul. In that instant the words of her sister came back to her. *Why don't you go after him?*

She rejected the thought for a second time as impossible. Paul McCoy had and would always think of her as the kid sister in the Duke family. He might have gotten over his feelings for Sara, but there was nothing to indicate that he had transferred those feelings to her. Not even that ridiculous business about him pretending to want an actual date with her.

"Here," he said, pressing a paper into her hand. "In

case you need me. Not that I think anything will go wrong—just a little insurance."

She glanced at the numbers on the paper and then gave him a puzzled look.

"It's my cell phone. If you need me, dial that number, okay? Not that you will—need me, I mean. I assure you that I'm not trying to mother-hen you. But just in case." He folded her fingers over the paper and held on. "You're going to be terrific, Rachel. They're going to love you."

"But?" Rachel knew that Paul would probably always view the world with a heavy dose of skepticism. With Paul, there was always a but.

"But it's a very different world out there. Things aren't always what they seem. People aren't always what they seem to be. I just want you to know you can always call home, okay?"

"Like E.T.?"

He laughed. "Yeah. Like that."

Rachel reached up and hugged him to keep him from seeing the tears that threatened. He was determined to look after her even if it was under the guise of a big brother. He was giving her his blessing in spite of the reservations he had expressed a few nights earlier. "Thank you," she whispered. "Thank you for everything."

He was standing with the others as the bus pulled away, but when she thought about it later, she realized that he was the only one she had really seen. She fingered the paper in her pocket, then thought about the money Sara had insisted on stuffing in her other pocket as she boarded the bus.

Rachel frowned and folded the note. Who was she

kidding? She had a crush on the good doctor while he clearly still saw her as somebody in need of care. She'd just have to prove herself to him once and for all. She was a full-grown woman, perfectly capable of making her way in the world. She appreciated everyone's concern—she really did—but she was so tired of being everybody's kid sister. The next time Paul McCoy saw her, he was going to have to recognize that little Rachel Duke was all grown-up.

Chapter Eight

True to her word, Rachel called home every night. She always called at suppertime, when she knew they would all be there but there wouldn't be a lot of time to talk. She told Maggie that this was the only possible time to call. She was so busy and the shows ran so late and there were pre-show interviews to be done and backstage guests to be met, not to mention rehearsals.

The truth was that she wasn't ready to share her experiences on the road with them. At first, everything was new and exciting, but that lasted only the first week. By the second, they had settled into a routine that was either boring or exhausting or both. Rachel tried to remain upbeat, but the truth was that being on the road was very different than what she had imagined.

Maggie and Sara plied her with questions, wanting every detail of her adventure. Rachel found that she needed time to digest how she was reacting to what was happening to her—the changes she was experiencing, the ways in which being on tour were different from what she had expected. The more they pushed, the more closemouthed she became. She knew that if she tried to provide details, they would hear in her voice how exhausted she was, how grueling the schedule was.

She wouldn't even have to tell them about the endless boring hours on the bus, trying to catch a nap sitting up or serenaded by the rumble of the tires on the asphalt. They would read between the lines as they always had been able to and they would know. Most of all, they would hear in her voice that she was lonely and homesick in spite of the many kindnesses of the Wilsons.

If Paul had stopped by for supper, he always got on the phone. Fortunately for Rachel, the location of the phone in the Duke house plus the fact that everyone wanted their turn to talk to her made any real conversation impossible. She knew that Paul was concerned. She could hear it in his voice. He, of all of them, would see through her efforts to be upbeat and cheerful. He would know that life on the road was—as he had predicted—not at all what she had expected.

After several rushed phone calls in which Rachel barely seemed to have time to say hello, Paul began to worry. She did not sound like herself. She was enthusiastic and upbeat, but as the days passed it sounded more and more as if she were putting on a performance for all of them. Her tone was too bright, and her laughter sounded forced.

After a week of this, Paul made sure that he would be the last to get on the line with her. The others would have their fill of news by then and drift to the kitchen or living room. Maybe he could really talk to her for a change.

"You sound different," he stated flatly.

"I am different," she agreed with a lightness he would swear she didn't feel. "It's a different life."

She sounded defensive, and that wasn't like her at all.

"How are you?"

"Fine. Great. Oh, a little tired, but we're traveling or setting up for a show or doing a show—the days are really full, you know. It's a normal kind of tired, Paul. I'm not sick again, honest."

He hadn't even been thinking of her physical health, but she had become instantly defensive. He realized that he didn't know how to talk to her over this distance that was both geographical and emotional. "I meant that in a general way, Rach. I know you're in good health."

"Oh." She sighed, then added in that bright, forced tone he had come to dread, "They extended the tour—how about that?"

"That's good. Isn't it?" *I hate it. Come home where you belong.*

She ignored the pointed question. "We've added four shows in Dallas and then two weeks of bookings after that."

"Really?" He tried to fake enthusiasm and knew that he had failed.

"Yeah. I mean, this is all so amazing. Well, I have to go. Tell everyone I'll call tomorrow—same time. See you."

The line hummed, and he slowly hung up the phone.

On the drive home that night, Paul asked his father, "Dad, do you think you could manage on your own for a long weekend?"

"You going down to see Rachel?"

"Yeah. I thought I'd surprise her."

Doc chuckled. "That one sure does know how to get under a person's skin. Are you going because you're worried about her or because you're finally owning up to the fact that you're sweet on her?"

"She's a good kid, Dad, and maybe under other circumstances…" He shrugged. "The fact is, she has her career and I have mine. The two don't really blend, but we're good friends, and that's more than a lot of people have."

"I see," Doc said slowly. "So you're traveling all the way to Texas because you want to see your good friend?"

Paul sighed. "Yeah. Maybe. I don't know. She sounds completely changed and not for the better."

"Yep, I think you might have a point. She's a little too excited and upbeat when she calls in. It isn't natural talk."

So Doc had heard it, too. Paul breathed a sigh of relief that he wasn't imagining things. "In addition to being my friend, she's also my patient, Dad. I know that physically she's fine, but I promised myself when I left Sami and the others back there in Kosovo that I would never again desert a patient if I didn't have to."

Doc was quiet for a long moment. "I'm sorry I pulled you away from that, son."

As Paul realized how his words must have sounded to his father, he reached over and clumsily grasped the older man's shoulder. "I didn't mean it that way, Dad. I was ready to give up. I was so frustrated by not being able to make a difference for those kids, those people…. The truth is I would have left anyway. Your call just gave me the reason I needed to do it without feeling guilty about it."

"But you do feel guilty."

"Yeah. At the same time I can see that I made the right choice. I'm glad I came home, Dad. I'm really glad you called."

"My being lonely wasn't the only reason I called you, son," Doc admitted.

"Why else?"

"I was worried about you. There was nothing in your letters I could put my finger on, but it seemed to me that ever since you left the hospital in Chicago you'd been flopping around like a trout out of water. No direction. No goals. You always knew exactly what you wanted, son, and how to go about getting it."

It was as close to the truth as anyone other than Rachel had come. Paul remained silent.

"Truth is, I've been thinking about that idea you had for a traveling clinic and rehabilitation center for the kids. I reckon we *could* set up a program here. I've done a little checking around. We could get the old abandoned hospital building and fix it up. That would give you the room, and it has a good layout for the center. I also ran into Hank Riddle over there at the dealership, and he might be persuaded to donate a van. Of course, we'd have to raise some money to outfit it, but…"

"How did you know about all of this?"

Doc chuckled. "Well, certainly not from you. Rachel took me out for coffee before she took off on tour. She gets pretty excited about this stuff—mostly because it focuses on the kids. You two have a lot more in common than you may think."

"She's got her own career to manage. Besides, even

if I could get the program going, what about you? You can't spare me from the clinic until you find a partner, and face it, nobody is exactly racing down here to operate a small-town practice in the hills of Tennessee."

"I've been thinking about that, too. I was talking to Sam Doolittle, the hospital administrator over there in Bloomville, last week. He got pretty excited about the idea of our working on something like this together—rotating residents through here. They could give me the help I need. Then we could work through him to make services available to poor kids here in the mountains and maybe also…"

Paul stared at his father. "Dad, I appreciate what you're trying to do here, but…"

Doc ignored him. "Seems to me you'd want to take things a step beyond treating kids in this area. Might even be able to see about bringing some of the worst cases from overseas here."

"The kids from Kosovo?"

"Yeah, I was talking to Sara about this grant stuff. Seems there might be money to bring some of the most needy kids here for treatment. Probably your Sami would qualify—him being an orphan and getting cut up by that land mine."

"You're serious."

"Well, yeah, I am. You seem to have taken to this idea, and I've got to tell you, son, that it's a load off my mind to see you finally get interested in something again. We all knew that it would take a lot more than just being a small-town doctor to keep you happy. If this project gives you a reason to stay, then I'm for doing whatever it takes to make this happen."

Paul couldn't believe what he was hearing. His dad had seemed so set in his ways. Now he was talking about developing a sophisticated program of services that many major hospitals would hesitate to take on. On top of that, he'd already done a great deal of work toward getting the dream on its way.

"You don't have to do this, Dad," Paul said. "I'm going to stay as long as it takes."

"This is no bribe, son. I've been watching you work, listening to your stories, reading the articles. Rachel tells me that you've kind of gotten hooked on treating the mountain folks around here."

Paul smiled. "They remind me of the people in the camps."

"I thought so. Look, son, this thing is something a lot of people need. Rachel's right. There's nothing to say it can't get started right here in Smokey Forge. We may not have the money now but we can get that. What's most important is that we have you here, and you are the person most qualified to build this program. Are you game?"

Paul felt an ember of excitement that had been banked far too long begin to glow deep inside him. His father was offering him the opportunity to make a real difference. More important, his father wanted to help build that project because he believed in Paul and what he could do.

"I'm game," he said as his father pulled the car into the garage.

"Then let's get started, son."

They sat at the kitchen table until well past midnight discussing ideas for the program. Paul was astounded at what his father had already put into motion, including the plan for residents from the hospital his friend Sam Doolittle ran to rotate through the clinic starting immediately.

"It's a temporary solution," Doc said, "but it will free you up to do what you need to do to get this thing off the ground. Besides, I think I just might enjoy playing the professor to these young upstarts."

Paul and his father had never been the demonstrative type. That was more Paul's doing than Doc's. Paul looked at his dad across the kitchen table and saw a man whose devotion and dedication to the science of healing was as undeniable as that of any doctor who had ever lived. "I'm really proud to be your son, Doc," he said, and his voice was husky with emotion.

They were both misty-eyed as they stood up and moved toward each other. "Let's get this thing built, son," Doc said as he pulled Paul hard against his chest and hugged him.

Long after Doc had gone upstairs to bed, Paul sat at the table making notes. He wished he knew how to get in touch with Rachel. He'd like to tell her about his father's surprising move. He'd like to hear the flood of ideas he knew would start to spew out of her like lava from a volcano. He'd like to see the delight in her expression, her eyes lighting up, her radiant smile. Realizing that, he knew that he had another reason for wanting to go to see her. He missed her. Rachel Duke had touched something deep inside him—something he had thought had died there in Kosovo.

"Sweetheart, you hear the reaction as well as I do," Todd Mayfield argued. "The audiences love it when you go a little rock and roll, a little funky. It's time we made some changes—the clothes, the arrangements."

"It's just not my style," Rachel protested as she eyed the costume Todd had thrown across the chair. The demo tape he was playing of a new arrangement to one of her songs pulsated in the small room. She had to raise her voice to be heard.

"Trust me, sugar. Your style is whatever you make it. Here at the start is where you want to set that, and believe me, those long skirts and buttoned-up shirts you wear are not going to win you any points with the audiences. You've got a way about you that could have 'em buying tickets by the thousands." He walked around her, sizing her up. "Show a little flash—the hair works, and you've got a great body. God gave you that body. Show it off a little."

"That's out of line," Rachel snapped.

"Okay, okay." Todd replied, holding his hands up to ward off her anger. "It's your call, of course. But if you've decided that you're happy playing country fairs and revival meetings, you don't need me. If you want to open for the Wilson Brothers, I expect you to pay attention or I'm outta here. Think it over."

As soon as she heard the door close behind him she snapped off the tape recorder and threw the offending costume across the room. Then she sat at her dressing table and buried her face in her hands.

"I thought my talent would be enough," she whispered. "God, what do I do now?"

There was a soft knock at the door.

"Come in." Rachel checked her face in the mirror and

turned to greet her visitor with a bright smile. "Hi, Pearl, what can I do for you?"

"I think the question is what I can maybe do for you, honey."

Rachel smiled at Ezra's wife. "You've been so good to me, Pearl. I don't know how I would have handled this tour without you along. It's..." She felt tears coming. "It's very different than what I expected."

"It's a lot to get used to, but it does get easier," Pearl assured her. She picked up the costume and hung it on the back of the door. "Todd Mayfield is a good manager. Unfortunately, he knows it, if you get my meaning. Over the years he's gotten pretty cocky about himself."

"He basically told me it was his way or the highway," Rachel replied.

"He does have a point, honey. Even the boys understand the drawing power of a well put-together body and a tight pair of jeans. The sad truth is that you gotta get their attention before you can expect them to really listen to what you want to tell 'em in your music."

"I want people to hear the music, not be looking at me. I'm just the messenger. It's the music that's important."

"But if they don't listen to the messenger..." Pearl let the sentence hang there for a minute.

"I cannot wear *that*," Rachel insisted, jerking her head in the direction of the spandex number Todd wanted her to wear. "Next thing you know, he'll be expecting me to show off my belly button."

"Maybe we can work together and come up with something Todd will accept. Do you want to try?"

* * *

Paul arrived at the theater just as Rachel was taking the stage. Pearl had left him a backstage pass and assured him that she would keep his arrival a surprise. He could not help but notice the difference between Rachel's appearance here and the one he had witnessed that first night in Nashville.

The stage was absolutely dark as an announcer's voice boomed her name. A band struck up a rocking introduction that he finally recognized as one of her songs. Colored lights played over the vast stage and settled on the woman who stood at center stage, a headset microphone hooked over her riotous red hair, which fanned out behind her as she moved from one side of the stage to the other.

She was dressed in jeans that fit her perfectly and a peasant-style blouse that shimmered with some kind of beading that caught the light. She was wearing boots with three-inch heels and she was belting out the song in rhythm with the band that backed her. He had to listen intently to the words to realize she was singing about God and His love and not some sexy rock song.

But she was good, playing the audience, flirting with them, going to the very edge of the stage and then backing up. At the end of the song she pumped one fist high in the air and brought it down for a final thundering chord on her guitar, then took deep bows and smiled broadly as the crowd shouted its approval.

"The changes are a start," he heard Todd Mayfield say to Pearl. "Good work, Pearl. We'll turn her into a hot property yet."

"I'm just trying to help her, Todd. She's got a big talent, and you know it. If I were you, I'd trust that and stop trying to make her into something she's not. Let her be the original she is, not some carbon copy of the latest teen queen."

Paul turned his attention to the performance. Rachel was talking, taking the time to catch her breath from that last energetic number. She perched on the edge of a high stool. The lights narrowed to a single spotlight on her. The band was silent. She strummed the guitar, tossed her hair and gave the introduction.

When she started to sing, there were a few rude calls from the audience, quickly shushed by others. By the time she hit the second verse, a pin dropping would have shattered the rapt silence. Paul peered at the audience and saw their faces focused on Rachel, listening to her, nodding in time to the music. A few were even crying. He looked at Rachel and wondered if she could see beyond the lights. He wanted her to know the effect she was having. He wanted her to understand that her ability to write and sing her songs was enough—more than enough. She didn't need any of the trappings Todd Mayfield was trying to lay on her.

The ballad was followed by two more heart-pumping, stage-strutting numbers, a guitar solo and a song designed to involve the audience. She ended with the song she had sung in Nashville but somehow it had been changed from the haunting ballad that had touched his heart to something he hardly recognized with a blues beat and a whining saxophone as backup.

"Thank y'all so very much," Rachel shouted above

the applause at the end of the song. "And now, it's my great privilege and pleasure to introduce the duo y'all came to see tonight—Ezra and Jonah Wilson—the Wilson Brothers."

The lights went to black, and Rachel ran to the side of the stage as the opening number for the Wilsons began. She didn't see Paul at first. As soon as she was offstage, the smile disappeared, and in its place he saw a frown and exhaustion as she reached for a towel and a bottle of water. She shuddered and draped the towel over her shoulders like a shawl. Todd Mayfield was at her side instantly.

"You were good, kid. By the time we get to Dallas, you'll be the name everybody's talking about. Trust me. The changes were great, and you carried them off like you were born to perform. Now, go get changed for the finale."

Paul watched as the agent moved on to berate the lighting technician for being a beat late in the opening. For a moment Rachel stood there in the shadows against the background of the brightly lit stage. She looked small and very much alone even as she was surrounded by people rushing around making sure the lights and sound were perfect for the Wilsons. Paul stepped forward.

"Hi, songbird."

She looked up in disbelief and then she hurled herself across the few feet that separated them and into his arms.

"Paul! How…what…why didn't you tell me you were coming?"

"And lose my one and only chance to be a groupie? Not on your life. Besides, I told you. I mean to collect on that date even if I have to follow you all the way to

Texas to do it." He held her and felt how thin she had gotten in just a couple of weeks. He felt something else. She was trembling. "Hey, what's this?"

She laughed it off. "It's nothing, really. I just get a chill after being out there under those lights. I can't believe you're here." She pushed herself away from him, and he could see that she was fighting to regain her composure.

"Did you see my act?" she asked as she wiped the sweat from her neck. "What did you think?"

"You've made some changes."

"Yeah, well, that's show biz. As Todd says, change or get left behind. What did you think?"

"The ballad was really nice," he said. "Can you see the audience or are the lights too bright?"

"I can see them, but sometimes I'm so scared by how many of them are out there that I have to admit, I try not to look."

"I wish you could see their faces when you sing that ballad. You move them to tears."

"Well, that's why the ballad is where it is in the program. It used to be my closer, but Todd says…"

If I hear Todd's name invoked one more time, I might have to shake her.

"Todd seems to have had a big influence."

"He knows his business. Pearl has been a big help, as well. I don't know what I would have done without her."

Come home, he thought. *Maybe you would have come home where you belong.* He wondered why he would think such a thing when all the while he had been quietly cheering for her success.

"Hey, I have to change for the finale. Come on with me to the dressing room. How is everybody?"

"Maggie sent cookies."

Rachel laughed, and it was almost her normal laugh. "God bless that sister of mine," she said and led the way to her dressing room. "I hope you've got 'em on you. Suddenly I'm famished."

"Now, that's the Rachel Duke I know," Paul said as he followed her through the narrow backstage area to her dressing room.

He waited in the small room while she stepped behind a curtained area and changed. "I like your hair," he said for no other reason than to open the conversation. "It's different."

"Pearl did it. She says that it's important for me to get it off my face a bit so the lights can pick up my features. She also has been a big help with my makeup."

"Sounds like she's taken you under her wing."

"How's Doc?"

"He's great." He wanted to tell her about the night in the kitchen, the night his father had encouraged him to find the funding and pursue his dream. The time didn't seem right.

The place was a madhouse with people popping in and out to bring her notes or let her know the time she had before she needed to be back onstage for the finale. "I thought maybe after the show you might have time to go somewhere for coffee."

"Sure." She emerged from the curtained area wearing white jeans and a fringed jacket left open over a hot pink tube top. She had piled her hair on top of her head in a haphazard manner. "I just can't believe you're here," she said again and smiled. "Oh, I get it. You have this fellow researcher here in Texas that you just had to see, right?"

"I'm crushed that you would think such a thing," Paul teased back, enjoying the repartee that felt like old times.

"Yeah. Sure," she said, and rolled her eyes. "Maggie got you to come here and check up on me, didn't she?" she asked as she touched up her makeup.

He noticed that as quickly as it had disappeared the edginess was back. "I came on my own, Rachel."

She paused in the motion of applying mascara and looked at him through the mirror. "That's really nice," she said softly.

Paul realized that they were both uneasy. Whether it was the place or what had happened to her since joining the tour he couldn't say. Maybe it was a little of both, but there was something plastic about her. The smile came too readily and was overly bright. She was too thin. The clothes were not in keeping with the woman he'd gotten to know. More to the point, the look and attitude did not seem to fit with her music.

"You sure have made some changes," he said and hoped she might take it as a compliment. She had to go back onstage. This was hardly the time to challenge her about what she had done to herself—or allowed Todd Mayfield to do to her—since leaving Smokey Forge.

"Five minutes," the stage manager called from outside the door.

Rachel pulled on one white high-heeled boot and searched frantically for its mate. Paul saw it sticking out from under a chair piled high with clothes and picked it up.

"Here, let me." He knelt and eased the boot onto her foot.

"You're making me feel like Cinderella," she teased, and this time her voice was less brittle and her smile was genuine.

He stood up. "Prince Charming, I'm not." He opened the door and stood aside to let her pass. "I'll watch from the wings."

The final number of the show was a medley of vintage gospel songs, a tribute to some of the groups who had made the music popular through the years. Paul could see that Rachel was perfectly at ease performing with the Wilsons. Part of that was no doubt because the two brothers were comfortable with their own fame and popularity. She was no threat to them. In fact, bringing her back onstage made them look even better. They were generous enough to foster new talent.

It was Todd's attitude that irritated Paul.

"You're watching a star in the making, my friend," the manager said, nudging Paul with his elbow. "If she listens to me I'll have her at the top of the charts and on her first solo road tour by next summer. Bet you didn't realize there was such a sexy body underneath there, did you, Doc?"

Paul entertained the thought of loosening several of the promoter's artificially whitened teeth.

"Look at 'em," Mayfield continued, calling Paul's attention to the audience. "The senior citizens all want to take her home and feed her, the women all want to be her, and the guys just *want* her. She's a triple threat.

"I thought it was her talent for songwriting and singing that was most important," Paul said fighting to keep his temper in check. "I thought that's why you wanted to represent her."

"Not in this market. It helps, of course, but the name of the game these days is sex appeal and how she'll play across audiences. I saw that she had what it took that first night in Nashville—until she passed out, of course. After that I did a little checking to be sure it was nothing serious and then gave her a call. The music—the voice—we can fix all that with enough amps and backup singers. Not everybody who comes to hear her is here for a religious experience—at least not the kind she sings about."

"So, you're planning to take her songs and make them more secular?"

"No need. Put the right beat behind those words and people hear what they want to hear. She can sing about loving God till the cows come home, and two-thirds of those folks out there will think she's singing about her lover. It's a real win-win situation."

The number ended, and Todd put his fingers to his teeth and whistled loud and long. "Way to go, honey," he shouted as Rachel came running to the side of the stage. "Now get back out there for an encore and sell it, sweetie."

Paul watched her trot back onto the stage, watched her face as the applause and cheers rained down on her. Did she know what Todd had in mind for her career? And if she knew, did she agree?

They ended up at an Italian place sharing a pizza. The Wilsons were there, along with several members of the band and crew. Paul was grateful that Todd Mayfield had stayed behind to settle up with the management of the theater and oversee the packing up of the instruments and sound equipment for the move to Dallas the following day.

"You look tired," Paul said lightly. They had taken a small booth away from the others so they could talk.

"It's just a normal letdown following a performance, and also knowing that we're moving again tomorrow." She smiled. "That's the one thing nobody can prepare you for. The constant moving from one place to another, never being anywhere long enough to see much of the town or meet the people other than those few who get backstage passes for the shows."

"You lost some weight."

She took another bite of her pizza. "The shows take a lot of energy. I'm fine."

He heard the edge to her voice and knew that she thought he was reprimanding her.

"I didn't mean anything by it," he said softly. "Just trying to make conversation."

She sighed and looked at him for a long moment. "What's happened? I mean, we always talked so easily, and now it's like…I mean I'm so glad you came, but…"

He nodded. "I know. It's pretty weird. Maybe it's just being out of our element."

She laughed. "I thought you were always out of your element, Dr. Paul."

He smiled. "Maybe we just need some time."

"How long can you stay?"

He saw her eyes fill with hope. *As long as you need*

me, he wanted to say. "I have to get back the day after tomorrow. I booked a flight out of Dallas."

"But you'll go to Dallas with us? You'll see the show there?"

"I'll go with you and watch the rehearsal tomorrow night, but I have to get the flight out at nine the next morning."

"Well, half is better than nothing," she said. She sat back and glanced over at the table where the Wilsons were having their supper. "They think you're my boyfriend," she said and gave him a mischievous grin. "Should we really give them something to talk about?"

He smiled at her. "It seems to me that you tried playing that game once before and it backfired on you."

Her laughter was wonderful to hear, and he began to relax. "Touché," she said.

"I've got something I want to tell you."

She leaned forward. "Tell me."

"Dad has encouraged me to go after the funding for the expansion of the clinic and setting up the mobile unit."

She sucked in her breath in surprise. "Oh, Paul, how wonderful. What changed his mind?"

"You played a big part in it. I don't know what you put in that coffee you had with him, but the man went into high gear. The other night he sits me down and tells me he's worked out this deal with a friend at a teaching hospital over in the next county to help with the patients at the clinic. The hospital will rotate residents through the clinic, freeing me up to devote full-time to this."

"For how long?"

"Forever. They seem to think it's a good deal for

their residents to experience that kind of setting. Dad seems pretty excited about it. He definitely likes the idea of being a teacher to these kids."

"And what about the program?"

"I have to find the money. Dad's already come up with a place, and we might be able to get the rent on that donated."

She leaned back again and drummed her palms on the table. "Well, isn't this something? You see, I've been kind of working on things from this end."

"I don't understand."

Her eyes sparkled. "Just wait," she said, and her voice was filled with genuine excitement. "Hey, Ezra, could you come over here for a minute?" The lanky singer pushed back from his table and ambled over to their booth.

"Boy, you folks sure did polish off that large pizza all by yourselves," Ezra commented. "Doc, did you ever see such a little bit of a thing eat like this one does?"

Rachel patted the seat beside her. "Ezra, remember me telling you about Paul's idea for a treatment program for kids from the mountains and from refugee camps overseas?"

"Sounds like a dandy idea, Doc," Ezra replied.

"Can we talk about the foundation?" Rachel prodded.

"Our tax guy told us we'd better find a way to start spending some of our money for good stuff or be prepared to hand big chunks over to the government taxman." Ezra grinned and took a long swallow of his soda. "Shoot, I figure they get their fair share. Why should I give 'em more if I can spend it on something that counts?"

"Like kids," Rachel broke in. "The Wilson family has a long history of helping needy children, and—"

"Well, now honey, we don't do anything special. But the Lord has blessed us a hundredfold, and we figure we ought to give back something. Who better to give back to than the young-uns who'll be our future?"

Paul was permitting himself to become cautiously excited. He wondered how much money the Wilsons could have earned singing gospel music.

"Paul is ready to start the program, Ezra—as soon as he gets the funding."

Ezra laughed. "Subtle, ain't she? How much do you figure on needing, son?"

"That's hard to say at this point. I mean, I've just begun to—"

"Do you figure two fifty would get you on your way?" Ezra asked.

He tried not to be disappointed. Every little bit would help—even two hundred and fifty dollars. "That's very kind of you, Ezra."

Ezra turned so that he was facing the table where the rest of the family was gathered. "Pearlie Mae, bring that bankbook I gave you to hold over here."

Pearl picked up her purse and came to the table. "Ezra, you know you complain about how much junk I carry around in this thing, but if you would just get yourself a safe deposit box somewhere or…" She rummaged through the large bag. "Here."

Ezra thumbed through the book. "Here it is. Get your phone out, Pearlie."

"They're not gonna be open now," she protested.

"Says twenty-four hours," Ezra replied. "Let's take 'em at their word."

Pearl handed him the cell phone, and he started punching in the toll-free number.

"Mr. Wilson," Paul protested, "this can wait. You can mail me the check."

Ezra held up a finger for silence. "Well, hi there, Amy. They got you working the graveyard shift, do they?" The singer chuckled, then continued. "This here is Ezra Wilson and the account number is eight one seven two six four nine zero. Then there's a dash and the number one eight four seven. Got that?"

"What a country," Pearl said in a stage whisper. "You can do your business twenty-four hours a day, seven days a week." She shook her head in wonder.

"That's it, Amy. Now here's what I need you to do, darlin'. Take two hundred fifty thousand and deposit it to the First National Bank of Smokey Forge, account of Doc McCoy—they'll know him there. Smokey Forge is just a wide spot in the road. Oh, you know it?"

Paul's mouth dropped open.

Ezra covered the receiver with his hand. "That'll be okay, won't it, Paul? Depositing to your daddy's account? I figure it'll simplify the paperwork."

Paul nodded.

Rachel leaned across the table. "You thought he was offering two hundred fifty," she whispered, "didn't you?"

Paul could do nothing more than nod as he kept his focus on Ezra.

"And you thought we small-town types were the bumpkins in this crowd." She giggled.

"I understand, Amy, honey. I'll be in Dallas tomorrow. You all got a branch bank there?" He nodded. "Well, then, I'll trust you to make sure they have the paperwork and I'll just drop by on my way into town and sign my John Henry on the dotted line. Will that be okay, then?"

He listened and grinned. "Why, yes, ma'am, I am *that* Ezra Wilson. My brother Jonah's right here. You want to talk to him?" He motioned for Jonah to come over and take the phone. "Say howdy to Amy," he instructed.

The Wilson brothers and Pearl moved away from the booth as Jonah and Ezra continued their conversation with the woman at the bank.

Paul looked at Rachel. "He just transferred a quarter of a million dollars to my dad's account."

Rachel grinned. "Yeah, when they get off the phone you might want to give Doc a call just so he doesn't have a heart attack when the bank calls him tomorrow morning."

"I don't know what to say."

Rachel covered his hand with hers. "Say that you'll stay in Smokey Forge doing the work God put you here to do."

Chapter Nine

It had been a long time since Paul had allowed himself the freedom of just having fun for a day. The bus trip to Dallas with Rachel and the Wilsons was a nonstop talk, song and eating fest.

Todd Mayfield saw them off the following morning, admonishing the driver to pay attention to the weather since thunderstorms were predicted. He would take a late morning flight to Dallas and meet them at the hotel.

"On our nickel," Paul heard Jonah mutter as they boarded the bus.

Ezra, Jonah and Rachel rehearsed the song she'd been writing for them to use as their finale. It would be introduced for the first time in Dallas. It was a song filled with hope and sung to a toe-tapping, upbeat melody.

> All the children
> Everywhere
> Give them hope and
> Loving care

> Teach them well, and
> Hold them near
> It's the children's song
> The world must hear

Pearl joined in on the chorus as the bus raced down the interstate.

> Children's voices
> Raised in song
> With God's own help
> We right all wrong.

Paul saw Rachel watching him as she repeated the chorus alone to the strum of only her guitar. Her eyes locked on his, and he knew that the song was about his plans for building a program to treat children.

> With God's own help
> We right all wrong.

Ezra and Jonah cheered the last chords and turned to each other to talk about harmonizing on the chorus. Rachel continued to look at Paul, waiting for his reaction.

"You wrote that for the kids?"

"I wrote it for you," she replied with a shy smile. "Ezra here thinks we might be able to release it on a CD and use the royalties to build the clinic."

Paul's eyes widened, and he turned his attention to Ezra and Jonah. "That's awfully generous."

"Aw, Doc, it's for the kids. Besides, the DJs eat this

sort of stuff up, so we know it'll get heavy air time. They play our stuff, we get better known and sell more of the other stuff," Ezra explained.

"Yeah, it's a win-win sit-u-a-tion, as ol' Todd likes to say," Jonah added.

Everyone laughed at Jonah's accurate imitation of the manager.

"I just want us to rethink that middle section a little," Ezra said, and Rachel and Jonah gave him their full attention.

"Paul, would you help me serve up some lunch here? I think they're almost done." Pearl nodded toward the trio of singers.

"My pleasure."

He and Pearl worked in easy silence against the background of the stops and starts of the revised music at the other end of the tour bus.

"She's very talented, isn't she, Pearl?" Paul asked as he spread mustard on bread for turkey sandwiches.

"She's a find, that one. Real star potential, and the best part is, she's as sweet as the day is long."

"What do you think of Mayfield? Is he right for her? To take her where she can go?"

Pearl shrugged. "Todd's one of the best. He has the contacts and the respect—those two things can make a huge difference." She glanced at Paul. "I wouldn't worry too much about Rachel, Doc. She may be sweet, but there's toughness to her. She knows what she wants, and she's got a strong faith to guide her. She'll be fine."

Paul smiled and added lettuce and tomato to the sandwiches. "When I knew her as a kid, I just thought of her as this cute kid with a fresh mouth on her."

"And what do you think of her today?"

Paul looked at Rachel, her eyes bright with excitement as she tried a new harmony Jonah had just suggested. "I think that I might be a little out of my league when it comes to Miss Rachel Duke," he said softly.

"Don't sell yourself short, Doc." Pearl loaded the sandwiches onto a platter and set them on the fold-down table. "Hey, music people, me and Doc are famished."

When they arrived at the theater where they would perform for the week in Dallas, Todd Mayfield was there to meet them.

"We've got problems." That was his greeting as they exited the bus into the drizzling rain. "Pearl, take Rachel there and get on over to the radio station for an interview—the driver's got the address. Ezra, the newspaper's entertainment and religion editors are inside waiting. Where the devil have you folks been?"

Paul found himself standing alone next to the suddenly empty bus as everyone scattered. He saw the limo drive off with Pearl and Rachel before he had a chance to say he'd come along. He felt out of his element. All these weeks since he'd come home, she'd been part of his world. Even the times they had spent at the farmhouse, more often than not their conversation had focused on him or medicine. She was always trying to find out more about him, prodding him to reveal little pieces of himself that he normally wouldn't share with anyone.

When had he asked about her—not her music or

her teaching—*her?* He had assumed that because he'd grown up with her sisters, he knew her. He had thought he knew how that upbringing would affect someone who had never really left the tiny town. He had thought his relationship with Rachel was one of doctor and patient with a little of the older, wiser, more sophisticated friend thrown in. When had that changed?

He thrust his hands into his coat pockets and walked away from the theater. He needed to think. He needed to put things into perspective. He needed to figure out how and when Rachel Duke had stopped being the cute little Duke kid and become a woman he might well be falling in love with.

Once they arrived in Dallas, it seemed to Rachel that there was no time to be with Paul. First, she was hurried off to the interview. When that was done, there were rehearsals and sound checks and lighting glitches to be corrected. Paul brought in Chinese food for all of them around seven, and then sat patiently in the empty theater while they rehearsed the finale again and again.

"Todd didn't like our arrangement," she said as Paul walked her the short distance to the hotel. She paused only a second before adding, "I really don't think he likes the song at all."

"It's a terrific song," Paul told her, and resisted adding that Todd Mayfield didn't know everything.

"You really like it?"

He'd never seen her like this, so dubious of her talent, so unsure of herself. "Now, you listen to me, Rachel

Duke. That is a remarkable song. Ezra and Jonah believe in it or they wouldn't, for one minute, let it be out there with their names on it."

"Well, that's true. But Todd says it's not right for the end of the show. He thinks we need to go out with something bigger."

"What does Ezra think?"

"Todd didn't talk to Ezra yet. He told me he's doing this for me—for my future. He says we need to think about showcasing me and that I should be what people remember as they leave the show."

"And what do you think?"

"I think it's more important that they remember the words of the song and that they spread God's message. That's why we're up there."

Paul let out a breath it felt as if he'd been holding far too long. "Well, I'm glad to hear you say that."

Rachel grew very quiet. "What is that supposed to mean?" she asked after several seconds, and her tone was filled with challenge. "You don't like Todd, do you?"

"Not a whole lot," Paul admitted.

"Well, he's not there to win popularity contests. He's there to help me get what I want."

"By turning you into something you're not?" Paul would have taken the words back if he could have.

"By turning me into a viable performer—one who can put people in the seats and get them to leave and head straight for the store to buy what they just heard me sing," she replied tersely.

Paul stopped just outside the hotel entrance. It was after midnight, and the street was deserted. He'd started this. Might as well take it all the way. "Are you listening to yourself, Rachel?" he argued.

She crossed her arms and glanced somewhere over his shoulder, refusing to make eye contact.

"You're letting this guy dress you up in three-inch heels and tight jeans and teach you to strut around like some rock star. I thought he was just changing the outside of you, but I'm really scared that he's beginning to work on the inside, as well."

"Meaning?"

"Meaning that Mayfield is turning you into somebody I hardly recognize, and I have to wonder if when you look in the mirror, you recognize yourself."

He saw in her eyes that he had finally hit the core of her emotions. She flinched as if he had struck her, and then her eyes hardened. "It's been a long day. I'm going inside."

"Not yet." He took her by the arm and started to walk down the street with her away from the entrance to the hotel.

"Paul, I'm tired. I'm not up for a walk, okay?"

"Just around the block. I just need ten minutes with you without Todd or any of the others around, okay?"

She sighed heavily but kept walking.

"Rachel, nobody wanted this more for you than I did. I saw that it was something so important to you, and I really hoped…"

"You don't think I've got what it takes to make it," she said flatly.

"I didn't say that. What I think is that this isn't right for you—something about it just doesn't work for you."

"It's one job—next month, I'll be with some other

group. God willing, one day *I'll* be the one out front with some other wannabe as *my* opening act."

"Is this really the life you want? Moving from town to town? Hours on a bus, arriving in town late at night and going straight to some hotel room that looks like the last one and the one that will come next week? You're a people person, Rachel, and…"

"I see thousands of people," she protested.

"Yeah. You're up there and they're out there and if you stretch you can touch a few fingertips during the finale. Don't you miss the real contact? The kids? The conversations?"

"We visit hospitals when we have a chance. We…"

"It's not the same."

"The same as what?" she demanded.

He struggled to find words. "Home," he said finally. "It's not the same as home."

To his surprise, she laughed. "You are hardly the one to lecture me about *home,* Paul McCoy."

"Well, then you'd better hold on to your hat, lady, because I'm not done."

"Oh, yes, you are," she replied, and strode away from him toward the entrance of the hotel.

He caught up to her, dogging her long strides. "You've always told me your music was about spreading the faith, about bringing people back to God. How can you do that if you let this guy lure you away from your own faith with the promise of big-time stardom?"

"He isn't doing that. God won't let that happen," she argued.

"Oh, really. Well, you might want to check in with

the Big Guy, because I don't think you've talked to Him in some time—not that I've heard, anyway."

"How dare you lecture me about religion? How dare you lecture me about anything when your own life is a shambles, or was the last time I looked."

"Things change," he said with a shrug and then looked at her directly. "People change, Rach. Some for the better and some not."

She didn't say anything, so he pushed his point.

"Look, I know what a jerk I was being when I first got back to Smokey Forge, but I've come to understand that I can make as much of a difference in and around Smokey Forge as I could anywhere else in the world. The difference is that I'm surrounded by people who care about me and believe in me. You can't buy that on the open market, Rachel, and you sure don't have to leave Smokey Forge to find it. You taught me that."

"I am the same person I was when I got on that bus four weeks ago," she said through clenched teeth in a voice that showed no emotion, just determination. "I have a job to do and it's hard and exhausting and I cannot please everyone all the time."

"All I'm asking you to do is make sure that *you're* happy with what's happening in your life, and the truth is, Rach, you seem pretty miserable."

They had come full circle and reached the entrance to the hotel. As soon as they were inside the brightly lit and busy lobby, she broke away from him and dashed across the lobby, catching an elevator just as the doors were closing. This time, Paul made no attempt to try to stop her.

* * *

Rachel closed her eyes and leaned her head against the smooth paneled wall of the elevator. Tears dampened her lashes, and as the elevator slowed at her floor, she dabbed at the tears with the back of her hand, just in case someone from the band or crew was in the hall.

She hated that she and Paul had argued, hated more that he had come so close to the truth. She didn't want him to think she couldn't handle things herself, but the fact was that Todd Mayfield *had* changed her in ways she didn't like. She had come to terms with it by deciding that it was all right to be one person onstage and somebody else in private, but lately, that person onstage had become who she was offstage, as well, and Paul was right—that was a person she barely recognized.

When she had walked off that stage the night before and seen Paul standing there, she had run to him as if he were a lifeline. It had surprised her how glad she was to see him, how much she had missed him even though she had only been gone a few weeks. Yet she still resisted sharing the details of her experience on the road with him. Why?

"God, he's my best friend. Why couldn't I talk to him? He did this really incredible thing—coming all this way just to see me, and what do I do?"

She felt none of her usual closeness to God. The room was completely void of any spirituality, but she plunged on.

"I ruin it. That's what I do," she continued. "What's the matter with me?"

She lay back on the bed and stared at the ceiling, waiting for guidance. The phone rang, and she grabbed it, hoping it would be Paul.

"Rachel? Todd. Now listen, kid, I'm not happy with the way this is shaping up—this finale number you wrote. I've got a couple of guys from the band down here in a meeting room just off the lobby. I want you down here so we can work this out tonight."

The minute he began talking, Rachel had automatically reached for her shoes and checked her hair in the dresser mirror. Something about the lifeless eyes in the face that looked back at her from that mirror made her stop.

"I've already undressed for bed, Todd. I—"

"Then redress and get down here."

"Not tonight. I'm tired, and I need some rest. We can fix the number at tomorrow's rehearsal."

"Maybe if you'd spent a little less time with your doctor friend—"

"Todd, I appreciate everything you've done for me and everything you're trying to do," Rachel said and meant it. "But you're pushing me beyond what I can do. I know myself, Todd, and I know I can perform up to your standards, but you've got to trust that a little and back off."

There was a long pause at the other end of the line. Clearly, Todd Mayfield was not used to being told to back off, no matter how sweetly the message was delivered.

"You're refusing to rehearse, then?"

"No. I'm doing what I need to do to deliver the very best possible performance tomorrow night. It's opening night, Todd. I want to be at my peak—I want my energy at an all-time high."

Again, a pause.

"Be at the theater no later than eight-thirty in the morning, understood?"

"Thanks, Todd."

"And no doctor hovering around, okay?"

"His flight leaves at nine. He'll be on his way to the airport."

"Good," Todd grumbled, and the line went dead.

As soon as she replaced the receiver, Rachel saw the message light blinking. She dialed into the system.

"Songbird, it's me." There was a pause and he cleared his throat. "Look, I was out of line tonight. I don't know where all that stuff came from. I just didn't want you to go to sleep thinking I didn't believe in you, because I do. You are an incredibly talented and gifted person—talented in your music, gifted in the person that you are…the friend that you are. I don't know what I would have done without your humor and your friendship these last months."

He paused as if expecting her to say something.

"Well, that's it. Get some sleep, Rachel. I'll see you before I head for the airport, okay?"

Rachel slowly replaced the receiver and switched off the bedside lamp.

"What if I didn't have Paul in my life?" she said aloud. "Or Maggie? Or Sara or Doc? I've been pushing them all away ever since I left on tour. What's wrong with me, God?"

The only answer she heard was the soft ding of the

elevator bell and hotel guests who had partied late giggling and shushing each other as they stumbled past her room.

The following morning, she dressed quickly and hurried down to the lobby. She didn't want to take a chance that she might miss Paul since he had to leave for the airport. Before their argument the night before, they had planned to meet for an early breakfast in the hotel coffee shop, but there was no sign of Paul.

Disappointed, she stopped at the front desk.

"Dr. McCoy checked out," the clerk informed her.

"I see." She started to walk away.

"Ms. Duke? This was left for you earlier. I was going to have it brought to your room, but since you're here…" The clerk handed her a blue vellum envelope.

"Thank you."

Absently she loosened the flap as she strolled toward the elevators.

Songbird,

It seems to me that we could use a little time by ourselves, and even though time is short, I hope you'll follow the directions in this note and join me for breakfast as planned—only in a slightly different locale.

Paul

The note directed her to take the elevator to the top floor of the hotel and then take the stairway just off the elevator to the roof. As she stepped into the bright morning sunlight, she saw a small round iron French café table with two chairs. The setting was bordered by flowering plants and afforded a breathtaking view of the Dallas skyline. Soft music played.

"If I can't get you back to the mountains," Paul said as he wrapped her in a beautiful shawl, "then I'll have to make do with the mountains at hand." He indicated the skyscrapers surrounding them and led her to the table.

"Paul, this is all so…the setting…the shawl…" She hugged the beautiful garment to herself. It was delicately woven of a fine woolen yarn. It was so lightweight and yet it warmed her, and it ended in a long fringe that drifted through her fingers like the rushing water of the millstream.

"It was Mom's. When you came offstage the other night, I thought the contrast of the drafty backstage and the hot lights onstage might give you a chill. When I called Dad about the money deposit from the Wilsons the other night, I asked him to overnight it so I could give it to you as a kind of a good luck gift for tonight."

"But last night you…"

He brushed aside further comment. "Last night I was being overbearing and overprotective. I understand that now. Last night was not about you or your gift, Rachel. It was about me."

He pulled out one of the chairs and waited for her to sit. There was a single long-stemmed rose on her plate. It was the color of the sunrise. She picked it up and savored its rich perfume.

"I picked that color because it matches your hair," he said with a shrug. He lifted silver servers to reveal eggs, croissants and fresh fruit.

"Paul, this is amazing," she squealed as she served herself.

"And *real* coffee," he announced, filling her cup with a flourish. "No green tea on this occasion."

"And what is the occasion?"

Paul sat opposite her and served himself. "The occasion is the morning of your biggest opening night yet, and that, my dear Ms. Duke, is cause enough for celebration." He lifted his coffee cup in a toast. "You are going to be a major star in whatever field you decide to enter. If that's rock or gospel or some combination of the two, you are going to be wonderful."

She felt the color rise to her cheeks. "Thank you, Paul. It means more to me than you can imagine to hear you say that."

He touched his cup to hers and took a swallow. "I just wish I could stay and be in the audience tonight—or maybe you'd rather see Dad there?" He grinned.

"It would be wonderful to see both of you there," she replied.

As they ate, they talked about mundane things—his flight, her rehearsal, the delicious food.

"What changed your mind, Paul?" she asked when the conversation had died and the plates were empty.

"I realized that in some ways I wasn't talking about you at all when I was warning you about people and difficult decisions."

"Who were you talking about?"

"Me."

She laughed. "That's ridiculous. You know exactly what you want."

"But not necessarily where to find it," he said softly. "It's because of you that I've found that. I guess I thought I was doing the same for you."

"But you did something far more important, Paul. I wouldn't be here today, ready to walk out on that stage tonight, if it hadn't been for you."

He smiled and covered her hand with his. "I guess we must be good for each other, huh?" He reached over and turned up the music. "Would you dance with me, Rachel?"

She tied the shawl around her shoulders and stood up. "I would be honored."

As they moved in time to the music, she saw the sun coming up behind the tall buildings and she felt its warmth. Paul tightened his hold on her as he twirled her around and around. They laughed out loud with delight, and she knew that the physical strength he used to keep her from falling as they danced across the rooftop was a symbol of the emotional strength she'd come to depend upon from him.

"Thank you for being my friend," she said softly when the dance ended, but he didn't let her go.

"Sounds like a song title," he teased, but his voice was unsteady, and he still had not released her.

She rested her head on his shoulder and felt his fingers stroking her hair. She wanted to stay there forever. She wanted everything and everyone to disappear except Paul and this magical moment.

"I have to go," he said finally. "Walk me downstairs to the cab?"

She nodded, retrieved the rose from the table and took his hand.

They didn't speak all the way down to the lobby, just held on to each other, their fingers entwined, their shoulders touching.

"Call me after the show," he said as the cabbie put his luggage in the trunk.

"It'll be late," she protested. "The time difference…"

He shushed her with a finger. "Dad and I will wait up. Call, okay?"

She nodded and ducked her head so he wouldn't see the tears. It was ridiculous to cry. He had come all this way, and she would be home in a couple of weeks. It wasn't as if she'd never see him again. But he already seemed so far away. All of the people who counted in her life seemed miles away.

Paul hooked one finger under her chin and raised her face to his. "Break a leg, songbird," he whispered as his lips brushed hers.

The kiss was brief, and yet in that instant she felt her life changing. She suddenly wanted to reach out, cling to him, beg him not to desert her in this hour of her need. Instead, she smiled and did a little buck-and-wing step, ending it with a bow.

As she had expected, he laughed. Then he got into the cab, and suddenly she was standing on the curb by herself. She looked across the street and saw the marquee of the theater. TONIGHT! The WILSON BROTHERS, Featuring Rachel Duke.

How many times had she dreamed of seeing those words, and yet she stood there staring at them as if they were written in a foreign language.

"There you are." Todd Mayfield's voice boomed as

he exited the hotel. "Where the devil have you been, girl? I've been calling your room for an hour."

"I had breakfast," she said softly.

"Must've been some breakfast. Never mind, come on, let's get this rehearsal going. We've got a lot of work to do before show time."

He strode across the street, and when Rachel didn't follow him at once, he stopped and looked back. "You coming or not?"

"Coming," she replied, but she took one last look down the deserted street where Paul's cab had gone.

"Rachel, what's the matter with you?" Todd barked the words impatiently.

She hurried to catch up with Todd. It was nerves and being with Paul, she told herself as she followed Todd down the narrow alley to the stage door.

As soon as the door slammed behind them and she found herself immersed in the sights and sounds of the theater, she smiled. It was another kind of homecoming, that was all. The people and places of Smokey Forge were one piece of her life. This was another. Surely, there was room for both.

She let the shawl slide off her shoulders and tied it around her hips as she strapped on her guitar and mounted the steps that led from the orchestra pit to the stage. Stagehands were preparing to cover the orchestra pit to allow for three additional rows of seating for the performance. The concert was sold out, and whether people were coming to see her or not, she was going to make sure they knew who she was by the time they left.

She half listened to Todd and Ezra debating the

staging of the number as she recalled something Paul had said at breakfast. They'd been talking about the rehab center.

"I've got to give it a shot," he'd told her earnestly. "I mean, look at you. It took real courage for you to go after your dream. You had no guarantees and yet you didn't let that stop you for a minute."

"I don't think it's the same thing," Rachel had replied.

"Yes, in a way it is. No guarantees and no regrets. Just go out there and give it your best shot. Isn't that what you've done?"

She couldn't deny what he was saying. "Yeah, I did."

"And it worked for you," Paul said, as if that were some assurance it might work for him, as well.

Rachel absently fingered the song she'd written for him as she thought about his wonderful plans—the good he was going to do.

"Thanks, God," she murmured. "Thanks for letting me be a small part of something so wonderful."

Chapter Ten

The plane was delayed. Paul could never figure out how bad weather in Denver affected a flight from Dallas to Nashville, but he had long ago decided that debating the point with airline personnel was a waste of time. He was in the airport café when his cell phone rang.

"Doc? It's Ezra Wilson."

Paul's hand tightened on the phone. "What can I do for you, Ezra?"

The man's voice shook at little as he delivered his news. "There's been an accident. Rachel's taken a bad fall."

"Where is she now?"

"We called the emergency squad, and they've taken her on to the hospital. Pearlie, which hospital was that?"

Paul heard Pearl in the background telling Ezra the name and location of the hospital. Immediately, he started walking toward the airport transit area and held up his hand for a cab even as he continued gathering information from Ezra.

"How did this happen?" he asked.

"Well, we was rehearsing the finale—you know, that nice piece she wrote for us all to do together. Todd had this idea that me and Jonah should start it real quiet like down front at the edge of the stage and then Rachel would come strolling down the stairs there in the background and join us."

"Okay," Paul said, willing the man to get to the point.

"Todd wanted her to just sort of appear up there like the angel she is, so she was climbing up from the back there. It's pretty steep, and it was dark. She was carrying her guitar and had tied some kind of shawl thing with long fringe around her waist."

If she had tripped on the shawl, Paul thought.

"Well, she made it to the top and then Todd had all the lights come on all of a sudden like. I don't think she expected that. She kind of took a little step back when the lights hit her, and that's when she fell."

Paul swallowed bile that threatened to choke him. "Are you telling me that she fell down the steps or off the back of the set?"

"Off the back."

Paul remembered the set from his view of it backstage at the previous stop. A fall from there was equivalent to a fall from a second-story window, at least.

"Was she conscious?"

"Yeah, enough to mumble your name again and again. Pearl still had your number from before when you needed the backstage pass, so we thought we ought to call. She's in a lot of pain, Paul."

"Who went with her to the emergency room?"

"Todd followed the ambulance."

Paul saw that the cabbie was turning off the expressway. "I'm almost there," he told Ezra. "I'll call you as soon as I know anything."

"We'll be waiting and praying, Doc," Ezra assured him.

Better pray I don't do something that puts Todd Mayfield in the emergency room, Paul thought grimly.

But when he reached the hospital and saw Todd Mayfield in the waiting room, he almost felt sorry for the man. Mayfield looked old and tired, and all of his usual bluster was gone. He'd been crying, but Paul was in no mood to offer comfort.

"Where is she?" he asked.

Mayfield nodded toward a curtained area down the hall. Paul nodded and went to the desk. He presented his credentials and asked the staff person to contact a doctor he knew who worked out of this hospital. Then he strode toward the curtained area.

The emergency team surrounded Rachel, hooking her to monitors, testing, probing, speaking to her in the loud tones medical teams used when the patient was dazed or floating in and out of consciousness.

"Rachel, can you wiggle your toes?" the doctor in charge asked. Paul kept his eyes riveted on her exposed toes.

Nothing.

"Okay, Rachel, we're going to get you ready to go upstairs, okay?"

Rachel moaned.

"I know it hurts. We're giving you something for the pain, Rachel. Just hang in there with us, okay?"

"Paul," she managed to say weakly.

"I'm here," Paul replied, stepping forward and grasping her hand. When the doctor in charge made a move to prevent him, Paul turned his attention to the team. "I'm Dr. Paul McCoy, Ms. Duke's friend and physician. What are you planning to do?"

The emergency room doctor motioned for Paul to follow him into the hall outside the curtained area.

"We need to get X rays before we can be sure," he began.

"You think it's a spinal injury?"

The young man nodded. "Maybe a broken back—too soon to know for sure whether the spinal cord is involved."

Paul's heart was in his throat. If the accident involved the spinal cord, Rachel could be paralyzed for life. Even if it didn't, there could be complications. Either way, she was facing a long and painful journey back to health.

"Are you a family member?" one of the women he'd met at the desk asked. "Because we really need to check on some insurance here."

"No," Paul replied, his eyes holding the gaze of the woman. "What we need to do is find out how badly she's hurt, whether or not she can be moved, who the best physician available is to do any surgery or treatment, and whether or not that beautiful young woman is ever going to walk again," Paul continued calmly. "*Then,* we'll talk all you want about insurance."

The woman looked stunned and glanced at the young doctor, who indicated with a nod that she should back off. "I'll handle this," he said quietly.

Paul relaxed slightly. He understood that professionally the woman was only doing her job, and the young doctor was trying to do his best, as well. "What's our next move?" he asked, turning his attention to the emergency-room physician.

It took most of the rest of the day, but by early evening they had a diagnosis and a plan of action. Rachel's neck was miraculously intact, but she had a dislocated vertebra. That was causing the paralysis in her lower body.

"We'll stabilize things and realign her spine by the insertion of a titanium rod," the surgeon told Paul as they studied the X rays together. "She's facing three or four hours in surgery, not to mention a long convalescence—and that's if she doesn't get pneumonia or some other complication along the way."

"And then?" Paul asked.

The surgeon shrugged. "I can't give you promises. My guess is that if she's willing to do the work, we can get her to the point where she can walk with a walker or maybe even a cane. The good news is that even though she has sustained a spinal cord injury, only the vertebrae are damaged. Since there is no direct damage to the cord itself, there is every likelihood that the paralysis will disappear once the bones are stabilized. Of course, from the look of these films, there will possibly be some level of permanent loss of function in the hips and legs."

That's not good enough, Paul wanted to say, and fully appreciated for the first time the impact a doctor's words could have on loved ones who were trying hard to understand what had happened and why.

As he walked down the hall toward Rachel's room,

he tried to find the words he would use to deliver the news. He imagined her questions. Could she go back on tour? Would she lose her big chance because she'd need to be away from performing for so long?

He thought about the way she had looked onstage— her long legs striding across the vast space as if she owned it all, her hair flying free behind her, her smile radiant and her eyes twinkling as she caught the eye of a fan and waved. Surely, they could do something to give her that again. Abruptly, Paul changed direction and headed for the waiting room. He wasn't ready to see her yet. She would see too much in his face.

By the time he got there, Ezra and Jonah and the others from the tour had joined Todd to wait. They all pressed forward when they saw Paul walk into the small room.

"You." Paul pointed to Todd. "I need a word."

The manager moved slowly toward Paul as the others stepped back inside the room.

"How is she, Doc?" The man's voice shook, and his eyes brimmed with fresh tears.

"She's strong and a fighter, which is a good thing since she's facing the fight of her life at the moment."

"Can I see her?"

"In time, and here's what you're going to tell her when you do see her. You're going to tell her that as soon as she's well enough, you'll be booking her for tours and engagements all over the country. She'll open for the best, and eventually they'll open for her. In the meantime, you want her to focus on her songwriting because you are going to set up a recording contract and get play time for her songs on every radio station in the country, understood?"

Todd nodded vigorously throughout Paul's instructions.

"And here's the kicker, Mayfield," Paul added. "You're going to mean every word of it. You're going to deliver and you're going to do it on the premise that Rachel Duke is a gospel singer—not a rock star. Do I make myself clear?"

"You blame me for what happened today?" Todd asked, his eyes widening with comprehension.

Paul looked the short stocky man up and down. "From the way this has shaken you up, I'd say it's more like you blame yourself and I'm offering you a way to ease that guilt." He brushed past the man and turned his attention to others, giving them the news and urging them to go forward with the evening's performance.

"Tell us how else we can help," Pearl said. "There must be more we can do."

"The best thing you can do for her right now is play the concert—sing her songs."

"And pray," Jonah added.

Paul stared at him for a long moment. "That, too," he said, and then left the room.

Later, after he had stopped by to see Rachel and reassure her that she was in good hands with Dr. Hogan, Paul called his father. Earlier they had spoken just long enough for Paul to alert Doc to what was happening and get his advice. Doc in turn had delivered the news to Maggie and Sara. Rachel's sisters were determined to catch the next flight to Dallas, and nothing Doc could say would stop them from doing so. Paul could tell that Doc wanted to come, as well.

"Somebody needs to stay there and hold down the fort," Paul said. "I'll call you the minute she's out of surgery."

Paul's colleague organized the best available surgical team, and the surgery was scheduled for the following morning. If all went well, they would be able to move Rachel to a hospital nearer to Smokey Forge in a few weeks.

"How's she holding up?" Doc asked when Paul called to update him on the plans.

"She's the same as always."

"Well, she's had quite a terrible shock, and it's not unusual for a patient to try to make everything as normal as possible," Doc replied.

"Maybe," Paul agreed, but he knew the emotional wounds had to run deep. What concerned him most was her unwillingness to talk about the accident. The nurses raved about her upbeat attitude and high tolerance for pain. Paul worried that she was pushing the physical and emotional pain inside. In his opinion, she needed to talk about it. She had to be frightened—as scared as he was, Rachel had to be terrified.

That evening he stopped by her room. She was dressed in a hospital gown that seemed way too large for her. Her hair had been pulled into a clip at the nape of her neck, but tendrils of it framed her face. Her skin was very white. Her eyes were shut.

"Rachel?" He called her name softly as he pulled a chair close to the bed.

Her eyes fluttered and opened. She gave him a quizzical smile and looked at him for a long moment as if trying to understand why he would be here at her bedside. He saw realization dawn for an instant, and then the mask was drawn.

"Did Dr. Hogan come by to explain what he plans to do tomorrow?"

She nodded.

"He's the best, Rach."

She smiled. "You doctors say that to all the patients," she said, and her voice was weak as if she was too tired to make more of an effort.

He moved the chair closer to the bed so she wouldn't have to strain to talk. "Well, we have to protect each other, you know."

"I'd rather go into this thing knowing you were holding that scalpel," she said.

"I'm not a surgeon, Rachel, but I'll be right there, okay?"

Again, the single nod. She closed her eyes.

"Maggie and Sara are on their way," he told her.

"Oh, they shouldn't," she said, her eyes open instantly and filled with concern. "The airfare on the spur of the moment must be so expensive, and who'll manage the school?"

"Rachel," he said sharply, and got the response he wanted. Her eyes were riveted on his face. "We need you to concentrate on *you*. We need you to fight, okay?" he said more gently. "I know it's the hardest thing you've ever had to do. But it's vital that you focus only on the surgery and getting well. You can't spend your time worrying about the rest of us, understand? We'll be fine as long as you are. Think about yourself, all right?"

She was quiet for a long moment. Her lips moved,

but no words came. She tossed her head impatiently as if rejecting several comments.

"I'm so scared," she whispered, and finally the tears he'd been waiting for, hoping for, came. They rolled down her cheeks, dampening her hair and the pillow, but she made no move to stem them. Instead she reached over and gently smoothed the lines of worry that creased his forehead. "You, too?" she asked.

Paul nodded, trying hard to suppress the emotion that threatened to overwhelm him. He couldn't let her see how frightened he was for her. That was totally unprofessional, and certainly the last thing she needed at the moment. How many times had he sighed in exasperation at family members who succumbed to their own emotions at the very moment when the patient needed their strength and reassurance the most?

"It's going to be fine, Paul," she said. "It'll all work out one way or another. We just have to get used to whatever comes. In time…"

He knew she was talking about God and the fact that in her view, He was in charge. Well, if He was in charge, where the devil had He been when she went tumbling off the back of that set? His anger at a God who would permit such chaos in the life of one as devoted as Rachel stopped his tears.

Not wanting her to see his anger at the God she clearly still needed to see her through this ordeal, he got up and went to the sink. He rinsed a washcloth in cold water and returned to gently wash away her tears. "I'd better go and let you get some rest," he said when the task was done. "You have a big day tomorrow."

"We have a big day," she said softly, and grasped his hand. "Could you get me my shawl? I think the nurses put my stuff in a bag in the closet there." She nodded toward the closet.

He retrieved the shawl he'd given her and covered her with it. "It smells like cedar," he said nervously as he straightened the edges, "because Mom always kept it in her cedar chest."

"It smells like home," Rachel replied softly, and pulled it closer to her face, fingering the fringe as she closed her eyes.

"Sleep well, songbird," Paul whispered, and bent to kiss her temple. He stood there a minute longer, watching her even breathing, knowing she was asleep.

Rachel had no idea what time it was when she woke. The room was very dark although a light shone from the hallway. Her heart was pounding, and she suddenly felt as if she couldn't breathe. She tried to get up, and then everything came crashing back.

Her legs didn't work, couldn't work because she was totally immobilized. The large wall clock showed just past three. Later this morning, they would operate. The doctors all assured her that because she was young and in excellent health, they expected things to go well, but she had noticed that they all stopped short of promising that she would walk on her own—much less appear onstage again. Even Paul stopped short of that.

She willed herself to take deep breaths and suddenly realized that what she was feeling was absolute terror. She had never felt more frightened, and for the first time in her life could find no inner strength to stem this panic. That frightened her even more.

"God, I'm so scared," she whispered into the darkness, grateful that at least the hospital rooms were all single-patient rooms. "I can't seem to understand any of this. Thank You for sending Paul back into my life again and again. I have come to rely on him so."

It was the worst sort of lie—she was lying to herself and to God. What she felt for Paul went well beyond relying on him as a doctor and friend.

"Okay, I love him," she whispered. "I know that probably wasn't part of the plan, but it's true, and I don't know what to do about it. Especially now. Oh, why has this happened? Why now?" She would not permit herself to wallow in self-pity and ask, "Why me?"

It was petty and selfish and it implied that her accident should have happened to someone other than herself. She refused to acknowledge that the shadowy concept of *why me* even floated through her thoughts in spite of her efforts to keep it at bay.

She waited. She stared at her lifeless legs. If only she had listened to Paul that night outside the hotel. If only she had admitted the truth of what he was saying to her and gone home with him. But her pride had stood in the way. Her stubborn determination to prove that she could make it on her own in a world bigger than the one her sisters had created for her had taken precedence over everything.

What if God had spoken through Paul and she had refused to listen? If she had gone home with Paul, perhaps they might have worked together on the clinic for the children. Perhaps in time he might have come to care for her as more than a friend.

"Perhaps," she said softly, but would not permit herself to imagine him loving her back. It was too late for that now. Even if there were some miracle that would make him love her, it would be tainted with the suspicion that in part his love grew out of pity, and she couldn't stand that. "Show me what You want me to do, God. I'm so confused and afraid."

She waited for the feelings that had always come to her in such times. The questions that would spring to mind and force her to think through her options and reach decisions. She wasn't necessarily expecting a sign, but there should be something. There had always been *something*.

She closed her eyes, and in the blackness the story of Jesus's anguished night in Gethsemane came to her. He had felt abandoned and alone. He had wondered why it was necessary to go to such extremes. She had no thought, of course, that her own outcome would be remotely similar to that of Jesus, but she suddenly understood that He must have suffered in a way she had never appreciated before. He must have been even more lonely and frightened than she was. Somehow He had found the courage to face what lay ahead. Somehow she must find her own courage and strength and do the same.

The longest night of her life passed, interrupted periodically by the arrival of the night nurse to take her vital signs. The longer she lay there waiting for morning, the more aware of her immobility she became. If she slept, her dreams were disturbing fantasies of life as an invalid, a cripple, her sisters waiting on her, the townspeople pitying her—day in and day out. She tried hard to summon the remnants of what Doc liked to call her spunk, and failed. All she felt was tired and scared. Every waking moment was a silent prayer. "Please, take this burden from me. Please…I don't think I can do this. Please…I'm not strong enough. Please."

They were preparing her for surgery when Maggie and Sara bustled into the room.

"We're her sisters," Maggie told the aide. "Hi, honey, we just saw Paul, and everything's going to be fine."

"Just fine," Sara chorused, and Rachel noticed how her middle sister stayed near the door as if she might at any moment need to make a quick escape.

"You didn't have to do this," Rachel said. "Come all the way down here. It must have cost a fortune."

Maggie's eyes widened. "Are you nuts? Of course, we had to come. Where else would we be?"

"What about the school?"

"The school can manage," Sara replied, and glanced at the wall clock. "They said they would take you up at eight. It's five after."

"That clock's not right," Rachel said. "Trust me, at three o'clock this morning, it was slow. Now it's fast. Go figure." She smiled to let them know she was kidding.

Maggie brightened immediately. "Well, it's good to see that you haven't lost that dry wit," she said with obvious relief.

No, just any feeling from the waist down, Rachel thought, but willed herself to maintain good spirits for the sake of her sisters. "You two look like you haven't slept."

"We had to take a red-eye, and of course, that meant we had to get up at three to dress and get to the airport," Sara replied, clearly glad to be able to discuss logistics.

"You could have skipped washing your hair and putting on makeup," Maggie reminded her. "I got in a whole extra hour of sleep that way." She winked at Rachel.

So, we're all doing the same thing for each other, for ourselves, Rachel thought. *Thank You, God, for bringing them here.* She squeezed Maggie's hand. "I'm glad you're here—both of you," she said louder, for the benefit of Sara, still stationed by the door.

"I see Paul," Sara said unsteadily and left the room.

"She's pretty emotional about this," Maggie reported. "Not that I'm not, mind you, but Sara is just plain scared."

"Tell me about it," Rachel replied with a wry smile.

"Oh, honey, what a stupid thing for me to say. I'm just chattering. Sara handles it by running away. I do it by saying stupid things." Throughout all of this she continued to stroke the back of Rachel's hand. "Paul says it's going to be fine," she added almost to herself.

"They all say that, Maggie, and we both know that whatever comes will come. If I'm meant to get better or if I'm not—that's not in our hands or the surgeon's."

"Here's Paul," Sara announced, sounding as if she were introducing a television talk show host.

"Hi, songbird. Ready to take a ride?"

Paul was accompanied by two aides who unlocked her bed and began the process of moving it into the hall and through the corridors to the operating room. Maggie and Sara hovered outside the room, then tried to keep up.

"We'll be right here," Maggie called when they gave up the chase. "Paul?"

"I'll let you know as soon as I know anything," he replied, and his face was set and tense as he kept pace with the rolling bed. He kept one hand on the side of the bed as if wanting to make sure it didn't get ahead of him.

Rachel reached over and clasped his fingers, which made him look at her in surprise. She was feeling groggy from the medicine they had already started through the intravenous drip into her arm. "It's going to be okay," she said and knew her words were slurring. "Really…"

The next thing she realized, she was struggling to come awake. It felt as if she were trying to come out from under a hundred heavy blankets. People were talking, and she picked up snippets of their conversation. Some of it was even directed at her.

"Rachel?"

A woman. Maybe a nurse.

"It's over, and you're in recovery."

"Rachel?"

A man.

"I'm just going to put this oxygen mask on you for a bit."

Don't! She was fighting hard to emerge from the blackness that seemed determined to pull her back. She didn't want anything more covering her, holding her down.

She heard the tearing sounds of Velcro and felt people doing things to her lower body, but she still couldn't feel her legs. In fact, she felt numb and weighted down all over.

"Rachel?"

The woman again.

"We're just putting these circulation pads on your legs, okay? You might feel them puffing up now and then, but that's to prevent blood clots, okay?"

Does it really matter whether it's okay with me or not?

"Rachel?"

A man's voice. Familiar. Concerned. *Paul.*

She struggled to open her eyes.

"It took a little longer than we planned, but it's over and it went well."

He was holding her hand, and she felt it slipping from his grasp. With a fierce effort she held on.

"I have to go tell the others," he said gently. "I'll see you back in your room. Dr. Hogan's here."

She felt herself falling back into oblivion, felt Paul's fingers sliding away again, and the panic she had felt the night before returned and brought her back to consciousness.

"Paul?"

"Right here." He took her hand again.

"Why don't I go talk to the family," she heard Dr. Hogan say. "I'll see you when you're more awake, Rachel," he added.

"Thank you," she croaked, and her mouth felt like cotton.

"Rachel, it's okay to sleep. You need to rest. I'm right here. I'm not going anywhere." Paul smoothed her hair from her face.

"Set that to music, Doc, and you might have a hit song," she said and smiled.

She had called him Doc, and yet he knew she hadn't mistaken him for his father. Maybe it meant that she was placing the same trust in him that she and dozens of others had placed in his father for years. If so, it felt good. It felt like something he could get used to—especially where Rachel was concerned.

Chapter Eleven

"Dad, I'm bringing Rachel home," Paul told Doc one night as they sat across the table from each other sharing a late supper. "It's been six weeks—she's not getting any better." His voice faltered as emotion overwhelmed him, and he bowed his head to keep it from his father.

Doc stood and put a comforting hand on Paul's shoulder. "The staph infection set her back quite a bit, son. You know that. It'll just take more time than you planned."

To say that Rachel's recovery had not gone as well as expected was an understatement. Following the euphoria they all shared at the apparent success of the operation, Rachel had developed an infection, requiring more surgery. Her surgeon had insisted on a four- to six-week recovery period with no physical therapy until he could be sure that she was completely out of the woods in terms of more infection or possible pneumonia.

The longer-than-anticipated recovery had left her weak and postponed the start of therapy to rebuild her muscles and strengthen her back. The truth of the matter was that the long recovery from the infection had caused her muscles to atrophy and set her even further back following the surgery. Paul had alternated between spending long weekends in Dallas and flying to Tennessee to work on setting up the mobile unit and expansion of the clinic during the week.

Frustrated with the lack of any real progress from one visit to the next, Paul decided Rachel might do better if she came home. He had sent Jan Stokes, the chief therapist he had hired to develop the program for the rehab center in Smokey Forge, down to Dallas to assess the situation with him.

"A lot of surgeons have doubts about the value of therapy in postsurgical patients," Jan told him. "The research that would prove efficacy is pretty sketchy, so it's not unusual that a surgeon would take a wait-and-see attitude."

"Can we move her safely?"

"That's up to the surgeons and the team there to decide."

"But would you move her?"

"Ordinarily, no, but given the circumstances…"

Paul had confided in Jan his concern that Rachel was becoming more emotionally fragile with each passing week. Her stubborn determination to maintain a positive outlook in the face of setback after setback worried Paul. He had only seen that eternally cheerful facade crack once.

It was the Wilsons who had seen to it that Rachel's entire family and Doc were flown to Dallas for the Christmas holiday when it became clear that Rachel would not be home as planned.

Ezra and Jonah had brought a huge fresh-cut long-needled pine tree to the hospital's private dining room for doctors—a space they had persuaded Dr. Hogan to let them take over for the evening. Pearl had provided the decorations as well as the food. Several members of the staff and other patients from Rachel's wing had been invited to the special trim-the-tree and caroling party— a party that would feature the famous Wilson Brothers to lead the carols and Doc as Santa Claus.

They had all worked together in secret to prepare the surprise for Rachel. When her nurse had wheeled her into the room on the pretense of meeting with Dr. Hogan before he took off for a couple of days, everyone had serenaded her with "We Wish You a Merry Christmas."

Only Paul had been concerned when Rachel started to cry. The others all found it a natural reaction to the surprise and the kind generosity of the Wilsons. Paul saw that beneath the polite smile and the tears, Rachel was not at all herself. Rachel was upset. He watched as she called upon some inner strength and threw herself into the festivities, but he saw that her eyes were dull and her smile was locked in place by two tense lines at the corners of her mouth. He knew at once that they had made a huge mistake in doing this.

She almost pulled it off until Ezra picked up her guitar and invited her to sing along with them the song she had written for their holiday concert tour. Rachel had stared at the guitar as if she'd never laid eyes on it before. At last, she took it, and Paul saw that the smile trembled unsteadily. She strummed her fingers across the strings, but the instrument was too heavy for her to support, and her efforts were awkward and clumsy.

Let it comfort her, Paul thought, unaware of the prayer he'd just conjured. *Let this be the instrument of her healing.*

To everyone's dismay, she burst into tears, thrust the guitar toward the nearest person, who happened to be Maggie, and rapidly wheeled herself toward the exit.

"I'll go," Paul had said quietly as the others looked on in stunned silence.

"It's just too much for her right now," he heard Maggie say as he hurried to catch up with Rachel.

She had cleared the automatic doors, which had swung shut behind her, leaving her alone in the empty hallway. When Paul came through the doors seconds later, he saw her shoulders heaving with sobs.

"It's okay," he said as he knelt next to her chair. "Everyone understands." He put his hand out to touch her, and she brushed it away.

"It's not okay, Paul," she replied angrily. "And *I* don't understand. I don't understand at all." She rolled herself a few feet farther down the hall, then stopped and sat there pounding the armrests of the chair with the flat of her palms. "I can't do this," she said, more to herself than him.

"You can," Paul assured her. "You're strong and you have more courage than anyone I know."

She answered that statement with a mirthless laugh that clearly indicated her disbelief, and refused to look at him.

"Hey, listen to me. We're going to get through this.

We're all here and we're all going to do everything we can to…"

She looked at him for the first time since leaving the room. Her face was wet with tears, and her eyes reflected the anguish of her deepest self. "That's just it. I have dragged all of you into this with me. What are you all doing here? What about the fact that Maggie and Sara and the twins have spent a fortune coming down here yet again? What about the fact that because of me Doc has shut down the clinic? What about the fact that the Wilsons are spending their precious holidays here with me instead of back home with their own family where they belong?"

"You're blaming yourself for what people want to do for you?" Paul was astounded. Then he understood for the first time. "You're blaming yourself for the accident," he stated flatly.

She jerked away from his touch. "I don't know who to blame," she shouted. "I just know this thing has happened to all those people in there as well as to me, and they don't deserve it."

"And you do?"

She stared at him and then turned away. "I don't want to talk about this."

"I do. Something has happened. Tell me what it is."

She looked at her hands for a very long time. "The doctors here are pretty sure I won't make a full recovery— I won't walk on my own again," she said softly.

Paul swallowed. Dr. Hogan and the others had told him the same thing. He had asked them to let him tell Rachel. "They told you that today?"

"Earlier this week." She gave another mirthless laugh. "It was my own fault. I just kept going on and on about the timeline I was developing for getting well, and poor Dr. Hogan got this expression on his face. You know, I think he's come to like me—to be okay with my kidding around with him. At first, he was so serious."

Of course, he likes you. The man is probably half in love with you. Who wouldn't be? You make everyone you meet feel as if they can move mountains.

"So he told you."

"He said he couldn't let me go on living on false hope. He said I was strong enough to face the truth and build a timeline on that."

The door behind them opened a little, letting the muted sounds of the party escape into the hall. "You two okay?" Pearl asked.

"Yeah," Paul replied. "We'll be right in."

"I can't go back in there," Rachel told him. "I hurt their feelings."

"Then go back in there and let them do what *they* need to do for you."

"Put on an act?"

"You were doing a good job of it when you first entered the room," he challenged her.

"I can't play or sing. I can't."

"I don't think that'll come up again tonight."

He saw her struggle with her natural tendency to do what was best for the people in the room behind her and what was obviously her wish to just be alone.

"Okay, if I go back inside, then after this, I want you to make up something that says they need to stay away.

I can't worry about them neglecting their own lives to hover over me."

He nodded. "Fair enough. No visitors for the month of January. How's that?"

"That means you, as well. You need to focus on getting the center going, and this business of being there during the week and running down here every weekend has to stop."

"No deal," he said flatly and folded his arms defiantly across his chest. "I'm not going to stop coming here, Rachel."

She frowned and then smiled. "All right, we'll compromise. Keep them home and you can come on the weekends. Do we have a deal?"

"We have a deal."

She sat very still for a long moment, then turned her chair so that she was facing the door to the dining room. "Okay," she said under her breath as if preparing herself for a race or Olympic event. She pushed herself toward the door.

He held the door for her and watched her enter the room. She smiled shyly and asked everyone to forgive her outburst. He saw the relief in their faces and knew that she had reassured them.

"What's wrong with this picture?" he mumbled to himself as Rachel accepted a gift from Pearl and made a great fuss over the wrapping. *She's taking care of everyone but herself,* he realized, and knew that agreeing to her terms was indeed the best way to get her to concentrate on herself instead of the others.

So he had gone every weekend and watched her fight

for every minute improvement. It had been six long weeks, and enough was enough. This weekend he would not come home without her.

Rachel leaned close to the window and watched as the plane circled the mountains—*her* mountains. Somewhere down there was Smokey Forge. Somewhere down there was home.

In the weeks since they'd made their deal for him to keep everyone away and stay away himself, she thought she had made real progress. Emotional progress—the physical side of things would come in time. She felt prepared to see her family again, to be with them and reestablish old routines.

She glanced over at Paul, his attention focused on putting away his laptop. For now, she was pretty sure she could actually be in the same room with Paul without fantasizing about what life might be like if he loved her. In the weekends they had spent together in Dallas at the hospital, she had worked hard at keeping things light between them. She thought she had convinced herself that being his friend was just as good as being the woman he would eventually love and build a future with.

Yet with each mile that brought them closer to landing, she knew that she was only fooling herself. She loved him, and maintaining a relationship based on simple friendship would be harder than learning to walk again.

"If you don't mind waiting until the others have deplaned," the attendant said as the crew prepared the cabin for landing, "I'll have a skycap assist you into your wheelchair."

Just like that, reality came crashing back. For a little while, she had felt normal again. Now, she had to face the truth and the future that came with it.

She used a wheelchair. She *needed* the wheelchair. In time she would become stronger and less dependent on the chair, graduating to a walker and perhaps—if things went really well—to a cane. The doctors had made it clear that such progress was not entirely out of the realm of possibility. Walking independently again, however, definitely was not an option in their minds. The aftereffects of the infection had been too severe.

She understood that she was fortunate. The doctors had told her that by all rights she should never have been able to walk at all. They were frankly amazed at her strength and determination. After meeting with Jan Stokes, they had also agreed that the program Paul was setting up for the children in Smokey Forge offered her the best equipment and professional help to achieve her goal.

"You okay?" Paul asked as the other passengers filed past them.

"Sure. It's good to be home." She laughed. "Frankly, it's good to be anywhere outside that hospital."

"I'll get your chair." He followed the last passenger off the plane, and Rachel collected her things. "God," she said softly as she bent to retrieve her bag from under the seat in front of her. "Even though I can't seem to feel You as close as usual, I know You are out there, and I need Your help more than ever. Please help me make this easier for them and give me the strength I'm going to need to get through the days and weeks to come."

"Ready, ma'am?"

The skycap and one of the airline attendants assisted her the short distance from her seat to the door of the plane. Each step was like running the hundred-yard dash. The pain was excruciating, and she had to concentrate so hard to make her legs do so little.

"Your chariot, Miss Duke."

Rachel looked up and saw Paul waiting with the wheelchair just outside the door to the plane.

"Thank you, kind sir," she replied as they all helped her into the chair.

"Your sisters await," he whispered as he pushed the chair up the jetway. "I'm afraid they insisted on coming." She knew he was teasing. There had never been a doubt that Maggie and Sara would be there.

"Just the two of them? Shucks, and I thought there would be a brass band at a minimum," she teased back.

As soon as they cleared the door and entered the terminal, Maggie and Sara rushed toward her. Rachel held out her arms to receive their hugs, and in that moment she knew that there were indeed many reasons it was good to be home at last.

"Look at you," Maggie said, bubbling excitedly. "You look fabulous. I like your hair that way."

Rachel touched her hair self-consciously. "One of the aides talked me into cutting it some and letting it be straight."

"Well, hallelujah," Sara added with a smile. "Ever since you were a kid, you've had this silky-straight hair and you kept trying to curl it. This is much better. It's you," she announced. "Paul, what do you think?"

"I think she could shave her head and she'd still be beautiful," he replied. "Can we go now or were you ladies planning on setting up housekeeping here in the airport?"

"The kids at school can't wait to see you," Maggie told Rachel as they all moved toward the exit. "They've planned a special assembly in your honor."

"I was thinking…" Rachel began.

"And wait till you see Paul's traveling clinic," Sara interrupted. "It is truly like a hospital on wheels."

Rachel looked over her shoulder at Paul, who was grinning with pleasure. When they were together on the weekends, he had shown her sketches and plans for the van and expansion of the clinic, getting her ideas, wanting her to be part of what she had inspired him to create. "I can't wait to see it all for myself," she said.

"You won't have to wait for long," Sara replied. "We drove it here today so you could see it first thing, and later—if you're up to it—we'll take a tour of the center."

"You are not going to believe the changes in the old hospital building," Maggie added. "Oh, honey, it's just so good to have you home."

The ride home flew by as her sisters talked over the top of each other, filling her in on the gossip and the happenings in Smokey Forge since she left. She relaxed and enjoyed it all. Family and friends—that was blessing enough for anyone, she thought as she listened to Maggie and Sara laughing at their own stories. She could rebuild her life. She could live with any residual disability, because other than her physical condition everything else was the same.

Paul drove through town, past the clinic and on to the

building that would house the center for the children. "We'll just drive by for now," he said. "Later I'll give you the full tour."

"It's amazing—just from the outside," Rachel said as he slowly drove around the perimeter of the building. "You've added that deck area—and oh, look at how it's all been opened up with the skylights."

"Your idea," he reminded her.

"But to actually see them…" She craned her neck to get a good view as he drove slowly past the clinic.

"When it's done we'll have a dedication, and the Wilsons have promised to come," Maggie told her. "Of course, there's lots of money to be raised before we can really get things going."

Rachel saw Paul cast Maggie a look in the rearview mirror, and Maggie suddenly was quiet.

"We're going to put up a plaque in honor of the Wilsons," Sara added, filling the gap.

"It's wonderful." Rachel sat back as Paul turned a corner and they started up the hill that led to the house. Rachel felt a twinge of nervousness as she turned her attention to the realities of being home again. The bedrooms of the house were all upstairs—her room was upstairs. Through all the trials and good times of her life, her room had been her refuge. How many hours had she spent lying on her stomach, staring out the window and planning her future? Now she supposed they had set up some makeshift arrangement downstairs, at least for now. She prepared herself.

"We've made a few changes at the house, as well," Paul said quietly as if reading her thoughts.

The first change was a temporary ramp off the gravel driveway that she could navigate to the porch. The second was a chairlift on the stairway inside.

"We thought you'd be most comfortable in your own room," Maggie told her. "It was Doc's idea."

"You went to so much trouble," Rachel replied, fingering the controls of the lift.

"Insurance can be a wonderful thing," Sara said as she began bustling around organizing the luggage Paul had unloaded from the van. "And it's a wonderful contraption for getting these suitcases upstairs," she added as she piled them onto the seat of the chair and pushed the button to send it up.

"Let's have something to drink," Maggie suggested and headed for the kitchen.

Rachel wheeled herself slowly through the house toward the kitchen. It all looked the same and yet different, and she realized that the difference was her vantage point. She was seeing everything from the perspective of the wheelchair.

"You okay?" Paul asked, coming alongside her. "Maybe you should rest. It's been quite a full day already."

He looked worried and a lot more like a mother hen than a doctor. She smiled at him.

"I'm fine," she assured him. "I've got lots of time to rest. I just want to be home and catch up on everything. Did you get the work finished for the center this week as planned? How close are you to opening?"

"The physical therapy area is done. Jan's been incredible in overseeing that."

"It was Paul's first priority," Maggie added as she

served them cold milk and gingerbread. "Can't imagine why."

"It's important that you be able to start your therapy as soon as possible," Sara explained to Rachel, unaware that she was stating the obvious. "Paul didn't want you having to travel to some specialty hospital for that."

"In addition to Jan, we've been able to hire another first-class therapist," Paul told her. "And after they saw the advantage of rotating interns through the clinic to help Dad, the university wants to use the center as a training ground for its physical therapy interns."

"Paul, that's wonderful. When do you start seeing patients for real?"

"First thing tomorrow," Maggie said before Paul could answer. "You're scheduled to be there at eight."

Rachel felt her smile falter. She knew Maggie meant well, but it was still hard to think of herself as a patient. "I'll be there," she said cheerfully and took a sip of her milk to buy some time to get her emotions under control. It was the one facet of her being that she felt she still did have control over and she was determined to make things as easy as possible for the people she loved.

As usual Paul seemed to see right through her. He reached over and covered her hand with his. "I would like you to come down and try out the equipment and the routine," he said. "If it's not right or if you and Jan don't hit it off, we'll make other arrangements, okay?"

"I'm sure everything will be just fine," she said, her sunny smile firmly in place. "And as long as I'm there I might as well put Jan through her paces."

"Heaven help the poor woman," Sara said, and rolled her eyes as they all shared in the laughter.

Paul had been watching her carefully ever since they had arrived at the airport. To all outward appearances, she was the same, but there was an edge to her. It was as if she were always on guard, watching herself, holding her emotions in tight check. He knew that her progress was not what she had hoped to achieve after all this time, even though she didn't say anything. She simply accepted the well-meaning compliments of others about how far she'd come with her usual grace and good humor.

He saw how sensitive she was to the wariness of others and how quick she was to put them at ease with a quip or a smile. That was the way she had always been. Still, something was missing. He studied her closely as Maggie bustled around the kitchen serving them. Sara stood off to one side, observing as usual. Everything was normal—except Rachel. She looked the same, and yet she was different.

He saw her reaction to Maggie's comment about her being the center's first patient and knew instantly what had changed. Her confidence was gone. That self-assurance that had been her trademark since childhood was absent. That thing he had first noticed about her— that she approached the world as if she had inside knowledge—was nowhere to be found in the person sipping milk and smiling at her sisters.

"I have another surprise for you," he told her later that evening as he sat on the side of her bed. She had finally admitted to being "a little tired" after the long day. Maggie and Sara had helped her get into bed and then insisted that Paul come upstairs to be sure that she was indeed all right.

"Another surprise? I don't think I can take much more. It's been a really full day."

She sounded polite and distant, as if she were talking to a stranger. He wanted to shake her and remind her, *This is me.* He had saved this news because he wanted to tell her when they were alone. He had imagined her face when she heard the news—the way it would light up—and he had selfishly wanted to have that moment for himself.

"Sami's coming here."

In that instant all the wonder he'd come to expect from her for even the most ordinary happenstance of life was reflected in the warm glow of her emerald eyes.

"Oh, Paul, how fabulous," she said as tears brimmed. "But, how?" She grabbed his hands and held them tight. Large tears plopped onto the backs of his hands. Her tears.

"Hey, this is *good* news," he reminded her.

She smiled. "I know. It's just that everything seems so laden with emotion for me these days." She shrugged and sniffed loudly. "I don't know. It all feels so strange— *I* feel strange. I feel like a stranger in my own body."

"It's your first day home, and so much has happened since you left," he reminded her. "I should have saved this news for tomorrow when you were less tired."

"No. Please, tell me about Sami," she urged, settling back into the pillows her sisters had insisted on piling onto the bed. "When do I get to meet him? How did you pull this off after all this time?"

"He arrived in the States three weeks ago, but he's been at Georgetown University having surgery. You two have a lot in common. Sami's going to need a lot of therapy now that he's had the surgery. I'm counting on you to help him through that."

"Who's with him now?"

"For now he's alone. His aunt has taken his two sisters and returned to their village. Sami refused to go back there."

"That's understandable. The memories must be horrible for him," Rachel said softly, then she realized the impact of what Paul had just said. "Do you mean that he's come all this way on his own?"

Paul smiled. "I told you he was resourceful. Somehow he was able to make the arrangements, probably by conning some of the relief workers to help him get where he needed to be."

"But the cost—the money…"

Paul looked away, and she noticed that his cheeks were flushed.

"You paid for this, didn't you?" she asked.

Paul nodded. "It's not nearly enough. I wish I could get them all out of there, but it's a start."

She reached for him, wrapping her arms tightly around his neck. "You are the dearest man," she whispered.

Having her hug him felt so right—like his own homecoming of sorts. "Well, Sami's first order of business is going to be to meet you," he said as she pulled away. "He's already made me promise that."

She smiled. "I'm looking forward to it." She leaned back against the pillows.

Paul stood. "Boy, some doctor I am. Here you are exhausted, and I'm rattling on and on when what you need most is to get to sleep." He bent and kissed her forehead as he clicked off the bedside lamp. "Welcome home, songbird."

Rachel was glad for the darkness that did not permit him to see how the nickname he had coined for her and that she had treasured suddenly seemed so foreign to the person she had become. After he left the room, she focused on Sami. As Paul had said, he was going to need a lot of support and understanding once he arrived, and that was one thing she could give him—one thing she could do for Paul.

Chapter Twelve

It was harder than Rachel had imagined keeping up the facade of cheery optimism with her sisters and well-meaning neighbors and friends who flooded her with cards, gifts and visits. Outwardly, she was determined to face the world as one who had faced the reality of her injuries and was getting on with her life in as normal a manner as possible. Inside, she was struggling to stay afloat amid the debris of her emotional and physical malaise.

She was surrounded by people who loved her, cared for her, and yet she had never felt more alone. To her chagrin, sometimes she had to fight to maintain an outward appearance of appreciation and gratitude for all their kindness. It frustrated her that she couldn't think of anything she might do to repay the kindness.

"I can do it," she snapped at Maggie one morning when her eldest sister insisted on helping her dress as if she were a two-year-old.

"I know," Maggie replied. "I just want…" Her voice

faltered, and she turned her attention to the bureau where she busied herself replacing a sweater Rachel had rejected.

Rachel realized that she had taken her frustrations out on her sisters more than once in the last several days. She pushed herself off the edge of the bed and, using the furniture as crutches, made her way to Maggie's side. "Don't mind me," she said, hugging Maggie, leaning on her. "I just got up on the wrong side of the bed this morning."

They shared a laugh, for it was true that in rearranging the room so that Rachel would have everything she needed at hand Maggie had moved the bed to the opposite wall.

"We could put it back the way it was," Maggie suggested.

No, we really can't, Rachel thought, and knew that she was no longer thinking about the arrangement of the furniture. She hugged Maggie once again. "It's fine. Something different," she assured her. *Like me.*

It was Paul who finally confronted her, and when he did, Rachel realized that the most upsetting thing about the way people had treated her was the way everyone tiptoed around her, afraid of upsetting her, afraid of saying or doing the wrong thing. Paul's anger came as a relief.

"What is your problem?" he asked one night when she had gone up to her room immediately after supper.

"I'm a little tired," she lied, knowing it would be hours before she slept.

"From what?"

His tone surprised her.

"What is that supposed to mean?" She didn't even try to keep the edge from her voice.

He sat in the rocker across from her bed. "It means that ever since you came home you've been hiding. Worse than that, you've been acting like an invalid. I know the infection and second surgery set you back a lot, but the time has come to get off your duff and work at getting stronger. You've given up."

"I have not," she declared.

"Really? When's the last time you came to the center?"

"Day before yesterday." She shot the words back and folded her arms defiantly across her chest.

He leaned back and pushed the rocker into motion with one foot. "I see. And the reason you weren't there yesterday or today or three days last week was because you just had so much to do?"

"I don't think sarcasm is necessary."

"I think it is if that's what it takes to get you to snap out it."

She pounded her legs with her fists. "I am not going to *snap out* of this…at least not completely. For an active person like me, that takes some adjustment," she said angrily. "And what would you know about it, anyway? The pain. The work that produces no results. What would any of you know about it? You're all whole—the picture of health."

He pantomimed playing a violin, knowing it would enrage her further. "Poor baby."

"I've tried the regimen your therapists have set for me. I know you've given them stuff to have me do based on your own research, your own consultations with your doctor buddies. Well, *you* try doing those exercises over and over. You try gritting your teeth against the pain. You try…."

He stood up and moved toward her. She shrank back against the pillows. "What have you done with Rachel, lady?" he growled angrily. "She was never a quitter. She was never one to let a little thing like adversity get the best of her. She looked at a situation and sized up what she needed to do and then she *did* it. Where is that woman?"

The look she gave him was so forlorn, so utterly without hope that it broke his heart. "I don't know," she whispered, her eyes wide with panic. "I'm trying to find her, but I feel so—" she faltered and swallowed hard "—alone."

She started to shake all over, and he gathered her into his arms and held her. "I'm here," he said again and again as she clung to him. "We're going to get through this. I promise you that."

Later, after she had promised to be at the center the following day and given in to the exhaustion of the outburst, he stood at the door of her room watching her sleep.

"God, where are You?" he whispered. "Now in her hour of need, where have You gone? If You really exist, why have You deserted the one person who has always put You first?"

No answers came. He hadn't really expected any.

Determined not to let Paul bear the burden of her physical and emotional rehabilitation, Rachel forced herself to get to the center early the following day. Jan Stokes, the lead therapist, was working with other patients, so Rachel wheeled herself to the hand weights and began some warm-up work.

As she lifted the weights, she watched the faces of the other patients. One was a teenage girl who had been in a car accident. Rachel saw the girl's fear as she tried each exercise. She understood that fear, understood the pain the girl was experiencing. She knew that subconsciously, the girl was thinking, "If it hurts this much, how could it be a good thing?"

She looked up and saw Paul watching her from the entrance to the therapy area. She nodded in greeting and turned her attention to the repetition of the hand weights. Out of the corner of her eye, she saw him cross the room. He paused to speak to Jan and the girl, offering some comment that made the girl laugh. Rachel saw in the girl's eyes that she was a little infatuated with Paul. It was normal.

"Hi." Paul bent next to Rachel's chair, placing himself at eye level with her. He smiled. "I'm glad you're here."

"You didn't give me a lot of options," she replied. Then she smiled at him. "You knew very well that I would be here after you practically accused me of being a coward last night."

He shrugged. "Whatever works. Why don't you try this one?" He handed her a heavier weight. "That one is way too easy for you. You're hardly exerting any effort."

"I thought Jan was the therapist," she reminded him.

"Yeah, but I'm your friend," he said softly. "And as such, I'm going to keep you honest to yourself." He kissed the top of her head as he stood up. "Got to get back to work. See you tonight?"

"Sure."

After Paul left, Rachel had her best session yet with Jan. When she finished, she was exhausted but exhilarated, a sharp contrast to her usual mood. Jan had kept her so entertained with stories of other patients and their excuses for not working at their therapy that she had hardly noticed the time and effort.

"You're making progress," Jan assured her as they sat together sipping orange juice. "They did excellent work with the surgery, and if we can keep building on that, you're going to be amazed at how quickly you are out of that chair for good."

Rachel recognized it for what it was—the halftime pep talk. She knew Jan believed in what she was saying, believed it was part of her job as a therapist to keep her patients thinking positively. The problem was that Rachel still had doubts. No, it was more than that. She had no faith in Jan's prediction. The truth was, she had no faith at all these days.

"I have to go," she said, forcing a smile for Jan's sake.

"See you tomorrow," Jan called after her.

Rachel noticed that it was not a question. She wheeled herself out of the room and down the hall.

"Oh, let me get that door for you, honey." An older woman who had obviously been bringing her grandson for an appointment retraced her steps to open the door for Rachel.

"Thank you."

"Oh, honey, you are entirely welcome."

Rachel saw the pity behind the smile, knew that the woman was probably thinking what a shame it was that she was so young and in that chair.

I don't need the chair all the time, she wanted to call out after the woman. *Most of the time, I can manage quite well with my walker, and it's not entirely out of the realm of possibility that one day soon I could actually walk with a cane and not need anything more.*

But the thought gave her little comfort. Walking with a cane was, in her mind, only a tiny step beyond needing the walker. She wanted to walk free again. She wanted to run. She wanted to skip and dance.

"I don't want pity," she whispered to herself, and gripped the arms of her chair as she fought to get her anger and despair under control.

At any other time, her attention would have been on the child. At any other time, she would have been touched by the older woman's concern. At any other time she would have engaged the woman in conversation, oblivious to her own condition as she focused on the woman's obvious worry about her precious grandchild. But she wasn't that person anymore.

"God, You have always been *in* my life, not Somebody I was waiting to meet in the hereafter," she said as she pushed herself determinedly down the hall toward the exit. "Where are You?" She paused to wait for the automatic doors to open. She looked out at the gray winter afternoon. "Where have You gone?" she whispered.

With a heavy sigh she pulled on her winter jacket, noticing in the process that the sweatshirt she had put on with no more thought than that it matched her jeans read, Expect a Miracle.

She let out a cynical bark of a laugh as she zipped the jacket closed over the words that seemed to mock her.

Paul had seen her leaving. His first instinct, as always, had been to go to her. She'd looked so bewildered as she wheeled herself out the automatic doors and down the ramp to where Maggie waited to take her home. Her thin shoulders had hunched with the effort of pushing the chair, or maybe it had been the effort of holding her spirit together. He had to do something.

They were all worried about her—Maggie, Sara, Doc. She was eternally cheerful and upbeat whenever they were all together. Maggie told him that with some rare exceptions, she maintained that facade even when she was alone with one or both of her sisters. Both sisters agreed that they would be far more comfortable with some cracks in that cheery armor.

"What are we to do?" Sara asked later that afternoon when Paul stopped by the school. "She's so stubborn and determined to take the burden off us by stuffing all of her feelings inside. Even Pastor Griffith hasn't been able to penetrate it. Why, when he stopped by the house the other day and prayed with us, I saw Rachel looking out the window."

"As opposed to?" Paul asked.

"Bowing her head, folding her hands, closing her eyes." Sara ticked off the list on her fingertips. "Rachel would never disrespect the Lord," she added.

"So, looking out the window was out of character?"

Sara released an exasperated sigh. "Yes, Paul, completely out of character."

Paul didn't find it particularly strange. He'd certainly been guilty of gazing out the window on many occasions. Then it hit him. He gazed out church windows or let his mind wander whenever the topic of religion was at hand because he had lost his faith years ago. Rachel was always either talking *about* God or, more likely, talking *to* God.

"Has she been to church since she got back home?" he asked Sara.

Sara shook her head sadly. "She always claims to be too tired or not feeling well. It's hard to argue with that, although, if you ask me—"

"Well, this week she's going," Paul interrupted, "even if I have to take her there myself."

On Sunday morning, Rachel was sitting by the living room window sipping a second cup of coffee when she saw Paul coming up the front walk. She blinked and looked again.

It wasn't that it was so odd to have him stop by. These days he seemed to spend every spare minute at the house. The thing was, this morning he was wearing a suit complete with a crisp white shirt and a tie, not to mention dress shoes. She could not remember ever seeing Paul in anything other than running shoes, and she certainly had never seen him wear a suit and tie.

"Maggie?" she called without taking her eyes off Paul. "Paul's here. I think something may have happened to Doc."

Maggie rushed into the room from the kitchen. "Why on earth would you think that?"

"He's wearing a suit and he looks serious," Rachel said.

"Paul always looks serious except when he's around you," Maggie said as she hurried to open the door. "Paul, it's freezing out there. Where's your topcoat?"

"I don't own one," he replied with a sheepish grin.

"I'll get you a cup of coffee." Maggie headed for the kitchen.

"You're not dressed," Paul observed as he came into the living room and sat down.

"You certainly are," Rachel replied as she wrapped her housecoat more tightly around her legs.

Maggie returned with the coffee. "I'll just be upstairs," she said, and escaped the charged atmosphere of the room.

"You should hurry. We don't want to be late," Paul observed as he sipped the coffee.

"For what?" Rachel eyed him with suspicion. His nonchalance did not fool her. In fact, it made her more certain that he—and possibly her sisters—were up to something.

"Church."

"Church?" It was a laughable idea. "You?"

"And you," he replied. "And Maggie and Sara and probably Doc and a host of others who make this a regular part of their Sunday routine."

"It's been a very long time since church was a part of your Sunday routine."

He shrugged. "I thought I'd give it another shot."

She turned away from him and stared out the window.

"Maybe you should give it a shot, as well," he suggested as if it didn't matter to him one way or another.

"You don't find God in church, Paul. You find Him in here." She touched the place where her heart beat. She heard him get up from the rocker and move closer.

"You know you don't want to miss this," he said softly, standing just behind her chair. "Think of it, Rachel—the surprised faces, the muffled whispers."

"Why are you doing this?"

He knelt next to her where she could see his face. "Because I think you aren't going because you know the first time will be hard. You know everyone will be looking at you, wondering about you, making up their own predictions about how you're *really* doing."

He had hit the nail on the head. Not returning to church had little to do with her sudden absence of faith. She had discovered that it was easy enough to fake piousness and pretend reverence. No, Rachel had avoided church as she had any public forum because she didn't think she could handle the looks of pity, the whispered comments about how she was so young and her future had been so bright.

"If I go with you," Paul continued, "then people won't know where to look first. They'll be so shocked to see me there that your presence will seem normal by comparison."

It was a gift. A wonderful gift from one friend to another. She understood that, and her heart filled with love for this gentle, kind man.

"Besides," he added with a grin, "it'll be fun. I mean, imagine Mrs. Spencer's face—and that's just for starters."

She couldn't stop the giggle that bubbled from somewhere deep inside. Maxine Spencer had made it clear that in her opinion Paul had besmirched—her exact word—his dear mother's memory by refusing to come back into the fold. Every time she saw Paul on the street or at some function, she gave him a look that left no doubt of her low opinion of him.

"She'll be beside herself," Rachel gasped through her giggles.

"And then, of course, there's the good reverend himself. He's been working so hard at this—"

"Now, that's just mean," she reprimanded him. "Pastor Griffith's heart is in the right place, and you know it."

"But even so, it's going to make his day, seeing me there."

She couldn't deny that.

"Come on, Rachel. Get dressed and come with me," he urged.

All of a sudden it was as if she could feel a weight lifting. "Okay," she said, and smiled. "Okay," she repeated with more conviction.

"Great." He stood up and fetched her walker for her. "Maggie," he shouted. "She's coming up."

He walked with her to the stairs and helped her settle herself on the elevator chair. "Going up," he announced as he pressed the controls to send her on her way.

"See you in a few minutes," she assured him, and she felt excited for the first time since the accident. She glanced down and saw Paul watching her ascend the stairs. She couldn't read his expression. There was something pensive about it and more. It was the more that she didn't understand.

Maggie helped her dress for church. As Rachel

brushed her hair, she caught a glimpse of the sweatshirt she'd been wearing a few days earlier. Was the miracle that Paul was actually going to go to church? Rachel smiled at her reflection and felt more lighthearted than she had in weeks. She'd give God one thing—getting Paul McCoy to darken the door of a church was certainly miracle material.

By the time they arrived at the church almost everyone was already inside. They could hear the strains of the organ as they entered the vestibule. Rachel had persuaded Maggie and the others to go on ahead and save seats for Paul and her.

"Ready?" Paul asked after he'd hung up her coat. She had insisted on using her walker rather than the chair.

She nodded and swallowed hard. It felt strange to be here in the church again, not because the church had changed, but because everything about her was different.

"That's my girl," he whispered as he pulled open the door to the sanctuary. He let her go ahead of him. "I'm right behind you," he told her as she took one tentative step.

She saw their faces first—the eyes widening as she made her way up the center aisle. Maggie and Sara had gone to the family's usual pew near the front. It seemed a very long distance to walk pushing the hated walker. She began to regret that she hadn't insisted on her chair, but Paul had reminded her that the chair would elicit even more pity than the walker. She pasted a bright smile on her face and moved forward.

Then, as Paul had predicted, she saw all eyes shift to him. She even heard a few gasps of surprise, and Maxine Spencer looked as if she might actually pass out. The fake smile blossomed into a real one as she realized that together they had pulled it off. Hardly anyone seemed to notice as she slid into the pew, but even Pastor Griffith's bushy eyebrows fluttered when Paul slid in next to her, folded his hands piously and gave his full attention to the minister's opening words.

"The psalmist records in Psalm Twenty-five, verse four, the following message." The preacher's voice boomed over the suddenly hushed congregation. "'Direct me in Your ways, Yahweh, and teach me Your paths.'"

Rachel leaned forward, her attention focused on the words. It was as if she had a great thirst and was looking for something to quench it.

"In Psalm Forty-three, verse five, the psalmist raises an important question. 'Why so downcast, why all these sighs?' he asks. 'Hope in God! I will praise Him still, my savior, my God.' Let us all rise and join in the singing of hymn number eighty-four."

It seemed to Rachel that Pastor Griffith looked directly at her as he quoted this last passage and then announced the first hymn. It was an old favorite that Rachel knew by heart. It was hard not to sing along.

As the organist played the introduction and the congregation stood, she felt Paul put his arm around her, helping her stand, giving her his strength to lean against as they shared the hymnal she held.

Paul sang, too, his voice tentative as he searched for the melody. Rachel sang by rote, her mind focused on the verse the preacher had just quoted. *Why so downcast, why all these sighs?*

Why, indeed. She looked around her and saw a

church filled with people who would count her as their friend or at the very least as their neighbor. She glanced to her left and saw Maggie, singing lustily, and Sara, more sedate, but nonetheless involved in the moment. She thought of her brothers off at college, sending her funny cards in Dallas and calling her now that she was home. She thought of the Wilsons and all they had done. She thought of Doc.

Most of all, she felt Paul's arm encircling her waist, felt his strength pouring into her, helping her stand without need of the walker for the duration of the hymn. *Why all these sighs?* She was truly blessed, surrounded by people she could count on to help her in times of need and to rejoice with her in times of celebration.

She felt a tear form at the corner of her eye, but it was not a tear of pain or despair. It was a tear of relief. If she was to recover her faith, she needed to listen, to pay attention to the world around her, to look beyond her own pain and see what was needed by others. As far as she could see there was no better place to start that process than here, in the third pew on the left on a wintry Sunday morning with her family and Paul at her side.

Paul felt her straighten, felt beneath his supporting hand the lengthening of her spine. He glanced at her and saw that she had entered wholeheartedly into the singing, where only seconds before her effort had been far less enthusiastic.

Maybe it was the way the light of the winter morning was spilling through the transom of the stained-glass window and spotlighting her glorious hair. Maybe it was the smile, the rapture in her gaze as she looked straight at the minister, but something had changed. She glowed, and the radiance came from within. He thought he had never seen her look more beautiful and he thought his heart would burst from loving her so deeply.

Thank You, he thought subconsciously as the last chords of the hymn died away. There was a general rustling of clothing and hymnbooks reshelved in racks on the backs of the pews as people settled into their seats. Paul was the last to sit, mostly because he was thunderstruck to realize that he had uttered a prayer. On top of that, it wasn't the first prayer he had spoken since Rachel's accident. In giving thanks he was acknowledging that his earlier prayers had been heard—and answered.

He barely heard the words of the sermon, was barely aware that twice more he stood with Rachel to sing God's praises. He was only aware of her, of the fact that something had changed for both of them by bringing her here. He felt for the first time since receiving that phone call in the airport that she was going to be all right.

The strains of the last hymn faded, and once more the minister stepped to the podium, holding out his hand in a gesture of blessing as he quoted one more verse.

"And the psalmist entreats us in Psalm Thirty-three, verse three, to 'Sing to him a new song, make sweet music for your cry of victory.' And let us say together, amen."

Paul glanced at Rachel and knew that the words were illustrative of what would happen in her life. Rachel would find that new song and she would triumph. For a moment he was afraid he might cry as he realized that.

He bowed his head and said amen, with the others, and perhaps for the first time in a decade, he meant it.

After church they were besieged by friends and neighbors who had not had a chance to see Rachel since her return from Dallas. All of them marveled over how well she looked, what progress she had made and how the doctors must be amazed at her recovery. Rachel received each compliment with a smile. She listened patiently as several people related tales of their own or a family member's illness or tragedy, and knew that in listening she was giving them something. One of the things that had upset her most about her accident was the constant need to receive the gifts of time and effort and caring from others and her seeming inability to give anything in return other than her gratitude. It didn't seem to be enough, and that had frustrated her.

"I understand now that it was an underlying cause of my anger," she told Paul later that afternoon as they sat together in the living room.

"I'm afraid I don't," Paul confessed.

"Don't you see? I kept trying to give back tit for tat—if you did something for me then I *had* to do something for you in return."

"Sounds rational."

"Life isn't all that rational, though. The fact is I achieve the same thing—in fact, I achieve more—by turning around and giving something of myself to someone who is more needy than I am. I take the kindness or the healing or the talent that you or Jan or Maggie share with me and I find my own version of that to give to someone else. Like when Sami gets here—I'll be helping him."

"But you give back to others all the time. You do that through just being you, through your teaching and your music."

She dismissed that idea with an impatient wave of her hand. "Making music is a lovely thing. It brings a moment of contentment or peace perhaps to some people at some particular moment. What I'm talking about is focus—a new song, as the psalm says. Maybe my calling is using my music to help others—not a big-time ministry, as I had once imagined, but in smaller doses."

Paul still looked puzzled.

Rachel grinned. "The truth is that I don't really entirely get it myself yet, but for the first time in weeks, I'm sure that I'm on the right track, Paul. I can feel His presence. What I need to do is think about my life in a new way. This accident happened for a reason, and what I need to do is figure out what it is that God intends for me to learn as a result."

"Just remember that sometimes God is a cruel teacher," Paul said, and held up his hands to forestall her protest. "I know what you think, but the fact is that an eighth of an inch in the way you fell and you could have ended up paralyzed for life."

"Oh, Paul, don't you see? That's just it—He made sure there was that eighth of an inch difference."

Chapter Thirteen

The boy was rail thin and missing one leg from the knee down, yet he walked along on his prosthesis with something close to a swagger. He had a mop of brown hair and enormous dark-chocolate-fudge-colored eyes that constantly scanned the room even as they seemed focused only on the person he was with. His smile came easily, and he had a distinctive deep throaty laugh that was not in keeping with a boy of his size. Rachel knew immediately that this had to be Sami.

"Rachel," Jan called to her from across the room. "Come and meet the newest member of our little community here."

As Rachel made her way slowly across the room using her walker for support, she saw Sami studying her, sizing her up. His gaze lingered on her legs and the walker.

"Sami, this is Rachel Duke. I believe the two of you have exchanged some letters," Jan said.

Rachel held out her hand. "It's great to meet you at last, Sami. Welcome to Smokey Forge."

"Why is it that you use the metal thing?" he asked.

"It's something I need until I can get a little stronger," Rachel explained.

"Can you play your guitar or do you need to sit down for that?"

"I…"

"Sami," Jan warned.

Sami's attention remained on Rachel. There was no malice in him. His attitude was simply one of open curiosity.

"I haven't really thought about it," Rachel admitted. "It's been a while since I played."

The dark eyes grew even larger. "But your accident was weeks ago. Dr. Paul told me himself. Does it hurt to play?" His English was perfect.

She knew he was asking about physical pain. "I've had other things on my mind," she answered lamely.

"Well, I cannot wait to resume my soccer career," he announced. "I will work every day as much as I can until I am once again able to score the goal."

Both Jan and Rachel worked hard to hide their smiles at his assumption that playing soccer was for him a career rather than a schoolyard activity. "Really?" Rachel said.

"Oh, yes. I met a doctor at the hospital where they did my surgery, and he said that it was most important for me to get an early start and practice. This is even though other doctors have said I will not play again. You had surgery, didn't you?"

"Yes, I did, Sami."

"And now you must work very hard to get back to your career, as well. We can do this together, don't you think?"

Rachel stared at him. He had been told—as she had—that his recovery would not be total. He had heard that and refused to accept it, at least until it could be proven. It occurred to her that the difference between her and Sami was that she had heard her doctors say she would never walk independently again and accepted it.

"Out of the mouths of babes," she said softly to herself, and saw that Sami was still waiting expectantly for her response to his challenge.

"We will work together, yes?"

Paul arrived before Rachel could form an answer. "I told you he was direct," he reminded her. "Well, Samir, my friend, have you managed to get everything reorganized around here?"

The boy laughed. "You are a kidder, Dr. Paul." He wagged one finger at Paul, but continued to smile. "Ms. Rachel Duke and I are becoming acquainted."

"And how is that going?" Paul looked at Rachel, then back to Sami.

"Quite well, would you not say so?"

"Very well," Rachel hastened to add.

"And now, if it will not displease you, Ms. Jan Stokes will begin my session. We have much work to do, yes?"

"Yes," Jan agreed with a laugh.

She walked to the opposite end of the room, and Sami followed her, swinging along jauntily on his crutches.

"He's incredible," Rachel said softly.

"He's determined, too. I wouldn't take that business about becoming a soccer star lightly. He's dead serious. He believes that that would be his ticket for staying in the States."

"I wouldn't think of belittling his dream," Rachel assured Paul.

"What about your dreams?" he asked as they watched Sami begin his workout with Jan.

"I told you—I'm rethinking them."

She saw the dismay in Paul's expression and laughed. "It's not a bad thing, Paul," she assured him. "I just need to figure things out now that I find myself in this new place in my life. Perhaps I'll talk to Sami. Clearly, he's very good at figuring things out."

"Well, all I know is that he made you smile, and that's good enough for me."

Rachel stayed much longer than usual at the center that day. At first she got caught up in observing Sami working through his session. After an hour of what Rachel knew had to be painful work, he took a break while Jan worked with another patient.

"How's it going?" Rachel asked. She knew that Sami had not seen her approach. He had been lost in his own thoughts and for the first time all morning his expression was pensive, even a little apprehensive.

"Fine. All right. Good."

The smile was firmly locked into place, but Rachel knew better than to believe the smile. She searched his eyes. "I was watching you. It's hard work."

He nodded and fought to keep up the cheerful facade.

"Does it hurt? Your leg, I mean."

"It's going to be okay," he assured her, but his voice trembled slightly.

"Sometimes my back hurts so much that I don't

think I can stand it one more minute, much less for a whole hour."

His eyes widened.

"Sometimes," she confided, lowering her voice to a confidential whisper, "I wish I could just stay in bed and never have to lift a weight or do another exercise."

She saw that he wanted to trust her, confide in her. She certainly wouldn't blame him if he decided against it. After all he'd been through, it was a miracle that he would let anybody come near him. He was used to being strong for his family. She understood that it would be hard to let down his guard.

"Sometimes I feel that way," he admitted, and his voice was barely audible, "but then…" He didn't seem to know how to finish the thought.

"It's okay, you know. It's really hard being strong all the time, being the one everybody depends on. Even grown-up people have to lay down their burden and rest every once in a while."

"Like Dr. Paul?"

"Sure."

"I always knew he'd send for me."

"He's thought about you every day since he left," Rachel assured him.

Sami nodded. "I just wish…"

"Say it, Sami. Tell me what you wish, and maybe we can find a way to make it happen."

"I worry about my sisters," he whispered. "My aunt is a good person, but she is not their mother and she is young herself and…"

"Let me talk to Dr. Paul and see what we can do."

Instantly his face was alive with excitement. "Really? You can do this?"

"I can talk to Paul. There are no promises beyond that. I know that you understand that, Sami."

He nodded. "I know," he replied in a tone resigned to the frustrating ways of the world. Then he smiled. "But Dr. Paul can do wonderful things."

Rachel smiled. "Yes, he can. Dr. Paul can indeed do wonderful things." She held out her arms to Sami, and he came to her.

Paul found them that way, holding on to each other, their whispered conversation making him wonder what these two might be plotting. Their laughter told him that it was probably something major.

"Well, you two have clearly hit it off," he said after Sami had left the room with Jan for a session of aquatic therapy.

"He is more wonderful than I imagined, Paul. We have to help him."

"We are helping him. He's here. He's had the surgery he needed and now he's getting the rehabilitation that will make him capable of things he couldn't even have dreamed of back there."

"He wants to bring his sisters here, and we have to see if we can make that happen."

Paul looked away.

"What is it?" Rachel's voice shook with anxiety. "Tell me they are all right. Please, don't say that something has happened to his sisters."

"They're fine. At least as far as I know. It has nothing

to do with his sisters. You have to understand that we can't bring every kid over here just because they need to get out of there." He sounded frustrated and edgy, and she realized that since she'd come home, they hadn't really talked as they had before the accident. She accepted her role in that. He'd been trying to keep her spirits up, and so, of course, would not tell her any bad news.

"Then what is it? Don't protect me, Paul. Tell me what's bothering you."

It was the last thing he had wanted to do, but he knew that he had to tell somebody. No, not just somebody. He wanted to tell Rachel.

"It's the funding for the center."

"What about it?"

"We used the donation from the Wilsons to outfit the van and update the heating and plumbing on the old hospital building. For this, we had to borrow." His hand swept the room, indicating the renovation and the expensive equipment. "And there's more to do if we're really going to build this into a workable program."

"You can't give up, Paul. This is your dream coming true."

"Expensive dream," he said wryly.

"What about grant money?"

"It'll come, but it takes time. Meanwhile, we have loans to pay with interest plus the day-to-day running of the program. It's possible that we may need to cut back on the services we planned to offer—at least until we can get the grant funding."

Rachel knew how hard it was to get grant funding. She'd watched Sara agonize over it often enough in trying to fund programs for the school. "Are you saying you might have to shut down?"

"No, we can do it, but we have to proceed within our means. We simply can't add bringing more kids out of Kosovo and other such places on top of everything else. As crass as it sounds, we may need to seek out some paying customers—some families who have insurance so we can get this place on its feet first."

"What about the kids like Henry and Sami and all the others? They're the reason you started this in the first place."

"That's pretty much the catch-22. We were in line for this one government grant, but then the program got cut. It was a five-year grant, and we were counting on it."

"Oh, Paul, I'm so sorry. What can I do?"

He handed her the walker that was always close at hand. "First, get well. I need you around to help me."

"And?"

He sobered. "And don't get Sami's hopes up about his sisters. There's no medical reason to bring them here that we know of, and right now I need to spend all my time just keeping this place running so Sami can stay here and get the help he needs."

"There must be something I can do," she insisted as he walked with her to the strength-building weight machines.

"You're doing it," he assured her when she had settled into place for the first exercise. "Just get well." He touched the tip of her nose and then waved to Sami and Jan as he left the room.

That night, Sami came to supper with Paul and Doc. He didn't even have to work at charming Maggie, and

Sara had him enrolled in the school almost as soon as he came through the door.

"I can be in your music lessons," he announced happily to Rachel at dinner. "I know your songs. Dr. Paul has played them for me in a…how do you say it? CD?"

Everyone else glanced nervously at Rachel. No one had dared raise the question of her music since the night of the Christmas party in Dallas. Doc cleared his throat.

"Well, now, son…"

"I think it would be a wonderful thing if you came into the school choir," Rachel said, focusing her attention on Sami but aware of the reactions of the others. "You don't have to know my songs to qualify. You just have to come to rehearsal on time."

"I can do that. I am very good at time." He held up his thin arm to show off a giant wristwatch.

Everyone laughed and relaxed a little.

"Are you saying you plan to return to teaching?" Paul asked her when the laughter had died.

It was Rachel's turn to laugh and put them all at ease once again. "Well, I would say it's about time I earned my keep around here, wouldn't you?"

Maggie started to cry, Sara became overly involved in clearing the table, and Paul just stared at her as if she had suddenly announced she was planning to try out for the Olympics.

Doc reacted as he had always reacted when life dealt him a pleasant surprise. "I think that's a real good idea, Rachel, honey. A *real* good idea." He reached over and covered her hand with both of his and squeezed to let her know how much she had touched them all.

"The children are going to be so happy," Maggie blubbered through her tears.

"This is a sad thing?" Sami whispered to Paul as he observed the gamut of emotions.

"No, a glad thing. Sometimes people—especially women—like to cry even when they're happy."

"Confusing," Sami muttered and frowned. "I can still be in the choir?"

"Definitely," Rachel assured him and put her arm around him. She noticed that he immediately curled into her embrace, becoming the little boy that he was for the first time since she'd met him. She felt him tremble and understood that the effort he made to convince everyone that he was in charge was even more exhausting for him than her emotional journey had been for her.

Watching them, Paul found himself thinking about what it might be like if he and Rachel were to marry and settle here in Smokey Forge. After all, even if she were to return to performing some day, it would be some time. Her rehabilitation was going well, but it would have to be accomplished in stages. Once she could give up the wheelchair and even the walker, there was still a great deal of work to be done.

He found himself playing the game he'd picked up from her—the what-if game. What if she could learn to love him instead of looking upon him as just a friend who used to have a thing for her sister? What if they could make a life together? Have children together? What if the way to help Sami and his sisters was to bring them all to live with him and Rachel?

Whoa, he thought. *You of all people have never been*

the settling down type and now you're thinking not only about a wife, but a ready-made family?

"Isn't that right, Paul?"

He looked blankly at Maggie, realizing that conversation had gone on while he'd been lost in thought.

"I'm sorry. I was…"

"Not listening," Maggie chided him in her best schoolmarm voice. "I was saying that I thought it would be a great welcome back for Rachel if the children performed a concert on the day she returns to teach."

Paul glanced at Rachel and saw that she was okay with this. "I think it's a very good idea," he told Maggie. "Can I come?"

"Of course," Sara told him. "And Doc, as well."

It was on that first day back at school that a plan for helping save the center first took form in Rachel's mind. Not that she had anticipated any such idea in this particular setting. Mostly, she was concentrating on not being overwhelmed by the excitement of the children at her return. They were all at the windows of their classroom when she arrived at the school, their faces pressed against the cold glass as they watched her wheel herself up the ramp that had always been there to accommodate any students or staff with disabilities. Rachel had never imagined that the ramp might be for her.

As she wheeled herself slowly toward the front entrance, she thought about all the times she'd used the ramp as a shortcut to her car in the parking lot or when she was late for a lesson. Those times she had run up or down the ramp never giving a thought to how it might be to navigate the ramp in a wheelchair or on crutches. She had never thought about the steepness of the slope of it until now.

Even later, as she sat in the front row of the school's small auditorium, it did not occur to her that later in the morning she would have an epiphany that would change her life forever. Her attention was on the children, the eighteen members of the school's choir. Maggie and Sara had impressed upon her how hard the children had worked on this and how important it was to them.

The children were dressed in their Sunday best and stood in three semi-straight lines on the low platform that served as a stage. One by one, they sang the songs she had taught them—spirituals, favorite hymns, songs she had learned in her own days in Bible school. Sara accompanied them at the piano, and Maggie directed.

As she listened, Rachel felt something happening inside her. There was a loosening of the tight knot that had occupied the center of her being ever since the accident. In truth, the knot had been there even before the accident. Throughout the tour she had felt it binding her, tightening its hold on her, changing her shape, her outlook. Even Paul had been unable to loosen it— although he had tried, and she loved him for his willingness to risk her anger to help her.

She turned her attention to the children. A choir of angels could not have made more beautiful music than those marvelous children did as they turned old standards into heavenly anthems. She recognized her own part in this concert. She had arranged the music in keys all the children could sing. She had taught them the simple harmonies. She had choreographed the hand motions they used. It was a wonderful performance and a fantastic welcome back to the school for Rachel. Listening to them, she understood that she had made some small difference in the lives of these children. Perhaps she could make a difference for others, as well. Somehow there had to be a way for her to help Paul get the money he needed to keep the program going and help those children who most needed its services.

At the end of the last number, Rachel clapped and cheered as the children took their bows. She saw Maggie and Sara exchange nervous looks, then Sara's mouth tightened. With a look of resolution, she turned to the piano and launched into the introduction to Rachel's song "This Little Child."

Before Maggie could react, the children in the choir had straightened and started to sway from side to side in rhythm to the music. Rachel felt her chest tighten. The blood rushed to her cheeks. She didn't know where to look or what to do. She had the greatest urge to flee but knew that she couldn't. She would have to get through this moment. Her sisters intended no harm. They only wanted to help, but as far as she'd come, she wasn't ready for this—not yet.

"This one, I also know," Sami shouted excitedly. He grabbed his crutches and rushed forward to join the other children, mounting with ease the two steps to the platform. Sara continued to play the introduction until he had found a place. In seconds he was leaning on his crutches and swaying with the others. The other children were startled at first, but then they closed ranks around him, including him in their circle as they turned their attention to Maggie.

Sara and Maggie exchanged looks and smiled broadly as Maggie gave the children the downbeat to begin the song. On the chorus Maggie turned and invited all those in attendance to join in, and the hall was filled with the joyous strains of Rachel's music. Rachel looked around and saw everyone singing—the children, their teachers and Paul standing by the door.

When the number was finished, there was a moment in which it seemed that every eye was on Rachel. Paul had not wanted to disturb the concert already in progress when he was finally able to get away from the center. He had watched her enjoy the children, her face luminous with delight. When he realized that Maggie and Sara intended to conclude with Rachel's song, he had resisted the urge to rush forward and protect Rachel from the pain of hearing her own music performed by others.

Then Sami had suddenly leaped up and joined the others, and Paul had thought that it would be enough to diffuse the moment. As Maggie turned and indicated that everyone should sing along, Paul saw Rachel turning in her chair, taking in the happy faces of the other students and teachers singing along. The expression on her face had been unreadable—a mixture of bewilderment and amazement. She turned slowly to face the stage as the song ended. Paul rushed forward and saw that she was crying.

The whispers spread through the audience as the children realized that she was sobbing. Sara and Maggie started toward Rachel, but Paul waved them off. He took the seat vacated by Sami and resisted the urge to pull her into his arms.

"Rachel?"

She motioned him away and buried her chin deeper into her chest as her shoulders shook with her crying.

Paul glanced helplessly toward the stage, looking to Maggie but finding instead that Sami was moving forward to take charge.

"It is not a sad thing," Sami announced, standing tall to talk into the microphone that Maggie had used to introduce each song. "People—especially the women—like to cry for happiness," he assured everyone. "This is happy even though it may seem sad. It is really quite confusing," he finished lamely and stepped back from the microphone.

Rachel was the first to start laughing. Her sobs gradually changed to giggles and then peals of laughter. When Paul saw that, he started to smile and then to laugh, as well. Then everyone was laughing, except for Sami, who looked a little bewildered but decided these crazy Americans must do things this way. Soon his deep foghorn laugh could be heard above the laughter of the others.

Sara struck up the chorus of Rachel's song, and everyone sang along. With Paul's help, Rachel stood and joined in on the chorus.

> And God was there
> And God could see
> This little child
> Was really me.

Paul didn't even care if he was off-key. He had never in his life felt more like singing. Rachel was filled with the pure pleasure of singing her own song again. Added to the commitment she had already made to return to teaching, Paul understood that he no longer needed to worry about Rachel Duke.

Not that he had ever doubted that she would find her way back. But he couldn't deny moments of skepticism. If Rachel, of all people, were to lose her way, then what possible hope could there be for the rest of them? It was Rachel he had come to count on to find the good in any adversity. In the absence of his own faith, he had come to depend upon the presence of hers to help him make it through the chaos of his own life. The fall and all its aftermath had left her reeling, and in her confusion, she had seemed ready to cast aside any facet of her life that seemed to have anything to do with the accident—including her beloved music. If she could regain her love of music and teaching, then he was sure that she would fully reclaim her faith.

He looked at her as they sang one last chorus. She moved in time to the music, joining the children in the hand choreography she had taught them. Her music not only touched others—after all these weeks it had finally touched her, as well.

"Welcome home," he whispered when the song ended and she hugged him.

She looked startled at first, and then he saw understanding dawn. "I don't know why I thought I needed to leave—there's far too much to be done here for me to even think of going anywhere else," she replied and hugged him again.

"I couldn't agree more," he whispered as he pulled her tightly into his embrace.

Chapter Fourteen

Rachel could hardly wait for her session with Jan to end so that she could talk to Paul. She had come up with an idea that just might work for raising the funds to bring more children to the center.

"You're really making progress," Jan told her, and she sounded impressed. This was no pep talk. This was genuine respect.

Rachel wiped her face and arms with a towel. These days she approached her therapy as if it were a good workout. She could see the results. She was able to do things that even a week earlier she could not have done. She was determined to make it all the way back. "I'm feeling a little stronger every day, and I owe so much to you."

"No. You owe it to yourself and your willingness to do the work in spite of the pain," Jan replied. "I have to tell you that when we first met, I was very worried about you. Some of my clients lose the will to do the work, especially those who—like you—know there's only so far you can go. Frankly, I would have pegged you as one of them."

Rachel laughed. "And you would have been right."

"What happened?"

"I realized that I had things to do and the best way to get them done was to get this business taken care of as quickly as possible so I could get on with my life. Putting it bluntly, I realized that I didn't want to give one more day to this than was necessary to achieve recovery." She pulled herself out of her wheelchair and made another trip up and down the stairs she had been unable to tackle two weeks earlier. "How much longer?" she asked Jan.

"Before your therapy is finished?"

"No, before I can graduate from the walker to a cane," Rachel replied, and saw Jan wrestle with an answer that was both honest and kind.

"I... Look, Rachel, there are circumstances—"

"Because I am going to make it all the way back, Jan, and I want it to be a surprise for my family and especially for Paul, okay?"

"We'll do the best we can," Jan assured her, but Rachel could see that she was skeptical.

"That's all I'm asking." She threw the towel over one shoulder and headed for the shower, ignoring the wheelchair as she half-carried her walker. "I'll see you tomorrow. I've got to make some calls and then get to class."

Paul was confused. He'd just had a call from Ezra Wilson, checking to see how things were going with the traveling van. They had talked for several minutes about the van, about Rachel and about the Wilsons, then Ezra had ended the call, saying, "We'll be looking forward to seeing you all next week, okay?" He'd hung up before Paul could ask what he was talking about. Clearly, Ezra thought that Paul knew.

"Dad? Are we planning to see Ezra and Jonah Wilson next week?"

"I'm not sure," Doc answered, "but it would sure be nice to have a chance to thank them in person for their generosity."

"Ezra seems to think we're getting together next week."

Doc shrugged. "Check with Rachel. Most likely, they've been in touch with her and she forgot to tell you."

More likely she had been in touch with the Wilsons and not mentioned it because she was up to something, Paul thought.

"I'm going by the center to pick up Rachel and take her home."

"Why don't you two go someplace nice for supper for a change? Someplace where you can talk without all of us around to interrupt?" Doc suggested.

Paul had gotten to know his father pretty well since returning to Smokey Forge. He certainly knew when the man was up to something. "What's going on?" he asked.

Doc handed him his jacket and pushed him toward the door. "Go ask Rachel."

At the center he found Rachel and Jan laughing together over some silly quiz in a magazine. Rachel had just finished showering, judging by the damp tendrils of hair that framed her face.

"Good session?" he asked.

"Great," Jan reported. "She's my star client." She helped Rachel put on her coat, and Paul noticed that Jan winked at Rachel in the process. Was everybody in on whatever it was that Rachel was planning?

"Ready to go?" he asked.

"Ready." She smiled at him.

Two could play this game, he thought as he helped her into the car and then started to drive away from town instead of toward the house.

"Where are we headed?" she asked.

"Dinner. I'm finally collecting on that date even if I have to kidnap you to do it."

"Paul, I'm really not dressed for a restaurant," she protested, indicating her sweatpants and running shoes. "Stop by the house and let me change."

"You're dressed perfectly for where we're going," he assured her. "How was school today?"

He kept her engaged in small talk until they reached the roadside diner on the outskirts of town that was known for its hamburgers and onion and chive fries.

"I'll be right back," he said, leaving the engine running as he hurried inside.

Rachel noticed that it had started to snow. Large flakes stuck to the windshield and flashed white in the headlights of the car.

"Here," Paul said, handing her a large paper bag that steamed with the delicious odor of hot food. He opened his door and got in, balancing two large milk shakes in the process. "I thought we'd have a picnic," he said, looking very proud of himself.

"In spite of the fact that it's February—not to mention that it's snowing?"

"Details." He placed the milk shakes in the cup holders and shifted the car into gear. "Ready?"

"Now where are we going?" she asked.

"Not far." He turned the car toward town, drove down the main street past the clinic and the rehab center, up the hill and past the school and on into the night. Along the way, he made small talk about his day at the clinic.

"Paul? The food is going to get cold."

"We're almost there," he assured her as he turned off the paved road onto the snow-covered gravel road that led to the mill.

Rachel smiled. "Oh," was all she said as she relaxed in the seat and enjoyed the rest of the ride. The mill was the perfect place to tell him about her idea.

Paul pulled the car close to the place where the water fell over a small dam. "Looks a lot different than it did when we first used to come here," he said as she took charge of unwrapping the food and putting straws in the milk-shake cups.

Rachel looked at the scene made light by the snow. "It's always been one of my favorite places. I wrote some of my best music here."

"Past tense?"

She smiled. "Okay, I wrote some of my best music *to date* here."

"Better." He took a bite of his burger. "I had a call from Ezra today."

"Really? What did he have to say?"

Paul took a long swallow of his milk shake. "Why

don't you tell me? Why is Ezra planning a trip here next week and why would he think I knew all about it?"

"Oh, that," Rachel said as she wrestled with opening one of the small packets of ketchup she found in the bottom of the bag.

"Let me do that," Paul said, taking it from her. "Talk to me, lady. What's going on?"

"Well, what if I were to tell you that Ezra and Jonah recorded my holiday song?"

"Without your permission?"

"No. They asked while I was in Dallas. I figured why not. I certainly was in no mood to record anything, much less a holiday song."

"Okay, so they recorded your song. What's that got to do with coming here?"

"Well, suppose they put out the CD with the understanding that all royalties come to the center?"

Paul forgot to swallow. "You're kidding."

"Nope. What if I told you that to date—after just six weeks—it's still climbing the charts?"

"That's good, right?"

"Well, so far it adds up to a year's worth of that grant you didn't get because the program was cut. Is that good?" She took a bite of her burger and gave him a wide-eyed look.

"It's incredible. Oh, Rachel, do you understand what this means?"

"There's more."

"There can't be—this is everything."

"Well, I talked to somebody else today." She paused a beat. "Todd Mayfield."

Paul's euphoric mood was instantly extinguished. "Todd? Why would you— I mean— Todd?"

"We had some business to discuss."

"Such as?"

"Well, I had been kind of mulling over this idea, and then after I talked to Ezra, I knew I was on the right track and…"

"What's the idea?" Paul settled back and waited.

Rachel moved to the edge of her seat, her eyes sparkling like the newly fallen snow. "What if we were to work together for the children?"

"Meaning?"

"What if I wrote songs and put together concerts with the kids and Todd got them recorded and got play time for them on all the major stations and the money went into some sort of foundation or fund and we could start to use that money to bring in the most serious cases from overseas, from wherever, and we could give the kids the rehabilitation they need and…"

"Slow down a minute. Are you saying you're going back onstage? Back on tour?" His emotions turned upside down. He should be happy. She had come back—all the way back, at least emotionally. Wasn't that what he had wanted for her? *No. I want her here. I want her to be my wife and sing in the church choir and teach little kids Bible school songs.*

"Well, yeah, in a way, I guess I am talking about performing again." She looked confused, as if that hadn't occurred to her until now.

"I think that's great, songbird."

"Really?"

"Really."

She leaned against the door and folded her arms across her chest. "Then why don't I believe you?"

"Really, I…"

"You don't think I can do this, do you? You don't think I can get back out there. Well, let me tell you something, Dr. McCoy, I—"

"Stop shouting at me. I'm not saying you *can't* do this or that you *shouldn't* do this—"

"Now, who's shouting?"

"I'm not shouting. I'm just saying that…" He paused, looking for a finish to that statement.

"What?" she shouted in complete frustration. "Spit it out."

He focused his attention straight ahead, looking at the falling snow instead of at her. Then he turned and said, "I love you. I don't want you to leave again."

The only sound for the next full minute was the water cascading over the boulders. They stared at each other. Her mouth was open, but no sound came out. He waited.

"Well?" he asked finally, his voice hoarse with fright at how she might react.

"Why?"

"Why?" He might have expected anything but that.

"Why do you love me?" She frowned.

"Are you serious? You are the most— You make me— Do you want all the classic movie lines or what?"

"I want a little honesty."

"A man tells you he's head over heels for you and—"

"You never said that."

"I'm saying it now."

"Oh." She looked as if all the air had suddenly gone out of her lungs.

"How do you feel about me?"

"I— That is, we—"

Paul grinned. "Not easy, is it?"

"We're off the subject."

"I don't think so. How we feel about each other seems to me to be very relevant to the subject of whether or not you go traipsing around the country making CDs and doing concert tours while I'm back here running the center, which is a lot more complex than helping Dad at the clinic, by the way." He gulped air and wondered how she was able to ramble on in those long, intense sentences of hers without pausing for a breath.

"I never said I was going back on tour, and I try very hard not to *traipse* anywhere."

"Now who's changing the subject? It's a simple question, Rachel," Paul said, cutting through the banter they were both using to get them past the shock of his declaration. "I love you. Do you have feelings for me?"

"Yes, but…"

He put his fingers against her lips. "All I heard was yes. I'm going to kiss you now, Rachel, okay?"

She nodded.

They leaned toward each other. Their lips met, clung for one long moment, then released on a mutual sigh. Their foreheads touched and their fingers entwined. They sat that way for a long moment.

"That was nice," she said finally.

He chuckled. "I thought so."

"What do we do now?"

"Well, why don't I calm down and let you tell me exactly what you have in mind?"

For the next couple of hours they talked through the details of her idea. The more she talked, the more excited he became. It might work, and the best part was, she could do it all from Smokey Forge.

Maggie was the first to take note of the shift in their relationship.

"Something's different," she announced to Rachel at breakfast a few days later. "Paul is here so often that he might as well move in."

"He's always been here," Rachel replied calmly.

Maggie studied her for a long moment. "*You're* different."

"Well, yeah. I can walk some without the walker and pretty soon I won't need that elevator chair to get upstairs."

"I'm not talking about physically." She strolled around Rachel.

"You're making me nervous, Mags."

"You're in love with him, aren't you?" Maggie started to grin. "And more to the point, he's finally owned up to being in love with you. Well, hallelujah. It's about time. Sara!"

Sara came rushing into the room. "What's happened? Has something happened to Rachel?" She glanced from Maggie to Rachel, who was calmly eating her cereal. "Well?" she asked, impatient at being interrupted.

"Rachel and Paul are in love."

"We knew that, Maggie. We've known it for weeks."

"Yes, but now *they* know it."

Sara started to smile. "Really?" She turned her attention to Rachel. "Really and truly?"

"She's not admitting anything," Maggie said. "She's probably afraid we're going to interfere."

"Ya think?" Rachel said, deliberately using the slang that the kids were so fond of tossing around at school.

"We do *not* interfere," Sara argued. "We simply want what's best for you."

Rachel got up from the table and put her dishes in the sink. "Well, I've found it in Paul," she told them. Then she grinned and held out her arms to them, inviting a group hug.

"When's the wedding?" Maggie asked.

"Whoa. We're not that far down this road yet. Let's don't try to rush this along."

"Does this mean that Paul intends to stay in Smokey Forge?" Sara asked.

"He has a practice here now—the center? The traveling health van?"

"You'll stay home, as well," Maggie said, and Rachel could see that it was something she had been hoping for but afraid to bring up.

"For now, we're both here," Rachel assured her.

Throughout the day she thought about the question Maggie had raised. *When was the wedding?* She couldn't deny that it had crossed her mind. Under most circumstances, it was a logical step for two people in love. But was it logical for Paul and her? Was it even possible given their disparate views of life and the work God had given them to do?

It was clear that even though Paul seemed to have

mellowed toward her faith in God, he had not embraced it for himself. He had not returned to church after that first Sunday, and while he accepted that her beliefs were a key to her recovery, he believed that it was the science of medicine and therapy that had brought her as far as she could come.

She had always thought that loving someone meant acceptance of the whole person, flaws and all. Trying to change another person would just destroy the relationship. On the other hand, helping a man find his way back to God might be the most loving thing she could ever do in her life, and if the relationship got sacrificed in the process, wasn't it worth it?

"No, God, it's not. Not this relationship, anyway," she argued as she worked out in her room, practicing walking without the aid of a walker or cane. "If he wants to marry, then I'm going to say yes, okay? You'll help me figure out the rest as we go along. No disrespect meant, but frankly bringing Paul back into the fold is really Your job, isn't it?" She glanced toward the ceiling and waited. "Okay, so I can be an instrument in that, but don't expect me to make it an ultimatum."

A few days later, Paul was driving past the school on his way home from yet another meeting when he noticed the kid on the field and the woman on the sidelines. The typical parent-child scene tugged at his heartstrings. As usual it made him think of Rachel. Everything made him think of her these days.

As he got closer to the field, he realized that there was something familiar about the boy and the woman, and yet what he was seeing was impossible. He pressed on the gas, urging the car into the nearest parking space so he could get a better look.

Sami was on the field, his crutches propped against a bench on the sideline next to where Rachel sat. The boy was working a soccer ball down the field toward the goal. Occasionally, he lost control of the ball but resolutely chased it down. Paul could hear Rachel's shouts of encouragement through the closed car window.

"You're almost there, Sami. Twenty yards," she shouted. "Ten."

Paul got out of his car and moved toward the field, his heart hammering as he watched the child he thought would never be able to play his favorite sport again move steadily toward the goal.

"That's it," Rachel yelled. "Come on. You can make it. Come on."

Paul glanced over and saw that she was standing, her body poised as if she were the one about to kick the goal. It took a moment to understand that she was standing without aid—no walker. No cane.

"You're there," she shouted. "The clock is running down. You have to make the winning goal. Five… four…three…"

Paul's attention swung to Sami. In amazement he watched as the boy sidekicked the ball straight into the net with his artificial leg. As the ball cleared the boundaries and caught the net, there was silence on the field, and then Sami and Rachel both exploded into cheers.

Still oblivious to his presence, they ran toward each other in an awkward hobbling manner but without aid.

They met and caught each other in a bear hug, their voices hoarse with shouts of victory.

Paul watched it all, knowing it was a moment he would replay for the rest of his life. Whenever he felt that life was unfair, that the world was narrow-minded and biased, that there was no God, he would remember this moment. There was no medical reason either of them should be capable of moving this freely. He blinked, wondering if he was just tired and hallucinating, but when he opened his eyes, there they were, standing unaided in the middle of the field reliving the moment. Impossible as it was for him to accept, there was no scientific explanation. Something greater than mere medicine had healed them both.

"Thank You," he whispered, and fell to his knees, unable to stay upright in the presence of such a miracle. "Thank You for this." He almost added that he would never again ask for anything more, but knew that would not be true. In the years to come there would be many times when he would need help beyond his abilities to manage the trials of life, and he would turn—as he had even when he was in deepest denial—to God for help.

"Paul?"

He looked up and saw Rachel and Sami standing next to him. They both looked frightened. "Are you okay?" Rachel asked, and when she saw his tear-streaked face, she knelt next to him.

"You can walk," he said.

"And I can play," Sami added proudly. "One day I will score the winning goal for real, right, Rach?"

"Right." She ruffled his hair.

"But how?" Paul asked.

Rachel grinned at Sami and together they unzipped their ski jackets to reveal matching sweatshirts that read, Expect a Miracle.

Chapter Fifteen

Rachel had been attending church regularly ever since the Sunday that Paul had baited her into going. She found what she had always found there—peace, solace and on this particular Sunday, cause for rejoicing. Sami was at her side. He was going to be all right, going to be able to play his beloved soccer. He was safe and whole and that was reason enough to praise God on this early March Sunday when the first hint of spring had flavored the morning breeze.

As she stood with the rest of the congregation for the opening hymn, she looked up to see Paul standing in the aisle waiting for her to make room for him. He gave her a sheepish grin as he took his place next to her, held one side of the hymnal and started to sing in his off-key baritone.

During the service, Rachel noticed that unlike the other Sunday, Paul concentrated on the minister's words. He read the congregational portion of the response reading with inflection and meaning. During the sermon, he sat slightly forward, his eyes riveted on Pastor Griffith as he listened to the message of the day.

Following the sermon there was quiet music for meditation followed by the announcements of church activities and meetings.

"Are there any further announcements?" Reverend Griffith asked, clearly expecting none.

"Yes." Paul raised his hand like one of the children in school and then stood.

"Well, Doctor, I…" Griffith faltered for words. "The floor is yours," he said finally.

Paul moved quickly up the aisle and faced the congregation. "When I was a boy, growing up in this church, there was a part of the service that was called Joys and Concerns."

Rachel saw people nodding throughout the congregation.

"People would come up here and talk about things that were happening in their life or to people they knew. Somebody was sick, somebody else had a new grandchild, that sort of thing."

The attention of every person in the church was focused on Paul.

"Well, the other day, I experienced one of the most joyous days of my life and pushing my luck—as most of you know I'm famous for doing—I'm going to try for a second such day right now."

Soft chuckles rippled through the pews as people whispered the explanation to others that Paul had always been something of a rebel—someone who marched to his own drummer. Rachel saw that for the most part people were very glad he had decided to do that again. They leaned toward him, their faces curious as they waited for whatever he might tell them.

Rachel assumed he was about to announce some major news about the clinic project. She looked at Sami and then at Paul.

"I would like to ask Ms. Rachel Duke to join me up here," he said quietly, his eyes on Rachel.

She reached for her cane, but Paul moved quickly down the aisle and took it from her. "You don't need this, remember?" he said softly as he hooked the curved handle of the cane over the end of the pew and offered her his hand instead.

Rachel stood as she accepted his hand and together they started down the aisle toward the pulpit. It was only when she heard the gasps of surprise and Maggie's muffled shout of rejoicing that she realized that Paul had released her hand and she was walking unaided.

"As I mentioned," Paul said when they had reached the front of the church and turned to face everyone, "I have already had a reason to rejoice this week." He told the story of seeing Rachel and Sami on the soccer field. "My good friends and neighbors, I need for you to understand and appreciate that there is no medical reason in the world why this happened. Rachel and Sami have both received the very best that medicine has to offer. Even so, they were not expected to ever be able to achieve what I witnessed this week on that soccer field and what you have just seen this morning."

The members of the congregation burst into spontaneous applause. People stood and cheered and whistled through their teeth. Paul motioned for them to be seated. Rachel could not imagine what was coming next.

"I told you that I hoped to recreate the joy I felt on that soccer field a few days ago. So here goes." He fumbled in his jacket pocket for a minute and then knelt on one knee. "Rachel Duke, you have changed my life. You have taught me courage and conviction and tenacity. Most of all, you have reminded me that we are not in this alone. You have brought me home. I love you with all my heart." He opened the stiff-hinged lid of the tiny blue jeweler's box. "Will you marry me?"

No one heard Rachel's reply, but when she flung herself into Paul's arms, they knew the answer was yes, and for the second time that morning, they stood as one and cheered.

"And let us all say together—amen," Pastor Griffith announced in the voice he used every Sunday for the benediction.

"Amen," the congregation replied, and it was Sami's foghorn voice that could be heard above everyone else's.

From the minute church ended, Rachel found herself in a whirlwind.

"There's so much to do," Sara announced immediately following the service.

"Well, it would be nice to start with a date," Maggie said, turning her attention to Rachel and Paul.

"The sooner the better." Paul looked at Rachel as if having gotten her agreement to marry him, he was ready to begin their life together immediately.

"How about April? I've always loved spring here in the mountains." Rachel looked to Paul for agreement.

"It could rain," Sara warned.

"Or not," Rachel replied dreamily. "An outdoor wedding up at the house with everyone gathered like a big old-fashioned reunion or picnic. I think Mom and Dad would like that," she added as if she fully expected her parents to be there.

"All right, April it is," Sara agreed with a sigh. "At least that gives us some time—a little more than a year should give us plenty of time to…"

Paul and Rachel stared at her openmouthed.

"Not *next* April, Sara," Rachel corrected her. "*This* April."

Both Maggie and Sara looked startled. "That's less than a month away, honey," Maggie reminded her gently.

"I know, but the time will go quickly," Rachel assured Paul.

"Oh, my stars," Sara moaned. "Well, I'm going to talk to Pastor Griffith right now and check his calendar." She hurried away.

"I'd better see if Mabel Woodward can get the bridesmaids' dresses done in time," Maggie said as she hurried off in the opposite direction.

Paul and Rachel were alone for the first time all morning. "You are incredible," she told him. "What if I had said no?"

He shrugged and grinned. "Then I would have been pretty embarrassed. Even if you had said no I would have spent as long as it took to convince you. After all, I know you love me."

"Pretty cocky, aren't you?"

"And why not? The most beautiful, incredible woman in Smokey Forge just agreed to marry me. Life is good, lady."

"Where should we go on our honeymoon?" Paul asked later that night. They had escaped to the front porch swing, unable to take another minute of Maggie's and Sara's making minutely detailed lists for the wedding and reception.

Rachel pulled the blanket they'd wrapped around their shoulders closer. "How about Kosovo?"

Paul laughed. "Oh, yeah, now that's really romantic."

"I'm serious. What if we went there and got Sami's sisters out?"

He was quiet for a long moment, but she knew him well enough by now to understand that he was actually considering the possibility.

"We'd have to have a very good reason."

"How about adoption?" she asked.

"You mean someone here adopting them?"

"I was thinking maybe we would adopt them—and Sami, too, of course." She turned her head and looked at him. "Could you handle a wife plus a ready-made family?"

"You don't have to do this, Rachel. We'll find a way to get them out."

"I want to do it—if you agree. I've been so blessed in my life, and think of the family we would be giving them. Maggie and Sara, not to mention Doc. Can you see him as a grandfather? He'd be absolutely wonderful."

"Maybe C.R. and Emma would agree to be godparents," Paul added, catching her excitement. "Do you really think I could be a good father?"

"I think you would be a wonderful father. You've already proven that with Sami. He adores you."

Paul grinned. "I'm kind of partial to the little guy myself."

"So we honeymoon in Kosovo?"

"Sounds like a plan. I'll start making the arrangements."

They were quiet for a moment, rocking gently in the porch swing as they enjoyed the night with its promise of spring.

"Maggie and Sara are going to have a bird when we tell them this," Rachel said with a giggle.

"Let's go tell them now. I can't wait to see their faces. I'll be very casual—'Oh, by the way, Rachel and I just decided on the honeymoon location.' They're going to think we've gone completely mad."

"But when they think about it, they'll be thrilled at the prospect of being aunties. They already spoil Sami shamelessly."

To their amazement, both sisters took the news in stride.

"Anything else?" Sara asked in her no-nonsense manner.

"Not at the moment," Paul replied.

"Good." Maggie sighed with relief. "I don't think I can handle any more surprises tonight."

The mountains were garbed in their spring finery on the day that Rachel married Paul. A predawn shower had left everything sparkling and fresh. The ceremony took place as planned, outside the Duke house. The wedding party walked down the front porch steps and into the yard through a bower covered with flowers entwined in dried grapevines. Serving together as Rachel's maids of honor, Maggie and Sara were dressed in ecru lace with forest-green satin sashes tied in a bow with streamers to the hem of their ankle-length gowns. They carried bouquets of deep green and rose mountain laurel spiked with twigs of pink and white dogwood. Rachel wore her mother's wedding gown with the shawl from Paul's mother tied around her shoulders. Her bouquet was made up of three white lilies and cascades of bridal wreath the sisters had picked from the yard fresh that morning.

The Wilson Brothers sang, and Doc sniffed back tears as he prepared to walk Rachel down the aisle to where Paul waited by the altar. C.R. served as the best man, and Sami and Henry proudly carried small white lace pillows with the rings tied in place by a satin ribbon.

As Paul watched Rachel appear at the top of the porch steps on the arm of his father, he looked heavenward and said softly, "Thanks, God, for sticking with me and bringing me to this place, this woman."

C.R. gave him a cockeyed smile.

Rachel saw Paul look at her and then at the blue sky above. She saw his mouth move and laughed happily. Throwing her head back so she could see the same blue sky, she said, "What he said, God, goes double for me."

Reverend Griffith delivered the traditional service, but everyone in attendance knew that he had never meant the words more sincerely than he did on this day. "And as Rachel and Paul share a kiss to seal their vows, let us all say together, amen."

* * * * *

Dear Reader,

As I write this, it is snowing here in my Wisconsin home, one of those made-for-TV snows—light and fluffy and blessedly silent. 'Tis the season of miracles.

I had a miracle of my own this year. Last spring, just as I was beginning the final writing of *The Doctor's Miracle,* I was diagnosed with uterine cancer. In the most harrowing two weeks of my life, I went from being one of those people who has always been blessed with perfect health to having cancer, having surgery and starting down that long road to recovery. I thought there was no way I could focus on writing—especially on a story about illness!

However, I found that writing this book was incredibly therapeutic. I looked at these characters with fresh eyes and a unique understanding. I thought about all of the miracles that had come to me in the form of this terrible diagnosis—friends and family, of course, but also doctors and nurses and coworkers and strangers who helped me face a moment of crisis and come away whole. I hope that you will also find a message of hope and healing in these pages.

Blessings,

Anna Schmidt

REQUEST YOUR FREE BOOKS!

2 FREE INSPIRATIONAL NOVELS
PLUS 2
FREE
MYSTERY GIFTS

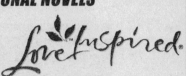

YES! Please send me 2 FREE Love Inspired® novels and my 2 FREE mystery gifts. After receiving them, if I don't wish to receive any more books, I can return the shipping statement marked "cancel." If I don't cancel, I will receive 4 brand-new novels every month and be billed just $3.99 per book in the U.S., or $4.74 per book in Canada, plus 25¢ shipping and handling per book and applicable taxes, if any*. That's a savings of 20% off the cover price! I understand that accepting the 2 free books and gifts places me under no obligation to buy anything. I can always return a shipment and cancel at any time. Even if I never buy another book from Steeple Hill, the two free books and gifts are mine to keep forever.

113 IDN EF26 313 IDN EF27

Name	(PLEASE PRINT)	
Address		Apt. #
City	State/Prov.	Zip/Postal Code

Signature (if under 18, a parent or guardian must sign)

Order online at www.LoveInspiredBooks.com

Or mail to Steeple Hill Reader Service™:

IN U.S.A.: P.O. Box 1867, Buffalo, NY 14240-1867
IN CANADA: P.O. Box 609, Fort Erie, Ontario L2A 5X3

Not valid to current Love Inspired subscribers.

Want to try two free books from another series?
Call 1-800-873-8635 or visit www.morefreebooks.com

* Terms and prices subject to change without notice. NY residents add applicable sales tax. Canadian residents will be charged applicable provincial taxes and GST. This offer is limited to one order per household. All orders subject to approval. Credit or debit balances in a customer's account(s) may be offset by any other outstanding balance owed by or to the customer. Please allow 4 to 6 weeks for delivery.

Your Privacy: Steeple Hill is committed to protecting your privacy. Our Privacy Policy is available online at www.eHarlequin.com or upon request from the Reader Service. From time to time we make our lists of customers available to reputable firms who may have a product or service of interest to you. If you would prefer we not share your name and address, please check here. ☐

LIREG07

CLASSICS

Enjoy these four heartwarming stories
from two reader-favorite
Love Inspired authors!

2 stories in 1!

Irene Hannon
**NEVER SAY GOODBYE
CROSSROADS**

Lois Richer
**A HOPEFUL HEART
A HOME, A HEART, A HUSBAND**